Kalki Evian

The Ring of Khaoriphea

Cover Art:
MLCDesigns 4U

Publisher's Note:

This is a work of fiction. All names, characters, places, and events are the work of the author's imagination.

Any resemblance to real persons, places, or events is coincidental.

Solstice Publishing - www.solsticepublishing.com

To those who ceased to trust their instinct
just because everyone told everyone else
that no one did.

Grazie...
Emerantia, Mark, Melissa
Giulia, Garima, Luigi, Shikha
& Shreiya

Foreword

Hypothesis #1: Every choice has its own unique consequence.

This would imply that at any given time, the choice we make leads us on an entirely different path from the one that any other would take us on. It is like driving a car. Once we turn right at any junction, all roads on previous left turns cease to matter. And that right turn takes us on to a new junction with a new set of turns, each with its own choice of left and right, and so on. None in particular is better or worse. It is just different. And these paths may even meet later on.

Hypothesis #2: Time travel could be possible at some time in the infinite future.

Time is a dimension like any other; only somewhat beyond our understanding. The day we evolve enough to comprehend exactly how it works, we may be able to travel in time and return to a junction/event that occurred in the past – our own, or maybe someone else's.

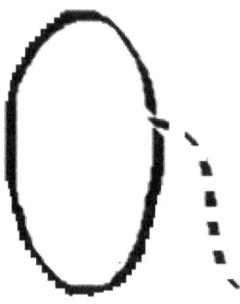

If we combine hypothesis #1 and #2, it would indicate that at least someone may have travelled back in time to warn Caesar of an oncoming conspiracy, or persuaded Hitler's father to allow his son to become an artist, or simply changed something in their own past. In each instance, that change would involve going back to an event, and may result in an altogether different set of affairs to consequence. In other words, the second path – one different from that which we took initially – could come alive.

That said, we do not yet seem aware of any such changes to our known history. Brutus continues to exemplify treason rather than honour. Hitler remains the author of Mein Kampf. And our life remains dotted with specific, unchanged events just as we remember them.

These two points mean that as a consequence of any active and influential time travel, one or more parallel realities must come into existence, somehow unknown to us.

Hypothesis#3: We do not yet know how to time travel.

That is a gap that exists . . . in common knowledge as per common beliefs. But then, news from many unknown corners of this world remains obscure.

Hypothesis#4: The relativistic view of time and space shows a warping of the spacetime plane, audience to the disparities in distance and time travelled with changes in velocity.

General relativity is Einstein's brainchild, whose applicability to this case shall be assumed to be hypothetical.

. . . So follows the journey of what was and what may be.

Chapter 1

"Is this where she falls?"

"Two miles further south."

"Then," the former hesitated but asked with hope, "is this where we save her?"

Wind blew perfectly in accordance with fresh traces of floating memory that lay in the latter's mind. The man smiled. Significantly taller and older than the inquiring other, he stood with a sparkle in his eyes, unmoved and unblinking and gazing ahead under the faintest crease of brows that stood in striking contrast to the amused pair ordained by one to his right and to the tense pair of a third who stood behind him, looking up, awaiting a sense of their plan.

It was pitch dark on a brazen land. Clouds usually decorated the sky at this time of the year but they had arrived today in galore, witness to a moment of particular significance that bore a perfect sense only to the one who had stood there without a twitch of muscle for over an hour. Metal cape was a rather unusual coat to adorn those heavy shoulders, but he wore it as if he had journeyed from a battlefield. The younger, chubby individual who accompanied him – Bree was his name – would have vouched that he had. The graphene, fashionably complimented his neatly combed silver hair. Uniform white stubble graced his cheeks, save for three short creases on the upper end of his cheekbones. Together, it all directed one's focus to his sharp eyes that he relied upon to speak out more than words could. Even under the dark shade of that evening, his face glowed not through a visible shine but through a perceptual radiance. Drizzle marked their borders, illustrating the elder's stern body language, with his hands neatly folded at the back and fingers clasping on to each other. Two in particular seemed to gently toy with a ring on one of his thumbs. Bree's younger pair of shoulders, meanwhile, heaved under his heavy breathing. They bowed smoothly on to fleshy arms that hung parallel to his thick legs positioned with utmost care to stand beside but half-a-step behind the pair in boots - as if to conform to the latter's authority.

As the first drops began to trickle from above, the metal-clad almost allowed himself to smile again – one fairly invisible to any who could see him. For, the sound of rain had been perfectly tuned to a faint rumble on the metal rails far in the distance, reflecting a coherence that was nothing short of little verifications that he belonged there in that moment.

The third - a doctor and the one with the questions initially - had heard the rumble too. He tried to stab his sight through the darkness to find its source. The effort had brought about a spark of excitement from within his exhausted body. His shoulders were straighter, the dressing sharp. Only a little pouch hung across on a thread-like string and repeatedly bounced off the waist in constant attempts to fly under the wind.

The little smile on the elder's face waned amidst continuing sounds of those drops on metal as he spoke, unflinching still, "Any issues?"

The task that the doctor had been sent for not many moments ago had drained sufficient proportion of his energy. He quickly gathered his breath to reply, despite having had enough time since his arrival, as if all air had stalled in his lungs during the anxious moments that had recently passed. "The information was precise. I reached just in time to warn them. Such carelessness . . ."

[11]

"It wasn't beyond the norm, doc," Bree spoke with an almost juvenile amusement, "It was an inevitable consequence of a long chain of cause and effect that perceivably began with a pack of milk."

"Milk?"

"Yes, and some superstition."

"I believe that is simply a misnomer for carelessness," the doctor quipped.

"It is one for precisely the opposite. Whether superstitions have any viable meaning is trivial. They are always true – not because they work but because they make us believe they do. It's a belief that often runs stronger than even any other faith. In this case, it was one that pertained to spilt milk - a bad omen in these parts of the world. But that story is quite unworthy of this moment and is rather irrelevant."

"How can it not be relevant, Bree?"

"Because subtle chains of cause and effect are too complex to decipher for an individual mind. There lies no beginning to such stories, no matter how many millennia one traverses back in time. The only matter of relevance then is to know that life is always, and exclusively, what it turns out to be . . . nothing more, nothing less and certainly nothing different."

"That explains your persistent sense of adventure," the doctor replied in an implied jest under a very serious face. "What's with the tweed cap?"

"My sense of adventure needs props, much like your little pouch" Bree replied, contrasting his comfort in the situation with the other's panic.

Two large bags lay almost kissing his wet feet. The doctor pointed at them, "I prefer mine to those!"

"Aah, yes. I would help if I could, doc. Sorry to spoil an otherwise perfect evening . . .."

It was then that the heavy voice intervened once more. "Perfection is a matter of perception," the elder said, "and there's much left in this evening. She's here."

The other two looked out into the distance. A yellow ball of light shone hazily through the heavy curtain of rain in the dark but was intensified by a deafening horn riding on a sudden screeching on rails that stabbed through the space. A red light in that area was never part of the itinerary for the train but that order stood defiant, facing the speeding frame of metal and forcing it to apply its brakes, perhaps unaware of the catastrophe that may follow for the souls seated inside. The distance, though, had worked in the train's favour as the driver sprung into action the instant the red light had come into view. The screech was unsubmissive, the shock unavoidable, but the tracks lay embedded within a slight cavernous stretch on the land. As short hills rose on either side of the tracks, the slopes might just cushion the near-fatal consequence that was soon to be. And so the train slid more than sped in those last few hundred metres with a wave of scream and confusion rippling along her entire length. The last few coaches bounced off but followed helplessly under the dual force of a roaring engine in front and the waves of elevated earth on the sides. Things rattled, tilted, inverted, shook, bounced and broke – all within the perceived parameters, all except one.

"Make the call," was the command. Bree sprung into action. He closed in the fingers on his left hand and gently rubbed the tips of the three-fingered glove he was wearing, with his thumb. As the tips illuminated under the charge, it seemed to the doctor as if light had stuck itself to them, for the thin spot of illumination stretched in between as the fingers moved away. Soon, the gluey spot of light turned into a ray between his forefinger and the little one. It broadened to produce a thin film on his palm, which immediately came alive with embedded blue lights. Bree tapped on the virtual phone.

[13]

The three scanned past the rough muddy terrain under the leadership of the pair of feet that seemed to outline two steps in advance, a finality of objective as to where they intended to land. As the three approached the only coach with a door thrown open, the anticipation on the doctor's face gave way to a flush of subdued panic. Secluded from the air of shock that prevailed around the train, someone lay unconscious, stained in red.

The victim was pulled to the other side of the slope as his rescuers got down to business; two inspecting the immediate wounds while the other stared at his blood-smeared face.

"You knew he would fall out?" the doctor asked in haste.

"Yes," the elder replied, his eyes fixed on what lay before him.

"How? What of the others?"

He asked with a calm blink of those eyes, "What would you say, Bree?"

The man climbed a few feet on the slope and began to scan the coaches with his naked eye. At length, he replied with eyes strained on those opaque walls, "Injuries sustained throughout but I see a conglomeration at only two places, both in the dismounted coaches. No deaths though, just urgent movements and significant shock."

"How long is it before the others arrive?"

"Half an hour for the emergency services; quarter more for the media. In two, the area should be swarming."

"Are we in position?"

Sweat was beginning to work its way, softening the crisp hair of the one nursing the body. The doctor's words then, were those of unparalleled concern, "His heart beats slow."

"But beats still . . ."

"Yes. But did you check him? Is it him?"

"To every detail," was the definitive reply. The mass of metal heaved with the elder's shoulders as he bent over the body and analysed it comprehensively with a blank stare that defied any form of indifference it may have been ordinarily reserved for. This one belonged to a trance. The body lay spread out with one palm clenched on to nothing in particular. The man held something in his fist, something that had been dear enough to have extracted every inch of endurance in him to keep it within his grasp even through the painful - and seemingly endless - course of his fall from the train. The elder looked at that fist as though he could conjure the invisible piece in his own imagination. "Hope," he uttered softly and blinked. The name had proclaimed itself louder in its rarity.

He stood up and spoke, with the usual heaviness back in his voice, "Prepare the cart." The doctor pulled one of the bags and dropped inside a miniature stretch of metal wound on two small rods. He placed the bag on the ground, stretched it wide, and began tapping on his wrist band. Streaks of blue shone and faded where he touched it, and the bag began to twirl from within. Inside, sand-like particles ran over each other as they encapsulated the little piece he had dropped inside. Once the rendering was complete, he took out the object, poured more of the particles, and tapped a few more times. Gradually, more and more particles joined in to form a large replica of the tiny object.

The doctor then turned back to the other sack and dropped another piece. The routine followed and out came a flat board. He then placed it near the body, and stuck a charge underneath. It slid seamlessly and activated itself. Another push and the two boards stuck together as the air was sucked out from between them. He then dug into his pouch to extract a metal frame that he attached under the contraption. A few wrist-taps later, it lit blue immediately and the light spread along the borders of the board as the entire mass began to float few inches above the ground.

[15]

He looked up once done. Bree was smiling. The doctor guessed, "Electro-permanent magnets, I suppose."

The reply was almost instant and familiarly amused, "Not bad for an expert in biology."

"The problem when you focus too much on one subject," the doctor countered, "is that you lose your grip on the rest."

"Unless the rest begin to converge . . ."

Bree had left a cryptic possibility free to implant itself in the other's mind and was aided conveniently by the elder's interruption to march forward.

The two men pressed charges near their torso while the doctor climbed on his contraption. With soles lifted inches above, the three began to move with the body. Many minutes passed before they came by a small instalment, few miles away from the railroad and everything else. The site of commotion had been left far behind and only ghostly whispers of the breeze continued, sans the drops of rain and their clinks on metal. The doctor questioned, all thoughts relegated in the face of a larger lump in his throat, "You took a risk."

It was as if the metal-clad elder had been anticipating it. His words nearly overrode those of the doctor's, "One that saved some two hundred lives; perhaps more."

"You facilitated one accident to prevent another."

"It was a necessary risk."

"Enough to justify this?"

The reply came almost immediately once again, but the voice was far gentler and had come from behind them. "Any act has its consequence. Every act changes the world."

Those broad shoulders turned to face the source of the sound with an unmistakable constriction in the pair of eyes above, as if in attempts to fashion a smile. A woman, dressed in a silhouette sharply accentuated by a short cloak that covered her head, came towards the three from around a little tent. She was nearly as old as the elder but carried a significantly warmer gaze. Her hair was wavy and grey and seemed to rest on her shoulders with the softest touch, fashioned with streaks of silver in the front locks.

She looked at the body that lay on the board, and sighed. A welcoming look then followed on to the man who sat upon it. The doctor ignored the warmth of that attention that lay bestowed through seconds of concern. He addressed the elder again, though with slight hesitancy, "I can't . . . just . . ."

"What happened?" Bree asked as if charged with managing the doctor's conundrums for the evening.

"Nothing," came the desolate reply, followed by a more professional concern, "A hospital would have been more appropriate . . ."

"That wouldn't be necessary. We can trust each other on this," replied the elder. His words were calm but bore a striking directive towards haste.

"How . . ." an argument attempted to ensue but gulped itself down its bearer's throat, switching instead to a taunt, "Are you really willing to watch this lad die?"

The elder did not speak. His eyes expressed a strange concoction of pain and calm as he was helplessly diverted to the lifeless body that lay in front. That entrapped chunk of oxygen in his lungs was measured immediately by the recently arrived. She spoke on his behalf, with a smile that was an answer in itself, "Of course not. That is why we have you here."

"But how do you know I will save him?"

"Because if you had not already done that, we would still be human."

Chapter 2

The eyes opened gradually. Light had not entered them for an age, or at least the brain had ceased to process it so. Any part of the world, then, should have been a beautiful vision to come across, but all he saw were streaks of blue running across in mid-air against a plain white background. Everything was hazy except these sharp blue characters, and a crystal clear voice of a woman, as if programmed to initialize the moment he woke up.

"Welcome. Default settings now active. Visuals confirmed. Data status, basic. Volume level: aligning . . . aligning . . . aligning. Saved. Thank you. Your world is at your service."

The streaks and the sounds faded as the background came into clearer view – a lone glass frame stood on a white stretch of the wall, with the words: *One hand washes the other; both get clean.* His pupils narrowed in trying to read it carefully, and immediately, little edges appeared out of nowhere to focus on the text. There they waited, and shivered with the confused movement of his pupils. Fidgeting to get the little blue edges away from his sight, he shook his head and blinked as he moved. The visuals hanging in mid-air twitched, lost focus and tried to target something else on that otherwise bland wall. He resisted but to no avail and then held his eyes static on the frame, waiting. Nothing happened. With eyes beginning to burn, he blinked once more with a perplexed gaze fixed at the wall. The projection of little edges joined together over the frame and gently faded away to display a copy of that text in blue, somewhere in the empty space, followed instantly by the words: *Curaçaon proverb. Origin: Former Caribbean.* He blinked again, and they disappeared.

"I've been waiting to see them. . ." It was a different voice, equally gentle but so much sweeter. He held still, expecting to see another series of obstructions, until footsteps sounded somewhere to his left. He turned to find white flat-soled shoes crisscrossing their way to him, carrying slender legs that rose up to partially visible fingers holding a tray, followed higher by a sparkling white shirt sprinkled towards the top with fluffy locks of hair bouncing around a young slyly smiling face. Their eyes met, and the books would have spoken of an emotional concordance. But the blue edges appeared again. Unable to draw his sight away, he quickly blinked. The projections displayed one line of text after another: *Friuli, Fridgeon. F, 25. Permissions denied. Possibly 1st.*

"Fri-uli-," he muttered.

"Those eyes," she interrupted matter-of-factly, "I've been waiting to see them."

"Huh?"

"Although now the perplexity seems equally catchy."

"Uh-I'm . . . sorry," he said with weak, broken voice, continually blinking and shaking his head to ward off the information displayed.

"You will get used to it. If you want it stopped, just tell it so."

"Tell what? Tell whom?"

"Your brain. The password's right beside you."

He turned to his right. A table lay at about his height with a little white card embossed with an alphanumeric code that was barely visible. He strained once again as the edges appeared, and managed to read out the letters: QIn45. Nothing happened.

She corrected him, "It is one word. They confused with the caps. Sorry for that."

He uttered it accordingly. The edges disappeared and nothing followed, drawing his eyes to move all around the room as if they had been let loose to absorb his surroundings. They stood wide open in anticipation of the source of what he had just seen. He fell back on his pillow, already exhausted under the stress.

"You should rest," Friuli spoke, smiling still. "Or you won't be able to handle it."

"Handle what?" He enquired.

She waited, looking directly into his eyes, letting him absorb her tease of curiosity, and then answered, "What we have done to your world."

The pupils changed shapes again. He was nervous. "You?"

"We the people, Qin. Welcome back, and good morning."

She walked out and the room fell back to a white stretch of space. He rose to look at himself, strapped and bandaged in a long robe. But there was no plaster, stitches or even pain. How long had he been there? The simplicity of that query dragged his thoughts back to the dreadful night. Nothing came back perfectly but in his blur, he remembered a sudden shock, a muscular effort, a short flight, a series of scratchy rollovers, and a determined fist. Attempts to think further strained his nerves as exhaustion overtook a bit more. Sleep dawned and he closed his eyes with troubled relief. The images came back in view, but differently so: a girl breathing heavily . . . he saw himself scream and run away . . . a train came into view shortly after, and with it came a feeling of uncontrollable rage. And then there was shock, a muscular effort, a short flight, a series of scratchy rollovers, and that determined fist.

It felt chillier and the surface his skin touched felt rougher than it appeared. He woke again and quickly got off his bed. His feet dragged and stumbled on their way to the wash basin. The water was a respite but felt nearly numb when it splashed against his face. He looked up in some irritation to find a long stretch of glass, in the centre of which stood a man many years older than him.

"Wh-," he jerked back in surprise. "Who are you?" he asked, feeling misled into believing it was glass. But the figure mimicked him to produce an unwelcomed realization. He looked down at his arms, closely and in disbelief. They looked larger, and older. He tried to take a closer look at his reflection. It was him, much older than he could remember. His fingers slowly crawled towards the mirror but the moment he touched the glass, more words rolled out, this time displayed firmly over his own reflection, without a sound: *Welcome.* Four more words appeared beneath as he half-muttered what he saw: *News, Weather, Sport, Emergency.* But by the time he pronounced the first of those, the characters disappeared and were replaced by a statement in bold: *Etna wakes up, and puts everything else to sleep,* followed by more texts highlighting the headings of various articles on the day. He nervously read them while trying to shake away the text on glass until he found a little series of icons beneath. He tried each with different results. A familiar voice read out the text at one, one translated it all in different languages, one changed the pattern of the text, a fourth stuck to his fingers and ran along as they moved, highlighting all text that came in its way, while another switched to a different screen that began to ask for his identification. With his head splitting, he drew away and shouted, "Stop it!"

Everything vanished, and he stood there, alone, in silence and decades older than he remembered. *"The card,"* he thought, and uttered, "Qin45." A beep sounded as he took a deep breath, focussed on his reflection and blinked. Texts appeared again, seemingly in mid-air, but they had no mirror image. He strained further until he noticed little blue streaks on the reflection of his pupil. The image was startling, but his focus was immediately drawn away on to

[21]

the text itself: *Permissions denied.* He tried again, to a similar result.

He would have screamed again, this time to an audience extending far beyond the bounds of his room. But with those very first steps that went backwards without any direction or intent, carrying a lost mind and a panicking body, the sweeter voice returned, "I told you to rest."

He turned in anger to face the face he could not help being intrigued at. He fought the diversion and addressed her sharply, the intensity of his voice increasing with each word, 'Rest?! You tell me where I am. You tell me RIGHT NOW!"

"Anger won't help you, Qin," she spoke softer still. "You know this better than most people. Nor would restlessness, or even solitude."

The last word hit him as hard as his confusion had, for it ran on inconvenient memories that came back distinctly. He breathed again and asked, simply but sternly, "Where am I?"

"I would tell you right now, but please spare a thought to this: you are alive. And if you can remember anything, it was quite unlikely."

He did realize the fact, for if nothing else, he did remember an excruciating pain that he had shut his eyes amidst. He remembered, if nothing else, that more painful had been his final regret that had stormed out from within all illusions of uncertainty and righteousness, as he lay in seclusion, smeared in his own blood and clenching on to what felt most dear in that moment. *I didn't see,* he had thought as his grip had tightened over a ring. And then, it had all gone blank.

The nervousness marginally waned as the breathing normalized but he was restless still when he asked, "Why do you keep calling me that?"

"Calling you what?"

"Qin, you said."

"Aah, but that is what we have had registered here. Is that not right?"

Qin thought for a while but could not explain his agitation under the severe headache. He exclaimed in agony, "I . . . don't know."

Friuli enquired, "Do you remember anything?"

"Only vaguely. Bits and pieces, but it's too difficult."

"It will come back. You need rest."

"What is all this, these screens? And what the hell is on my eye?"

"So you activated it again?" she asked, walking up to help him back to his bed.

"I had," he said guiltily, feeling much easier with her very first touch. ". . . switched it off." He continued, as he looked at the smooth stretch of her fair skin, "Couldn't take it."

"You have been in a coma for quite a while, Qin. Things have changed as they always do with time. So it is not that the world is upside down now but as you can see, there have been a few developments. What you see are automated projections designed to assist you with any information you need in real time. Some you can switch off while others are ingrained in the objects."

"But why on my eye?"

"*On* your eye is nothing spectacular. Most have it. As to why we put you in such a shock with it, I extend both my apologies and my sympathy. These were orders, intended to help you accommodate with what has come to be. Quite naturally, you wouldn't have allowed the implantation once you woke up, given that you are still," she hesitated, "a bit old school."

"This thing is implanted?!" He asked with a sudden high pitch.

"Well, of course it is. Is it really that bad a thing, considering how bad your eye was after that fall?"

[23]

"H-how bad was it?"

Friuli gave a gentle smile as she tucked the sheets around him, never taking her eyes away from his. She whispered, pointing to the whiteness of the entire room, "Let's just say all white is better than all black."

He knew panic would not help things. He was just too oblivious at the moment. Friuli walked around his bed, setting the table straight, replenishing it with fresh water and taking a good look at everything else.

"The water-," Qin said, under subtle hiccups, "doesn't taste . . . very well. It doesn't taste at all actually."

"Well, I guess it's absolutely pure then! I'll put that on record for the maintenance staff," she mused, and spoke with greater sincerity, "Sleep Qin. Get your energy back."

As she approached the door, he interrupted again, almost shaking in his voice, "*Quite a while*,' you said. How long is that?"

Friuli stopped to take a heavy breath. Few seconds passed in silence before she answered with a decisive effort, "Twenty three years."

Chapter 3

The sounds in the world outside were decently audible. A superbike or two would roar by periodically, breaking through the intermediate whirling of a dozen cars moving around, which itself was superimposed on a continual swish that seemed to sum up all other sounds prevalent in the environment. Occasionally, a welcoming wind would create an interruptive crackling of leaves on thin stems of trees rising up to his 5th floor apartment, until the crackle would turn to a generic swish before subsiding altogether to leave the former sounds at ease with their flow. The sun had begun its rise, warm in its indirect shine on the western balcony that his room faced. He had pulled the shutters halfway down to yield a translucent glow on the walls that were now draped with several thin rows of light that radiated from the opposite building and reflected from its windows, escaping in beads through the metal frame. His laptop screen, transparent and as thin as thick paper was not of much use to his wavering mind. He needed a grip on the eventless situation to cater to what he was attempting at. So he decided to restart.

He put on a pair of earphones to play a poetic number recited by a grave voice against the keys of a piano. But first he listened keenly to the melody of all noise in the environment that seemed distant even in its omnipresence as a constant sound that one had come to live in. It was as if there had never been such a thing as perfect quietness. To think of it, there really had never been such a thing. Just the way cleanliness had its own smell, silence its own noise. Cars and bikes had come to be equipped with absolute noise-cancellation, but to the proponents of style and fandom, their roaring noise still seemed tasteful. The classic earphones appeared then to be no less than a marvel to deliver a sound of relevance that could magically cut off everything else outside its perimeter and fill one's auditory world for the entire length it played. And so he waited for the poetry to float in clear voice as if someone had begun to whisper in his ear:

And who did live in the very beginning
when there was nothing at all?
Only a first flying duck,
one that flew along.
Settled down for the night,
she laid an egg that broke.
The liquid then formed the lakes,
and earth from an emptied cloak.

He marvelled at the words as he sat back with arms folded at the back of his head. The eyelids slid back to show a faint illusion those beads of light had been creating on the wall. The song was inspired from the beliefs of the Tofa people from the far stretches of Siberia. Those were curious words, words of men who chose, above all else, a duck; ones who chose, above all else, the night, and ones who believed, as per this metaphor, that there was absolutely nothing of significance once. *How ironic it is*, he thought, *when one traverses the lands and hears the stories from the southern end.* For, he had looked through just that and now recounted the first few lines of their text:

"Never was there a time when I did not exist, nor you, nor all these kings; nor in the future shall any of us cease to be. As the embodied soul continuously passes, in this body, from childhood to youth to old age, the soul similarly passes into another body at death."

What of this, then? He inaudibly asked. These people clearly referred to a subset of the former. Both spoke of relevance, in different ways: one in terms of elements and the other in terms of time. And therein lay a clue to how the mentalities had diversified from then on, just as it also suggested how events that do not concern us need not be inquired into.

Convenient. It was, indeed - enough to revel in the fact that we lived, laughed and cried. Yet, he was never entirely satisfied with this uni-dimensionality of human existence. Words were boring to him if uttered categorically as part of conversations that he had witnessed over the years. Gossip was spicy but only enough to fill in the empty seconds, which themselves shrunk in length with time. Issues, as they prevailed, bore a certain degree of engagement but soon became an encore of what had always been, and would continue to be, part of our daily lives.

The state of affairs worsened when the category began to consume even the seemingly tragic global roadblocks of financial, political or simply, human nature. And so he had turned to the future, for that was the only space left for him after a while where one could never find all the answers and hence, was obliged to keep looking. Soon, though, it had become necessary. The world around him had felt as if it would crumble, and later, as if it had gone berserk in the face of possibilities that had flown in out of nowhere. Truth was that they had always been on their way: opportunities that come as the human mind evolves. And one in particular had caught its imagination in entirety: energy.

He walked out beyond the glass doors that slid back the moment he came close, to a wide balcony dressed in red tiles laid under an open sky. Far below, the streets ran between two little roundabouts lined and laden with trees.

Beyond them, as the eyes climbed back up, stood several buildings in Art Nouveau with columns of long windows on beige walls under a sloping tiled roof, each catered to by a little balcony hyphenated with carvings of flowers and of little circles. The ground floor stood distinct as a fundamental base in grey bricks, beautified solely by carvings that were relatively grander in nature, with bold pillars, corner gateways and more flowers. Meanwhile, the red tiles gave way to a blue sky littered with white puffs of clouds that hung without any apparent movement. A part of the beige wall was covered under the shadow of its own roof. On the outer edge of the shadow, he noticed a movement in black – a smaller shadow crawling up in haste. As he watched, the shadow of what seemed to be a bird curled up from beak to claws. The little black ball began to roll, gradually gaining speed as if on a slope until it came to within an inch of the edge, at which point a large wing flapped out in the midst of the roll as an arm would flay when a sleeping man was turned from his side. The bird wasn't asleep. Yet it fell, or so the rolling shadow seemed. He instantly looked up to the roof, but saw nothing.

Nothing is not insignificant, he thought. What he had seen was sheer beauty to him – colourless, unassumed and unknown, exaggerated further by the absence of details and effort. For, such beauty or an understanding of it had come to be rare. His thoughts came back to the details already at play around him and to those that were just beginning to. He noticed little wind mills guard many balconies and he observed solar panels play on most of the windows. He looked at the sleeker curvature of cars and at the near-invisible security cameras lining every structure.

I should go out today, he thought, and considered it quite comical. It was an act he did not like. His mind scanned the seconds gone by – nothing but the faintest wind had crossed his way. Yet, for some odd reason, he felt as if something had beckoned him, and despite all his reasoning, he yearned to step out on to the streets. The dislike did not belong to what lay outside but to what it symbolised – a chain of formalities essential to qualify as suitable for any activity that belonged to the public domain. It did not make sense to him. It never had. In the last ten years though, he had come to make peace with this interpersonal divide.

It was all customary, and familiar to one who lived in the area. Although if one were to run an imagery of how he saw it, the entire walk was an art of superimposition. There was first the superficiality, where one could see buildings, roads, parks, shops, trees and cars. And then there was the subtle, where one began to see the sounds, the creatures, the orchestra of little fateful events from one conversation to another and from one person to another – each moving around, oblivious to how he, she or it was contributing to the whole set up of that existence.

The place was not overcrowded so early in the morning. He noticed two young men greet each other at the roundabout as another cycled by to the other side where a pretty young woman stood in short pair of lycra over stilettos, waiting to cross the road. The former greeting had been casual, given that both men looked to have woken up not many minutes ago and to have agreed to a cup of coffee downstairs. They sat at one of the little round tables placed outside the café at that juncture, on small woven chairs with gleaming metal hand-rests that curved inwards. As the first sip of Cappuccino tuned itself with the first puff of smoke, their voices grew, and that itself was tuned with the arrival of the woman from the other side of the street. They turned to glance at her as she walked across with persistent clicks of her delicately disciplined steps, compelling her to drop her head and readjust her blouse as she stormed by, unaware of the oncoming collision when the waiter stepped out of the shop with another tray of coffee variants.

"Ma che cazzo!" the guy shouted, watching his morning labour requirements suddenly increase.

[29]

"O Dio, mi dispiace tanto! " she replied, stepping away from the broken cups on the floor to check the coffee spill on her clothes, with her steps gone awry for a couple of feet. (Oh God, I'm so sorry!)

A tram arrived across the other street just in time to pour our many pairs of feet that made their way to the little tragic turn. Perhaps each ex-passenger had planned on a quick breakfast at the café on what appeared to be a mutually shared morning rush. The pair of eyes that had been observing this looked back to find the woman on the phone en route to recovering from her little accident, delirious and half-screaming to whoever held the device on the other end. She hung up with a frown implanted firmly upon her face until the moment one of the recently disembarked passengers arrived, screaming one good word, "Fra!" She looked up with hope and all stress was alleviated in that moment of respite when hugs returned and she breathed easier. "Hey! Che bello vederti! Oggi è stata una mattinata d'inferno" she said. (Hey! It's so good to see you. It's been a terrible morning.") As they began to walk, her last audible words, now at ease and in control, crawled up to a distant but keen pair of ears, ". . .Non avrei dovuto alzare la voce. Credo che dovrei mandarle un messaggio. . ." ("I shouldn't have shouted. I think I'll text her in . . .")

All that the watchful protagonist offered was a little twitch on the corners of his lips, thinking of the chain of events that the foul phone call must have sparked off on the other end. It stretched further by the sight at the café where the cashier and the coffeemaker were suddenly a lot busier, having to compensate for the temporary absence of the lone waiter on his morning-shift, who was probably trying to wash the stains off his apron, to the dismay of a lot of coffee-hopefuls whose energy and enthusiasm for the morning, and subsequent behaviour in the day, had rested upon that first sip of coffee.

[30]

"Ciao amico," came the first interruption, "Ti ho aspettato tutto il giorno e ancora non hai comprato niente in una settimana!" ("I wait for you all day and you haven't bought anything for one week!")

A grocer had addressed him from a nearby shop. His addressee smiled and waved back with an adjusted reply, "Scusami, Driss, guarda che passo oggi piu tardi." ("Sorry, Driss, see that I come by later today.") The grocer laughed and waved back, all the while settling payments at the counter.

The superimpositions returned to view – tangible objects of the environment and ignored frivolities of its characters. Yet, not all was trivial. For, there lay a third layer visibly hidden but fast taking shape within those walls and upon them, running like veins in the system. Much had changed with time within the familiar architecture. He walked along, now gazing around as if looking through the walls – a feat he both wished for and foresaw as attainable at some point of time. The "transparentized" imaginations reflected pulses of electricity continually crawling up the buildings and onto another in all directions. Its role had evolved and with it had evolved its recipients. Was the evolution complete? How could it ever be! Evolution, by definition and interpretation, was an act of natural continuity spread over time, often invisible but eventually pronounced. Energy was no different. But how did it all ever begin?

He had traced that path a million times, but it still filled him with glee. Lost therein, he arrived at an entrance to the subway and stepped in without much thought. "*Production. Communication. Energy,*" he murmured but before much could follow, he stopped still. More of that generic buzz – this time populated with random voices – had surrounded him. A train had just arrived in the subway and people were flooding out of it, crossing each other's ways in hasty steps on the shiny floor as they made their

[31]

way out. Most of the space, though, had been carpeted with moving walkways – or flat escalators – to ensure order amidst the chaos and a successful tracing of each person by the cameras as necessitated with time.

Several three-dimensional virtual projections dotted every path with an interesting blend of ignorant indulgence, relaying information on various brands and offers. People continually aimed their phones at ones they found of interest, allowing an immediate transfer of order, catalogue, data or cash as they passed by on those walkways. It was no crime, of course, to just step down and take one's time. But then, who had it anyway? People were busy, or had found some way to be so, as always yet more than ever.

And thus it was that exceptions continued to bring a welcome garnish amidst the persistent rush. One such anomaly in the criss-crossing mobile mesh of speeding legs was a girl, curled up in a corner with her face dug between her crouched legs. Her stationary obstruction was rather dramatic and amplified just how fast and how many pairs of shoes greeted each tile of the subway floor at that instant. The girl was dressed well enough – too well to grace that spot. Short turquoise sleeves flowed in a gentle current of breeze that seemed to channel itself through the subway gates above to land directly upon her. It eclipsed her knees in radiant blue and had managed to ward off any dust. But all that was just an illusion. She intermittently rubbed her face against the bare skin of her forearms and that was enough to give a glimpse of her smudged eyeliner. The black had once clouded her eyes as if the sun were to shine through them. The clouds themselves had produced a rosy fog that had warmed her cheeks even as they stood competing hopelessly with her bright red lips. Several feet away, this man, bent on one knee, observed the hallucination amidst the relentless interruption of walkers around. The interruptions proved worthy though as they brought into clearer view the smudge of black that had now enveloped her cheeks, cleaned further by disciplined rows that her tears had followed for a while now. And yet, after the prolonged display of this tragedy, not one person had stopped by.

He walked up to her and kneeled down. With both hands cupping his knees, he inched closer and asked, "C'è qualcosa che non va?" ("Is there something wrong?")

She continued to sob softly as he waited. He enquired again, "Che c'é?" Noticing his presence even after a few reluctant minutes, she raised her face, looking away simultaneously, and replied in what was barely even a whisper, "niente." ("Nothing.")

"Guarda, io non so cosa sia successo ma ho capito bene che si tratta di qualcosa da non sottovalutare. Dimmi cosa c'è che non va." ("Look, I do not know what happened but I know well enough to not underestimate it. Tell me what's wrong.")

She caught a glimpse of his slightly creased eyebrows over eyes that looked straight at her. He continued, "Magari non sarò capace di capire quello che stai passando in questo momento ma di certo startene seduta qui non ti aiuta per niente. Lascia che ti aiuti." ("Maybe I will not be able to understand what you're going through right now but surely, sitting here will not stop it. Please let me help you.")

She turned her face towards him but kept her gaze fixed upon her knees. The first thing she noticed was a ring on his right thumb, prominent in its glossy black shine, with letters engraved along its rim, unintelligible at first. It said: KHaor. She read it twice and looked away. At length, she spoke with some effort, "è . . . solo che . . . lui . . . I have nowhere to go." With those words, the tears began to roll down once more. Four short words were all that she had spared but they were enough for Kanha to discern that she had not switched languages simply over of a lack of words.

[33]

She was afraid of possibly being watched. He was quick to respond.

"He, who? I'm here. I'm here to help and I'll be here till you're okay. Just tell me what happened."

It seemed as if a fresh bout of hope had surged through the woman, possibly in light of having faced someone who really was listening – not only the bare minimum that was, as is always, being spoken through words but also the more important bits that she had managed to communicate through alternate abstract channels. Her tone was strengthened when she spoke again, quick and hushed. "I don't know. I cannot be with him anymore. I am scared of him, scared for my life," she said in between her continuing sobs, "If I go to the police, he'll find me. They'll do nothing. Where do I go now?"

"I do not know. But look around. There's no one who looks interested enough or worth so many of those tears that you've shed. And if you stay here, the police will find you anyway. I'm surprised they haven't already."

She raised her eyes to meet his and stopped to sob with substantial effort. They looked at each other and found a trace of companionship that had been obsolete for both, by will or by chance. The weight on her chest had clogged her throat as much as her heart. She silently nodded, acknowledging the perceived bleakness of the situation not through agony but salience. She took out a napkin to wipe her cheeks clean.

He looked around at the faceless faces, witness to their unspoken thought. *She's a fraud.* He looked back and found a face of utter dismay. He turned towards them again. *You're weak. A nimble heart, one such frauds make use of . . . a fool.* He looked down with a sigh and smiled under the certainty of his response to the common logic – one that had never changed, despite all his previous attempts. *So be it.*

"You'll work it out," he said, extending a palm with fingers boldly stretched out to her, "c'mon." She weakly held the side of his palm with all four fingers as he pulled her up. "Kanha Evian," he said and jested, "Though that's not the only lie I'll ever tell you."

She chuckled at the muse against her wish, blinking twice as she continued to look down, and replied, "Fridgeon Friuli."

Chapter 4

Twenty three years. How could it possibly be? Qin lay there staring at the top-right corner of the room. He kept his eyes open for as long as he could. Inconvenient images would return every time they shut. It was as if his brain was urging to reboot. In truth, his system felt flustered under the uneasy agony of the years that he never got a chance to live through. How much could the world have possibly changed? Did it, in fact, change at all? What he saw in the room was certainly all new. He had switched his lenses on several times and scanned through every inch of the space, trying to gather all the available information. The blank white walls had returned nothing. The mirror too had hardly proved significant in content – presidents, soccer, rains and a bunch of information he could not make much sense of. *What on Earth is Bionism supposed to mean?* He irritatingly asked himself, as it came up each time he flipped through the relatively uneventful news. He had tried different combinations of credentials that he could muster on the identifications-page, hoping to gain a greater insight, but none worked. It did not surprise him, given the larger surprise at play. And amidst all this confusion, it felt like several days had passed while he was regularly fed and attended to by a charming girl that he both smiled and frowned at, from time to time.

"Better?" Friuli asked, as she entered his room with fresh white linen one morning.

"Three dimensions," he said, still staring at the top-right corner of his room.

"Huh?"

"I still see only three dimensions," he reiterated, outlining them in air with his forefinger, "So it's not like the world has turned itself inside out."

She looked up at the corner, then at his fingers and eventually at him. Her lips parted as if words were destined to drop out but she decided against it, after some prolonged analysis.

"The mirror still can't identify me," he pointed out.

"I had put in a word. They'll fix it soon."

"But there is no "they", is it? Just you," Qin said, looking at the linen in her hands now.

"What are you talking about?" She asked, with a half-chuckle.

"You know what."

"What makes you . . ."

"Say that? Look at the walls," he said, pointing towards one with his eyes. "White. Not a speck of a stain. I do not smell paint or plaster. So clearly nothing as such has been applied in recent time."

"So?"

"I kicked at them, several times. There was no mark. I looked at my slippers only to find them clean as new. I touched the floor and it was the same. Nothing ever gets dirty here."

"So?"

"Yet, you change the bed sheet and the covers every day." They looked at each other, one with simplicity and the other without expression.

She responded with a moment's noticeable delay, "So you want to sleep on the same old sheets."

"Nothing ever gets dirty here, Friuli. Not even me. I don't sweat, no matter how much I exert myself. This is not an ordinary accommodation. That's not all. I fall asleep frequently even though I keep my movements to a minimum so as to preserve energy. Every time I do, I wake up with a sweet taste in my mouth. It's like clockwork . . . except that quite curiously, there is no clock around for me to see. It is an observatory, isn't it? The question is why. What are you playing at?"

She attempted to continue nonchalantly, "You are . . ."

"Anonymous. It's intended to be so, from what I gather. So you can either choose to continue the little play without pretending anymore, or you can tell me the truth."

Friuli looked at Qin, with a stern expression as if her brain was computing several variables. She spoke as her somewhat muscular jaws rose half-an-inch higher, "But anything I say could still be a lie." Qin nodded. She gave a crisp little smile and said, "Then the only way for you to know is to see for yourself."

She walked out, leaving Qin with a sense of anticipation even as his eyes turned back to the top-right corner of the room.

Several oscillations of sleep and stare passed by through what he could only guess to be another couple of days. Qin managed to keep his head turned away each time Friuli walked in. Her sternness, meanwhile, had mellowed back to a tone of empathy. She spoke each time she came in, filling him with random trivia on human behaviour and the weather outside, but it all stood a greater chance of receiving a reply from those bland walls than the person that lay staring at them. It was so until she finally uttered what compelled Qin to turn back to her with hope, "Good morning, *Signore*. Today we leave." It felt like the first drops of rain on drought-stricken land. Under that first impulse, Qin felt a curiosity he had assumed dead for good some twenty-three years back.

She gave him a pair of tight-fitting trousers, a sweatshirt and a jacket to go with it. His face wore a constant expression of angst hiding well the oodles of nervous excitement. He walked out of the room to an empty corridor, the walls of which were made of tinted glass, slanting away from him. He had tried to see through them several times before but had hardly grasped anything more than clusters of flickering lights. He reached one end of the corridor that stood partially ajar. He pushed the door to find her dressed in leather pants and what resembled a cross between a polo shirt and a black jacket, tucked in, expressing well her slim waist. The boots didn't make much sound as she walked towards him.

"That is a weird material to wear," he commented.

"Biocouture," she answered with a smart smile, to a perplexed Qin. He had spoken to her after ages. "Come, it's time to show you around."

As they approached another tinted door, she touched it with her hand. Once the identification processed, it slid open and they walked out. "All right, here's your phone," Friuli said, handing over a three-fingered glove. "Your details have been entered. It'll pick up the rest as we move along."

"What details?"

She raised an eyebrow, letting him feel the needlessness of his question. "We had to keep your identification to a minimum for the sake of simplicity, Qin. Imagine if you woke up and the first thing you were told is that you are already middle-aged and in some God-forbidden land."

"Are we?" Qin asked, pulling the glove down his palm.

"We could've been but as of now, no. This is rather interesting."

"So where are we?"

"Too many questions, Qin. Have patience. For now, pull your fingers close, rub on the tips over the glove, and stretch them apart. Your fingerprint has been registered." He did so, and observed a luminescent spot widen to reveal a phone of glowing air. Words appeared, starting with:

Welcome, Qin. She continued, "Now scroll around to Maglev and click on it."

He did as was told. Immediately his boots began to lift up and float inches off the ground.

"Pretty much how you imagined it, right?" she asked with a childlike grin, and then simply uttered the word to her phone for the same result.

Qin was trying to balance himself, nearly falling off several times. He said, "You could have asked me to practise first."

She looked at him and chuckled. "Every inch of what you are wearing is in communication with each other," she said as if it were the most natural thing to happen, and added, "And don't worry, it won't show or spoil your fashion statement." Her eyes turned back, as if escaping away with their shadow left implanted on Qin. The creases on his forehead straightened. She continued, "Now let's see if you still remember your skating skills."

He was enjoying it, regardless his perceptual frown. As they gradually approached the main doors of that construct, she scanned her fingertips at the keyhole and it swung open.

"I remember that," Qin said, both arms thrown out in trying to float straight.

"Of course you do. These are derivatives of technologies you already know. There is no such thing as an "in-thing" in the new world; only new and ordinary."

"What do you mean?" he asked, but did not wait for an answer, for his head had bobbed around expounded by eyes that could have popped out any minute, all initiated by a gush of fresh wind.

It was night but in the face of all anomalies that lay before him, he could not decipher whether the sun had set or a blanket had been weaved over the city, such was the perceived shock his commonplace expectations had received at the very first glance. The first set of entities registered were the towering buildings, pretty much at par with any future one had imagined. But they should have been gleaming with glass throughout their length. Instead, they lay carpeted with plantation on one or two faces, while the others exhibited the more stereotyped glass walls bearing the pleasure of balconies randomly scattered through their length. On the entire span of those high rise glass walls, advertisements scrolled through in text, images and videos. His neck craned as he looked up at the urban jungle fitting literally in its definition. His eyes stayed glued to everything above twenty storeys until his neck craned. He strained further and noticed those random balconies move with its resident as the latter went in or came out. He looked more carefully at one such window pane high above. Even as blue advertisement continued to flash all over the building, one pane turned black. It's lower half then slid out of the wall along with a thin roof like a sheet from the two upper inches of that black rectangle. Gradually the remaining half slid sideways to reveal a yellow hue inside. Someone walked out to this newly formed "cabinet", looked around and then hastily returned. The extended structures slid back to yield plain glass once again, in continuum with the rest of the building and now drenched in colours of the ongoing advertisements.

He would have expected movement of which there was much, though thankfully less clustered than what that expectation had carried. Up in the sky at those higher storeys, flying cars should have occupied all space. There were none, only occasional drones that seemed more maintenance - and other function-oriented than catering to the whims of some fanciful owner. These occasional drones were fast and floating along fixed directions, visibly reduced in size as compared to any carrier and in sync with the streets far below.

What of the people? He thought. Finally, his eyes climbed down that eclectic mix of shimmer and greenery.

The ground still fashioned good old roads. Once again, though, there was no dirt. It seemed unnatural. Several cars were moving along but these were occasional and driverless. What was common was the smooth surface that even his sight could slip against. Each car was sliding an inch above the ground but this did not display some disconnected loathing towards the poor roads. Instead, every now and then he observed sparks between the base of the car and the streets. It looked scary at times for the walkers, for they were aplenty and to his utter relief, still looked human, at least as he had remembered them. Most of them floated on Maglev, comfortably at home with their mid-air skating. Yet, weirdness lacked only in relative amounts. For, while floatation itself was an unusual activity, he also witnessed most wearing clothes that just did not seem static. They were not unconventional in structure but Qin could swear he saw one change design while its wearer moved on. There existed a general level of fitness one would have hardly come to expect – probably the most cheering fact of all. Cheerful, though, was also the unexpected greenery on the walls of the buildings. The streets were still lined with shops on either side, each with a version of salespeople standing outside, like the old-fashioned beckoners who screamed out the entire catalogue as one walked by as in the greasy downtown areas of the old world.

He turned to glance at Friuli, the head still angled upwards and the mouth slightly open. She had been watching him with sufficient glee. They began to move on the footpath relatively slower than everyone else as if on an evening walk. "These people," he pointed out, "the ones reading out the menu. They are just projections, right?"

"Yes, they are. Far cheaper than hiring staff, when the job profile only requires speaking out to an uninterested mobile audience. Of course, they can handle conversations too, if you wish to speak to any of them."

[42]

"Speaking of mobility, what of these cars, err . . . cabs?"

"They are hardly used for human commute but are helpful as a back-up and for logistical purposes. Energy is being transmitted to them via metals embedded in roads each time those coils resonate at the frequency of the cars' movements. The roads allow wireless recharging in effect."

Qin was silent, observing everything he could grasp in the brightly-lit and buzzing area of the city. The setup was addictively dynamic but he was lost. She stressed with some enthusiasm, "It's all very catchy, isn't it?" She had a spring in her voice and her grin spoke of her apparent fascination for the place. It was only apparent, for as convincing as it appeared to Qin, he could hardly notice her clenched fist tucked in the pocket. His eyes were glued to everything at least three feet above and beyond.

"Hmm," he replied. Then noticing Friuli's rather immediate attention to his reserve, he added, "very catchy."

As they moved further, more buildings began to emerge. They were fascinating indeed, especially in their versatility. Not only did each building look strangely active, it also exhibited a relative lack of convention, in architecture above all else. While most had at least one face draped in green, the glasses found themselves in a competitive position. Only a few were straight-walled while the rest curved and tilted in their attempts to resemble daily objects. One bent out on each floor on both ends to accommodate a transparent bowl of blue water superimposed with yellow in its glow, thanks to some underwater lighting. Yet, this relative glowing charm was just a minor indulgence as lighting was what built up the interiors more than metal, cement or glass. These private swimming pools were being utilized well but were just a snapshot of what lay indoors.

Friuli waited, never taking her eyes off him. She had expected a prolonged analysis but had been divided on the nature of that analysis. Barring the initial shock-imposing jaw-dropped moment of fiction that he had expressed, he had been drowned in the magnanimity of the place but with an unusual diffidence. She waited, and then asked, "Questions?"

"Too many," he replied, still not taking his eyes off his surroundings.

"Shoot . . ."

He thought a little over where to begin but did not want readymade explanations. He remarked, "So much energy . . . how did we ever come to afford it?"

"That's too direct, Qin. Renewables, of course."

"Yes, but how could we pay for it? Did everyone suddenly get rich . . . and fit?" She laughed but it was hardly audible under the noise around from projections, the overhead advertisements and the people. "I mean, look at them. This is excellent, if you come to think of it: not one bad physique or figure. How?"

"Is it making you uncomfortable?" Friuli quipped.

"Uncomfortable?" he asked, looking at her, and then affirmed with a nod, turning away again, "Maybe, yes."

"But you are not in that bad a shape," she teased.

He looked at the twinkle in her eye and ignored it, lost in thoughts, "It's not the good looks. Give me a moment, Friuli and I'll explain. Let me just soak it all in."

"Sure . . ." she said, blinking several times under a straight face and letting him journey through his mind as they floated ahead.

"Qin," she interrupted his meditation after another long break. He replied with an unintelligible sound. She looked away and added, "Nothing."

He turned to her, by now relatively calm and more at home with both the floatation and the continuous wind, "I'm sorry, Friuli. I've just . . . been lost, I guess."

"That's not surprising."

"How fast can this thing go?"

"Quite, but you don't want to crash do you?"

"No. You said it works on magnetism against the surface, right?"

"Yes."

"Well, catch me if I fall," he said and before she could respond, turned into an alley and took off. The streets were lined with what appeared to be cobblestones, guarded on both sides by layers of green plants planted horizontally on the walls. He sped along the long alleyway until it opened up to another street, relatively silent. He quickly took a step on to the side walls and surely enough, the magnetism held him against it. For a moment, he thought it would hold his full weight running on the walls, parallel to the ground. With hope, he jumped onto the left wall to a nearly horizontal position. The magnetism held, his body did not. He crashed immediately against the stony pavement, with his feet still in position against the greenside of the building. His arm rubbed against the walk for a couple of feet, while the head hit it twice. Friuli arrived immediately behind him, blocking his crash midway, screaming, "Are you out of your mind?"

He turned to her with a foolish grin, "So we're not Supermen yet!"

"What? Are you insane?" she remarked, as she helped him sit up, checking for any damage.

He sat up with the grin long gone and both hands resting on his knees. "Anything? Any scars?" he asked.

She looked at him with a sudden jolt. "Qin," she said, trying to calmly talk sense into him, "Look straight at the building after that crossing. Glass walls, you see them?"

"Yes."

"At any point, a balcony could slide out from one of them. If you were caught midway, it could've broken your damn leg!"

"Hmm . . . true," Qin answered nonchalantly.

"Look, I know this is all a bit overwhelming but it is what it is. Now it'll take time, but I'll be with you. I'll fix you, I promise," Friuli spoke with earnestness, her hand gently resting on his shoulder as her head bent to one side trying to look squarely at Qin.

He turned to her with a sense of guilt. He had achieved what he had tried to and as he did, anger had risen within him. But in that moment when he looked at her concern, it all vanished. She had taken care of him thus far and he was healed way beyond what could have been imagined. Those were facts he could not deny. He smiled at her for the first time and it was worth every moment she had passed in anticipation. The smile was genuine way beyond expectations, for it wordlessly expressed his thankfulness. Hidden beneath, though, was a more compelling reason: a foreseeable answer to one among his many questions. The answer should have brought the anger back but he simply could not feel it at that moment. Somehow, for some unexplainable reason, he felt as if she was there to balance out a debt long overdue.

All his years, Qin had chased a sense of control over things where he could calculate situations and install his actions upon them. Yet, somehow his equations had gone horribly wrong and had cost him twenty three years. So it was in that moment of cluelessness in an unfamiliar world that he felt sensitized to a different sense altogether. He let it play, and decided to play along.

Chapter 5

He slid his card along a single crevice on the door and turned the knob. The door pushed open and they entered the apartment on the 5th floor.

"What was wrong with the keys?" she asked almost absent-mindedly.

"This is safer, I suppose," he replied.

"I don't care," she continued in the same lost tone, "I don't like so much change that one has to adapt to every other day. What's wrong with the old ways?"

"As you said, they are old," Kanha replied as he helped her to the couch. "Let's see . . . you'll need something beneath the left eye. It's turned black," he said as he began to check her wounds, "Here, too, beneath the ear . . . actually, this entire stretch that carries on behind till . . . oh, and the neck."

Fridgeon pulled away, obstructing his inspection. He immediately apologized, "I'm sorry. I was just . . ." She shifted an inch and half-turned to her side, pulling the neck of her dress a little further down her back. Stems of scars zigzagged their way down her shoulders. He turned away to spare a moment. Strangers rarely bore any logical incentive for him and this one had not revealed any particularly enticing essence of character either. Yet, his gesture a couple of seconds later was conventionally unexpected. "I will fix you. I promise," he said solemnly with words that seemed laden with a paradox of indifferent concern.

"I could do with some painkillers," she said.

"We'll start with those. That should help you be able to wash yourself and rest well." Those last words wavered

[47]

under a mix of sympathy for her, and anger for the one who had done this. That could be addressed later. She popped a pill, gently washed her face and went back to the couch while he prepared tea. By the time it was ready, she was fast asleep.

Kanha's steps instinctively switched to tip-toe once he entered the living room. He inched closer to her and bent on a knee with the teacup in one hand. She slept as if an age had passed over the last few minutes. The sun was nearing its western half and the room was beginning to glow as the intensity of its shine increased. It was fitting, given the clarity it offered to look at the marvel that had unfolded before him. The couch had hardly ever been a space large enough to offer comfort to every inch of his body without bias but it had comforted her fairly well, evenly accommodating her entire length that seemed habituated to crouch in any given space, so as to minimize the obtrusion it may cause to its surroundings. Maybe it had been forced into such a subconscious effort. Obtrusion, though, was exactly what that delicate body deserved to impose upon any space it lay in. There she lay softly wrapped in her dress that seemed to love every inch of the skin it touched. It had been bestowed with the responsibility to take care of her. It had failed, of course, and was now doing its best to impart nothing but the grace that seemed so natural to her being. The dress extended till her knees, at which point its loose ends flowed like feather under the slightest of winds that prevailed at any time at such heights. Yet, not more than a few inches of the ends slid around, as if they knew the degree of respite that could be afforded while their bearer slept. He looked at the cloth curve along her sides up till those arms that lay crossed and held each other firmly as if each hand was trying to assure the other of its presence. Her body waved with each breath, making the cushions seem softer and springier than he had ever imagined them to be.

He felt strangely insecure at that moment to look at those lips, thick and luscious, parted with the space in between guarded firmly by sparkling teeth. They seemed to create a setup that allowed oxygen she desperately needed but blocked all thoughts from translating into audible words. What was she scared of? Her eyes were gladly shut, her lips reduced to faint shiver instead of the lush they were born to revel in and softness they were meant to exemplify. In those lips drenched in natural rosiness, he found beauty that were meant to be protected. That was not all. What swayed him above all else was the innocence he found spilling from her face as she lay unaware and fragile; an innocence meant to be preserved. He did not know how. To think of what lay for her outside the perimeters of that room, he grew steadily concerned, almost laughably so. The steam rising from his cup seemed to make her cheeks wave along, and in that moment, he found himself in a feeling he thought was long lost. He found himself care.

"No . . ." he remarked and stepped back. His breathing had grown heavier and sweat had beaded, partially due to the heat and partially due to memory. "I can't," he said. Can't what? He had learnt to stay detached but had fallen prey to that which ran in his very genes. Why could he not care, when more years had passed fighting that feeling than acknowledging that feeling itself. How could he not care when it sat upon the very objectives that had come to drive him. *Because this is not about a vulnerable feeling amidst self-uncertainties; and because he was there to make up for inadvertent errors.* He got up and took one last look at his guest. Calm had returned to his decisive eyes. He walked out, sipping the tea and relishing its flavour.

Days passed under the heat as two souls filled the apartment with mutual silence. Fridgeon slept as frequently as she could while Kanha lay submerged in thoughts and simple set of metals stocked in a separate room that often

[49]

stood locked. A strange emotion prevailed in the house. Most interactions between the two in those initial days took place around breakfast. Fridgeon would wake up to find the food ready, with Kanha sitting at the table, having already finished his portion. The usual menu included a fresh bottle of milk, an assortment of bananas and apples in a yellow boat-shaped bowl and a box of dried multigrain cakes. "Rich in fibre and the best way to start a day, if it has to start tastelessly anyway," Kanha once said, busy reading the news on a wafer-thin transparent screen and perhaps unaware of the rhyme-induced smile across the table. At times, though, he would notice Fridgeon flinch at the sight of that food. The next day, eggs would lie scrambled and salted as an accompaniment to the usual rest.

"You are not a big fan of food, are you?" She asked him once. He mustered a bleak response garnished with a more informative: "I am. I just don't like to cook."

His dietary intake really did look a compromise between what was essential and what required minimal effort. Yet, their lunch and dinner were not entirely without interest. The food was but the gesture wasn't, at least to her. Weakness had crept over her. Many hours of her days went by in unscheduled sleep but the oven would always be inhabited by something new when she woke up. Yet, regardless the unspoken welcome, Fridgeon could simply not restrict a part of her that was becoming immune to such warmth. What concerned her more was that it was not just the human but even the material that her heart was shutting itself to. She did not want it but was reminded of the fact every time she entered that kitchen.

It was a beautiful culinary space. The entire wall opposite the door fashioned a translucent stretch of silver. Had it not been for apparent cuts in between, she could not have distinguished the various cabinets. One gently pressed on any one to have it sponge out. A touch and that particular cabinet would turn from translucent to a transparent screen filled with digital information as to its contents, a potential list of recipes, the storage temperature and date. Each item could further be tapped on to reveal its ingredients, expiry date and manufacturing details, all scanned automatically from the barcode on its label. The information was processed every time a pack was placed inside, given the delicate nature of preservation for various articles. The cabinets were all formatted according to a person's needs. Despite all this, the meal-heating routine marked her most indifferent moment of the day laden with an essence of hurt. She had operated such kitchens for a long time with an act of love and affection for one who would return, hoping that he would look forward to that delicious meal she would serve. Yet, all she had to show for it now were those scars. So even though the oven was just one among the many sections of beauty extending on that wall, she rarely ever used it. This pretty much balanced the overall effort that went into the meal as preparations that began with care in one culminated with spoonfuls of revulsion in the other.

Not all could stay gloomy, though. There was another time in the day which the two spent together. This is when the emotions would trespass into the realms of oddity. It had begun in a rather unassuming manner.

A faltered bolt and soft gasps of quick, hushed air is all Kanha had heard on the third day, but he had heard it too often until then. Unable to let it go, he moved towards the bathroom door - a bold move that his feet seemed unconscious to. It wasn't love in any form or manner, unless love was a moment of concern that overtook all obstructions of one's conscience. And so he pushed the door open and walked inside, without a word. She half-looked at him and abandoned any effort or pretence. He grabbed a sponge as she put on her towel. She turned towards the window as he sat near the edge. He bent forth towards her bare back as she dug her head between her crouched knees. And with a controlled calmness in his sensitized grip, he began soaking the scarred stretch of her skin. With an uncontrolled pause in her heartbeat, she let him soothe that burning sensation in her wounds with soft jets of cool blown air that had perhaps found a direct way to enter her. The heart, unfortunately, continued to beat. Those few mystic moments desperately strove towards an unspoken alienation, ruined by the alarmingly heartfelt machinations of his rock solid resolve to help her but to stay away. How ironic was it that neither could see each other then! For each had a contradictory incentive to indulge in kindness; each had a contradictory incentive to stay detached. And so they let it become a daily routine, secure in the knowledge that she could not sense love in him and he could not sense revulsion in her.

To him, beauty lay in lack of deliberation unless deliberations were an act of innocence. So while few eyes would have bothered to strain themselves past those ugly scars, he did turn weak to think of how much such fragile exquisiteness had managed to suffer and evade. It was neither fascination nor love that hooked him but the preservation of her poise that made those occasions as worthy of his indulgence as very few other things could be.

To her, it need not have carried so many complications; it was simply a matter of much-craved care – one she had yearned for unknowingly. It was only with his first touch that she ever realized this and she could have withstood a hundred times the pain she felt from her scars to go through those passing minutes of affection. How long was it ever: a minute, two or maybe five? It did not matter. She lived out those few minutes under a pleasure that guiltily rose out of all the agony she had to bear each time the water flowed down her scars. In fact, those few minutes assured hours of sound sleep that would follow.

So the days passed while the wounds healed. Her strength returned, as did her smiles. The breakfast continued to be a monotonous treat except for scrambled eggs that she would introduce in his cooking every alternate day. This continued until one day Kanha woke up to find a faint hint of smoke in the house topped with a roasted smell. He rushed to the kitchen to find her dressed in a lovely cotton suit that fell down her back with ease, pressed against her waist by his apron. She was busy putting the final touches on her crème brulèe while freshly cut peaches and melons sat on the table along with two empty cups and a potful of hot tea beside another tiny one with milk. An additional jar carried orange juice that seemed to have been freshly squeezed out. Equally fresh, going by the aroma, were the breads. With these in the centre, two plates rested on the opposite ends of the table. On each lay two thin omelettes.

He stood there looking at the spread, until she noticed his presence and turned in partial surprise. "Buongiorno," she wished him in a highly casual tone that showed hardly more than a little smirk.

"It suits you well," Kanha remarked, looking at her attire. "Too early for the dessert, don't you think?"

"Huh? Oh, this?" she asked, lifting the container roofed with a uniform golden crust, "These are not for now," she said, covering it with a lid as she turned towards the table and took off her apron. "And thank you for the cottons."

He looked at her and smiled in return with pursed lips. They sat down on opposite ends, as he helped himself to some juice and cut fruits. She sat staring at him, with her chin resting on her palm, without an expression except for two highly curious eyes. He hardly noticed it as he finished the first set and dug into the omelettes.

"You made this?" he asked, immediately realizing the needlessness of his question. She just smiled and continued to look at him. He glanced at her and went back to the knife-and-fork frivolity. After a couple of bites he asked, with both hands firmly holding the utensils upright, "What?"

"What?"

"Your omelettes feel quite neglected."

"Would you like to have them as well?"

"No, I mean you should eat them."

"I will."

"When? Once I've finished? That hardly counts as a shared breakfast." She smiled and poured some juice for herself. He added, "and the fruits."

"I will . . ."

"It's not enough. I see you have gained your strength back, but that doesn't mean you don't need more," he said, pointing at the fruits with his knife. Her eyes smiled as she gave him a glance before they returned to her plate. She did as was told and silence returned to the table. He broke it a while later, "Now that you are feeling much better, I think it's time for you to tell me a few things."

The words had been overdue, and a part of her short-lived fantasy seemed to crumble under their imminence. She exhaled heavily, followed by the words, "What do you want to know?"

"Everything that can be told. To start with, there has been no report of a missing female, nor any related news or other development. On top of that, you are not carrying any phone, which is a curious thing. Won't your husband . . . boyfriend . . ."

"Husband . . ."

"Right. Won't he be looking for you?"

"I'd be surprised if he even knows I'm gone," she said, focused on cutting out a piece of her omelette.

He slowly put his fork down and sat with elbows on the table, fingers rubbing against each other. He asked quite simply, "How so?"

"Because by now he might as well be lost, somewhere in the Alps."

"The what?"

"Or maybe feeling at home more than being lost."

"In the Alps?" he repeated.

"Yes," she continued with a helpless tone, "Look I don't know what happened or how it began. I just don't. It was probably his accident."

"Tell me."

Her eyebrows creased under the memory, as she summed up, quick as she could, "We had driven across town to a mall at the outskirts. He dropped me there and reversed to go park the car somewhere. Just then, this trailer came out of nowhere on his end and hit the car's rear, dragging it along for several metres."

Her story broke off midway when Kanha frowned. "What?" she asked. "You didn't see a big trailer arrive," he replied.

"Huh?"

"People just love to decorate a drama with one that fits a script worthy of perceptions."

"I'm sorry?"

"Out of nowhere, you said. The trailer couldn't have just appeared," Kanha replied softly.

"It's an expression," Fridgeon quipped with some restlessness.

"Fair enough, but expressions tend to blur the lines of realities when rehearsed subconsciously."

"What makes you think I'm rehearsing it?"

"What makes you think you'd know if you were? It's the subconscious."

The restlessness peaked as Fridgeon shifted in her chair with unease. "I don't think this breakfast is a good idea!"

"No," came the reply tad too quickly. The next words fumbled their way at a slower pace, "Sorry, I tend to-. . . forgive me, please go ahead."

It could have been a keenness to share her conundrum with someone but that incentive coupled itself to the realization of her alternate eagerness to draw an earnest attention from Kanha Evian. If fresh breakfast wasn't going

[55]

to achieve that for her, then let it be his momentary guilt. She was glad and satisfied, and she continued, "To be honest, it didn't look that bad given that the front half was very much in shape and standing still. The sudden jerk would have been enormous, but still. Oh, I don't know . . ." Frustration had returned as she concluded, waving her hands in mid-air.

"What happened then?"

"I ran, as fast as I could," she continued, massaging her forehead with both hands now, eyebrows stretched under the stress, "Two guys helped him out on the other side of the car. By the time I reached him, he was unconscious with a lot of blood soaked all over his right, and on the ground. They said they needed to take him to an emergency ward immediately. They had to operate him the next day."

Kanha looked at her through his constricted eyes, with no specific response but with those fingers continuing to gently rub against each other. "Go on."

"But there is nothing to go on with, Kanha . . ." she almost pleaded, seeking some help. "When he came out, he looked quite normal. In fact I was so relieved to find him that way after all that I had feared. For the first couple of months, there was no significant change. But then as days passed, he began to grow violent. First I thought he was having bad days at work, but then he became more erratic. I began to fear he was having an affair or that I was not goo- . . ." her voice choked, "good enough for him." She began to sob with her face buried in her palms. Kanha didn't say a word. She continued, probably under an impulse to get it all out of her system, "But I have known him and this wasn't his way. A bad breakfast and you use it against me – that I understand. But a perfectly normal breakfast and you complain as to why it tastes so "humanly good"..? I just don't get it!" She grew increasingly animated with those last words. Kanha raised an eyebrow. She went on, "From then on things only intensified. Every now and then, I would notice him stare in mid-air and wave his hand as if trying to swat a fly. The very sight of it irritated me. Yet, for some reason, he never showed his anger in those moments. Anyway, there was also his skin: it had turned to a weird shade. It looked thicker . . ."

"Where had he been operated," Kanha interrupted her.

"It's this hospital," she said trying to remember its name, "on the outskirts itself . . ."

"Where, Fridgeon," he nearly requested, "where on his body?"

"Oh, umm . . . leg, torso, arms – mostly internal, except for the fingers which were broken, and a chipped off elbow. His eyes too; they said blood had gorged them."

"What happened on the morning I found you?"

"It was the night before," she corrected. The clock ticked on as she tried to regain her voice and then spoke with sarcastic amusement, "Those are excellent love stories we keep hearing as we grow up. What's more amusing is how we are so willing to believe in them. It's not the real deal, I guess. Our love had never really prospered until, ironically, sometime before his accident. Yet, only a few months ensured every trace of it was wiped out again. On that night, it became a matter of an unresponsive love against my own life. So I chose one."

"As a result, he escaped to the Alps," Kanha concluded rhetorically.

She explained, staring at nothing in particular, "We had taken a break from the daily routine. I thought it would do him good, let his mind drift from the usual. We had ventured to our summer house in the mountains. But the vacation only lasted till that evening." By now she was visibly shaking. "That evening, I heard sounds from the kitchen and rushed in. There he stood . . . I saw him . . . against the window on that dark night . . . he resembled an animal. He sounded like one. I mean, don't get me wrong. I

[57]

am not saying he had turned into one. I'm not that stupid.
But he felt like one. Oh, maybe I was hallucinating."

"That's when the scars came?"

"He nearly jumped at me and his nails did what you
have seen already. He screamed and screamed but I ran
towards the door and he didn't follow me. When I came out,
I heard the window shatter on the other side. I didn't stop
until I had reached the highway."

"Thereafter you took a lift and reached the city by
morning, but with no money in hand, were compelled to
stay out. . ."

"I was afraid to go home. I still am."

Kanha's face finally allowed an expression; it was
one of sympathy – born out of her troubles or her naivety,
one could not say. He asked in a subdued tone, "What did
he do?"

"Meaning?"

"His job…"

"Oh, he was just a manager at Scinoi Bee."

Kanha's eyebrows suddenly straightened. The
following blink was relatively long. He asked, with eyes
shut, "Which department?"

"Marketing."

"Any contacts with R&D?"

"I wouldn't know. But there wouldn't be, right? For
a company like that, I mean his job was concerned more
with public relations. Finished products – energy systems –
electronics . . ."

"Well, marketing and R&D often go hand in hand.
Any promotions in sight?"

"Again, I wouldn't know. Why are you asking me
all this? You think it was some paltry office politics?"

"One would fancy approaching that answer, but no
I'm not implying anything like that."

"Kanha, thank you for everything. I mean no disrespect, but what difference does all of this make to you?"

"Curiosity, perhaps. I didn't mean to force you but maybe saying it out could have helped."

"It did," she said with painful thankfulness flashing across her teary eyes. "I'm sorry but that's all. I do not know about any promotions but there were plans of a reshuffle that he was quite excited about . . ."

"Due to Scinoi's recent acquisition?"

She paused for a moment and confirmed, "I guess."

"Thank you, Fridgeon, for an excellent breakfast. I hope my plate finally clarifies how much I love good food."

She smiled under the last tear that was shed and forgotten. She replied, "It's not your plate but how you eat that does."

The corners of his lips yearned to stretch further than he would allow but he pulled them back as he got up from his chair and remarked, "I would like to look further into this, if you wouldn't mind. Consider this your home for now. Just one last thing . . ."

"What?"

Kanha spoke, direct, unblinking and measurably solemn, "You probably weren't hallucinating that night."

Chapter 6

"Where are we?" A very exhausted Qin asked, staring at the little house that stood before him.

"Home."

"But this is not where we were earlier . . ."

"No, but that was a little too bland, wouldn't you agree?"

"You have two houses?!" he exclaimed in an excited voice, despite all the effort it took to merely utter the words. There was no reply except for her customary smile. She held him with one hand and waved her gloved fingers at a little knob from a distance. A beep sounded as the knob turned green and the door opened. "Sleep," she ordered him.

The little fall had not hurt but had instigated severe difficulty in Qin's breathing. She had dragged him along to a different residence and was now helping him to his new room.

"What? No. I need some medi-"

"Just," she emphasised, "try to sleep."

Qin lied down and shut his eyes. Sleep dawned abnormally quickly and he woke up after another indeterminate period of time with a sweet taste in his mouth.

"Better?" Friuli asked, sitting beside his bed with one leg crossed over the other.

"Yes, much."

"It was probably the sudden shock. It's an expected physiological problem."

"Well, for good reason."

She was there to attend to a splurge of curiosities he bore in his heart, or maybe just to tease them a little. So she waited until he asked, "That greenery . . ."

"Vegetation growing on walls, the plants usually sit on a soil-free setup. Irrigation channels deliver the nutrients." She clarified, waited a while to allow his curiosity to instigate her smile, and explained, "It started with experimental decor and Eco-friendly advertisements. Bonsai on office desks or plants in balconies have always been soothing to our eyes but none of these could counter the increasing pollution, and maintenance was quite an issue. So a desperate need for the greening of all inhabitation arose. However, there was no space in the cemented spread of cities and planting trees in one corner of the world was not really efficient, even though effective on some levels. So we were forced to transcend our mental fixations with vertical growth."

Qin nodded in agreement, "I knew things would get that desperate sooner or later."

"But it was not just pollution," Friuli reasoned, "you see, one good thing that happened with time was an increase in our ability to equate seemingly unrelated factors. In this case, for instance, a bigger concern was not the physical damage to our health but a psychological one. A polluted living coupled itself to our constant engagement with digital information at which point, our eyes and brains were left with minimal escape route to rewind since we had already robbed them of proper sleep. This created an omnipresent sense of irritation that led to regular tiffs and constant negative inclinations. The latter was especially aided by greater competitive nature our being had come to entertain – owing either to an increased population and fight for limited places or to newer avenues like social media that subconsciously necessitated a constant attempt and empowered us to create and maintain a certain social image."

[61]

"Was there a way to measure them then?"

Friuli was taken aback but she fashioned it with a smile and commented rather cryptically, "Feeling right at home, aren't we? That should make things much simpler."

"Like what?"

"There wasn't one at first," she answered, ignoring his most recent question as purposefully abstract, "and so a new system waited to take off until we found a repercussion that could be measured in black and white - efficiency. With a continuously distracted and tired mind, our work efficiencies reduced visibly, as did the utilization of 24 hours that had begun to look smaller than ever. There were other forces at play too but none looked obvious at first. Anyhow, point is that one of the things we did was carpet our walls with plants. Trivial as it sounds, its initiation and duplication worldwide was very much generally consented to in light of an increased sense of relaxation it brought to our minds. Its expansion took time but gradually, it became necessary by law. These little crawlers soaked up the pollutants and gave us a visual treat, made our oxygen easier to come by, cleared our brains and made us fall in love with the concept."

"It is neat, indeed."

"That is not all that went green. I mean, well, many more obviously did. One among them, to your interest, is what I wore this evening."

"That was leather," Qin remarked with sarcasm.

"Yes, but it was biocouture devised from organic materials – bacteria, yeast, etc. That's quite a far cry from being a product of some tragic sacrificial significance." Qin was suddenly much alert and very awake on his bed. "Take, for instance, one that you've been wearing. It's a normal cloth but treated with detergents awash with catalysts that cut airborne pollution much in the same way as those greens on walls do."

"As instead of producing an entirely new line of clothes, that just turns every existing one into an anti-pollutant," Qin concluded, establishing well his level of agreement with this ingenuity. Friuli just gave an acknowledging nod. He asked, "What else did we end up innovating?"

"Oh, this is just the beginning." His eyebrows creased in doubt at the overt gesture. She continued, "Is it that hard to believe? Try to recall the times you can. Scan through the ten-twenty years that preceded it. Weren't there so many things that had bent our collective thinking and had consistently produced the "next amazing thing" within the span of a generation?"

Qin thought over it. It was true. It was always difficult to notice change when one constantly looked at it. The magnanimity of any such difference was only pronounced when considerable time had elapsed in a complete lack of awareness. Qin wondered if he was fortunate to be in that unlikely situation. Yet, the proportion of change he now witnessed was far greater than any he could think of.

"It's equivalent to several decades of change that I remember," Qin said, partly in response and partly to himself.

Friuli argued, "Well, as times pass, we evolve in intelligence, capability and experience and build up on previous ones much faster. It's like a snowball effect."

The argument was not complete but Qin accepted it, under the lack of any foundation to attack it on. He had, after all, just woken up and was yet to see much else.

"I noticed some of the dresses just . . . change themselves in design?"

"Well, they also transmit data and help their wearers stay online at all times. But it's also fashion. I'm afraid that is as socially misdirecting an influence as ever."

Qin looked at her with interest. Friuli realized she had given herself away in part with the heightened tone of her words. She stopped abruptly when he asked in a disguised manner, "So you don't like it either - the social misdirection."

"Well, I just think it's a little extravagant; something like the feeling a renaissance prodigy would get if he came to a different time."

"But you haven't. You have been with the current times all along." Friuli did not reply. He continued, "It's amusing, considering how excited you seemed out there."

"Excited? If you must know, I do approve of the electrification of clothes, even if flashy LEDs are too far-fetched."

"Why is that?"

"Because it's handy: a data transmitter cum wireless charger on-the-go. Your body is a material like any other, Qin."

He did not immediately speak next and Friuli was only too happy to observe his state of thought. "So if the body is effectively transmitting information, it can transmit just about anything between devices it comes in contact with . . ."

"Yes, and it does. Once you look closely, you'll realize that the world we built was one of a very different kind of automation where minimal human intrusion was just a psychological fact. In actuality, it is us that make all the functioning possible. The devices, if I may say so, are using us."

Qin was uncomfortable. There was no denying the fact to any who could see him. His worries were justified, especially for someone who had not been introduced to the detailed functioning of the place. He asked again, "So we lose all control over any such thing."

"We never had complete control anyway. Perfect control was an illusion at best and we collectively ensured it. Even if one could have such perfection, the use of that control was an obsolete theory. But this is a much more intense argument, Qin. You'll have time to look over it. Believe me," she said with a strangely intensified look in her eyes, "it is important that you do. First though, you must get a three-sixty degree understanding of the human space as it exists today."

Qin nodded, although he hadn't really understood. He was solemn and still thinking about how everyone came to employ all this so fast and enjoy such vast levels of consumption. It led his mind drift to a more personal issue. He inquired, as if suddenly realizing the novelty of the room, "Where's all my stuff?"

"You don't have any," Friuli answered, underlining the triviality of the inquiry.

"What?"

"Relax. Few you'll get. Others you shall buy."

"Buy? But I don't even have any money."

She expressed some sort of an understanding towards his concern but could not hide her inclination to giggle, which translated itself to a harmless grin. She stood up and replied, "You won't need any."

His assumption of an intended attack at his self-esteem was anticipated even before he was through with the thought. "Don't worry," she said, "had you not taken that little tumble today, you'd have already had the answer to this one by now."

"What do you mean?"

"Only that an entire world changed while you slept, Qin. Tomorrow you'll see exactly how and why."

She walked out and left him to rest. It was a far-fetched expectation though. He was not only perpetually restless as long as he was awake but now also filled with curiosity. He scanned his memory to find leads but it only aggravated the pain in his head. It was a nice trick – as it seemed to him – which Friuli played each time, leaving him to think of answers, knowing he would not be able to for more than a few minutes. He eased down and looked around.

The room felt far less evacuated than the previous one, and mysteriously dynamic. The wall he faced was covered in mahogany – an unusual choice for an architectural era that seemed to have shunned all materials with a high perceptual density. The floor was wooden as well, lined in diagonal pattern of thin and long blocks. The two walls on either side were earthier, wearing a uniform rough texture in shades of soil and shadows. Driven by an anomaly that only added to his overflowing curiosities, he activated his lens once again and focussed it on the wall in front. It read:

Theme: Terra. Developed by Yuefen Zang. Glasswork by Veneziani. Informatics by Scinoi Bee.

He wondered, *Theme?* and turned the mute off. A voice read out the entire message to him, followed by a suggestive *"You may state your choice."* He looked at the first word projected in mid-air, and blinked. A new message read out, this time in a very energetic voice: *"Now you can choose from over fifteen hundred themes submitted from all over the spheroid and including the works of artists like Yuefen Zang, Sirita Nostri, Angle Manning and many more. You may design and personalize your own themes and sell them to over eighty five thousand other users in this community, or you may become a premium member and gain access to Scinoi's worldwide community with, well, nearly everyone worth noting – all of this starting at as low as 200 carbons."* The voice died out significantly more excited than it had begun. There was no further intrusion. Qin blinked on 'Terra' and a list of themes appeared in alphabetical order. The names were mostly uninformative since they had probably been designed by random users. Instead, he blinked on 'categories' displayed further left, and ran through a considerably shortened list. It was useless to decipher much. He chose 'Aqua', followed by a randomly chosen 'Baarish21'.

It must have taken the span of one blink. It seemed as if the wood had begun to dissolve on the walls and for a split second, he observed a blank coating of what was now revealed to have been some form of glass all along. But immediately thereafter the colours emerged again on those glassy walls and began to curve with fluidity and to spread as waves, resembling a drop of ink diluting itself in a bottle of water. He tried to wave off the projections on his lens to get a clearer view and shut it down, but even this panic-ridden act proved to be too long to observe the process that had unfolded. For, the room had turned to a rainforest on the edge of a lake. The latter came to view first on the front wall as he saw a body of water stretch out three-dimensionally till a very distant horizon where it merged with dense rainclouds. The surface was rippled with raindrops and bore little still waves of flowing water. On either side of him, the walls fashioned few huge leaves surrounded by many smaller ones stemmed on to trees and hedges that made up a dense jungle view. The show stealers, however, were the static rainfall and those crystal clear raindrops hanging by the edges, which collected onto the grooves of those bent leaves whose very veins shone under a faint hint of light from above. The resolution was so clear that his eyes did not dare move and explore the rest of the room, smitten as they were by the degree to which he could see a hint of his own shining reflection in each miniscule drop. He slowly turned to the roof, trying to figure out the source of light, but could see none. Instead, the roof carried the rainclouds along its length with gaps through which sunrays seemed to appear even as the giant star stood hidden behind. He lay still, soaking up the enormity of what lay in view. A few minutes later, he switched his lens back on. Details appeared, automatically muted, but this time there was an additional option: *Play*. He blinked.

Slowly he felt the virtual leaves beside him begin to twirl, bend and spring back under the force of virtual raindrops that had begun to fall around into oblivion. They simultaneously shook, led perhaps by a sort of wind that seemed to push the rainclouds as well. He would not have noticed it had the imagery of a gap in the clouds not passed right over him. For, right then, directly upon him shone the sun that had emerged strong and pure – the source of light. It was virtual, electronic and confusing. The lamp, bulb or LED that had flashed itself a while ago on those leaves was now prominently on his head, as if moving along the walls with those clouds, under a perfect computation of artificial intelligence. He turned on the sound. Leaves began to crackle. The wind began to blow by as the ripples spread on the lake. The raindrops began to hit an invisible ground, the clouds expressing their thunderous intent. The entire transition had been smooth and Qin remembered how auditory and visual adjustments had been made the very first time he had opened his eyes, back in the earlier white room.

He had been marvelling the sights and sounds that had transported him across continents when one sudden, deafening thunder jolted him up from his bed with ferocious intensity. All sounds fell back to normal the next moment and amidst efforts to settle down, he heard someone laugh. Friuli entered in splits and apologized.

"That was not funny," Qin shouted, or tried to.

"I'm sorry," she said, with her laugh subsiding, "I heard the sounds and couldn't stop myself."

"I thought I carried the control to these."

"In your head, yes. But physically, the room is multi-user, like everything else. Also, well," she underlined, "I'm the mistress of the house."

Qin sat back against a pillow stacked apparently along a broad brown bark of a virtual tree. "That you are, sadly. What else does this place do?"

[68]

Friuli looked around and tapped things in mid-air. Soon the place grew chilly as wind began to physically hit Qin from one corner. The settings were ambient though and Qin smiled against himself. "I get the point."

Friuli switched back to the former setting.

Qin inquired, "But . . . what about these moving lights?"

"Most walls are either integrated with LEDs or just fluorescence or radiant properties. There are few basic inclusions in every structure, Qin: lights, speakers and computers, as you can see. The intention is to allow two things to any resident: connectivity and convenience. So every flat surface that you see is potentially a screen for any kind of computation, equipped with everything you ordinarily expect to find. The other major addition is sensors – the good old technology but seamlessly integrated. These are what account for the comfort you feel on every bed, every chair or wall in the house. The ones in the furniture adjust the surface – seats, cushions or agility – according to your body shape or the force that you apply. The walls change shades of light to keep everything soothing to your eyes, and if you'll notice clearly," she said, winking, "they hide all damages; keep things looking new. That, naturally, saves a lot of shopping. Though, people shop nonetheless."

"Well, this is . . ."

"I see you are not impressed."

"I am. I mean, I just can't get my head across these. I'm constantly unable to understand how all of us came to afford such extravagance."

"By making extravagance sustainable."

"How? Did a chunk of population just kill itself and reduce the inflating demand?" Qin joked. Friuli, though, took a deep breath under creased brows, all of which drowned amidst the dense environment. She was suddenly very serious and disturbed. Her face straightened moments later and she replied much more empathetically, "Wait till tomorrow." She looked at him with relatively greater love. He could not figure out a response or deduce much from the sudden change in her mood. She relieved his hesitation by continuing, "Can I ask you something, Qin?"

"If you don't know the answer already," he said.

"This one I would like to hear from you."

"Ask me."

She framed her question, direct as she could, careful not to twist it in any way, "You have been awake for some time now. Why have you not inquired about your family?"

He stared at her, his heart spelt out in behaviour he had already expressed. Now he was being asked to explain it, and he could not. In any case, he was in two minds on whether he should tell her anything. He asked with hope, "Do you know where they are?"

"No," she said simply.

His heart sunk again. It was not about family as much as about the truth that surrounded him. Something was unsettled, unexplained, and even in her most touching gaze, he found hesitancy. Yet, while he was busy configuring a response, she probably sensed the lump in his throat, put a hand on his shoulder and gently pressed it. Her little smile and that touching gaze were no different but in that moment, he saw how her support had probably been his life for a length of time he could not measure. And all feelings of suspicion and analysis took a back seat against that simple truth. She dimmed the brightness in the room and walked out. Qin kept looking at her. *There's one who did matter, even when I was asleep,* he thought, *just like them, in their own little way.* They had cared with their life once and yet, he had not inquired. *Why indeed?* It was not like he had not thought about them . . . about hope. Had it been longing, or actually, worry? He had opened his eyes after an undefined period of time and would have wished for them to be around. Those initial moments had passed by in a heavy state of seclusion and headaches. He had not pondered much. He had learnt not to. But as he gradually recovered in strength and in adaptation, he had wondered . . . and avoided. They were people who had loved him and he felt a sense of overwhelming guilt at having been questioned. But how could he explain? What explanations could possibly summarize why he had boarded the train and why falling out had inexplicably entwined relief with remorse and realization that it was all too late?

That was so until he had woken up from his coma. Time had shown its mettle to him. 'Too late' had been rendered a word of theory. So he had delayed that piece of information till he could grasp onto a flood of novelties that had been thrown at him . . . rather, ones he had been thrown into; he had resisted the temptation to inquire till he could quench the other, more immediate ones. For, his family would not be looking for him – of this he was sure. How could he explain the complexity of human thought and of its strange motivations? How could he tell her this and yet emphasize just how much he loved them; just how much they had probably gone through due to that love?

How could he tell her that fate had rendered him dead in his family's memory?

How could he tell her that the only one who could answer her questions was a mysterious fly . . .

Chapter 7

A chair stood in the middle of the room, isolated from every other object as if it had been shunned out but forced to exist within the limited perimeter of that space. Many had arrived bearing a greater panache, few of which adorned the house itself while others were both popular and on the rise; yet this chair stood defiant in its simplicity and utter rejection of all that was new and fantasized about in the world of furniture and entities of human use. It did not bear any arms and stood on four thin legs that curved outwards, connected by equally thin leg rests, much as the seat itself which was made of a mesh of woven cords. The back shaped out a gentler curve as it rose from the seat with intermittent horizontal rods. These were thin and the backrest would not allow such meekness to spoil its image, for it rose like a crown, proud in supporting the tired body of the man that sat upon that chair, as if it were trying to stamp upon every other object in its vicinity that it still bore strength; that it still bore some meaning.

The man sat with one leg closely crossed over the other. His elbow was hooked around the left edge of the backrest with the thumb and forefinger resting on his forehead as if to guard a splurge of thoughts, while the other three spread out, covering his eyes from all view. The room was an ordinary affair, both dingy and partially stained. There was no complication on its walls, meant to prevent any drift of thoughts that oscillated within its bounds. A singular table and a small bed lay on the northern side, adjacent to each other. On the wall opposite the entrance was a full-height three-fold door that opened up to another side of the common balcony. Three-quarters of its height was covered by a metal shutter while the remaining was positioned out of view by the cemented guard outside. Beside the door lay a small couch covered in white artificial leather, followed by an open cupboard that covered the entire eastern wall. Newspapers and files lay spread all around – the floors, the bed, the tables and those few inches of cupboard racks. Amidst the old sat the only gleaming trace of new – his laptop with its lid thrown upright and ignored, as its screen displayed some twenty tabs, filled with the latest updates on research and global news. Five in particular were dedicated to Scinoi Bee.

He had been sitting there for several hours now, drenched in effort and hope. The former announced itself in the mess that lay around even as more continued to brew in his mind. The latter was more simplistic and succinct. Every now and then, the walls would echo with the words, *"Not her. Please, not her."* She had been a distant and often indirect subject for many years now – like a soul that had departed and was lost in the pages of time. There were no issues that could cause a flutter in him, but the memories were a different bargain. The former were external agents that he had learnt to ward off and detach himself from. The latter, though, lay within him. Every now and then, faces flashed before him, doused with an expression of decaying pride that had been stabbed with pieces of broken hearts. She had turned away from him once, for the last time ever, and imaginations of those jaw muscles tightening under resolve still haunted him every time he closed his eyes. He would have tried to rescue her and mend those broken strings of emotions that lay buried deep within its stakeholders. But efforts had been put to rest even before he could expend them, for her whereabouts had come to him on their own, and rather publicly so. He had heard and read all he could to as much detail as could be mustered, and his emotions had settled-in deeper. Any effort then, was a waste of time until time itself could proclaim its worth.

His thoughts returned to the contemporary as hours ran their course. His muscles had tightened as his mind raced through those passing minutes, slowing down time itself. The breathing grew heavier and the scratches of memory began to chisel out a stronger heart. *Au fait*, he said, finally raising his eyes to look beyond those fingers directly at the cupboard in front, standing in brown as a memoir of the very Earth that he loved. A resolve arose: There shall be no collateral damage.

Many moments later, he walked out to his original room, now occupied by Fridgeon. She was not there. He looked out to the balcony and saw a woman stand against the railing, looking out at a height that was way above any structure in the neighbourhood. A little breeze was gently striking her stance. Her dress in grey satin waved by it, accentuating the sides of her legs upon the smooth stretch of her bare feet. Her hands were crossed around her waist, held one over the other but the fingers periodically ran over her upper arms, trying to comfort their owner against a cloudy sky. The cloudiness was partial and the sun had almost set, throwing by the last traces of its radiance on her. She stood there with those silken strands of her neatly brushed hair teased continually by that breeze. Her eyes had not blinked for quite a while.

His eyes relaxed, as did the corners of his lips. He walked up to her and she adjusted her pose at first notice. "Temperature's dropped," he said.

She continued to stare straight ahead, "Hmm . . ."

"Did you sleep well?"

"I did," she said with a little nod. Silence prevailed for a while. She broke it, "I can't thank you enough for . . ."

"Don't," he said, emphasizing it with his palm.

She gulped her words down to his acknowledgement and then voiced her concern, apparently only after having won a silent debate with herself on whether she should say it at all. "I don't know what I'm going to do. I left everything back in the woods – my phone, money . . ."

"You won't need any." The words came upon his lips faster than he realized. He could understand the nagging sensation of uncertainty that could have dampened any person's spirits. "Its fine," he assured her, "You'll work a way out. Until then, you are my guest." His words were supposed to carry a smile that he would not show. She returned it with a half-smile that was expressed more in gratitude from her body language.

Few seconds passed as he finally breathed under a realization of his own aloofness, and continued as if to make up for it, "Besides, in a few years, none of us might need any anyway." It turned her smile to a question, prompting further clarification, "You can have all my cash if we could only jump in time a bit."

"What do you mean?"

"I mean history tells us that the money, as we know it, might soon die out. It'd be heartless of me to explain to you in detail since that may exponentially add on to your stress."

She smiled a bit more openly as her eyelids batted through one extended oscillation of her pupils between him and the sky. She said, "Leaving me hanging in curiosity is not very helpful either."

"True. Well, look at those shops below," he said and pointed at a chain of them across the street. "Almost all of their transactions happen through cards. Cash, even though still existing, is already almost phased out."

"Of course, but that's not something we need history lessons for."

"No, not at all," He said with a slight chuckle.

"Then what makes you say money will die?"

"Money as we know it," he corrected and proposed, "let me tell you a story, shall I?" An uneasy wait in courtesy followed. He then narrated, "Once upon a time, there were two men. Let's call them Prehistoric Uno and Prehistoric Due."

"Do we have to?"

"Well, it helps us shorten them to PhU and PhD, if you like," he said in quite an uncharacteristic tone than the one as she had come to identify him with. He continued with words that were preordained to carry an implied smile. "They were pretty happy going about the usual affairs of their day. They woke up, made weird sounds, hunted and ate what they killed, made more sounds and slept again; until one day PhD, being busy in educating himself of course, ran out of a good kill. Now he was quite hungry and without food. So he proposed to PhU that the latter give PhD some of his game and in return, PhD would cook it for them both using his newfound talent of creating fire. A piece of meat in exchange for warmth and cooked food – "*It's a deal*," said PhU, and so began a system of trading. Thereafter, knowledge and skill would exchange hands with physical wealth and utilities. Gradually, companionship began to evolve. Soon they began to grow crops and feed their family in ample proportions. Now PhD, and you'll be surprised at how he still lives, continued to sharpen his cerebral skills while PhU honed his physical worthiness; until one day PhU suffered from the possession of an infertile land. So PhD gloriously rose up to the occasion and came to the rescue, sharing his knowledge of growing crops on that seemingly unyielding land – let's call it smart farming – on grounds that he be entitled to a larger share of crops grown. Gradually thus began a system of bargain. Years passed by, with crops and cattle allowing a shared prosperity of the most intelligent species known to Earth. It rose and evolved. The two gentlemen lost a lot of hair and began to find their own ways of sophisticated survival. Slowly, possessions grew; they were no longer bones or edibles but seemingly useless solids that later came to be addressed as gems. Now these were excellent ingredients to build tools with and also novel objects with novel definitions and hence, revised values. The two naturally grew greedy, competitive and flashy. No pun intended."

Her smiles never ran their full course but she could not help notice his attempts as the darkening sky found itself suddenly ignored. "This story better be going somewhere . . ."

"It is. You see, this was a crucial time. For, when wealth comes into picture, consumerism and bankruptcy are always 'round the corner. Now PhD had accumulated a lot of goodies but they can't be eaten. So naturally, he gave PhU some of his possessions in return for the latter's hard-farmed crops. But this could work only up to a limit, for those objects were limited in number. Soon, PhD ran out of all things interesting to the other. All he had now were basic metals that resembled stones. So he came up with another idea – or was compelled to – one that would change the functioning of this world, again. He went to PhU, gave him a small piece of an ordinary base metal and told him that while it may not be something PhU would like to keep, it was something way more valuable. It was carte blanche; an object that could be exchanged for anything that PhU did actually want, and he would not need to give up his crops anymore. But since there had to be a limit to what it could be exchanged for, he engraved a mark upon it – say, 1 – declaring that as its value. In effect, what PhD had given him was a random stone that held value only when donors and recipients believed it to. So they did, given the limitless possibility of consumerism that came with it. This was the origin of . . ."

"Coins!"

"Soon, paper was invented, and PhD replaced the varying metals with a single universal material – paper, which was consistent and easy to carry. Thus, we ended up with promissory notes – cash. Now fast forward the time to one not so long ago when, for some odd reason, PhD ran out of all metals and papers he could have hoped to exchange. His demands, however, were still in continuous supply. So he went up to PhU this one last time and told him – on account of the good relations they had held for so long – that while he did not have any more material entities to exchange, he had something of unparalleled value thus far . . . a promise."

"A what?"

"A promise that he would return the value of goods he owes to the other person sometime in the future. While it might seem dicey, it wouldn't be so if everyone followed it. Sure enough, the new approach caught everyone's fancy and the evacuated exchange of value prospered. This last one, dear, may be addressed to as Credit – one you now so obviously see as being put to use in those shops through credit cards."

She looked across the street, having comprehensively forgotten about the clouds. Her lips parted twice in anticipation before she revised his story, "Crops, cattle, coins, cash, cards . . ."

"Fill in the blanks."

"So you think there will be a new one?"

"Do I think so? Look back at the years gone by in our time – financial crisis, debts, bankruptcies . . . don't you think we've saturated our capacity to handle this latest goodie?"

"But we have advanced as well. Look at the elaborate nature of our financial systems."

"That is true, and perhaps rightly so. A new level of wealth would certainly require a new level of sophistication and the ability to handle it."

"What would it be?"

"I do not know. Something," he lied. She looked away and took a long breath. Her amusement levels had run consistently low but she was glad to receive those little diversions that he provided each day. With the bleakest sense of longing, she looked down upon his hand resting on the short wall, fingers spread out and intermittently touching the cement surface. An inch of blackness that wrapped itself around his thumb stood distinct against the grey around. She asked gently, "What does it mean?"

"What?" He inquired, turning back to her.

"Those letters on your ring. KHaor?"

He looked down upon it and two noticeable changes occurred. The smile shrunk back while the eyes drooped. His lips parted without words and he looked away. She did not force him, surprised at her own sudden appreciation of a person's need for silent space.

It was his turn to breathe deeply. He answered with the information of greater contemporary interest to them, "It doesn't seem like your husband–"

"Jelzan . . . with a J."

"Right. Yelzan. It doesn't seem like he suffered from any particular hatred towards you, I want you to understand that."

"I hope so."

"From what you have told me, it could have been a case of nervous breakdown but while that would explain his mid-air hand flicks – which we can assume to be some sort of acute hallucination – it wouldn't reveal much about his growing frustration. You said he didn't behave rough in those times. The other cause could be personal grudges of a particularly violent nature against him, which could indicate conspiracy and solitude, but then that wouldn't explain the former."

"What's your point?"

"My point is that it's time for you to go . . ." he uttered with a blink issued above his pursed lips.

"I-"

"Do you know of a concept called bionism, Fridgeon?"

[79]

"Partially."

"It's not a radically new thing in town but only just beginning to have a mass appeal."

"Wait, he did mention it and seemed quite excited. Do you think my husband-?"

"No, I strive to avoid unhealthy judgements for the sake of quenching one's inherent need for spice."

"But chances are so."

"Yes, they are, as they are always, as are many others, as are also the ones that we couldn't possibly ever imagine. The point here is that there is only one way to find out and it's a twisted way, crucial as it might be. Would you be willing to cooperate?"

"Without a doubt," Fridgeon said, ready to take whatever measures might have been necessary to explain her loss and to get Jelzan back, if there was even an ounce of possibility.

"Very well. Tomorrow I must return to work, which I now believe would prove even more exciting. Meanwhile, you shall head to Scinoi Bee."

Chapter 8

"So what's the plan?"

"Consider it a date."

Friuli persisted with her cheekiness as she led Qin to the front door. The latter, clueless and brimming with energy, had kept those expressions at a minimum. He quickly recited the directions of movement as the door opened and they floated out. Friuli, a step ahead, turned to look at him as they turned right and headed out to a long alley of tall green buildings, now resembling a more natural urban jungle on that incredibly sunny day.

"Interestingly enough," Qin remarked, "it doesn't feel as hot, despite the sun. In fact, it's like last night, isn't it?" He added on seeing Friuli nod, "some sort of temperature control?"

Friuli continued to move with a sly smile. They went on for a distance without a word. The vertical greenery looked glossy. Greenery, though, was just an expression, given how the natural colours spread out in shades of red, blue and yellow too. The leaves shone, shadowing the ones beneath to create a wonderful gradient on those walls. The glasses were no longer blackened and streaming with videos. Instead they fashioned still images in solid colours upon the sober negative space. The balconies, meanwhile, continued to move back and forth at random as per their residents' movements.

"Did the financial crises of your time worry you?" Friuli asked, as they bathed under the pleasant sun on an idle morning of gossip, feet gently floating over the silent pavements.

"Partially, yes. But I couldn't do much about it anyway."

"So you were fine with watching money fall before you, as poverty, unemployment and other such social discords prospered."

"No, certainly not, but I never really believed that it would decline completely."

"Why not?"

"Well, entire nations or human species couldn't just crumble because of this. It was not our survival so much as the quality of our survival that depended on that money."

"You wouldn't have been able to purchase varieties or get a decent housing . . ."

"Maybe so, but we would have found a way, even if it took us back to pseudo-animalism."

"But?" she egged him on.

"I didn't really think that it would come to that. We have brains, and we have evolved."

Friuli smiled. "It is not just we who evolve, you know."

"Everything does."

"Correct, things - living or not. Some are automated, others we force."

"What do you mean?"

She looked at him half in anticipation of a self-constructed answer to his question, let him ponder and then said, waving her hands around, "Your biggest confusion is how we came to earn all this, right?"

"Yes."

"Well, money was that something else that evolved with us."

"You mean, in value?"

"In a way."

Qin brainstormed further, "In its usage, from cash to cards?"

"Go on."

"Well, cash, cards and virtual money are all based on currency as we know it. These are still money – the Dollars, the Euros et al – that is being used differently."

"Indeed," she said and with an almost girlish excitement in her voice, asked, "do you know what the difference between these were?"

"Tell me."

"Crops and cattle," Friuli began with a novel perspective, "were commodities of direct use to us. So whenever we traded with these, we received something we could consume immediately. When coins were introduced, however, we began to use an object that was of no real value. I mean . . . you couldn't eat the piece of metal for dinner or use it to make tools. All we could do was trade it further to buy what we actually needed. What this meant was that we had based all prosperity on an intermediary entity whose importance itself was defined by us and varied from place to place and from object to object. It gave us tremendous flexibility in adjusting the value, definition and commodities we could purchase as per our convenience. When the world expanded and collaborated, many such adjustments and accompanying calculations became too complex for anyone to perfectly handle, and more importantly, stabilize. Stability could only be achieved if we discarded these intermediate anomalies and went back to dealing with direct goods. That, though, would necessitate finding something that every consumer in all corners of the planet could use, and that was available everywhere, just like money itself. In other words, a universal demand and supply for the massively exploded population of Earth. It couldn't be crops or cattle. There was, as it seemed, just one."

She waited once more to let him absorb and process her words. His mind raced, as she continued from a different end, "It was in the final quarter of the second millennium, anno domini, that we saw the beginning of a techno-

[83]

economic paradigm that was to define our growth over the next centuries. It showed how the world grew on the back of a new technology, in cycles of half a century or so. It was like clockwork. Growth occurred on established technologies and managerial principles until every fifty years or so, things reached a point of crisis, of instability, of recessions. Such period propelled newer measures, approaches, creativity and innovations. Within a few years, an insurgent technological innovation – initially too expensive for mass adoption and silently lurking in the background – would mature enough to take charge and prosperity would begin to build up again."

"The way water mills made way for steam, which enabled railways, which ensured connectivity, which ensured mass production of goods?"

"I mean precisely that, Qin. Production, communication and energy were the three main sectors where growth occurred. Each evolution was either a dramatic change or just an increase in efficiency . . ."

"Fordism to Toyotism," Qin nodded in agreement.

"To mass customization. Energy, meanwhile, was a more curious entity. Steam gave way to electricity to crude oil & chemicals to processed oil & natural gas, to finally . . ."

"Renewable energy."

"The Renewables they were indeed, and in ample proportions, but tricky. They required expertise and it took us some time to reduce the size of wind mills or the rigidity of solar panels. It was beautiful, really, because the day these tools became sufficiently scaled down and significantly more efficient, we looked around and realized: everything in the past had been building up to this." Qin smirked, shook his head and looked up, ecstatic at the knowledge Friuli was showering him with. "Decades of infrastructural work had presented us with a system sturdy enough to carry a commodity of universal demand and

[84]

supply, like money. For, once we learnt to capture all available renewable sources of energy coherently in our homes, it became our surplus asset – one we could produce enough to give out to others in exchange for goods or services."

Qin's thoughts were now synchronized with Friuli's words, "As you said, anything that could even think of replacing money had to be equally in demand, irrespective of geography."

"It was necessary too. You see, despite all our fantasies and boastful proclamations, we as humans were still not rich enough – not even close, except for a miserly few. A lack of power, after all, was the bane at most places." A slight pause intervened to allow the thought to settle before Friuli quizzed, "Do you know what Edison's biggest challenge with the light bulb was?"

"Inventing it," Qin declared.

"Not quite. The product required an extensive singular effort, yes, but the concept had been developed much earlier by quite a few. It was its application that proved tricky, for that depended on everyone else accepting this new technology. To do so, people needed easy-to-reach shops selling this new invention, a readymade electrical connection to plug it into, and of course, affordability. Thousands could not simply shift from kerosene lamps to a light bulb overnight. That required an all-round ecosystem."

"So, the same thing happened with renewables?" Qin asked, simultaneously noticing a drone cleaning up the side of the road while another appeared at a table of customers in a nearby café. Both stopped for a fleeting second, as if to look at him, before returning back to work.

"It did so with their simplification," Friuli continued, "It was only when we had begun to generate enough in our homes to share that the funny thought occurred: Why not send out a portion of energy to the nearby grocer in exchange for one's purchase? However, an entity as

[85]

complex as this would not only require suitable tools but also a sophisticated management system." Qin's grin widened at the snowballing scheme of affairs as Friuli went on, "The anomalies of money-handling over the years had forced the financial system to evolve. Online networks had ensured pre-profiled consumer data whose use we had already consented to. Most appliances already ran on electricity or batteries. To complement it – and rather ingeniously so – logistics had become dirt cheap and exceptionally quick. In essence, a new system stood waiting – almost mocking our delay – complete with an entity in demand, an entity in supply, actors as producers, actors as recipients, actors profiled and ready to engage, a network in place with infrastructure at hand, and as if this wasn't enough – and it never is – a series of crises to spur us on."

"Quite a number of them, I suppose," Qin acknowledged with his enthusiasm firmly in place.

"Financial crisis – debts and bankruptcies, social and anti-political uprisings, disgruntled and hungry consumers – yearning to consume more as they had been habituated to but without enough money or supplies, the shortage of energy itself and of course, the larger climatic danger. And so it was – our journey from crops to cattle to coins to cash to cards to-"

"Carbons," Qin sighed with the words.

"Or carbon units, as we had been calling it for a different measure. Good word to go by, although coincidentally so. It makes you wonder about the true nature of coincidences, doesn't it?"

Qin did not reply. He was looking up at the buildings, as if the rays entering his eyes had shifted in the spectrum from visible light to x-ray. He whispered, "Qin45." Immediately a barrage of virtual information punched its way across his eyes with an enormity that was at first incomprehensible. He did not flinch this time, and began to work his way through them, shifting away words and focussing on ones he wished to look upon to dig deeper. "So there is energy in generation and transmission through each of these structures as we speak?"

"Much beyond that. For starters, think of all visible architecture as part of a body. Energy, in different forms, flows through it like blood in our veins – with high and low pitched pulses, varying with demands of each little entity in the system. Look at the roof of each building . . ."

"Wind mills. I can see them."

"Miniature ones. Now look at the windows; actually any and every glass pane that you can track, including," she paused, "the ones on cars."

His lips parted an inch to allow the words, "Solar panels."

"There are rods lining the corners of each structure to harness geothermal energy and had we been closer to the sea-"

"We would have witnessed tidal energy," he concluded, his eyes widened as he began to grasp the practicality of all he had heard so far.

"Now look at those little tubular structures, also at the roof, constructed at multiple levels. They collect rainwater – and in its scarcity, manually filled water – which is then dropped on to the level beneath to yield hydroelectricity – again a miniature version."

"Micro hydro. I guess you then drop it further to hydrate the plants on those walls," he said in a lower pitch, assembling the overall functionality of the system at play.

"Yes," Friuli confirmed almost childishly, enjoying his dive into the pool of fantasies that seemed to have come alive.

What Qin saw now was an organism. Without perfect sight, he was free to let his imagination run as the city pronounced itself quietly but with great dynamism. The current of energy flowing through every inch of what he saw was relentless but obedient. *Was this concoction*

[87]

beautiful? A sudden doubt pinched him out of his thoughts, and he asked, "Is that what spurred the whole thinking behind using energy as money? Utilizing every bit of what lay around us to support our own survival?"

Friuli had sensed a tinge of aversion in those last words. This was probably not where she had intended to take things, for she snapped back almost immediately, "Every bit of what lay around us was already an active participant in our survival, Qin, as was the case with all else that existed in the world. We were just too ignorant to accept it or understand how." Her words broke to a halt and she added as an afterthought, "Still are."

"What do you mean?"

"That it was an appreciation for Nature that brought us to this," she said, pointing out to all that lay ahead. "Come with me."

They went to a nearby café and sat around a little round table shaded under a huge red umbrella. It was contrastingly cooler within the span of its shadows. She tapped on the table and a menu appeared, displayed in full on the glossy surface. They scrolled through the choices as he took his time inspecting the images of each in high definition. After a third set of revisions, she intervened, "Here, try it this way." She clicked on "Latte macchiato", manoeuvring her way through few other clicks. A 3D image, complete with the style of glass and the pattern on the foam, rose upright in front of them. "Now go closer," she said. As soon as he did, he felt a certain whiff of its aroma. He jerked backwards and gave Friuli a puzzled look. She said, "Sensory-systems are a different domain altogether."

Once the order was placed, complete with hand-swiped payment of a certain amount of Carbons, she shut off the display and began to digitally draw something on the table. While her hands moved in practised strokes along the outline of a simple figure, she simultaneously spoke,

[88]

"Leonardo DaVinci once said: Human subtlety will never devise an invention more beautiful, more simple or more direct than does nature because in her inventions nothing is lacking, and nothing is superfluous." She waited to complete the figure and then exclaimed, "Behold, the Leaf."

Qin looked down upon a cluster of arrow marks structured as a simple leaf with alphabets and numerals printed upon it:

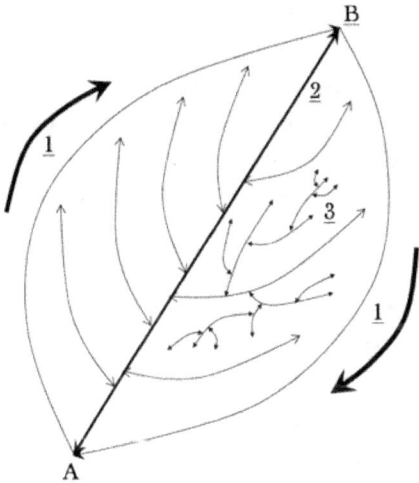

Friuli explained, pointing at the corresponding positions, "The day each one of us began to generate energy in our homes, we all became both consumers and producers of this currency. Consider our home to be at A here, dealing with a recipient at B – say, this café – which may also be a producer. Now suppose we wish to pay for our coffee. The first way to do so is to transmit energy through the direct route, marked 1. I can validate a transfer online, and any energy stored or being generated back in my house gets transferred here directly."

"But that would require an electrical carrier of some kind."

"Or batteries that can be manually transferred. Bear in mind that this can take place in either direction, like all other routes in fact."

"It may not be feasible though. What if you cannot generate enough energy at this time?"

"What about those other times when I may have generated too much and did not use it?" Friuli asked rhetorically and explained, "That is where a second way comes into the picture – the intermediary route or route 2. This is the one that moves via the Energy banks, positioned at any or all of these junctions in between."

"Shouldn't the very idea of an alternative currency with little leverage value threaten them? I mean, when their primary product is what makes them powerful, why replace it?"

"Because there *is* no primary product. There never was. What did banks do really? They enabled the management and investment of money to help it grow for those interested – practically everyone."

"Yes and that money is their product."

"Did they produce it?"

"They made it grow."

"How? Did every single currency note come alive and give birth to another note secretly in their vaults? The whole idea of banking was based on a play of time. There existed an assumption that if I continuously borrow money from everyone – investment you may call it – in the name of returning it with interest at a later date, I'd have enough at any given time to return to the few who ask it back. In simpler words, lenders, donors or investors would always outnumber the borrowers. Banks ensured it. It worked because it made practical sense – nothing unnecessarily scandalous but more of a necessary evil in an overpopulated, over consuming world of limited resources."

"Hmm. What you imply is that my return on 100 dollars after a few years is equivalent to receiving those 100 dollars, plus a little from someone else's pocket, who in turn would get his invested sum plus extra from someone else's at a later point, by which time, I'd have re-invested a higher sum, thereby making the amount available again!" Qin was gradually recovering to his more outspoken self. In that moment, Friuli drifted from the topic at hand to a momentary celebration at having drawn him out of his shell. He added, "Sales increase and markets grow after all. That is the objective of any business – to make money."

"They do but my focus is on the system of banking. It was one not loyal to a particular concept or limited to physical attributes. It was a play of time, and of willing people, regardless the entity in use. Although, I suppose this is harsh. These institutions did play a crucial role then, much as I detest them, and they certainly do so now that their prosperity is not virtual."

"So they have come to deal in renewables?" Qin asked but was startled by a drone that approached them with a tray. Their drinks were served, but for a moment, he felt as if the robot was looking straight at him, reading him with purpose like a mesmerized man. Qin stared back but recovered from the ephemeral trance as soon as he realized that the perception was simply a figment of his imagination. Little did he know that his heart had sensed something his mind wasn't yet aware of - one that would not reveal itself just yet.

"Yes, coming back to our Leaf," Friuli concurred, "what they may have done is collect energy from our house at regular intervals just like cash deposits. Only, in this case, they are more concerned with the physical handling of the entity rather than just our virtual accounts. There are other secondary actors that come into play here, but let's just stay on the surface for now. The banks may store the energy, transfer it to this café when asked for or carry out a similar transaction with any of these many other producer-

[91]

recipients marked by the arrowheads on the other veins – numbered 3."

"Yet, that problem must exist on the other end too, I suppose. This place may not require any additional energy at this time," he said, taking a sip.

"Of course, which is why most of the times, banks do not need to make an actual transfer. They just entitle the recipient's account to those many Carbons. The transfer is made when he or she needs it, unless he or she wishes to transfer it elsewhere."

Qin studied the image for a while as he sat bent forward over the Leaf with both his elbows resting on the table. Having intently spent several minutes, he fell back against his chair. Friuli adjudged his feelings in time and countered them in an attempt to keep him glued to normalcy amidst the extremities he was oscillating between.

"It's not the only inspiration of its kind to have come by, in case you find it exemplary," she said in an attempt at mitigation, "Seeds stuck to a sweater inspired the concept of Velcro; painless bites of mosquitoes inspired syringes; and mussels inspired a water-repellent glue. It is not about developing an intelligence quotient of a certain unparalleled level, Qin. It is about developing a sense of humility. It is about taking a step back and sparing a moment or two to prize the simplest of phenomena that take place around us, that life treats us to without a price. As it turns out, even a simple sense of appreciation as this could have only occurred to us once we had evolved sufficiently enough to realize the subtlety of importance in our being."

"Did we? Did we truly turn that humble?" he asked.

Friuli clasped his palm with hers and answered in a gentler tone, "I know how you feel, but I wouldn't bet on such a turnaround. For, humility, like all other such abstracts, is a relative term. Its definition changes with time and scenarios. This is why it is a matter of personal priorities and judgements. What matters is how humanity in its entirety, just like individual countries or any other holistic system, develops. Amidst all that seems erratic and random, there is something perfectly tuned and set almost on an "auto-pilot" – something that changes and grows or dies precisely at a preset time with a preset pace."

Qin cleared his throat as he brought himself to calm. He looked at the people moving around. They sat under the shadow of not just the umbrella but the neck-breaking expanse of greenery over and along the wall of the building the café lay under. It was a narrow street with two lanes, beyond which lay another building, facing them with its glass walls. The balance between the sheen and the green carried a high aesthetic quotient. Alternating vegetation and glass walls lined the rows on either side of the street. One wall was perfectly angled to receive the sunlight for its plant growth while the other building received it on its glass panes for the generation of solar energy. The roles were carried out by different faces of each building as the day moved on. The whole attempt had been directed towards creating a balance in functionality, aesthetics and economy, for advertisements needed their own all-glass space amidst the greenery around them. It worked well. Perceptually, the irritation at the sight of flashy advertisements continuously running along the entire length of a building was absorbed by the soft effect of pseudo-plantations on either side. Likewise the excessive wilderness on one was mitigated by the smooth glass-walls immediately around. In addition, the dynamic lighting effect of digital visuals cast a colourful radiance on the plants, thereby avoiding an entirely black-and-green visual.

Qin studied these with a casual glance. In that moment, it did not matter as to where he was or where he had believed himself to be. People looked fit, well-endowed and above all else, sufficiently happy – and that itself stood in complete opposition to all that he had ever heard being predicted about the future. It seemed too perfect to be true by his standards. *It couldn't be,* he thought. Times could change eventualities but not fundamentals. He steadied himself up with the momentary expression of satisfaction now gone and stated, continuing to look at the people, "This is wrong."

"What is?"

"Something. I do not know but this is all too perfect."

"You think it's impossible?"

"Yes," Qin replied without a hitch.

Friuli looked at him as he looked at the others. She studied the movement of his eyes, and had he turned to look at his initiator, he could have sworn her lips had twitched to a little smile. Her eyes were at ease, bright and blinking in an orderly fashion. She asked, "So what's wrong, Qin?"

"This perfection. It is perfection as we would have always imagined it – perfection by our standards."

"So?"

"Nature doesn't work that way, and it is nature that holds the key to all that functions. It is her obvious priority to keep things perfect on a grander scale and that perfection implies a balance – one for our own sake. It involves tragedies that can teach us lessons and help us grow. Those things are necessary for us to truly value what is good and achievable."

"Well, this is good and achieved by us anyway."

"Yes, but treasured by those who have seen the past, not by ones who will come in the future. For them – the successive generations – this will be nothing more than the ordinary. It is about our character. We are born to learn through mistakes and to strive to achieve what we do not have. All the anomalies and imperfections are inherent in us and absolutely undetachable. So as long as they exist, we need a seemingly imperfect world, for our own satisfaction if nothing else. Are you telling me that we have changed as a species?"

A shudder ran through the other's spine. Qin continued, "You said the problem with cash was that we handled it on credit on an assumption that there would always be an inflow of the same. Well, nothing guarantees an inflow as well as energy does, Friuli. It is limitless. It could potentially be the greatest promissory currency and hence, our biggest risk."

It was not just memory and facts that she knew but also Qin's deliberate critique that seemed to tear through all that lay before him. There were not many ways out towards procrastination. She said, "Do you remember your doubt over the distribution of authority and control in the energy network?"

"I do."

"This would probably only bolster your criticism over the perfections around but the Leaf model produced an interesting outcome: When practically everyone became a producer as well as a consumer, we reached an unparalleled degree of individualistic independence at a time when social boundaries had been diminished by globalization. This broke down the power barriers and singular control that had been traditionally exercised by specific stakeholders in any economic or political network. Yet, as you rightly said – those anomalies of imperfection inherent in our character continued to exist. So while the power play was theoretically flat, power itself was still chased above all else." She paused until he turned to her, and added, "The energy network itself might have had a certain degree of uniform fairness, but it was not the only big insurgence. There was also ICT."

"The internet?"

"All technologies of data and its transmission. Advanced. The next generation of seamless and spontaneous communication – automated and integrated in our lives like our own breathing as you already see to an extent. The beauty of this phenomenon was in how it forced our voluntary participation. One could hate it but not escape this worldwide web. Of course, it did help handle the Energy network better, for after the debacles we had experienced with the virtual management of money, we were now dealing with Nature directly and no one wanted to owe big to Her."

"Some still would," Qin said, staring at the air between him and Friuli, around three inches over the table surface. "Incredibly interesting; it seems as if the whole money-age had taken effect to teach us how to handle the next entity, and those crises had been like practice."

"In Nature's plan, it always is. How do you know you are not in one such build up even today?"

Qin passed a momentary grin at her. He certainly was, but if that was so, what followed this current phase of adopted utopia? Was that why Friuli had brought him there? Was she simply throwing breadcrumbs for him to follow and deduce? His mind raced back to the little accident the previous night. He had decided to wait and watch, and it appeared as though he had now uncovered a motive. Yet, unconfirmed as it stood, he looked up at the sky. There was just the ordinary occupation of sparse clouds and a bright sun on display. It was heightened perhaps by the sharp aroma of his drink that part-entered him and part-waved over to merge with that sky. Watching the vapour mimic the make of those moving clouds, he was suddenly compelled to question his simplistic reliance on whatever those eyes saw. He asked, "So what did ICT do?"

"Well, the online world was an addiction and had caught our fancies big time. So everyone was linked in virtually. Quite obviously, the companies that could own that space pretty much controlled that particular world of people."

Qin was still staring blankly when Friuli stopped talking. He reasoned further, "They would have all the profiles, registered and consented to, which itself would be a major selling point for marketing. Then they would also have all other forms of authority, because, well: it is information. And that is power."

"Does that really surprise you?" Friuli remarked with an almost mocking face, "Considering how eagerly we used to rush into adding every bit of our personal lives on social networks and everywhere else, from demographic data to our whereabouts to photographs to all our opinions – all dated and noted. Did you really think the firms were so much in love with your best interests so as to keep the laws perfectly tuned in your favour? We signed up in agreement to a particular policy of data use and in a few years, by the time we had grown quite dependent on it, those policies would undergo a change, at which point, we were given the option of accepting them or closing our online account altogether. Most did not care. Other could not disagree."

"Surely, global laws must have arrived with time eventually?"

"They did. There are privacy levels that need to be maintained and we have had a deluge of laws pertaining to this. But in an age of streamlined Big Data, things became much more elaborate than that and difficult to control. Energy and ICT were the new pampered kids. When the former became universally available, governments lost control over the entity. They could tax it at best. It was fine, for while this development had robbed the central authorities of a major source of income and power, those associated with energy had themselves taken a drastic fall. Effectively, the central powers were gaining more in terms of good image, reduced burden, relative international independence and incoming tax flows."

Qin looked down at his glass, trying to figure out a trend in all that he had heard. The beverage was half done. He had taken in its awakening smell, basked in its sharp taste and devoured several sips through their conversation. Yet, the mask of froth that had capped the top of that glass initially, still held on its own, preventing direct exposure to the principle content that lay underneath. Floating harmlessly, the humble, decorated foam, fashioning a smile on its face, actually proved to be the most obdurate guard in that container. To view past it, Qin would have to stir things up. First though, he decided to take another sip. "So what went bad?"

"Nothing went bad, evil or scandalous. Well, maybe the last one. The other entity – the digital one – was out of their complete control in its very character. No law could entirely cover the virtual space where people were participating, consuming and contributing voluntarily. It would have been like controlling the air around us. Together, these two segments were largely independent. Energy was so due to its fragmentation and coordination of multiple stakeholders of the Leaf model while the online space was so precisely because of the opposite – for its holistic offer of services to its users – a complete experience, as one would say."

An amused look resided upon Qin's face, for he was finally beginning to excavate what he believed were the first hints at imperfections around, which ironically, put him at some ease. Friuli noticed this and added, "You have seen the energy network. I think it is time you got a taste of the other big network in play."

"The pseudo-evil conglomerate?"

A sneer quashed his guess before she clarified, "Focus, Qin. Nothing surpasses the power of people. A small shop or a multinational conglomerate – they are all run by individuals at the end of the day; humans with their own motivations and choices. Only the banners change."

She was right, he thought as his sight shifted to the citizens. Amidst their murmurs, laughs and constant - mainly floating - movements, he noticed a sense of indifference. It was each one of them, including him, that had willingly shared every second of their lives online at the same time as they were dispatching data in every walk of life – at the grocer's, at the doctor's, in office. There were individuals within that crowd who had then carried out the analysis to make sense of vast amounts of data, find trends and make conclusions. So the scandals did not lie in conglomerates or large visible powers – those were just the beneficiaries. They lay in an unintended conglomeration of smaller, invisible ones. Subtle spasms of shock returned under the guise of misplaced excitement. Friuli did not have to explain, for Qin could see where the problem lay. He could see the "healthy and happy" people around.

Chapter 9

The grasses were longer than usual, partially discoloured and flowing flat. Fridgeon watched their restlessness as they waved in position with the flowing water that seemed to have drowned them eternally. The current was notably strong and she had never bothered to check where it came from. For, the canal had been artificially made centuries ago. It had served its purpose well, though the purpose itself had altered from time to time. There were two, to be precise, threading across the south-western parts of the city; straight lines meeting a couple of kilometres south of the centre of this radial city, carving out a piece angled approximately at thirty degrees from a largely circular piece of pie that Milano was.

Fridgeon stood on the right bank of one of these – the Naviglio Grande – a few metres away from where the two streams met. She remembered having taken numerous walks on the narrow streets that lined both banks. She could recall the knocking of her stilettos, like many others, on that charming pebble-draped surface of the road. The tiles, though, were now embossed with sensors that scanned the footfalls to immediately activate messages or projections of a particular shop every time a person crossed its perimeters. That was the order of this new world – one that bore shiny new elements embedded in structures that continued to fashion traditional exteriors.

Cars were not allowed and it bode well for the walkers as well as the chain of restaurants that set up their tables outside for multiple rounds of *apertif* – a kind of buffet – that the Milanese fancied in summer evenings. She remembered having spent hours popping in the dozen varieties of those little savouries, baked or fried and topped in familiar ways, while she held on to the thin stem of a conical glass graced with *il vino* that regularly moistened her lips as she idly chatted with Jelzan, feeling every wisp of the gentle cool breeze at play. *He loved the apertif,* she thought and remembered how she had craved it herself. Why wouldn't she? It was her outlet from the confines of a home that had come to comprise her world for most part. Jelzan had never been one to socialize much but his reservations ever since they had moved to the city had particularly dwelt upon. Nonetheless, he usually managed to balance the lack of comforting family friends. So prey to her own naivety, amidst her forgetfulness and a generally unassuming line of thought in the little period of her residence in Milano, it never occurred to her to question his state of affairs.

She looked at the stretch ahead. It was early morning and the sun had swathed the pavements and the water alike. The tables had been stacked inside the shops and the street was largely empty except for a few tourists. She looked at the opposite bank. A thin stream of water – barely a foot wide – flowed into an alleyway like a distributary of the canal itself. It was housed under a slanting red-tiled roof supported on bamboo sticks with several large slabs of stone placed slanting along its left bank. The place had been used for laundry once but now served purely for aesthetic purposes. The canal itself had been aimed to allow trade of goods to and from the city but now lay idle, tasked with reminding one of the richness of local heritage.

Her slender arms looked quite out of place on the metal fencing. The arms converged to fingers that gripped each other with an unusual firmness. She was staring at the long underwater plants that had been allowed to grow, then bent almost entirely so as to minimize their overall reach above the soil and as if that was not enough, submerged in flowing water that would not offer a moment of respite. That was, until winter came when the water would be drained and the plants left to shiver and freeze. Fridgeon felt amazed at this thought – she had never considered the Navigli as anything short of beautiful. Suddenly she found herself too aware of the ironies at play.

The canal had changed functions, which itself was an unimaginable eventuality for those who must have toiled for months and years to build it. Those workers had had a singular objective in mind, one they had consented to, found a valid reason in and had clung their hopes with. Little could they have known as to what becomes of their efforts long after they were dead. That, in a nutshell, seemed to be the truth with every human invention. Objects evolved and changed, either in structure or in functionality. "Things in this world often take a turn you never expected them to, even long after you are gone," she mumbled. The words had unsettled her further. She stood uneasy and straight, looking no longer at the water but keenly into the distance. *Is this what is at stake now?* She wondered as she stepped back and took a deep breath under tightened jaw muscles over her slightly raised chin. There was no time to waste.

Fridgeon walked up a sloping alley to reach an elevated main street. A yellow tram arrived just in time to take her to the central station. She did not like it, for the moment she stepped in, another sensor tried to track and identify her. She carried no ID, for that lay lost in a jungle, but validated her fingerprint to allow an automated online payment. It felt like a cage - the world wherein one lay immobile unless one abided by its rules, in which case one was trapped, and exposed, anyway. Half an hour passed before Stazione Centrale came into view, buzzing with activity beyond its tall gateway that was lit by a pyramid-shape arrangement of tube lights hanging from above. The station was settled in three levels above the ground. She could not help but feel a sense of liberty as she headed forth towards her train, stationed in the uppermost. Once inside, she tapped on the scanner implanted on one of the seats, entered her destination and sat down. That was her ticket. As the doors of the coach slammed shut, and she began to move, a weight seemed to lift off her momentarily. Even though under a definitive objective, to be able to leave the city comfortably positioned in a train with a valid ticket was a security that offered her a precious second's worth of respite. For that, she could only thank Kanha Evian.

The train moved through a melody of grey and brown before the former gradually made way for green. As her head rested on the thick stretch of the glass window, she looked blankly at the outside world passing by in haste. With her back facing the direction of movement, she allowed with mellowed eyes for the scenery outside to come by unannounced. She liked it that way: to stay unaware of what was to come next, just letting it all pass by her. Her tired eyes drooped in silence of the coach and muted slideshow of the scenery outside. At the very moment they closed entirely, the face of Kanha crossed her mind. She woke up immediately and looked out, thinking.

He had seen as many years of life as she had. Yet, his face held firm at all times as if his adolescence had been interrupted and never allowed to run its full course. His experiences had left him somewhat with a mature demeanour over a juvenile look, or perhaps, with the opposite. All she could be sure of was that there was something that seemed divided in him . . . on him. There was a noticeable chip on the curvature of his neck and right shoulder. A scar carried on to his back too. It seemed uncalled for that her mind had continuously wandered towards him in the past few days. She believed it to be her sense of gratitude towards all that he had done for her, and was continuing to do. She had felt warm on his couch and had been lured to sleep despite all her resistance. His food had been tasteless but she had looked forward to it each day.

While she had slept, she had felt as if he was watching her. *All that, though, was just a fantasy*: she thought and shifted in her seat. Moments passed before he returned, as she began to think of the times he had spent bathing her. An appreciation topped with helplessness at the rising warmth with every such touch was unavoidable. She had welcomed it with guilt, then with multiple justifications and then simply with soft breaths, letting it pass by just as those green fields currently did, covered under a blue sky that was gradually darkening. She looked around. There was but one ray of light she could see. It was him. He had saved her in body and soul and she could trust him. The knowledge gave her power in every moment of weakness that had followed her on this day and she was sure it would continue to do so.

The train arrived at a relatively smaller station, apparently more orthodox in its plain cement walls and undecorated edges, though not without more projections. She decided to switch to the road for her destination – Mongrando. She had heard about the place but had never had an incentive to visit. It was a small town in the commune of Biella with nothing worthy of note and housing, among others, a small factory. An hour's drive took her on a rocky terrain amidst a dense covering of trees. It might as well have been a hill station or an uninhabited forest. She was torn between her craving for such a view and her horrible memory of the recent past. A single lane curved through the woods for several miles until it arrived at a massive cove in which an old structure lay nestled, mostly out of view. It felt as if she had travelled back decades in time. Birds chirped loud and clear all around on those tall trees and the waning summer months had yielded them lush with leaves and with flowers that were beginning to charm their way through the numerous colours of autumn. Soon the green would turn into the yellows and the reds and the oranges and would bathe the long white structure that lay in the radial centre of that wide curve of the road, stretching behind and away from it. Few cars were parked outside and no sound came from within the factory. Smaller towns with uncluttered traffic and few, planned roads had come to accommodate driverless cabs, but they were still risky and experimental. She registered her cab to wait and walked in with some doubt.

The path that broke off the main road sloped down to the entrance of the front office in that cove, beyond which lay a short open space covered under the same roof, followed further by the long stretch of the factory itself which was beginning to spill out some noise as she came closer. Her steps hesitated as they arrived at the door. There were no signboards or indicators around and the plaster had come off the walls at several spots. She knocked on the wood. There was no response. A few minutes later, she quietly pushed it open to find a small empty lobby lined with a thick wooden staircase. A little ahead lay another door that stood partly ajar. She walked up to it and peeked in, but the room was empty. Her feet were about to turn when a faint creaking caught her attention. She looked up. One of the fans at the far end was moving. That portion of the room, though, was hidden from view by a wooden cabinet. There was no other sound. She walked up to it slowly, unsure as to why the place bore such an abandoned look. Hope must have risen within her, mixed with an unexplained fear, but it was all washed up soon after. All that stood there was an open window, throwing in the sounds of the birds outside flying on that of a gentle breeze that intermittently disturbed the window pane. She went out of the room and up the long curve of thick wooden stairs. Halfway through, she could have sworn she heard something again. She hurried up. There were just two doors on the upper floor – both washrooms. She checked each but no surprise of a human presence came by. One of the taps had been running, or possibly leaking rather fiercely. She came out, somewhat perplexed. The door was jammed now and would not shut but she tried nonetheless. *Perhaps, the factory,* she thought and turned. And then, her heart dropped.

A woman stood in the lobby staring up at her. 'Woman', though, was a stretch of definition. She stood motionless and did not blink; she could not. One of her eyes almost bulged out while her forehead bore a deep scar stitched over. Her hair was partially turned back but mostly splattered around. She wore some kind of a very thin uniform and stood almost directly under the spot where Fridgeon stood. "Lei . . ." she said in a coarse voice that accentuated her creepily abnormal demeanour. Fridgeon began to gradually step down, never taking eyes off the other. She opened her mouth to reply, "Sono-", but the words never came out. It felt, at that moment, as if all air had sucked itself out from Fridgeon's lungs and she nearly lost her balance midway, thrown back against the wall with one hand cupped on her mouth. It should have covered her eyes, for what they saw eviscerated all voice in her throat. The sunlight splashing through the window had filtered through the woman's uniform to reveal an outline of her body or in this case, an absence of one. There seemed to be just rod-like structures beneath her chest, with the internal system resembling tubes and sacks. And yet, she looked alive and human in conduct, if not so much in appearance. She moved forward towards Fridgeon with a step that creaked with legs that had bent outwards. The sunrays sprayed across to extend the view, and the last thing Fridgeon remembered was a painful crash. She had fainted.

Hours passed, given a significant shift in the position of the sun outside. Fridgeon's eyes opened partially and with great effort. Her head felt as if it had split into two from her fall. Four individuals stood over her as she lay on the lap of another. "Va bene," exclaimed one of them gently, "Ora va tutto bene. È una ferita minore." ("All is okay now. It is a minor injury.")

"Wh- How long?" Fridgeon mumbled.

"Non sappiamo," came the reply. ("We do not know.") The speaker was sitting on his knees with hands neatly tucked inwards. "Si può sapere a cosa è dovuta questa visita?" ("May I ask the purpose of your visit?")

"Who are you?"

He looked up at his colleague standing on one side with his arms folded, as if to decipher the appropriate response to a seemingly simple question. The latter replied in a grave voice, "The person in-charge of this facility, and at this moment, of your well-being. Now, please answer his question."

"I- I came to inquire," Fridgeon explained with a cracked voice, holding her forehead in pain, "I came to inquire about my husband."

"Has he disappeared?"

"Yes."

"Did he work here?"

"No."

"Then why would you suspect to find him here?"

"Because before he disappeared, something felt terribly wrong in him, just like that-" she stopped as her memory flashed back, and exclaimed, "Oh lord!"

"What?"

"That lady. Where is she?"

"Who?"

"The woman with no body."

"I'm sorry?" She could hear collective chuckles at her words.

"That woman. She was quite old, with wild hair, bulging left eye, a deep stitched forehead and," Fridgeon hesitated, desperately trying to sound credible, "no body!"

"I do not mean to startle you but I hope you understand the utter senselessness of your statements."

She looked up at them. They all wore plain clothes – shirts over trousers. The younger two stood with a bottle of water and some other liquid, while another held forceps that gripped on to some red-soaked cotton. He was the first speaker, still on his knees. The fourth now stood bent over her with both hands held behind him. She protested to the latter, who had just spoken to her, "Look, I know exactly what I sound like. I also know what I saw. Now there was a woman exactly as I have just described her to be. I want you to tell me where she is."

"With all due respect, m'am, I do not say that you are lying," replied the caretaker, "but as the in-charge, I'm fully aware of the personnel in this space. There happens to be just one woman here. You are lying on her lap."

She jerked forward to look back. The lady sat with eyebrows raised, concerned and awaiting a sense of the situation amidst all the confusion. Fridgeon looked at her properly and uttered, "You are, fine."

"Well, of course she is," continued the caretaker, "and she's the reason you're fine too. I hardly see this as a way to express gratitude."

"I'm sorry," Fridgeon addressed her, "Thank you."

"Not a problem," she replied softly, "May I add that the woman you have described sounds awfully lot like her." She pointed towards the opposite wall. Fridgeon turned to look, and saw a glass enclosure that housed what appeared to be a sample model of some kind. The face perfectly matched the ghastly one that Fridgeon remembered as having seen before.

"No," she said, disbelieving. "How could it be? Who is she?"

"A fake model for an abandoned test. Actually, just a showpiece now that they have shut down the facility indefinitely," replied the caretaker rather frustratingly. "One error and they cancelled the whole project."

"It was a failed experiment, Az," the other woman replied, "Lives were at stake."

[108]

"Aren't they still? How are we supposed to save them until we learn and correct the errors?"

"Hold on," interrupted Fridgeon, "what kind of test?"

"It doesn't matter. The question is why you came here to inquire about your husband."

"Why I feel something or don't is not your concern. I am truly thankful for your help but it is my right to explore all possibilities."

"Yes, but this is a closed facility. You are lucky that the few of us were here today to save you from your little fall. We were taking rounds of the facility when we heard some noise and rushed in. How did you come here?"

"I took a cab. It's waiting back there."

"I'm afraid there's nothing like that outside."

"That can't be! I had programmed it to wait."

"Apparently, the software changed its mind then. It's okay. One of us will drop you wherever you wish to go. Now, for the umpteenth time, why are you here?"

Fridgeon looked dazed, as though she had still not recovered from her fall. Her inconsiderate reply only bolstered that view, "What experiment was it?"

"A minor test on one of our specimens. Why are you so interested?" Az, the caretaker, was growing impatient, his gesture animated, tone high-pitched and temper beginning to fray.

It jolted her to normalcy as she finally answered, "Because I suspect that my husband went through a similar tragedy."

"Oh," he said rather loudly now, "You surely don't imply that. I mean, first a mystery lady and now a human experiment. Honestly, do you guys just sit at home fantasizing such stuff? We do not know about your husband."

"Jelzan. Jelzan Friuli. That was his name. He wasn't a 'nobody' at your company, this I know."

[109]

"Maybe not at the company. This, however, was a laboratory, miss. Our only connection with Scinoi was through the R&D head."

"Who was that?"

"Archer Piscoli. I do not suppose he will be of much help to you though."

"Why not?"

"Cos he is set to retire and is currently stationed in Dubai. It was his deputy that shut us down, just before she took over the reins of our new company."

"The IT one? What was its name?"

"It's anyone's guess," replied the one with the forceps. "Word is that they were shit – a social networking parody at best and yet to take off. All they had managed to develop was something they called an Incentivizer. Don't ask me what it did."

One of the younger men interrupted for the first time, and rather studiously so, "Energy. They hoped to incentivise people to record the production and consumption of renewable, along with many other entities."

"Yes," the former continued mockingly, "But who on Earth has the time or patience for all that? Anyway, the lads probably realized this and were more than happy when Scinoi approached them. Although why we did, I can't understand. We now call it the Beehive – the headquarters are in Milano."

"Via Turati, I know."

"Well, I suppose there isn't much for you to do here then," Az concluded, "You want the answers and she is the quickest way to get to them. Now we'll drop you at the station but then we suggest you go back and take some rest."

"Thank you, again," Fridgeon said, as she helped herself get up. They walked out to the couple of cars parked outside. She noticed on her way, a huge lock hanging over the doors of the factory. Now that it had grown darker, she could tell that there was no light inside and possibly no activity. It did not make much sense. She could have been sure she had seen the woman alive, but it was beginning to fade away under the headache and the cloud of doubt over her. The place lay abandoned, except for spiders. The trip seemed an utter waste, and a painful one. She asked the other woman walking beside her, "Who is this deputy that you speak of?"

"Not deputy. She's the Head now, and apparently very particular that everyone acknowledges that fact. Her name, if I am not mistaken, is Hope Leosword."

Chapter 10

"We could just float, you know?" Friuli suggested.

They stood out in the crowd as a couple walking on the shiny footpath instead of the usual floating.

"I like it this way," Qin replied. "It's been long." The logic was justified. Friuli did not argue further.

They were slow but seemed to enjoy tapping their feet around. The simple pleasure of human effort still bowled her over easier than others did. They were on the outskirts on a hilly terrain and a huge park lay in front, sloping down to the flashy settlement. They sat at the top, overlooking the habitation; their feet gently brushed against the carpeted grass ruffling noiselessly under an unusually constant breeze. Twilight had arrived and the city was already filled with a thousand colours of running light at a distance at the foot of that landscape. Even though the grass gradually darkened under the nightfall, true blackness never really enveloped anything around. The flashing advertisements and all other lights combined to shower all visible space with so much radiance that every surface looked like it had been draped with several rainbows. To him, it was still all new while to her, it was a change – a break to observe some things she hardly ever noticed otherwise. She sat supporting herself on both arms stretched at the back, while he sat with both folded over his raised knees.

Qin asked, "Why are you with me, Friuli?" They had spent most of the walk in silence.

"What do you mean?"

"It's a straightforward question. Why show me around?"

"Because you have to be introduced to the place." She answered equally sternly before softening up a little, "One can't just leave you alone, right? I'm your nurse and it is my job."

"What about your other patients then?"

"I work for one client at a time and that currently is you." Qin looked at her with eyes that declared how unconvinced he was. She said, "You are a long way away from home. You had ensured that before you met with your accident."

"Did no one try to contact my family?"

"Initially, maybe - tried to find them first, I mean. You did not carry any ID and there were no inquiries about you from what I hear."

"That can't be!" he exclaimed with a straight face.

"I feel so as well, but I do not know the whole story."

"Who does then?"

"Someone," she declared, "with a very keen interest in you. I cannot tell you much but as of now, you are to be acquainted with the place you are in."

"I do not understand," he argued, "Why prepare me for all this?"

Friuli sighed. Oblivious as he might have been at that moment, she knew what he was looking for and what would convince him. So she decided to be as forthcoming as was feasible, "Because it is important to someone, and to you. It will take some time to understand why. For now, you must trust me."

He looked at her and knew that he would do exactly as she had asked. He could not explain why he could trust her so easily but felt an unmistakable and unexplained intuition that she had put her faith in him in return on some level. It felt as if she was doing so even at that moment. It

[113]

startled him. He had consciously known her only for a few days. The only extension of their bond lay between her and his unconscious self, which was irrelevant. Yet, once again, it felt like chasing a balance that had been overdue. He looked away, drawn to his own calculations, eyebrows creased. "Do I have a choice? I have to blindly invest my faith in someone I know nothing about!"

"You do know something," Friuli reasoned and installed a yearning look upon him with those words. "You are alive and well, and I am here."

That was fact, and a crucial one. She looked at him and saw a young face with no scars that could testify to his accident. His lips had retained certain uniformity in their outline but it seemed as if every moment was a conscious effort to keep them shut. Suddenly she felt very aware of her appearance, wondering if she looked convincingly similar in age to him. She looked into his eyes. They were familiar and she knew about them. She had spent years striving to understand the most expressive element of a character like his. Her words had calmed his nerves and he used it immediately to assuage her in return, "If it's any consolation, I think you have done well for yourself. That's a nice house you have back there."

Friuli, though, was far detached from such gestures in that moment. "It's nothing extravagant. The measures of status have changed because the international laws forbid over exploitation of energy generation and use in order to avoid restricting our dependence to one entity. That would be a risk we learnt of the hard way."

"Still, it's nice. At least, you get to have a place to call yours," he said, significantly solemn, and was surprised to find her visibly hurt by that simple gesture. "What happened?"

"A catastrophe," she answered, "The culmination of one phase of human standing. A war the world fought with itself."

[114]

There lay the genesis of the mutation civilization had undergone. It was the key that Qin had been searching for in trying to identify the whip that had sparked human race into its ongoing sprint. "World war III, I suppose," he guessed.

"No," came an instant reply as if she would have preferred the idea. "There were no country-specific rivalries as much as there were ones with Nature. She nudged us back to our senses just when we were on the cusp of a proper political outbreak. It climaxed with a kind of supervolcano on the other side of the Atlantic, as if She had awakened to remind us that this was Her home and that we were just misbehaving guests, creating a ruckus that disturbed everyone else in the house. It worked. That period was the last recorded series of major calamities."

His mind hooked itself to those last words. He sensed an error and a simultaneous clarity but would not express it just yet. His immediate concern was for his own home, but before he could question Friuli on that note, a faint disturbance in the background occurred as if the city had suffered a power shortage. The little interference left behind a thick black spot hanging in mid-air, gradually closing in. As it came into focus – still distant and small – Qin saw a pair of compound eyes, and shivered. To an onlooker, it was an innocent fly, but a hundred images suddenly flashed past Qin's memory, none of which he could imbibe.

"What is it?" Friuli asked.

Qin didn't answer, save for a long, hard blink. He had tried to ward off traces of unpleasant recollections but had been nudged back in. He would not push them away anymore. He decided to let them linger and that did the trick. From the depths of fears that lay embedded all over his past, emerged a potential motive behind his ongoing training: He had believed he had lost ground on all that lay in the present ever since he had woken up, and was playing catch up on most things. So while his motivations belonged to the new world, all his sentiments ascribed to old memories that dated back over two decades. That was the duality that had to be beaten. He knew he could not trust himself to do it alone. Suddenly, it was clear why he could, and had, put his faith in Friuli.

"Hope," he uttered blankly but failed to notice what that word had done to his companion. She sat frozen for seconds that went without measure. In the absence of any incoming remark, he explained, "one that I had held long as a blanket over fears of what may happen if I could not uphold it."

She had now shifted forwards and was sitting upright, looking straight at him.

He continued, "It was a fear of what a woman, unlike any other, may turn herself into if adapted professionalism was all that was left to her. If all forms of love and incentives of sentiment that normally keep her shining, were snatched away, each day would be nothing short of war that she would constantly try to win as she tried to perfectly adopt a behaviour, out of her natural domain, in an almost robotic fashion. Such an individual would be like creamless Canneloni. Do you know what that is?"

"Just the shell and no fillings?" Friuli replied, amused but hiding a rising discomfort.

"A shell whose identity now is singular and immutable. It retains its structure but without the smooth sweet cream to guard, its crust is left without a role. And the very crispiness that made that Canneloni so much better than an ordinary mousse now turns into a stubborn appetizer. It is no longer subservient to its filling but is tasteful only if accepted on its own inflexible terms. More importantly, it is now willing to accommodate a new filling far riskier and unknown than the familiar sweetness we had craved it for. And when that happens-"

The tables had turned. Qin's cryptic words never met an end, despite an absence of any interruption except his psychological turmoil. However, he had unknowingly stirred a very different memory, one that belonged to Friuli. Little did they know, lost in their respective internal wars, that the culprit they were both now focussed on was the same; the only exception being that one thought of her with hate, the other with love.

The fly had worked again. That little spot of black hanging in air had been Friuli's creation. Clearly, for reasons of her own, she had felt she had the upper hand in this argument. She had assumed that she knew all that Qin was going through even if he did not know it. She had wanted to channel his vulnerability with the appearance of that fly but could not have possibly fathomed how her play would spur his thoughts to an extent that would instead return to hit her heart. Yet, nothing could have contrasted that more than the look on her face. She had smiled, her eyes laden with non-existent tears. She felt choked and blinked for longer stretches of time but managed to muster an answer for the answer's sake, one that, unknown to her, resembled what a certain woman had once rehearsed at a canal in a certain Italian city in a different time, "Things in this world often take a turn you never expected them to, even long after you are gone."

As those words transcended across an ancient dimension governed by time itself, they brought along the truth that Qin's present had failed to provide him with. He did not know why, nor understand how, but he had encountered a multitude of opinions drenched in a wave of emotions in the seconds gone by. The hovering fly was now close enough for him to look directly in those compound eyes. They were reflecting his forty-something self back at him. The last time he had faced those eyes, he had been a worn out youngster; and suddenly, twenty three years had vanished in thin air. Qin began to search for an objective essence to his sentimental overflow. He could not find one. Those were behaviours of that long gone past that had led him to his fall, slowly but surely. Now at this distant turn of things, he wondered whether that emotional upheaval had been necessary at all. What had he achieved? He had initiated corrections to stubborn anomalies in his life and those around but as fate would have it, all of that had been cut short in the pages of time. His train had met with its accident and here he was – a forgotten victim of that drama called life. A tear strained to drop out of his eye, but it never appeared. To Qin, his inability to cry was shattering but that realization gifted a simultaneous paradox as the melancholy transformed into a disciplined calm that men feel when they feel they have lost everything. Friuli lay lost in memories of her own while he strived to accept the reality of his situation. Gradually disappearing from view was the now-forgotten and ever-trivial house fly.

They did not speak for a while but he had never been more awake in recent times. The trail of coincidences had him stuck. Within seconds, the puddle of lights down in the city came alive and brightened the darkening sky. But the stars - they felt extremely unusual in the face of that glimmer on Earth which seemed to have magically oriented itself to bring the twinkling whites into greater focus. He noticed them at once but the dispassionate marvel culminated in one of empathy when Friuli exclaimed, co-incidentally tracking them too, "They are so ironic." Sadness had engulfed her eyes.

She had turned to face the city, looking very much in a strained control. And even though his eyes were now fixed upon her, the face his mind projected was entirely different. Momentarily, a different girl sat there and as he looked at her, all thought drifted away. A heavy dose of red splashed across and the cheeks glowed under it. Her quietness only aggravated the slopes of those upper lips while the lower one tucked itself warmly under the former. To feel mesmerized after over two decades was a welcome change for him, as was his consequent intervention for her, "Let's go, shall we?"

"You want to?"

"Yea, why not? It's been a long day."

"Sure."

They left and made it silently back to the house. Once there, Qin uncharacteristically went to his room, specifically requesting her to leave him alone. It was all very unwelcoming but she let it be, given the depth of revelations he had been through all day. She lay down on her bed, staring at the blank roof without a sight or sound of difference.

An entirely different individual now crossed her mind with relative ease. She vividly remembered how welcoming the prospect of nursing had been, but only now it occurred to her: the senselessness of it all – the actualization of a fantasy that was never meant to be realized. Now that she was here with Qin, she no longer craved it. What she did crave was to be back with one who really mattered – her employer. What she craved was a resurrection of lost love. She craved for the mending of the gap that had left that love hollow for so many years when all she had wanted was a reciprocation of her sentiments. Qin, to her, was a chance at redemption and she would do all she could to enable it; so that if a lonely girl ever came across a silent soul again, she could have a definitive judgement of her relationship pronounced then and there. *But then, the wait was perhaps what made it all so beautiful,* she thought and found herself equally thankful for the life that she had led. It was her chance to repay what she owed and she would do so with love.

Thoughts remained hazy and many minutes passed until she heard a knock on the door. The prospect of moving felt like too much effort. So she simply used her own version of the mid-air frivolities to unlock the door. It was pushed open and Qin stood there, hesitantly peeking in.

"Yes?"

"Umm," he hesitated, "could you come with me for a second?"

"What is it?"

"Please, if it's not too much trouble."

She forced herself to get up and asked, walking up to him, "What did you do now?"

"Well, I tried," Qin replied and led her to his room. He opened the door and bent forwards to check inside while she waited behind him. He then stepped back and signalled her to go in. She gave him a scrutinizing stare and walked in restlessly, only to have her feet stall at the door.

The room was as dark as darkness could allow without losing out on charm. There were just two distinct divisions in its ambience, physically divided midway through its height. The roof and the upper half of the walls seemed stretched out into an infinite space, showcasing a starry night, populated with little sparkles beyond count but not without meaning. There lay clear patterns of constellations and distant hints of planets and moving asteroids as if the room had lifted itself up into Earth's exosphere. And yet, it could not possibly be as the lower half of the room was submerged in soft waves of water, lit up underneath with careful streaks of turquoise light. The projection lay complete with a glimpse of the waterbed superimposed on the floor while their bed lay risen inches above the surface, in between like a hammock. The three-dimensional theme had come alive with slight sounds of water hitting against the surfaces around even as they moved in little waves. As she stepped in, ripples began to radiate out from her legs. It was all very magical and yet, all very real.

Friuli stood in a trance, unmoving. She then turned towards Qin, her lips still parted but with eyes far more at ease than they had been. He took her hand in his as he led her to the bed. He moved along to the northern end of the room while she lay down. Both her legs bent backwards and her head rested on her palm which in turn rested on the pillow. She looked at the sky, wordlessly staring at the stars – static and shooting across – while the sounds of the water filled her senses. She then murmured as if to avoid disturbing the ambience that prevailed in the room, "Thank you."

Qin looked at her and smiled. He followed it up with an equivalent counter, "Something happened to you back there." Friuli looked at him and turned back towards the stars. She did not really wish to talk much but then, he deserved to be answered.

"What you said was absurd," she joked, "but unfortunately, it carried traces of an inconvenient reality. The group of companies that came to nearly monopolize all digital space, through acquisitions and a very smart play of marketing that spanned many years, were led by a similarly ruthless drive of ambitions that marked perhaps the only emotion left in its bearer."

"From what I see so far," Qin said, pointing out at the theme at play in the room, "it is all quite beautiful."

"It definitely is. People wouldn't accept change if it did not appeal to them."

"Yet, you speak of it as if it were decadent."

"All that glitters, Qin," she left the proverb hanging.

"Ah, I am surprised gold has retained its privileges even in this age," he remarked but it took him a couple of seconds before his smile disappeared under the realization of its true significance: Gold or diamonds should have lost their status in such an age as this. He did not stretch the thought but let it implant itself well within him.

Friuli stammered, clearly acquainted to that realization only now and out of her comfort zone, "I . . . thought you would, umm, be able to identify with it."

"And that would mean you are mindful of what would and would not affect me," Qin quipped, now with some idea as to the source behind the appearance of the fly. He waited, she stared and the turning of tables ended soon after. Qin was careful not to damage a rare moment of an unexplained dominance he had stumbled upon. "Quite an exceptional and caring nurse you are," he said on a lighter note, "So what was wrong with the changes? Short-sightedness?"

"Yes," Friuli answered quickly, "A concoction of technology that no one could have imagined, and no one did, except perhaps one," she said with some thought. "We were mostly oblivious to where it all headed as we became an unassuming part of another worldly evolution, this time more personal in effect." She obstructed her own statement with an impatient expression and turned to lie on her back with both her palms held over her stomach and feet stretched out straight. "Let me soak in this place for now," she exclaimed, "These are two of my favourite themes but it never occurred to me to try them together."

It was easy for him to stop questioning. His mind was stuck on her discomfort. It was something personal to her and yet, he felt it clog his thoughts more than whatever had happened to the world itself. He fought off the urge to inquire further. She now lay deep within the projected space. He let a few moments pass before suggesting, "You should rest. I will sleep in your room. Just try to get the bitterness out of your system for now." She turned to him and smiled. Qin's reply was quick, "okay, so you won't."

He did not ask why, even though his eyes did. She continued to smile but did not answer. It slowly faded as he left the room. In her head there was just one sentence running across – one she whispered as if with hope that it would get lost in that dark sky, *Cos it were the wild ambitions of a loveless woman that took away what once mattered the most to me.* That was Friuli's experience with a creamless Canneloni.

Chapter 11

Beehive. No other word crossed Fridgeon's mind in the hours that followed, until she had reached the apartment. The offices were closed by the time she arrived in Milano and thought it best to head to her new home. It felt funny to address it that way. She was a guest and nothing more. Yet, it was a pleasant thought – one she found herself reciting several times.

The fifth floor, once she was there, looked quite rugged with bits and pieces littered around. She rang and knocked on the door but no one answered. Fifteen minutes passed on an irritated note, not helped to the least by her headache. Desperately, she looked around in case Kanha had left the card somewhere before leaving. *He wouldn't,* she thought but searched nonetheless. It appeared most unexpected then when one lay hidden in a little crevice on the top frame of the door. She would have sniffed something fishy but the bump on her head restricted her focus to getting in. The door opened to a pitch black house. She called out his name but there was no answer. The darkness seemed to bear a resemblance to the eerie factory she had visited earlier and it aggravated the pain. Her fingers scanned the wall for the switch and though it was a relief to have found one, the sudden light brought with it further aggravation. Everything lay in tatters. The furniture had been thrown apart, papers spread out on the floor and dirt enveloped the surfaces. It would be no surprise if the place had remained deserted for years.

Had she come to the wrong apartment? Of course she hadn't. Fridgeon stressed and strained over it against the constant nudge of her headache conspiring to drive her away from any thought. The out-of-bounds room was still locked. She tiptoed her way around the house, but there was no note, no indication of what had happened. A toppled chair and a glass of water looked like urgent necessities: she needed to think. An hour passed before there was any further movement. Her little plan to take Kanha into confidence had vaporized and been replaced by concern not only at the state of the house but at a more pressing thought: *what if something had happened to him*? It had thoroughly unsettled her and yet, much as she would have liked to instigate investigations, exhaustion overtook her whims and she fell asleep. When her eyes opened, the sun shone a little over the horizon and the birds had come back. Kanha had not.

She pulled herself together with a sense of undeniable discomfort. She had resigned to the idea of having lost Jelzan for some time now but Kanha should have never been part of that tragedy. Yet, somehow, it seemed as if he had. Soaked in natural light, the apartment was beginning to reveal its details. Nothing seemed right. It was as if someone had gone extra lengths to create a duplicate of the place she had stayed in and then dismantled it to hide intricate flaws that may have given them away. Her feet nearly shook on their tracks until sense returned and relayed directives to install normalcy. *"Don't lose it,"* She murmured and quickly shooed the thought away. Now wasn't the time to air speculation. There were too many to deal with anyway.

Fridgeon geared up and walked down to the streets, her steely resolve matched with the permanence of those steel tram rails that had embedded themselves on ground. The morning rush of people was prominent and the cafés were significantly active. She walked along looking at those moving around her. Every couple of steps, a shrill voice would rise and die down, leaving behind widely grinning faces. She had always found the level of excitement that typically accompanied an Italian greeting quite unnecessary and irritating, especially when all she would prefer was a cup of coffee in peace, to start off her day. This morning looked different though. The smiling faces and hearty salutations seemed to ease her mood. Not everyone was embroiled in her agony and the generic sense of joy and indifference to her affairs seemed the perfect sponge to absorb her thoughts.

She walked by under a flurry of *Buongiorno's* and occasional hugs around her and noted a sense of peace that prevailed amidst the larger issues that troubled life in general – through numerous empires, religious torment, dark medieval kingdoms, uncertain industrial expansion, state-wide unifications and subsequent World Wars. The citizens had lived through times of financial and ethical agonies, had accommodated numerous immigrants and had braved frequent natural disasters. It had all come and gone but they had survived. The latter was a generic trait of every successful civilization but the Italians had done so with glee. Every individual carried a certain despiteful taste against the prevailing system. While it was the norm against any oversized establishment, underneath the constant film of complaints and dissatisfaction, there lay pride and an almost stubborn love that no tragedy had managed to thwart over several millennia. Marvellous landscapes still graced the nation's Toscanian cheeks while her Puglian heels continued to sparkle through its white walls. Her islandic foot remained in the simplistic harmony of man and Earth while the north lay cradled in the security of the unwavering Alps.

Fridgeon listened to all that was said around and while none of the words concerned her, she felt herself float for a moment with the waves of their tone. Whether it was to express anger or joy, each person tried to sing in voice and dance with his hands in a persistent effort to accentuate the life that he carried within. She looked around. She found no exception.

Via Turati lay at a considerable distance but walking seemed preferable to the public transport. She needed time to gather herself and needed sufficient distractions to keep her from thinking too much over it. People had been under her radar; so were now the structures that shaded the street she walked upon.

It had been a premier city for most of what she could remember. She did not grow up in Milano, or even in Italy. It was Jelzan that had led to her transfer. The city did, after all, carry the juicy bait of a chic lifestyle. Sure enough, people seemed very conscious of the same not only when they walked out but even – out of some inertia – when they were alone. Yet, the overall image had been a matter of some very successful branding, like all things Italian. There was no flashy exterior laid upon a useless piece of junk in any product. It was, to an extent, the opposite.

She searched through the length of the street. None of the buildings carried the glossy effect of modernity. They were old, built in periods of cultural resurrections and edited as per the tastes of multiple regimes that came and went. They carried layers upon layers of thought that had prevailed among the masses through centuries, often ingeniously mixed together. Efforts were hardly ever spent on contemporizing it on par with the megacities the world boasted of. On the contrary, every measure was taken at all times to preserve the historic depth that every edifice carried. In effect, they were carefully dilapidated.

The dilapidation lay sustained and the structures restored to pleasing effect. They had been internally complemented with all technological necessities of modern livelihood, to stand in no way inferior to the quality that was offered elsewhere. The exterior, meanwhile, still proclaimed stories of mythology and architectural evolution on walls – with grand demons, angels, florals and even minimal intrusions hinting at the beliefs that each specific period of construction had carried during its long history.

That period of time, she thought. Things changed and took even the sturdiest beliefs with them, as was plastered as proof all over the city. People defined the socially acceptable constants as per the convenience on offer in any age. Without protest, we all followed and judged our life by it. Mass killings and conquer of foreign lands were acceptable and honourable acts of men in the age of kings and that itself stood in stark contrast to what was considered so today. Out of the blue, she felt an inclination to laugh. It all seemed to make any tragedy so meaningless – so much part of some larger plan and barely anything more than experience in a life whose rules and regulations were being twisted at all times. The thoughts eclipsed her mind for most of her journey, with her brain set on an auto-pilot to guide her through the streets to her destination. Consequently, it took several extra steps for her to realize she had crossed her spot and had reached the end of Via Turati. She walked back and faced a Gothic construction, carrying a square board with two lines of inscription embossed in gold that sparkled under the sun:

Scinoi Bee

The Beehive

Six long semi-circular steps took one to a huge revolving door standing within gold-rimmed borders. She walked in to a mini lobby and was greeted by a receptionist on the far left. No questions asked. The door in front was as tall as the first and as thickly framed. Yet, it opened with a gentle touch and she entered to a passing greeting by a gentleman dressed in suit-and-smile. She kept walking as a miniscule object moving around a grand circular lobby marbled in curves of brown on shiny bottle green surface. A massive chandelier hung above, covering nearly half the overall height, straining the neck of any who bothered to look at it. There were few onlookers, for they were all acclimatised. Hardly ever did one who wasn't, walk through those doors. He would always be instantly tracked and registered by those omnipresent sensors. Fridgeon checked the area. There were no other doors or windows. Only two crescent shaped stairways curved up to the first floor from either side, with nearly all of their twelve feet of width heavily carpeted in maroon and held in place by thin rods plated yet again in gold film, although sufficiently scratched. She climbed up, peeking through the thick cemented guards shaped as flower vases on the upper floor. Her hesitancy went unnoticed, except for a few curious pairs of eyes who were too busy to give her additional thought. The corridors were relatively empty, lit in intermittent yellow and lined with several non-gold polished-brown doors – all of which stood shut. She heard muffed voices from the third door behind her and knocked.

"Hope Leosword, per favore," she addressed two men sitting inside, in a strong voice.

They observed her for a while before one of them answered, "In fondo al corridoio dopo la porta grande. Ma serve un appuntamento . . ." ("Down the corridor, past the big door. But you will need an appointment.")

Those last words faded into oblivion as she walked off, with her utter disregard for the men prominent enough to hold their attention for several seconds after she had left. They did not protest, save the raised exclamations and a relatively more violent wave of hands. Fridgeon covered the length with steps that echoed with a sense of definitive resolve. She was stopped by a lady just beyond the stated door. The anonymous asked, "Si?"

"Hope Leosword."

"Non c'è," she answered, matched with the rude entry Fridgeon had made, clearly considering any courtesy towards her as undeserved.

"That won't work. I will meet her."

"Huh?"

"Look, first of all, she is present. I know this. Even if she isn't, I will wait here until she comes back."

"I'm sorry ma'am," the receptionist rejected the idea with her strong Italian accent persistent, "but must I remind you that this is a respectable place and some manner of courtesy is essential. We cannot allow any random individual to walk through and you do not look uneducated enough to not understand that."

Fridgeon did not expect such a sharp reply. She took a deep breath, staring equally deep into the other's eyes. The woman was right. She could not get across with blatant hard-headedness. She blinked and tried to reason, "Well, then let's avoid a scene. I'm the wife of Jelzan Friuli. How about we start with that? Could you just pass on the message and then let her, or whoever else, decide on whether it is of any importance?"

The receptionist studied her for a while and replied, "All right. But you must wait."

"Fair enough."

Fridgeon sat on the couch facing the reception desk, hidden in view from the little corridor that followed in that part of the floor and any other offices that fell within the range. It should have been a test of her patience but under those stiff brows and a buzzing mind, minutes ticked without notice. There was too much to grace her thought. The receptionist walked out several times indifferently, continuing with her work. She was, however, mindful of Fridgeon staring back at her. An hour passed before she came with an update, "I insist you talk to her deputy, Mr. Usafa. The second-last door on the right."

Fridgeon wanted to protest but decided to go on with what she had. Several employees had walked across multiple times, passing a dubious look at her. She walked in the suggested direction and was about to knock at the said door when a man in a tight-fitting grey striped suit opened it. He was huge and his eyes shone against an ebony skin

[129]

through his thick-rimmed glasses, exaggerated further by his perfectly set teeth showing prominently through his broad smile. He extended his hand, easily enveloping Fridgeon's.

"Welcome, Mrs. Fridgeon. Friuli, is it?"

"Yes," she said and walked in. He closed the door and they seated themselves adjacent to each other at one end of a long table.

"So how can I help you?"

"This is regarding my husband, an employee of your company. He has disappeared."

The man looked at her with a grave expression. It seemed news to him. He replied with a tone of genuineness, "I'm sorry for your loss, Mrs. Friuli, but surely you do not mean vanished, do you? I mean, I just checked with his office and – Mr. Jelzan, I believe – has been on leave for quite some time now. We have tried to contact him over the last few days but to no avail. It appeared as if he had resigned without notifying us."

"To disappoint you then, sir, Jelzan is neither on voluntary leave nor has he resigned. He has disappeared."

"How?" Usafa asked in subdued shock. Fridgeon briefly narrated the story to him. He heard in silence and pondered over it with his chin supported on his fingers. He then declared, "Then you should have informed us earlier. Anyway, we will notify the authorities immediately."

"Actually I came here hoping for an answer from you."

"Answer to what? This now sounds like a police case. I don't understand how I can help."

"You do not know anything further in this matter?"

"Officially, I'm afraid not. Personally, we did not work in the same department. So there's little I could have known about him."

"A prominent manager of your company vanished and you guys-"

"Let me stop you there, madam. 'Vanished' is quite an inappropriate term to use here. From what we understand, the last he was seen was when you two went on a vacation. I fail to see how we could help with that beyond registering the case with the police, and of course, extending our deepest condolences."

"Sir, are you aware of the circumstances under which he disappeared?"

"As far as you just told me. I'm afraid we will need to verify that as well. It's a procedural obligation."

Fridgeon observed him for a moment and then described the unusual behaviour that Jelzan had shown in the final days. Usafa did not reply but continued to ponder over it, gently rubbing his chin with his thumb. All he said in a while was a ponderous, "That is unusual indeed." She let him think over it further until he asked, "How did things come to this?"

"I do not know."

"Anything that could give us a clue?"

Fridgeon told him, in further detail, about the accident and the operation and noticed the creases on Usafa's forehead unexpectedly ease a bit. He had, after all, drawn her into narrating her entire story. He allowed himself a moment of prolonged inhalation at the end, excused himself and walked out. Nearly half an hour later he returned with a directive, "Mrs. Friuli, if you would, kindly follow me."

They walked a few steps to the last door in that short corridor. He tapped a card against it and was subjected to another scan, upon which a door unlatched to reveal an elevator. They stepped into the stuffy space, nearly dark but beautifully shining through the glossy black glass. There was no keypad to enter the floor number. The cabin moved automatically once they had got in, with only dim blue-lit borders to accompany them in the near-black darkness. It was absolutely silent. The elevator stopped a few seconds later and opened to a smaller lobby. Everything was black here, covered in shiny marble all around and lit only by indirect tubes of dim lights – mostly blue. A small reception desk lay on one end of this mini lobby, behind which a bald man stood with half his face glowing under an indirect yellow bulb somewhere beneath. He raised his eyes to look at her and then at Usafa, and keyed something behind the desk they weren't able to see. He then raised a hand with outstretched palm, pointing them and his eyes towards a couple of seats on the other end. Without a word, he went back to his work. The sofa gave an impression of volcanic glass but compressed like a sponge as they sat. It was comfortable but cold.

She watched the clock tick for several minutes. It was interestingly placed as the sole analogous gadget in a largely futuristic space, bringing in the only sound that could overlap the grim buzz around. Soon enough though, a door carved out from the seemingly plain black glassed-wall that stood nearest to the couch. The only way one could tell there was a passageway was by an eight-foot rectangular absence of black sheen in between that glossy stretch. Usafa nodded to the bald man and led Fridgeon inside.

The room, if it could qualify as one, resembled outer space – polished and lit up with thin, sharp flame-like streaks. The volcanic glass effect had carried itself from the lobby, and had now spread out to lengths that made the room seem boundless. The indirect blueness continued to offer an excuse for lighting, with rays at various points on the walls which seemed to define the curves and corners of the room. This would have seemed logical to Fridgeon had it also fit the conventional contours of a closed space. For, the positioning of these lights stood at complete odds with the three-dimensional framework of a room. If one were to assume that they hinted at intersections and boundaries, then one was clearly looking at a master play of architecture that had managed to create holographic exits. They were oriented at unfamiliar angles. To a novice, it was impossible to figure out the contents or directions in that area. To a novice, it was a trap.

Fridgeon had some difficulty making sense of anything around at first. That was the whole point of the room, for everything lay in a black illusion, helplessly drawing any pair of eyes to the only presence within that space that made sense – a seat behind a desk that was stationed at some distance with a hidden source of light that bore some strength in it, tasked with highlighting that one spot in the room that allowed – and invited – constant attention. And there she sat, pretty and voluptuous in a coat with long collars that slipped down her shoulders to a partially plunging neckline of her frilly shirt, with unbending authority and loud, daring control, with elbows resting on the desk and converging up till outstretched fingers that joined together at their tips, and with an aura that, even when her body language was at ease, seemed to issue a warning to anyone who dared to lay eyes upon her in ways she would not permit. In that pitch black existence, Hope Leosword glowed in red.

The woman had let sharp ends of her hair settle themselves in a disciplined pattern, with only a few allowed to grace her face on one side and in one long curve. They were cut short and pretty much summed up the features of her face – all of which stood distinct and sharp. Her eyes looked at her guests in amusement and a smile all but spread across. She addressed the man first, "That will do, Usafa. Thank you."

He half-bowed and left the room. The door slid back to render the glossiness complete. "Please, do not just stand there," she requested. Fridgeon walked forth upon being addressed and seated herself across the desk on one of stiffest seats she had ever come across. Clearly, guests were not accorded any respite within these bounds. Hope

[133]

continued, "I take it that you have had few difficult days recently."

The other, visibly out of her comfort zone, replied, "Yes."

Hope passed a quick smile and said, "Tell me, Fridgeon, what happened?"

"I think you know well, ma'am."

"Oh that I do, but please, I would like to get a first hand narrative."

Fridgeon sighed and told her all she could. Hope listened keenly and remarked at length without a change in expression, "So?"

Fridgeon felt unsettled. She wanted to scream at the cold behaviour she was being subjected to. The utter callousness of Hope made her want to shout but she controlled herself and asked, "Do you guys have no sense of humanity left in you at all?"

"We guys?" Hope enquired with pursed lips and a raised eyebrow.

"You and your management."

Hope smirked, positioned herself more comfortably in her seat and returned to her pose of frigidly connected fingertips. She poked the burning mind that faced her from across the desk, "I suppose you have generalized your assessment to cover the management everywhere. So what do you think goes on in our famed boardrooms, Fridgeon?"

The other replied immediately, "Cons-," but was cut short by Hope's equally immediate follow through:

"-piracies?" The latter concluded with a short smile. "Do you picture a group of fat men, immersed in jubilant puffs of smoke rising continually from their cigar, wearing an evil grin with raised eyebrows that altogether makes them look like magicians? Do they sit down at the first sight of an opportunity to roll out a new evil, a new 'game' directed purely at making a fool out of the more ordinary men and women?"

[134]

Fridgeon answered back, "Clearly women seem to be as much a part of that group now."

"Oh, yes. You should feel proud about that, shouldn't you?"

"Do I look proud?"

"No you do not, sadly enough."

"How can I be if the one who manages to take that seat gives up on vital virtues?"

"What might that be?"

"Empathy! Where is your heart? A man – your employee – has disappeared. Do you not care about that?"

"Well, foremost, he is not my employee. This is the Beehive, as I am sure you know, which actually perplexes me as to why you have come here."

"Were you not the deputy to Mr. Piscoli? And was he not in charge of your facility at Mongrando before it shut down?"

"Aah, Archer. That he was, not directly but liable enough. I feel it is quite right that he was dispatched to Dubai. Much as I respect him, clearly he had not done the best of jobs with that factory."

"You mean, a laboratory."

Seriousness dawned over Hope as she asked, "Why don't you tell me what you seem to fear?"

"You wish to know?"

"Oh, certainly. Do not be afraid. As I said, I like to have the full picture once an issue is brought under my consideration."

"Well, I think you are running experiments of quite a dangerous nature in your facility, the subjects of which might have also been humans," Fridgeon spit out in one breath.

Hope sighed and said, "It is extremely easy to voice out an opinion on grounds of a random controversy theory, Mrs. Friuli. We all like to do so about things we do not yet

[135]

know. After all, they fill us with spice and a feeling of reasoned maturity."

"It does not mean it is entirely a lie . . ."

"Nor that it is entirely the truth. I agree that the facility was shut down indefinitely because of certain accidents of an uncontrolled nature. We had to step back and think over. That is what we are doing, even at the partial expense of livelihoods of our employees stationed there. The larger picture is more important. You do not know what went on in there or what we were after, and I promise you it was something far more important than anything your dramatic apprehensions can conjure. But for now, I invite you to consider the decision makers that seem to suffer your anger at this moment. Do not forget that half of what we hear are notions that may be true but still do not imply tragedy on a scale that our pessimistic minds incur. In truth, these evil boardroom guys are at times more pitiable than anyone else. Tied in routines that are far less flexible and far more damaging, they live without rest amidst all pleasures available to them like a tease and with plastic smiles plastered upon their face out of necessity, snatching every bit of their originality day after day as they lead each other, driven by none other than those very "common men and women" seated way down in our supply chain, to take decisions that most would shy away from not because the risk to reward ratio is high but because the necessity to risk ratio is. Are these the men you feel you are prey to?" Hope, with her influential precision, had to be careful not to stretch the bounds of realism that could be followed sans any doubt. She added, "Indeed, their actions may cause as much a downfall as they cause progress, but that is the inevitability of mankind in general. They don't necessarily swear to buy their next villa solely from what they steal from you. Consider it a respite for all that they lose every day, which others have cunningly deleted from all definitions or measurement."

The diversion seemed easier to effect upon the other than she had thought. So she considered her position and threw in her veil of support, "Of course, I won't deny entirely. There are those who do just thrive through their day on account of exploiting us. However, I assure you, they are not the ones so far up the ladder. They are much closer to you and hardly beg an exaggeration of sorts that our pessimism yields."

Fridgeon tried to clear her mind to focus on what mattered. She could not blindly attack the argument that Hope had just put forth but there was no need to. Her concern was Jelzan. He is all she cared about. Or so she thought, until their conversation drifted to an unexpected domain.

It was Fridgeon who started it with the words, "Look, I simply wish to know what happened to Jelzan in the operation theatre?"

"Very sharp, Fridgeon. I see that you have substantially narrowed down the possibilities already."

"Yes, I have and so would you, had it been your husband."

"Oh, but it's not. I'm careful enough to avert that."

"Of course. Such things can only happen to one who knows how to love."

It seemed as if the room had suddenly radiated a chunk of chilled air from all corners. It must have been Fridgeon's perception, for Hope gave out a shrill sadistic laugh and stood up from her chair with a thud of her palm eclipsed by a sound of metal. It drew Fridgeon's attention to a silver ring that shone for the faintest moment against the blue light. Before she could spare another thought, Hope half-shouted, "You wish to know what happened to your husband? He was grievously injured after that little accident. The two men who held him up were fortunately, employees at that facility you seem to condemn so ruthlessly." Fridgeon tried to think hard and suddenly felt a striking similarity to the two young guys who had helped her recover back to consciousness after her fall at the factory. Hope continued, "When your husband was brought to the hospital, he had lost so much blood already that it would have been impossible to save him. Even if he lived, he would be severely handicapped. You could not have withstood the trauma of living with, literally, remnants of your husband. You want the truth, Fridgeon? What happened in the operation theatre was of our doing and you should be thankful that our R&D had solutions at hand, if at all. We saved his life and hoped, more than anything or anyone else, for all to go well. You think we are devious and business minded, right? Well, think further then: Wouldn't it be in our own interest to have him walk, talk and behave like a normal guy after an accident so ghastly? The success of that operation, carried out of necessity, could have meant billions of dollars in earnings and a revolution – mark my words, no less – in human era."

Fridgeon's eyes went wide. She asked, shivering at the prospect of having her theories nearing confirmation, "Why is everyone denying it?"

"Cos no one would understand. It would create a controversy that would put an end to years of effort into what has always been meant for the genuine good of people. Medicine is a risky field, Fridgeon. It takes ages to get the right product to shelves. An operative procedure is nothing short of a sophisticated invention. When you combine the two, the risks and rewards tear through the sky. What we are talking about here is quite complicated-"

"What was it?" Fridgeon asked, looking at Hope almost pleadingly.

"The next generation of biomechanics, with limitless possibilities if it were to work, which it will, sooner or later. Of this, I can assure you," Hope said and tapped on her desk. A section of the surface rose up, holding a computer screen. She asked, "Do you know what this is?"

"A computer."

"Magnetospirillium magneticum. That is what underlies this inanimate piece of metal," Hope said in a more reserved fashion.

"Magneto-?"

"Bacteria. Several years back, it became quite difficult to reduce the size of hard drives and chips beyond a certain point while adding more and more data. Computation had become quite a necessity for us – mobile computation. So scientists tried to use a particular breed of microbes that could ingest iron and turn themselves into tiny magnets. It is a work of proteins and their naturally occurring property of matching up with Earth's magnetic field. In short, they gave us biological tools in more than one way. The cell membranes, for instance, were similarly used to produce wires. What I imply, Fridgeon, is that once you approach Nature, the inspirations for our daily functioning know no bounds. So we started applying these in more unique ways, inspired further by more experiments that scientists carried out across the globe. One such application was Bionism."

"What's that?"

"All that concerns you right now is a simple fact. Imagine the limited options we had with Jelzan. Should we have let him die, as would have been the case under any other circumstance in any other hospital? Would you have preferred otherwise even if by sheer coincidence, he found himself in the hands of those who had this one way of saving him as something more than a limbless man? So we tried."

Fridgeon did not reply. Hope continued, "That is why we have not approached the police yet. We might do it, if you prefer. They will try to find him while we will engage in a decade-long legal and ethical battle. But what would you gain out of it? What would Jelzan gain? Even if he were to be found, do you think anyone will be able to live with

[139]

what has possibly become of him, God forbid?" Silence prevailed. Hope said in a softer tone, "Now think of the other possibility. The same guys who developed a partially effective procedure can now work on tying off the loose ends. They have expertise and experience and they can fix this – fix your husband if there have been minor glitches left over. We will deploy all our resources – and you have my word on behalf of the highest authority at Scinoi – to find him and cure him. It is, after all, in our best interests. We want this breakthrough more than anything else."

"Then why have you shut the place down?"

"Because we need a convincing non-controversial permission to go ahead. Being the current Head in the location, I have resolved not to proceed with a dangerous work as this until I have the consent of the one who stands to lose the most – you. Until then, my focus remains on the Beehive."

"Me?"

"Yes. While I had guessed at what had caused Jelzan's absence all this while, I could not make a move unless you raised the issue and consented to it yourself. I was quite curious as to why there had been no word from you while we tried to keep things low. For obvious reasons, we could not let it slip out or it would have led to false rumours and a lot of trouble. Now that you are here, I leave it in your hands. We shall abide by your decision."

Fridgeon looked at her in shock. Suddenly the previous night seemed to make sense, and her concern grew manifold as another person entered the fray. She stated, partially scared, "You had all this already arranged. It was you . . . You thrashed Kanha's house. Wh-what did you do to him?"

"Excuse me?!"

"Kanha Evian. Where is he?"

Hope stood up straight and frozen in time and space. Her sleek shoulders took an age to twitch and slowly began to heave with great intensity. The lights were hardly enough to cast a proper glow or Fridgeon would have seen those stern lips part and the eyes constrict to the slightest. She felt subjected to a terrifying threat as Hope cast a look upon her for an eternity, as if with a storm of thoughts crisscrossing her brain. The latter verified, "He is here in Milano. That is what you said, did you not?"

"What? Of course he is," Fridgeon replied and realized that someone with such an objective bearing would always perceive any third party as a substantial risk. So she pleaded, "Would you please stop this? He is innocent. He does not know anything. Nor will he let out anything, I promise. Just tell me if he is fine."

Hope let out another short laugh, audible and boastful in that otherwise silent space. Her jaw outlined itself prominently against the backlight as she looked up at the sky-like roof and shook her head. "I cannot believe this," she said, as if lost in her own thoughts. A couple of head shakes later, she spoke, "Oh, but you should tell me, Fridgeon. How is he? Still prefers his space?"

"Huh?"

Hope continued, teasingly, "What? Don't be surprised. You have known him for a while now, right? How do you know him anyway?"

"I," Fridgeon cleared her throat, "we met at the subway shortly after Jelzan disappeared."

"Did you now? Is that where you have been staying?" Hope asked, almost with another burst of laughter. "Is that why no one has been answering calls at your home?"

Fridgeon could feel the bite of that grin stretched across the desk. Her suspicion did not help her nervousness. She hesitantly answered, turning it almost into an inquiry, "Yes."

Hope looked down, sighed, and began to move around. She came out from behind the desk and walked a

[141]

significant length of the room. Fridgeon was amazed at how far the place actually stretched. At a distance, Hope stopped and stood with arms folded and her back facing her guest. The moments that went by seemed more of a play to Fridgeon and she could not stop her imaginations from snowballing. She looked intently towards Hope and felt the latter's mind race. She could feel the flood of thoughts that traversed the zones of the unnecessary and the possible in that strategist's head. She had sensed urgency but Hope seemed to be taking her time, for this was an important turn of events – almost a gift and one Hope may not have foreseen. The Bee stood there, lost in thoughts, eyes closed, while the other sat looking at her back, careful not to interrupt despite her inclinations. At length, Hope let out another sigh and turned to Fridgeon.

"Doesn't it all seem a bit curious to you, Fridgeon?"

"In what way?"

"To find one person so caring among so many indifferent others - doesn't it feel as if something is wrong?"

Fridgeon thought over it and replied, "No."

"And I do not blame you. A caring wife as I am sure you were - are - such behaviour would naturally appear, well, natural."

"What are you attempting at?"

"I am simply trying to bring to your attention an anomaly that you have come across, clearly without realizing. What you consider a natural coincidence does not exactly look so if you take all the facts into account."

"Which are?"

"For starters, such goodness does not exist in the world. We all like to believe in one, because well, who would like to think that they are living in a pool of shit? Sadly, that is pretty close to the truth, whether one accepts it or not."

"I do not see your point. Are you-?"

[142]

"Kanha Evian, Fridgeon. There is just one. I should be surprised that you have not heard of him but then, it is understandable." Fridgeon simply looked at Hope, seeking some clarity. The latter continued, "You wanted to know what Bionism was, right?"

"Yes."

"Yet, you are oblivious to the fact that you have been living in its lap for some time now."

"I'm sorry?"

"Oh no, dear. It is me who is sorry, for you. So innocent, you almost make me feel sympathetic. It is a pity that despite so many technological inventions that drive the world's economy and carry human growth year after year, few individuals in this field enjoy prominence. With Kanha, of course, it is different, given how he prefers to keep himself distanced from any such acclaim." Fridgeon was listening keenly. Hope continued, "Kanha Evian is one of the pioneers of Bionism, sweetheart. He might not have invented it but he surely put in the accelerator. Have you noticed a scar or two on him?"

"One that nearly looks like a horse, yes," Fridgeon said silently.

Her words sounded unfamiliar to Hope but she let it go, continuing instead on the larger discussion at hand, "He got them in India." Fridgeon's brows creased as the other continued, "Oh yes, that's where he once lived. It was an ugly clash, to be honest. He shouldn't have been alive now but he managed to survive, somehow." Hope was serious now as she spoke, "Such an irony that a brilliant face as his should suffer such brutality. Alas, what can we say about what one deserves!"

Fridgeon noted those words with caution and partial disbelief. She remembered his face well and it did not fit the descriptions that fell upon her now. She tried to make her own calculations and asked, "Is that why he still looks so young, almost in his early twenties, although in a maturely adolescent sort of way?"

"Perhaps, courtesy the treatments he must have gone through over the years. There were further damages, ones that should have left him crippled for life. The cracks could heal and cuts could be stitched together but what was broken – or even lost – was beyond remedy, unless, a new technique could be devised. Now Kanha had always been all for novelties and it did not take him long to sink into an upcoming phenomenon called bionism. Till that time, the concept was plagued with imperfections. It could work only in minor ways, at best."

"Erm sorry, but what is this exactly?"

"A biomechanical alternative to transplant , in the simplest words. We had mainly restricted ourselves to bionic eyes on a commercial scale initially. Patients took a while to recover full sight but it worked nonetheless. Kanha improvised, for his requirement was not an eye – not just an eye – but also parts more mechanical and sturdy, for instance, an arm. Only Kanha developed it into a kind of superarm. Fancy, isn't it?"

Fridgeon did not nod to the rhetoric. Hope affirmed, "It was. He had equipped it with two additional 'ingredients' – a microchip, complete with a thin film around his wrist, and a metallo-casing that was far stronger than any human arm."

A sudden incongruity occurred to Fridgeon. She was in conversation with an extremely busy boss who had, for some reason and with extreme interest, decided to devote her precious time on every little detail to bring her guest to terms with reality. Clearly, Fridgeon's participation was extremely crucial. It was a thought that made the naive feel important, powerful and even more interested. "So a strong implanted computer in effect?" she asked in doubt.

"In a way. The computation was basic and he ensured it could easily be operated, replaced or removed."

"How did he power it?"

"Our body is a good enough conductor of electricity. Let's just say there were nano-battery capsules under his metal casings. It was very risky, but I think he must have enjoyed that part a lot." Fridgeon looked down in thought and confusion. Hope continued, "Don't worry though. Now we have much better mobile sources of power. Of course, you don't see them because the concept is not very common and highly expensive to commercialize. In a few years, you would."

Fridgeon revised it passively, searching for gaps, and then asked, "What about the nerves? How could he feel his arm?"

"Not just feel but also control it - two extremely important functions that should accompany any body part. These were foundations of bionism. Barring the overwhelming details, let's just say that the affected nerves are positioned around the more dormant muscles. The signals generated work via sensors on the skin surface. As years passed, developments took place around the globe and the bionic arm could connect to the active nerves wirelessly, reasonably simplifying all the fuss. Most interestingly, Kanha worked on reading nerve impulses travelling outwards towards the muscles and the good old EEG for brain activity. Soon enough, he could govern the functionality with his brain. All he had to do was make the connection based on the chip in his arm. Feeble mechatronics could do the rest."

Fridgeon spent extended moments of silence, oscillating between interest, concern and doubt, and then heeded the latter, "If you have really advanced that much, then why is Jelzan in danger today?"

Hope walked back to her desk and spoke in a grave tone, "Jelzan's condition was not purely mechanical, or even superficial. He had suffered internal injuries, loss of blood and significant damages to his nervous system. It was a case of complete paralysis, even if he would have lived. We tried on him a stage of bionism that is an evolution in itself. I do not mean to scare you, Fridgeon, but even if I were to continue explaining things in further depth, what good would it do?"

"I need to know what we are dealing with if I am to agree to your proposal, Ms. Hope."

"Yes, definitely, but that would then require years of education. If you have to know in brief anyway, then you know enough already. In either case, what do you hope to accomplish by disagreeing? You may have your husband found and see your hated managers behind bars, and then what?"

Fridgeon quietened down and turned to face Hope's vacant seat. It was a helpless situation that she could not find a way out of. Something, she wished, looking around in the darkness when her eyes fell on the screen that lay directly in front of her, shining in black and reflecting Fridgeon's face back to her. She read the depth of what she saw, and froze under the realization. "That's it," she mumbled.

"Huh?"

"Nothing," she replied, in a tone hardly more than her previous mumble.

It was her turn to think and make a decision, quick as she could. Hope wouldn't let her, and said, walking back and forth as if analysing within, "This makes sense."

"What does?" Fridgeon asked, diverted in mind already.

"The debacle, that little hitch in our hard work. The unexpected results when everything should have gone perfect."

"I don't get it."

"Jelzan's operation, sweetie! A perfectly set operation goes surprisingly bad with side effects that come forth only after several days have passed as if he were on some post-op medication. Meanwhile, somehow Kanha is found living in Milano; and he also, somehow, manages to find you – aghast, deserted, vulnerable. Tell me, Fridgeon, how did he find you?"

Fridgeon briefly narrated the proceedings at the subway as if out of some inertia in the ongoing analysis. Hope smelt victory and smiled at her words. She then asked, "That doesn't seem curious to you?" She let Fridgeon think over and added, "The one angel that came out of nowhere at a random subway in this big city. How coincidental could it all be? In fact, if you think about it, your husband's accident itself seems a peculiarly unfortunate incident, given how he also happens to be the employee of the same company that is working on solutions to his problem."

"Don't you dare."

"Oh, but think," Hope argued, coming close to Fridgeon in quick steps as if to manually drive sense into her, one hand stretched out with the inch-wide silver upon it reflecting the blue light directly into Fridgeon's eyes. "Two men who save your husband happen to be the same guys working in Scinoi's lab – so far from their town. What were they doing there? I mean, a couple of things may be passed off as chanced upon, but who could have possibly devised such a sophisticated orchestra of coincidences?"

Fridgeon reasoned in pain and asked, desperate for an answer, "Who was it, then?"

"Kanha Evian, the great conjurer of his own fascinations, you fool. While you blindly look up to a man you have hardly known except in a tragic vulnerable phase of your life, do spare a thought as to why he would be so well placed to begin with. In all your time, did you ever ask how he seemed like the only one to be concerned with your troubles? Did you ever ask who he actually was or what he did? Have you questioned anything that has come your way ever since you found that 'perfect man' to take care of you?"

[147]

She argued feebly, "I don't need to. Don't think you can trick me with this. I know where I am."

"Where would that be, Fridgeon Friuli?"

"In a-"

"-plan of some sort?"

A gasp of incomplete breath almost choked her. Things that had been clear felt hit by a touch of faintness. Fridegon thought in disbelief: Only two people had discussed her plan. She had not divulged the details to anyone and Kanha was clearly a distant adversary to Hope. *So how could she know?* The nerves tightened again, as she confronted her, "If you are so informed, then what is all this about?"

"It's precisely a matter of being aware. The question is – are you?" She waited for a clear introspection amidst an abstract conversation to result within the eyes that gazed straight at her. To draw focus upon something, all one needed to do was obscure everything else. Hope knew its mechanics all too well. Having caught another flicker of uncertainty, she spoke again, "Evian plays many games together at any given time, as he always has. I say 'game', for I define it as he would . . ."

"He saved a life; many more too, going by what you have told me of him. He tries to make a better future . . ."

"He amuses his interests, and terms it as hardly more than a play. Worth wondering why, isn't it? Do not indulge in circumstances beyond your understanding. You do not believe me and I can't care less, but I do care about unsettled scales. I do care that it was Evian's unbound curiosities that cost more than it gained."

"Cost whom exactly?"

Hope's sights had wandered away but they dashed back upon Fridgeon. She contemplated and decided to spill the beans that were called for. It may be all that was pending to seal her guest's confidence in her. "Kanha Evian grew up in times of action and uncertainty that was accentuated by the manner he grew up in. The whole world had always been skipping stones to get to a destination no one was aware of. Those were times of unprecedented change and they sparked the initiation of what you see today. Things were torn not only between capitalist fundamentals of vertical growth and communist fundamentals of horizontal stability but also between a 'new' way and an 'old' way to an extent far more intense than had been seen in recent history. Kanha grew up in a society just like any other, perhaps more rooted in reality than most would anticipate. I believe this aided him a great deal in getting a grasp of the versatility this world contained. What was strikingly different, however, was his upbringing. He grew amidst technological insurgences and simultaneous bedtime stories of religions. Fickle minded as he was, his inquiries never really met an answer. In fact, they grew more expansive and complicated."

"What kind?"

"Just like the ones you have. You question what exists. He questioned why it exists. Those were queries that hardly bore common sense, at least to those who were banking upon him to make the kind of difference that mattered to them. You see, Kanha developed with time, an uncanny curiosity to twist the general guidelines in play in a society. His quest for answers that did not exist had driven him to such corners of his mind that all his energy always focussed on flipping what he saw upside down. He was never satisfied. It was as if he was challenging existence itself. His loyalty to experimentation was so strong that he was willing to suffer losses and suffer embarrassment even if he knew them in advance. I think this cycle of paradox that he exercised upon himself gave him some kind of sadistic pleasure."

"You speak of him today in soft whispers of achievement, Hope. That doesn't seem like a man who liked to lose."

"I wish. I wish it were so," Hope said, looking away, gritting her teeth. "I wish there was a way to explain just how losing was his way to stay in a game far more complex. It cost many, especially those who went through self-inflicted suppression. It was like giving someone your life and realizing that you feature nowhere in his. It was like a great mask of genuine love that destroyed the very meaning of genuineness from the dictionary. It was like a tease, hanging right in front of you, making you chase it in unending circles until you realize its reins were in the hands that lay behind you. He was a human that deleted humanity with the expression of his humanness. Yet, it seemed, it was all just a game."

Fridgeon heard a sigh, the faintest there could be. She sensed the rise and fall of those shoulders and saw Hope's fingers fiddle with something she could not see but felt the entire focus of its bearer directed towards. It seemed like fascination. It seemed like hate. It seemed hallucinating. She pulled herself out of it, and asked, "What did he do to you?"

Hope ignored the question and went on, "Kanha, as I said, was possessed with notions of eras, birth, death, rebirth and human cycles from various cultures. To him, the idea of religions was one to have suffered misinterpretations over the ages. While the truth remained constant, our understanding of it was in a state of periodic transformation. So sometime during the close of the last century, when most were busy predicting doomsdays in light of our directionless progress on Earth, Kanha believed that it was a matter of beliefs alone. He believed that while some historical change might surely occur, its impact and consequence will depend on what we genuinely believed in our hearts. He was certain that if each one of us came to truly believe that the world was going to end on a certain day in the future, then it would, indeed, end for us but even that singular event would be seen, would mean and would incur different results to different individuals depending on how they had set up their mentality while facing it."

"Why was this so relevant? Everyone has beliefs of some kind or other."

"Because somehow Kanha, in his delirious ways, believed that he could change something."

"Change what?"

"I don't know. He felt that once people learnt to be humble and believe in existence over actions alone, they would be braced for all "doomsdays" in the future. To achieve that feat, he was willing to journey far. He was willing to take risks, blinded as he was by his pointless passion. I suppose such blindness only grows over time. That is what fanatics are made of. Kanha believed that the end of human era would be one embraced with love and not fear. He wanted to quash our perception of destruction and evil, of ghosts and demons. It's quite ironic really," Hope smirked, "Misinterpretations are what he wanted to eliminate. Misinterpretations are what he gave way to. History testifies that power in the lap of such blind fanaticism is immune to empathy, regardless the consequences that others may suffer. It's been years since I last saw him. Who knows what heights his incentives have now reached!"

The grit of her teeth echoed around her laser-outlined room, sending an added wave of chilled air cruising through the cold that lay amidst those shiny furnishings. Fridgeon inquired involuntarily, almost sedated, "It was you who paid for it, wasn't it?"

Hope turned at those words with her silhouette almost that of a rising beast. She bent close enough for Fridgeon to feel the whips of air coming through her cold whispers. She spoke as if in a sermon, "The day you interfere with the established order in the name of some righteousness, you simultaneously open doors for others to interfere too. When that happens, the world spins out of control, order fails, chaos results, and hope turns to a source of dismay. So I ask you now Fridgeon Friuli, are you not afraid?" She looked at her, inviting her to doubt what she had said. She had thrown an idea at the mercy of her calculations. This was the moment Hope had bargained for with her words right from the beginning of their ongoing tryst.

Fear had closed in on Fridgeon and only remained partially at bay due to an implied villainy that Hope carried through her image. It was then that the former caught her first good glance at Hope. She was older than first perceived and as she pressed her look upon Fridgeon, the latter asked, inevitably prey to the first caution of a human mind, "Why should I believe you?" And at those perfectly ordered words, Hope threw out her perfectly ordered response, "Why indeed? But then, who else?" She left the words hanging in mid-air. It was her turn to sit back and follow.

Fridgeon sat gently massaging her forehead, purposefully locked in a certain space of her mind. She asked with eyes shut, "Bionism. Was that it? Was that the key to his plans?"

"Who knows? Maybe. It doesn't sound so massive a change now, does it? That is the catch with such thinking. Anything you think as super important today would be nothing more than a trickle in history years later. There is no such thing as a permanent change. People are fine as they are."

Fridgeon let another set of minutes pass before asking what seemed most important and yet, significantly delayed, "How do you know so much about him, Hope?"

Hope smiled. "I have told you enough. Why don't you let Kanha answer this one?"

Fridgeon was not sure if she wanted to see him at this moment or many that were to follow. She could not decide whether she felt anger or concern for him. Fact was that he had disappeared like her husband. Fact was also that she could not deny all that Hope had said. The more she thought, the more she tended to agree with the latter. It seemed like an elaborate set of coincidences indeed. "Why," she asked Hope, "did Kanha do this to Jelzan?"

"A shot in the dark? Well, only one incentive seems to make perfect sense to me. Our inventions could have put Kanha's efforts in bionism in danger, but then he is not so much for the acclaim. Yet, he is all for exploring – almost droolingly so. Perhaps, he wanted to carry out the experiment more than us. Seeing that he had some of our people on his side, perhaps he had decided to edit the procedures in his quest to improve it. Could he really be that evil? Unless," Hope carried on, flooding Fridgeon's mind with every reason before the latter could think of it, "he had another incentive – in this case, of a rather personal nature."

"Like what?"

"Two birds in one shot," Hope pondered, ignoring the question, "That sounds more like him now, doesn't it? Maligning the company and its personnel – both which he stood against, and getting a firsthand experience into a new concept, although to level that, whether he would go to such extremes is beyond me!" Hope shook her head, laughing almost gleefully. "Why else would he be here? What else could Kanha secretly be doing in Milano?" Hope stopped in her tracks with that question as if to round off the circumspect analysis. "Unless he already has the antidote to an unfavourable result, if it were to occur, which it did. Perhaps he was filled with guilt as to what he had done to Jelzan and to you, which is why he helped you to compensate while he worked on the antidote. Meanwhile, of course, the Mongrando facility has been successfully shut down, which I'm rather sure would have pleased him immensely. All you have to do is notify the police, the obvious thing to do in this case, and his coast would be clear. Once they find Jelzan, he can use his antidote to fix him and have us nailed down at the same time!"

[153]

Fridgeon was close to tears. Her love had been made the bait in a play she had nothing to do with. The purity of evil on display made her nauseous. She suggested, "Then I think we should tell the police. If Kanha has the antidote, that's all I care for. I want my husband back."

"Does he? This is just a guess, Fridgeon – a guess that banks upon the assumption that there is some good in him. A man who can experiment on humans on both physical and emotional levels might not exactly fit that argument. All that I have told you is what I once knew of him. Many years have passed and he may have changed entirely. Moreover, what happens when the cops find Jelzan? It is a risk too big to play with a life at stake. We might not have the perfect remedy but at least you have the certainty of whatever we do have – and that is pretty close if only we could start working on it again. To do that, though, I will need your written consent."

Fridgeon reasoned long and hard, in every way she could. At this point, she found more arguments against Kanha than she could against Hope. One of them had to be trusted if she wanted Jelzan back. She was inclined, despite all she had heard, to follow her intuition and trust the man who had taken care of her, but even that felt like little more than an assumption now. An age passed when she finally came to a decision. She took a heavy breath and said, "All right."

The formalities were completed. Fridgeon stood up and walked out, cheeks soaked in tears, heavy hearted and with steps that seemed to weigh in several tons. As the glass door slammed shut and the room was obscured from outside view once more, a shadow emerged from a curious fold within the laser frame on one of the walls. To a casual observer, the stretch of tinted glass wall would have seemed like a plain extension but it bore a curve that disguised itself under the three-dimensional laser boundaries such that the wall never really began at the point where it seemed to, but further backwards. From within that curve, the shadow that emerged was lanky and moved without a sound. Hope, however, never turned to grace it as her sleek shoulders stood unmoved and facing in the direction in which Fridgeon had headed. The only acknowledgement was a sigh.

The shadow spoke in a crisp, grainy voice, "You shouldn't play around with love."

Hope replied, without turning around, "Nor should you."

Chapter 12

"Are you dead?"

Her eyelids would not budge. She looked lifeless for the first several minutes, then shrugged and ignored Qin's calls, and finally, tried in vain. It took him another fifteen minutes to get a response.

"What is it?" Friuli asked, drowsily.

"The first fat man," Qin said, somewhat enthusiastically.

"Huh?"

"I just met one, Friuli although the hype feels quite stupid now that I hear myself."

"It *is* stupid, Qin," Friuli assured him. "What's with the enthusiasm?"

"I don't know. It's an evil paradox – my body aged as years passed but my mind is still stuck back in time," Qin joked.

Friuli ignored the introspection and asked, "So where did you see this guy?"

"On the next street."

"You went out?" she exclaimed in shock, "How?"

"Your glove, or phone, whatever it is - you left it on the table in your room."

Friuli spat out at his audacity, "You used *my* glove and went out all by yourself?"

"Well, I tried not to but mine could not open those doors. I waited for you to get up until nearly afternoon." Friuli gave him a heated stare. He added, "It was just a walk anyway. Plus, I wanted to try out the things this lens can do. Absolutely brilliant it is, once you get used to it."

"Qin, you are not supposed to go out there alone. It is not safe."

"Why? Do you have happy and healthy dacoits out there?"

"No, the technology; It's risky. There's a barrage of sensitive information around for people to capture if you do not handle them carefully. That is the problem with having everything universally connected round the clock. It is like an ocean – with data floating around unless you keep them held onto reins."

Qin was taken aback at the idea. He could not reply under guilt but was appeased by a diversion from Friuli, "What about the fat guy?"

Qin felt a little hiccup and passed a sly smile, which was astonishingly well taken. He explained, "He was sitting at this café and well, it was just good to see a more orthodox figure amidst all the others. Although, at first, I was distracted by the amount he had ordered to eat. It made me think: I haven't been feeling very hungry or thirsty at all. Weird, isn't it?"

"Well, it's the pills. They are designed to provide all the nutrients you require. You have been on a liquid diet for many years now. You can't just jump on to heavy solid food without adapting to it again, right? It'll come back. Don't worry. Tell me about the guy though."

"He was preoccupied, puffing on some sort of a cigar. It was just very unsettling to see him sitting there like that on a chair. He was looking up at quite a height, surely lost in thought but at ease, indifferent to the heads turning all the while. At least that is how it was until he caught me."

She turned at a neck breaking pace and asked in disbelief, "You spoke to him?!"

"Yes, I mean, a little." Qin narrated in his feeble attempts at pacification, "Just listen."

He told her how he had stepped out in a kind of nervous excitement. He skipped the minute details in his

[157]

narrative but could not help silently recount them while his lips and throat worked in synchronization.

      Qin had chosen to head in an unknown direction with the very first step outside the house that morning. He used to love it once. Love was a travesty to be used in this case, for the behaviour had been like second nature to him at the very least. As the steps had grazed the layer of air above the ground, he had marvelled each breath he was taking with every inch he travelled in distance. Within a few metres though, he had stepped on the ground, his toes aching to feel the surface and play out their role in communicating a sense of simplistic freedom to their master. He remembered how his walk would create a perfect coherence running through him – from the pressured touch of toes to the inflating bronchioles in his lungs while his eyes looked and ignored the surroundings simultaneously, providing his mind just enough space to think of things that could keep his ease intact. It was the satisfied walk of a loner and it had seemed like a privilege ordained to an entirely different era.

      Qin had been using his blinks to good measure when he arrived at a different section of the town. There lay a park, smooth and soft to the knees of the carefree kids who played in a distance. A rectangular dugout that resembled a pool of sorts lay on the far end while the adjacent corner, under a row of thick trees that lined the entire length of the park fence, was lined with a few cafés. Partially lost in his blinking, he covered half the ground's width, bringing into clearer view the nearest café and the unusually ordinary man that sat upon the outermost chair.

      The tables were small and further intensified his bulging shape. The man wore plain trousers that stretched up to his knees and ended several inches above his ankle to reveal his wrinkled striped socks that disappeared in formal brown shoes, strung tight with thin laces. His shirt fit him loosely despite the relative expanse of his belly, and was equally uneventful by definition – though being considered to the contrary by his onlooker. He sat there like a sample that had been sent in time for Qin to experience a sense of the good and the old. A tweed cap rested on the man's head, shadowing half his face while he blew out puffs of white smoke delivered by the tail of his cigar.

Qin blinked, the quickest he could pull it off and still as the air around. The man was snapped and stored by the time the inhaled oxygen had left his lungs and Qin immediately turned to face the park. But he noticed movement at the café that lay some ten metres away. The man had turned his head and was now staring at Qin while he tried to ignore and act as though he had done nothing. Few heavily lengthened seconds passed but Qin could not ward off the feeling of discomfort. He shifted his pupils to the farthest corner of his eyes, trying to glimpse if the man was still looking at him. He was. He raised his tweed cap, then half raised his hand and bent two of his fingers twice – a gesture to invite Qin to his table. The latter walked.

"You are new," the man said, "please sit down."

Qin hesitated but meekly pulled a chair and asked, "How do you know?"

"You are taking pictures like a tourist. How many others do you see walking around, craning their neck at awkward angles?"

"I'm sorry," Qin exclaimed, "I was just-"

"-surprised to see a fat guy?"

Qin felt embarrassed and not many words could alternatively explain the situation. He said, "I was just interested in how differently you are dressed."

"Well done, Qin."

"Excuse me?"

[159]

"Have you never received a compliment? I said, well done."

"Not that. How do you know my name?"

The man laughed, "Even the brand of your inners is flashing distinctly."

"What!" Qin exclaimed, drenched in a new shade of red.

"Now I'd understand if you are new to the city. But are you entirely new to Earth as well?"

Qin looked over his head and waved the air as if to erase the information on display to the lenses all around him. Suddenly he was very aware of every second eye implanted on him with the leftovers implanted on the man that sat in front. It was a table of nearly blatant ostentatiousness.

The man eased himself in his chair, crossed his legs and observed Qin's panic with an unconcealed grin that subjected the latter to an unflinching stare, squeezing out all entertainment that he could from the passing moments. He then suggested, "The password."

"Right," Qin said and shut his lens off. They sat there quietly for a while with Qin looking everywhere but at the man while the latter continued to look at him, and grin. As the redness began to fade, he asked, "How could you see so much, when I can't see a thing about myself?"

"Bad lenses. So basically, everything you wear is a cheap brand." The man rhetorized.

The cheeks were beginning to redden again, though under fury now. Qin stood up and bitterly remarked, "I will take your leave now and I suggest you stop looking at other people's clothes."

The man replied, equally tastefully, "Oh, I seem to forget. Why exactly did you take my pictures?" It was like a festival of embarrassment and Qin thought it best to silently walk away but the man interrupted, suddenly very serious, "Where are you off to with my pictures?"

"Yours?"

"I believe you are not fully aware of the laws that govern one's conduct in a public domain. It is illegal to snap up any individual without his prior consent. As a staff of Securities in the town, I can and should take you in right now." Qin gaped at him. He added, "Surely you didn't think the x-ray visions or snap-and-transfers would be let out to people without imposing prohibitive restrictions on their use, did you? There would no such thing as privacy left anymore."

He was right and Qin quietly sat down in his chair with yet another shade of red on his cheeks.

The man added, 'Relax. I do not like fuss early in the morning. You are new and that might just be your saving grace. Have some coffee and breathe." Qin refused but ordered one when the man insisted. The latter then added, back to his amused self, "It's on me. You are funny, I like you."

Qin sipped on his coffee in silence as the man looked on at him, barring a few diversions once in a while. The latter asked, "So you were interested in my clothes?" Qin semi-nodded and semi-shook his head. The man semi-smiled and stated, "Well, I like them, probably cos they are different."

"Or is it because they stand out?" Qin interrupted.

"Either. Mainly the former though. I trust that you find my belly equally misplaced here?"

"That, not so much actually. On the contrary, I find the others uncomfortably coherent in their, err, shape."

"I think so too!" the man agreed with sudden animation in his body, "That is why I choose to stay fat."

"Why exactly?"

"To bring into this world some balance," he enthusiastically stated, and added, "And why is that?"

Qin followed like a student, "I don't know."

"Because it is the so-called negatives that make the positives considered so. Bad is needed to see and value good. You need dirt to appreciate what's clean. Etcetera."

"I don't think fat is negative."

"Oh, now don't swallow my words without chewing them up. It is about the perception, that being fat means one unhealthy and unfit. Being fit and healthy is of paramount importance, is it not?"

"Then why don't you value it so much?"

"There are just too many perceptions to value in life. It gets too burdensome. So I try to value my first sip of coffee in the morning and allow the rest to come naturally."

"Does it? Does the rest come naturally?"

"Well, I sure hope so," the man stated indifferently and chuckled. Qin looked unamused and stared blankly at him. The latter then asked, "Do you know the first thing that happens to us every day?"

Qin did not understand where that question had come from. He replied matter-of-factly, "We wake up."

"Aah, excellent. You are not half as dumb-witted as you portray yourself to be," he said, testing a helpless Qin's patience. He then added, "As soon as that happens, we are faced with a choice – either to believe that we are, in fact, awake, or that we are still in a dream. Do you know what each of us chooses to believe?"

"That we are up."

"Correct. To the lucky many, it proves true. Some, however, are rendered a brutal shock when they wake up again, realizing that they had been in a dream earlier. Once again, they are faced with the same choice. Do you know what they choose?"

"That they are not dreaming anymore."

"Correct again. This time, they actually aren't, except for the really-unlucky few who open their eyes a third time, with their mind blown out of its wits. Yet again, they are required to choose, and-"

[162]

"They believe they have woken up."

"Do you know what the amusing thing about this is?" The man asked with a grin and answered before Qin could reply, "Each time, they are absolutely sure that they are up and even if they were to be proved wrong thrice, they would still believe in the fourth go, with equivalent surety, that they were in the real world."

"Well, what else can they do?"

"Exactly, the alternative perception is not really a choice to believe in. So no one ponders over what the truth is because, well, there is no point doing so even if it were theoretically possible. Yet, this is not where the amusement ends. It gets even more interesting after this."

He waited to let Qin ask, "How so?"

"As we begin to go about our day, more such perceptions follow. We believe that our house would not suddenly collapse, that no one would drop something on our head from their balconies, that no drunk driver would ram his car against ours, that the person beside us would not bitch behind our back or that the noodles were cooked in a rat-free kitchen. Contrary to popular perception, we actually perceive the world as quite a perfect place to live in, even in terms of things that are not in our control. We believe, above all else, that we will stay alive at least in the moment at present and in the one immediately after – even if we swear by future doomsday stories. Every such prophecy translates into a day of nervous excitement and is followed by fear of another."

"So what should they do? Believe that they will die the next second?"

"Oh, no. As I said, it is not exactly an option because the alternative choice is just so unthinkable and wasteful. I am simply talking about the nature of perceptions, for it continues further. It turns eggs from an essential dietary ingredient one day to a source of some cancer on another. Every new study is perceived as a proven theory unless

[163]

proven otherwise, which itself is then challenged until an entirely new theory appears. Our understanding of the world is limited by time and evolution of our intelligence. So meanwhile, we naturally perceive all that we do not know in certain ways."

"Naturally."

"Also, convenient. The cell phones people used to carry in olden days were at times, dirtier than toilet seats. Yet, who knew and what difference did it make to those who did know? Cell phones were an important tool and somehow managed to break the barriers of hygiene requirements. You believed till some time ago that you were smartly, and secretly, capturing vital visible information, all the while unaware of the data that you were giving out to others. Perceptions, Qin, are amusing little entities of our nature. We live under such illusions, and believe they are real."

"They ARE real," Qin shouted, and many turned around to look at him, each with his own perception of what those three words had meant.

The man laughed, apologized and confessed, "I'm just fooling around, my friend. It's about time I had a laugh at somebody's expense, don't you think, considering how contrary it has been." He puffed on his cigar, looked around at the people floating past while Qin sipped on the remaining foam of his coffee.

"Look, I'm sorry I took your picture. We are even and this is no longer funny."

"Yet, it is surely entertaining, no?"

"You can't exploit someone just because you are a cop. Don't they have any law for that?"

"They would but I'm afraid it would not apply to me." Qin was surprised at his audacity. "You see," the man clarified in a subdued voice now, "I'm not really a cop. But it was totally worth the lie to have you as my company."

Qin stared at him, without a word or expression. The man pursed his lips with a sly smile pasted on his face. Qin could not decipher whether he felt relieved or angry, and it all fused into one when he finally reacted. A laugh broke out of him as he dug his face in his hands.

The man exclaimed, looking quite impressed, "So you do appreciate a good laugh. That just beat me, Qin."

"How so?"

"You need good sense of both confidence and humour to let others laugh at you. It's an elite club and I could have sworn you belonged to neither. That's good. I like you." Qin smiled and sunk in his chair. The man added, "It's only fair that you get a chance to make us truly even. I guess we have another meeting in store then."

"I do have better work to do."

"No you don't," he said, and ordered coffee for himself.

Another hour had passed at the café before Qin finally bid farewell and came home, only to have found Friuli still asleep. Back in his room then, he finished this narration with a final remark, "A curious man."

Friuli had listened intently to the story and was now well awake. She sat up on his bed with a confusing narrow-eyed expression with her lower lips tucked inwards. Her hair had tried to throw itself in disarray but had failed. Although drowsy and clouded by the black waves, she looked fresh.

She asked, "You guys did not shake hands by any chance, did you?"

Qin thought long and answered, "No, I don't remember." Friuli heavily exhaled but stopped when Qin added, "Wait. Uh, we did actually when we officially introduced ourselves."

[165]

Friuli slapped her forehead and spoke in dismay, "Qin, my dear, you had my phone with you, didn't you?"

"Yes," he said guiltily.

"Well, remember the part about our body transferring data once a connection is made?"

"Uh-oh."

"Yes."

"But it was locked. You had kept it that way, hadn't you?"

"I had but basic functionalities like keying in, ownership etc. normally remain available."

For the umpteenth time, Qin felt a sense of guilt and apologized, "I'm so sorry. I had no idea."

"Well, of course you didn't. Could I have it back, please?"

"Sure," he said, handing the glove over. Friuli's glove did not have the heavy contours as on Qin's. They nearly hybridized with her skin in look as she wore them on. Qin asked, "But how will you find him now?"

"You didn't think I'd leave my phone without some security measure in place, did you? Phones are generally activated to register the available details of any gadget they connect with, with or without manual permission, for instances such as this. Now, let's see." Friuli tapped on an app and scrolled through the information, muttering to herself, "C'Mon now. Don't make me hack you."

Qin looked on as creases began to develop across her increasingly strained face. He asked, "anything serious?"

"This definitely is."

"What happened?"

"There is no name. A concealed identity is never a good thing."

"I see three names clearly."

"Exactly. Three. These are profile names."

"Are they fake?"

"Not at all. Unless he is, in some way, above the law, which he wouldn't be given the records. They are misleading nonetheless."

"Wait," Qin spoke with a sudden surge of memory, "He did give me a name. It was different. I thought it was a joke or a random comment, the way he said it. To think of it now, it might just have been his real name. It was short, something," Qin said, deep in thought, 'Ree, or something like that."

Friuli scrolled through the available information a few times, each time with greater care. "I can't find any such name in here." Somewhere on her fourth attempt, she stopped and let out a short gasp. "See this?" she asked Qin, pointed at his demography and inquired, "You said he was middle-aged but with an old-fashioned taste."

"Yes."

"I don't suppose that description would fit a man born more than fifty years back."

"What?"

"A guess, under the assumption that it is the right data. I looked through the updates in the local network profiles. There are always a couple of idiots who keep everything public and let you in to their data and to those of their connections. Turns out you were not the only one snapping him up. Here's his picture. This is him, right?"

"Yes," Qin agreed in surprise.

"Well, I looked for this in the records at Beehive. There are not many that would fit in his shirt, after all."

"Where did you say?"

"Unnecessary. A platform. Now focus. This man-"

"Wait," Qin interrupted, "he could clearly not be that old."

"No, he couldn't," Friuli agreed and sighed. "Looks like we have a bionic in our hands."

"A what?"

[167]

Friuli shifted on the bed and solemnly expressed, "Sit down. You need to know something."

Friuli briefed him on the essentials of bionism, from its origins to eventual evolutions. Qin listened with interest and concern, for what had been a day of trivial guilt and amateurish frivolities had suddenly shifted to grave possibilities and an unexpected discovery. He listened to every word he could grasp while his brain processed algorithms on its potentials. Every moment since he had woken up had tested his patience. He had dealt in half-breaths as an entirely new world was unfolding itself in extremely measured steps. Perhaps it was the best, but Qin was reserved about who it was best for – him or an anonymous employer whose intention and now, the very existence, was beginning to cloud itself in doubt. Qin stood up, his enthusiasm drained out and calm returned amidst an internally violent brainstorming. He could be patient but the jokes were past now. The unfinished prospect of what men had possibly done to themselves and how innocently it had begun, had left him shaken. He needed to think, and think hard. This was exactly what he had needed after two decades of immobility that he had been subjected to. Suddenly the brighter aspects of his old self flashed in the slightest before vanishing once more, having delivered its message. He needed a challenge and only that could bring life truly back into him.

"Do not fret, Qin," Friuli consoled him, "We have it in our control as of now. Frankly, I am more concerned about this evening."

"Why? What's wrong with this evening?"

"We were scheduled to watch football. I thought it would be an enjoyable learning for you, but now I think it may be quite a risk."

"It's just football," Qin said. A faint trace of cheer had crept in him.

"It's a stadium and that means thousands of supporters. A place as public as that may not be the best idea on a day when you seem to have leaked so much information about yourself. Things can get grossly misused."

Qin could not anticipate what she was talking about but his eagerness to explore the missing elements of the world was too strong to be hindered by such niggles. He assured her, "When you wake up after twenty-three years in a world of complete strangers, Friuli, social courtesies tend to take a backseat."

She nodded and took a deep breath. It was in her interest to show him around, and both were driven under a sense of unexpressed urgency anyway. Qin inquired, changing topics to those of interest, "So where are we going?"

"San Siro."

"Italy?" Qin asked, his disbelief evident.

She wanted to bring him to terms as quick as was possible. Yet, this was not that moment. "My dear Qin," she tried to clarify, "your sleep has been longer than what you may have thought."

"I haven't perceived it as short in any way," Qin replied to her dubious statement. "But what do you mean?"

"In simple words, countries do not exist anymore."

Chapter 13

Life was fragile. Just when everything finally fell into place to yield a perfection we could have only dreamt of, the vulnerability would show itself. A simple wake up call, news of an accident, death and suddenly every little thing that we had bet on and planned for would drown itself in triviality and crumble into pieces. How could one be happy then? It was an accurate thought, for truth was that we had not really learned to be happy after all our time on Earth, unless we were ignorant. Perhaps this was, then, the genesis of the adage: ignorance is bliss. What was it really? What bliss were we looking for, a life of absolute cluelessness where we could never learn or evolve? The melodramatic monotonousness of a unidimensional wake-eat-party-sleep cycle? If not, then bliss seemed quite an evil thing by our definition. Happiness, then, was a hesitant moment filled with fear or doubt that it would soon die, somehow, and render us terribly hurt. So how could we learn to be happy then? How much longer would it take us as a species to experience a feeling we had devised and termed as important? How long would it take us to truly connect with our own creations – good, bad, right and wrong?

Fridgeon walked past the short corridor, and the longer one, down the curvy stairs, past the revolving doors and out on the stony streets that shone no more. The sun had been clouded out, without a clue or warning. Its enormity looked weak. In the face of all that she had heard and all that was on the verge of a freefall, the clouds could not stir her insides no matter how hard they cracked. It was a thought of insolence and lasted an entire minute until she was robbed of it. For, they roared and sent a shiver down her spine in one flashy moment. That was life to her, a prolonged battle. She looked up with a tormented smile and addressed something invisible, "My resolve towards happiness and meaning, against your resolve to quash it."

She walked through the now-busy streets populated more with cars than pedestrians. Her thought was fixed on Kanha. It was now a matter of instincts. They fought in his favour. They were absent for Hope. Instincts, though, were unmeasured figments of a life obsessed with tangible evidences, and hence, often just a passing thought. *Was there any good left at all?* She wondered, and looked around. Those faces of neutral smiles and innocence suddenly seemed to carry a hidden layer of mischief and inherent controversy. They were no longer just people who fell prey to evils of their own nature but ones that purposefully cloaked it over. *Was there any exception at all?* Her eyes scrutinized everything that came into view, and then they found the rocks.

The statues stood firm and towered over the inhabitants of Milano, mingled with the figures that walked and structures that stood, like the air itself. They were the inhabitants of history, drawn into the present to watch over the future. With bent arms, shocked eyes, canine jaws, rocky torso, stagnant cloaks, or crippled legs, they were there, all around and all seeing. She remembered how they had caught her attention for the shortest of moments the first time she had set eyes on them – an unavoidable subjection. The awe had passed over then to the more interesting things. Yet on this shaded day, the statues had come alive in their coherence with the grey that had blanketed the city. They humbled her under a stare of thousand emotions. They hung on walls and could not move, but constantly warned her as if they would. *What if they did?* She walked on, unable to take her eyes off every stoned face that stuck itself out onto

[171]

the streets below from the layers of parapets that lined them, on every storey of every building. Flowers adorned a few while few were left to hang out in depravity. Yet, some among the latter were built to extract pride from that loneliness, for these were gargoyles, built to protect the town and its structure from evil eyes. They were soldiers who resembled demons, while the demons themselves had been left to the viewer's imaginations.

Such a thing called precaution; she thought and felt vindicated for the shortest of seconds. It had led our long-gone predecessors to create demonic faces and knight them as protectors of the city against an evil that they had only imagined and feared for. There could have been no such thing for all we could know, or even if there was, perhaps in a very different way, lay hidden within those very gargoyles, hidden within their creators – us. That had not stopped us from plaguing the city with faces that would fill us with dread in the name of averting it. "It's a different kind of shit," Jelzan used to say, "that we give to others in the name of protecting them from some other kind. That's our nature." It still was.

She looked on at the sentiments that poured out of each figure. Most were stressful, tragic and internally deformed in their make. Yet, some were sober and silent at best. It was a subtle plan – one which made people value the sobriety as something immensely positive in comparison to all else that stood out. That is when she saw how, for some reason, people had managed to find happiness in such slightest of positives, satisfied and unwilling to trade for 'a greater something'. Most others had even managed to find it in those catastrophic figures. It was heritage, it was precious, and it brought them peace. The wide-eyed shock on those bodies of stone under attack with spears were reflections of a brutal past and passers-by smiled at how they still stood untouched, watching what were in simple terms, statues. And that, then, was happiness: an undefined emotion that found itself cradled in just about anything, tragic or marvellous, if one chose to see it that way. In times of inescapable ironies, we all did.

Who were these stone figures a portrayal of? Ordinary men and women of the past, or ones who had accomplished something; even if it were a bleak moment of torturous victimization or brutal murder. It could have been neither or both. These were the faces imagined by their sculptors who could only have drawn inspiration from what they saw or had seen. What their bodies did was a memoir of what had been done once upon a time in the vast history or perhaps, a then-present one. Both time and its characters had merged in this singularly active portrayal that was to last and reflect through centuries to come. And that, then, was humanity. Everything merged in the pages of time as all deeds and beliefs crisscrossed their way to yield a somewhat rough estimate of our social growth.

She saw how she could try all she could but would not detach herself from the nature of her species. She could establish herself as the epitome of all goodness on Earth while they could collaborate to present an evil metaphor. Yet, as years would pass, it would all melt into one memory – namely, the age that was, remembered as much by emotions in a generic sense. Heroes would be forgotten in the dark ages while the villains would suffer ignominy in the golden era. One or two would emerge untouched but that they would be only in our imagination of their character. In the end, it was humanity that was progressing as good or bad or both and not its individuals. The latter simply provided the sharp manipulative edges.

These were her thoughts as Fridgeon walked by, traversing corners and alleys of the town she had hardly every checked into. She went to a park near the centre that pillowed the back of a circular church. This was her purposeful delay of home-coming. The spread of green was one of the few familiar elements of an old life that had not changed. Still warm under the direct sun, sliced midway by a street buzzing with cars and occasional buses, nearly cushioning the multiple brick brown curves of the walls of the church that resembled a small castle in unison, and littered with couples sunbathing with coffee, cakes, beer or chips in a stand-by during moments of mush. Littered they were, for Fridgeon could not see them in other ways, though she had been very much a part of the idlers' community for most of her Milano weekends. Dogs ran across, summoned by their masters but let loose at most times. Kids played on slides, ladders and swings on one end of the grassy plain. These were merely accessories to the men and women who had come to celebrate a life gifted with kids, pets, food and love. None were part of Fridgeon's privileges anymore. She neither undressed nor put down a towel but lay down on the bare grass as though she had fallen upon it. She let the sun die down until the surface became too cool to offer comfort, stood up and walked on to the other side of the church. Its front face should have been godlier and commanding greater respect and attention from souls that otherwise ignored it on the opposite end on that park. However, that was its irony. The latter, sitting with their backs to the church and quietly devoted to their familial or personal being, were perhaps closer to the divine than the mêlée of drunkards who sat facing the Gods at its gates.

Divinity, though, was as collective as religion itself. It arose from an essence of convenience sprinkled over a socially upheld faith. So while it remained a church, with steps, statues and pillars of divine proportions, its meaning as often defined by its upholders, lay lost.

The courtyard was a stony affair. It was open from the three remaining ends. Tall, unroofed pillars lined one end of the space, followed by a pair of rails for trams. More brick walls stood on the left end, with a short straight bridge that ran over the tracks. It was an arch of historical prominence. Few buildings covered the other two sides. A

Caesarean statue stood in the middle – a crowned man, though in a robe of Greek inclinations, flexing his muscles while he stood in an awkward angle, with one leg semi-bent, on a six-foot tall circular platform. His eyes had darkened over the years and were now left mostly to one's fixations. Years of rain and snow had blackened most parts of this blue-green stone. Flat seats that lay in front were cemented, occasionally carved and partially decayed. A three-feet tall and two-feet wide brick wall served as the platform for the pillars, as if coordinated with the boundary of buildings on the sides. These buildings housed cafés and pubs on the ground floor, stacked up with enough alcohol to serve the crowd that thronged the area in the night. It was after sundown that a police car stationed itself on one side of the courtyard and trams slowed down as young men and women came from all corners of the city to hangout in what would become a lazy party. With drinks in hand and lighters in few others, they would chat, sing and clap along as the hours would pass well past midnight. The place would buzz with bodies, sound out with voices and intermittent shrieks, haze itself in smoke and smell of weed, vodka and bad breath that concealed little pockets of pleasant perfume drenching itself in splashed alcohol. Altogether, Fridgeon had always loved this gathering. It was almost a culture in itself – a mini-religion that came alive at nights and was ardently followed by individuals who barely knew each other, without question but with a great deal of happiness. On this evening, Fridgeon had decided to offer her devotion.

She stayed there till late, concentrating on sips of alcohol. Midnight arrived as haphazard steps finally carried herself drunk to a home she had secretly called hers until that morning. The 5th floor looked higher than it was and the elevators felt claustrophobic. *Why am I here?* she wondered. It was because she needed to verify what she had learnt about Kanha and was desperately hoping for one to the contrary. She found the little card hidden in the crevice on

[175]

the top frame of the door and entered in anguish. "Where is he?" she asked herself and went straight to her room, picked up a towel and headed for the shower. It was a plunge though, as she sat in the tub while the water rose inch-by-inch on her skin. As it touched new heights on her back, memories of those fingers that used to soak it up came flashing by. How could those gentle fingers of absolute affection bear a mind so cunning and nerveless? She sat crouched in there for almost an hour, looking at nothing in particular but also hesitant to close her eyes. She dived in, immersed as long as she could hold her breath, until she was forced out for a massive intake of breath. It felt as if it had driven her back to senses. She stood up, wiped herself with some care even though the scars were now more psychological and walked out with purpose.

She went to the kitchen first, hoping to find something – a note, perhaps. There wasn't any. Two glasses of water were quickly gulped down, some splashing over the towel that had wrapped itself around her. Her hair, wet from the shower, stuck to her head and back, crisp and devoid of all cosiness. She turned towards her room when the locked one came into view. It had been Kanha's private abode – a study of sorts – out of bounds to any other soul under any circumstance. Yet, it bore a simple latch. The lock was now gone. *Or had it not been there at all?* She could not remember but moved nonetheless. This was no time for courtesies, they were undeserved.

It was a study indeed. She entered the room as if she had come to a different time. The time machine that the door was had transported her to a housing of old. Technology had been shunned out as if to leave a space on Earth as 'pure' – if the technological insurgences were to be considered otherwise. Considering how they had come to continuously breach our privacy and a set lifestyle, purity could certainly be perceived as under constant attack. So these walls had shunned it all, in rhythm with papers – lots of them and of all varieties – and a system that resembled the long gone days of 15-inch-screen laptops. It was nearly worn out with the colours on the palm rest faded, a transparent screen riddled with scratches and the flat touch-keys heavy and stiff, though their edges still shone in metallic black. The system had been running on batteries, with the cord neatly folded and kept at the corner of that short table. The room bore a slight stench that was gradually lost with the prevalent air, but a gloomy darkness prevailed. She felt a momentary concern about the dirt around but it was forgotten once her eyes fell on the nearest pile of whites. They had been recently rambled through, journals and cut-outs from newspapers which had evolved drastically. Thus, some papers fashioned miniature chips, barcodes et al. but there were many that belonged to an older age. Most were headed with a word in common – Scinoi.

Several carried photographs of groups of men, with glasses of wine, either suited in black or cloaked in white. Among them, in a few of those, stood a lady with a familiar face, although it was much clearer now than it had been in her laser-lit office. As Fridgeon began to flip through those articles, Hope began to move in pictures – from the back row to the front seats, from a serious face to smiling one, and from white coats to black ones. Fridgeon moved slower, reading through what she could, though with slight impatience. The headlines spoke of what she had heard from other sources over the years –

Scinoi promises to be the new Adrianna Bios – reserves SEI status.

Scinoi on the cusp of revolutionary biomechanics.

Welcome the new shark in town – Scinoi is now Scinoi Bee. Management shakeup at Bee expected.

Scinoi Bee assembles world's first superleg.

Scinoi jaws in another. Anonymous researcher cries foul play.

[177]

Muscles flexed in Milano – Mongrando to defy state orders.

Do they qualify as us? Scinoi Bee unveils living prodigies of ten years of research and billions of dollars.

Scinoi Bee makes headway in the Energreen case. Court allows the merger to go ahead.

From a company to conglomerate – Scinoi Bee and its travels from biolabs to Biofuels.

The Bee ventures into IT in style. Welcome to the Beehive.

Fridgeon had reached the end of the short stack. These had been stapled together and tagged '4'. She looked around, once she had read through some of them. Amidst the disorderly spread of paper, she suddenly found meaning. They were an assembly of small stacks, each bearing a numeric label.

Her eyes scanned through the bold black headlines printed over so many sheets that had nearly turned yellow. They stopped, however, on one that lay further across the room. It contained neither journals nor newspapers. Those were torn pages from a notebook, single ruled and the yellowest of them all. She strained her eyes to read the characters hand-written on the cover. It made no sense. She stepped over a couple of piles to take a closer look, but her feet hit a small figure of porcelain instead. She bent under a subtle concern to not damage what could only be defined as mess anyway. It was a lightening feeling to watch a sense of care for something that belonged to someone who had come under intense scrutiny in the past few hours. It felt as if somewhere deep within, the house was still very much the new residence she had come to consider it. The bubble of sentiment, though, was short lived. It burst rather crudely in the minutes that followed as her eyes first set themselves upon another stack, labelled '3' and emboldened with the word 'Bionism'.

She picked it up and flipped through. Technologies, landmark inventions, change in regulations, key players, scientists, ongoing efforts – all had a mention followed by briefs either as cut-outs or handwritten in short. The stack looked incomplete in its information, although it was far thicker than any other she could see and heavy enough to command the employment of two hands. She did not read through in detail, curious to find where more information could be stored. The stacks were all limited in their scope. They could not possibly hold unlimited data spanning vast periods in history, unless they had a library to fill for themselves. This was why technology was important after all – simple ones like computers, even if it were like the unfamiliar one that lay on the table. Fridgeon froze with that thought, nearly slapped her forehead and rushed to the laptop. Each stack carried a number. What else could it mean but an index in a larger directory stored in the system? The logic was simple and precisely why the very first step required authentication. She made attempts with diminishing hope for ten frustrating minutes but none of her guesses worked. She gave up, accepting that she just didn't know Kanha that well yet. She went back to the stack numbered '3' and read through carefully. It revealed more of the world of bionic implantations that she had never known and she could see how fast the technology had progressed under the radar. With each new body part under review, she felt as if an infection were crawling up on her body, taking over those parts one by one. Slowly the droning read of largely over-the-head details began to thin out her patience altogether. Beads of sweat were beginning to pile up and slide down her cleavage, partly soaked by her towel. She hastily turned through the pages that didn't seem to end when halfway through, another freeze resulted. This one was prolonged.

Placed between two pages was a photograph. Three men were smiling ear-to-ear, hair wet under the rain that had moistened the grass around, sweatshirts muddied to the very last inch at the end of a day's play. One face was immediately recognizable. Another looked older but she could not identify him. The third was faint in her recollections at best, and demanded contemplation through memory. It was a short one nonetheless, for out came from the closets of recent past, the man that had bent over her fainted body a couple of days ago. His face in the photograph was measurably young, along with Kanha's, possibly dating back a few years. "Mongrando," she whispered. It might as well have been a spell as the words appeared on the very next page. An exhaustive outline of the factory came next, followed further by photocopies of balance sheets, escape routes, personnel profiles, photographs and then, experiments. They were graphical – sketches and labels, one organ at a time. As Fridgeon began to tremble, unaware of the lack of any blink in her eyes, recorded details of the works followed. Few pages later, a form lay pinned in, filled, signed and attached with a photograph of a woman's face – very much alive and well. The eyes did not bulge out, the collarbones looked in position and the hair was neatly combed. This old lady was, by no means, a lifeless sample to be displayed in a glass cage in a factory.

It was all very clear. Trust was a buried carcass now. The man she had found solace in the arms of had thrown her life out of gear and then garnished it with emotions she had been naively vulnerable to. She had fallen prey to the most lethal nature of any villainy. *And so had Jelzan,* she thought and cried once more. It was well past midnight and the streets had fallen silent as if to mourn her status. The tired eyes shut with ease, defeated and blank, once she had latched the study door and had hesitantly graced her bed. When she woke up in her towel at the first fresh sound of dawn, her crouched body had gone numb and stuck stiff to the leg end of the mattress. Having dressed and ready within an hour, amidst the heavy morning traffic and while the sun was yet to outgrow the tallest building around, she walked out and headed to the Beehive.

It was a journey hundred and eighty degrees apart from the one the day before. No individual could manage to take her focus away, nor did the greetings, the buildings, the rock figurines or even the sparse clouds. The trend continued as she walked in on Via Turati. The personnel were friendlier and the receptionist greeted her at first notice. She agreed to her wish to meet Hope Leosword with an immediate phone call and the magical words, "Please follow me," and led her to one of the doors in the corridor. Fridgeon was impressed with her cat walk distinctly reverberating the tapping of her heels in that hall.

"Excuse me. Mr. Usafa." She signalled to him and took her leave.

He excused himself from a meeting and came out with his usual smile. More cheerful, though, was his bottle green suit. The large hands enveloped Fridgeon's with former sturdiness and he led her into the elevator. She could smell a strong accent of citrus as he stood with an arching back and hands neatly joined in front. *Were they expecting her?* It all looked like a smooth preset movement of set pieces as she found herself back within those dark contours once the elevator doors opened. The gentleman behind the desk stood stern and silent, much in contrast to the reception so far but also much to her relief, given the normalcy of his conduct, or that of a lack of it. Usafa excused himself immediately. The following wait on the squeezy couch was customary. The silence, deafening.

Half an hour passed in statuesque seconds. When she was finally called in, Fridgeon once again found her eyes transfixed upon the walls of Hope's office as soon as she entered. The blackness was now gone. In tune with the day so far, it lay in complete contrast – brightly lit, too much so to be considered a closed space. There were clouds in the roofless top, white and scattered upon a rich blue sky. The room was bathed in indirect sunshine but no sun was visible. The ground itself was green and lush till the horizon which appeared to be miles away. Zaveras had grown through the ground during the night on a distant patch, blossoming wide and yellow. In every which way, she found herself in countryside. Hope let her stare to her satisfaction and answered only when half a question came across, "H-How . . ."

Hope replied, stationed behind her desk with her back resting comfortably against the chair, "The future. These are first samples of the projections that we might come to live in, assembled in our lab. Like it?"

"It's lovely," said Fridgeon without thought, still gazing at the sky. She gradually walked towards the desk and finally looked down at Hope with a drip of shock. The woman who had flamed across the blackness in red last night, now sat under the bright, clear sky, in black.

"You didn't think I keep myself perpetually in the dark, did you?" Hope jested, bent forward with her elbows back on the table, and asked, "So what is it that you know?"

Fridgeon sat down; taking a good look at the figure that had churned her insides the previous night without ever revealing itself entirely. Her hands looked strong for a largely sharp character that oozed out of her. There were no frills that adorned the neatness that she seemed to adore on herself, from the crispness of her soft, yet disciplined hair just as before, to the single fold of her sleeves that revealed a radiant blue on the black suit, firmly in place as if scared to budge. Her actions were equally poised and definitive. If an arm had decided to seat itself on the table, all other parts performed accordingly without an intermediate change of plans. The crispiest of them all was the smile she wore, shining but simultaneously bringing into view the silver ring that had stood out in its anonymity the previous night. This time though, it was clear and engraved with letters – upside down, such that Fridgeon could easily read them out from the opposite end. She asked, "What is ıphea?"

"Huh? Oh, this," Hope clarified, looking at her ring in an uninterested manner, "It's a brand I used to love. It died out. Anyway, Fridgeon, please tell me." It sounded more like a command.

Fridgeon explained, "I saw some material in his study – Kanha's. You were right. He seems to have a connection with Mongrando." Hope shut her eyes, gritting her teeth rather visibly and following it up with a heavy, almost audible breath. Fridgeon narrated how the five individuals at the factory had tried to convince her of the deformed lady that she had seen and fainted soon after and how she had found her photograph in Kanha's study, resembling a normal individual. "They must have known, or someone would have said something. I think they are all-"

Hope stood up in frustration. She looked around, lost in thought, and then pressed the side of her table. A bunch of virtual images appeared. She tapped on one and spoke, "Find out whoever is available in the Apiary and set up a conference in an hour." She then fell back on her chair, took a deep breath with her fingers dug in her eyes. Moments later, she looked at Fridgeon and quite literally out of the blue, smiled. She then said, surprisingly softly, "Thank you, Fridgeon. Your help will not go unacknowledged. Is there anything else?"

"No," she said, "just that there must have been more files on his laptop, although I couldn't access them."

Hope pondered over it and replied, "You must." Fridgeon gave a questioning look, to which she added, "You are the only way to extract whatever damage he intends to do. If he has made advances on your husband's cure, it's even better. We must take a look at those files."

"Why me?"

"Because it's Evian. He would have taken every measure to preserve his privacy, especially if forced upon by strangers."

"It's a simple computer. Snatch it, steal it, hack it. Everything in that room is decades old."

"Speaks even more of an immaculate disguise," Hope snapped immediately with a half-smile. She shifted closer and spoke slowly, "We may do all that, if required. Two of my men are already stationed there. They will act at the first 'go'."

"Two-what?" Fridgeon screamed.

"They followed you yesterday and have now taken up residence in one of the other apartments on your floor. I could not put you in harm's way without guard, Fridgeon. Your safety is important to us."

Fridgeon thought over it and did not protest. This was quite quick on Hope's part. She gently asked, "What do you want me to do? He is not even there."

"He will be back. My guess is he's home already."

"How do you know?"

"You fiddled with his things. I just hope you had the good sense to put everything back in its place."

"I did."

"Good. Now you don't need to worry. Much as important and now almost necessarily urgent this is, I shall not force you."

Fridgeon sighed and stated with an earnest voice, "Thank you, Hope. I admit I had preconceived notions about you. I guess anyone who is not part of the higher camaraderie does."

"They do indeed," Hope said and smiled. They stayed quiet as Fridgeon looked at the projected horizon on her right while Hope looked at her. The latter added, "You should know that we had initiated a search for Jelzan much before you came to us. We had to be subtle as I'm sure you can understand. In his absence and a lack of any response, we had to assume the worst. Sure enough, it was soon confirmed that he was missing and we let our dogs out, so to speak. For obvious reasons, we could not wait for him to worsen the mess."

She was right again and her sole audience could not argue, given the latter's helplessness. Fridgeon said, "I understand."

Hope continued with empathy, "If Jelzan were to be found, you still would not be able to meet him immediately. You know that, right?" Fridgeon softly nodded in understanding. Hope added, "But you would naturally feel inclined to."

"Of course."

"Well, it will take us a few days to wrap things up once we have him back. His tendency seems psychic and should be controlled with our antibiotics. We have in our hands now, an extremely advanced method to cure nerve functions," Hope added, quite proudly. "I hope for the best of the both of us that this is tied off quickly."

Fridgeon concurred and asked, "What must I do?"

"Nothing complicated. It is best to keep your plans simple when dealing with someone as erratic as Kanha. So we shall be patient but quick as is possible."

"Before you tell me any of this," Fridgeon interrupted to get a pressing query out of her mind. "Do we have any chance of finding Jelzan?"

Hope blinked and gave a short smile before revealing, "To be honest, Fridgeon, we already have."

Chapter 14

It was early evening and the sun lit the streets in yellow, marking its lasting images with an orange hue. It was setting perfectly in line with the orientation of each street that ran east to west in parallel with the rays soaking those mega-storey rows of green leaves. Friuli met Qin in the living hall that spread out plush with glossy ceramics and glasses twinkling under the selective rays of light falling on them.

"Ready?" she asked.

Qin was remarkably reserved. He asked, "The game?"

"One of the finest ways to show you the other critical element of our lives. We should leave now, if you are ready."

The two had taken it easy the entire day. Had Qin not been so preoccupied, he would have noticed how flustered Friuli had been even though she had concealed it each time they had crossed ways, almost purposefully keeping their meetings short. Qin had welcomed it, for he could have his space and time to think things over. Friuli, meanwhile, coped with her own set of thoughts; feeling punched more on account of an emotional upheaval. Thus it was in the house as the sun passed by in silence – with one member in search for facts; the other, in woe of their remembrance.

Friuli did have more than just one case on her head. From time to time, she would cross Qin's room and watch him sitting on the edge of his bed with fingers frayed through his hair. At times, he would be pacing around as if to dig out a channel with his feet, supposedly lost in the visuals of his activated lens. She did not disturb him.

The wind was strong outside and she could see wave after wave of the short vertical outgrowth of leaves bend under its force. There was no sound – such was the basic capacity of the walls. It was a neat guard and it inspired her hearty resolve that brimmed with empathy. However, the myriad of abstract thoughts that continued over subtle psychological hiccups were predetermined and out of her control. After all, the scars of yesteryears hurt still. She would have chosen any way other than what she had been compelled towards because of that very hurt but her employer deserved her obedience to the plan. All she could do was follow, and secretly scar herself more.

Yet, not all was burdensome. There was solace to be found in the choices she made. In this one in particular, she was glad she had limited the imposition upon Qin of the weight of excruciating moments in his past. *At least, he would have a cushion,* she had consoled herself. In any case, once again, it was her employer who had every right to dictate the terms of Qin's situation. The one who knew the other best, naturally did so. She found it to be an encouraging thought, though it might not have been enough to govern her piece of mind, had it not been for her employer's insight towards her subconscious. For, she had found her concern, born out of a historical bump, astonishingly anticipated and enacted upon. So it was all really tied off then and that emptied her of the momentary concerns that had plagued her wavering heart. She had left Qin alone and was now on to the next part like a soldier that she was.

As evening grew, Qin and Friuli prepared to go to the game. It had been the only uplifting grace to prevail in their conversation for much of the hours that had gone by. Friuli was visibly excited about the play now and Qin could not tell whether it was the prospect of showing him around or the one of watching football. To go anywhere had not really been his immediate preference. So he was pleasantly astonished when she only took him to a different room! They seated themselves on a couple of extra-comfortable sofas.

"What's this?"

"Seats 23 & 24 – Row J in the 2nd tier of the Red section. Activate your lens and follow my lead."

Qin did as was told while Friuli began to tap around in mid-air. All lights faded until the space was barely lit by a faint hint of bland meaningless projections. A translucent one floated out and hung in front of them as she entered their details. "Hold my hand," she said to allow verification via charges that ran through them and the physical retrieval of associated data from the glove she was wearing. Pitch darkness fell back in the room and an icon appeared hanging in front, glowing in yellow with the intermittent stripes of a bee. Welcoming sounds, customized with their names, followed. The glow gradually disappeared and was replaced by a loading bar, which was more of an oval cluster of hexagonal pieces, transparent and bordered in gold at first and gradually filling up in solid gold colour. Once the download was complete, the beehive glowed, disappeared and a world replaced it.

Qin found himself stand in a dim yellow-lit passageway. The path began to slide forth as they were led forward amidst muffed cheers that could be heard in some distance. Gradually, the projection of a giant cuboidal structure came into view, angled with one of its ends towards them and pinned to the ground by four tall pillars on its corners. Both the pillars and the sides were patterned with floors of passageways – curving around the pillars or slanting straight along the sides. Each ended somewhere along its base to a gateway – entry or exit, while the other escaped somewhere within the walls. The exterior was all in glass, flashing with running bands of colours as they covered the distance – major sponsors, details of the organizers, rules of conduct et al.

"This is San Siro!"

"The good old."

"Il Quarto Internazionale?" He asked, "What is it?"

"The Fourth International. It is the Vesuvian brainchild of a marquee international tournament held every alternate year, before the season kicks in."

'Vesuvian?"

"Consider it the area covering the central half of Italy."

"Oh," Qin said with all effort to channelize the questions that branched out from that answer.

"The name refers to the international games that former Europe used to play. Remember the world cup, Euros and the friendlies? This was the fourth. The name was not their creation, really. In fact, it was made up by those outside and referred to the non-grammatical Italian translation of what the tournament was called only casually. Slowly it caught on, and the organizers realized it had come to enjoy far greater brand recognition than any other. So they started calling it this, though rather hesitantly so."

The wide space that stretched between the stadium and the first set of metallic fence creased in, bringing along a growing wave of cheers that came from within. Qin felt his pulse speed up as they approached the gate. Once in, escalators carried them upwards with more advertisements flashing by the sides, and sounds that sufficiently eclipsed all else.

"These are surprisingly limited in range," Qin exclaimed.

"They are personalized. The advertisements are cherry-picked to suit your profile, except for the main sponsors, of course."

"Is that why they are so localized? I mean this one here is for tenants looking for apartments in our area; as if they know I am your guest."

Friuli smiled and replied, "Of course. Localization is a key element of their effectiveness and the main advantage of being profile-specific. You should be glad they are limited. To be honest, they were – and are – a pain in the ass."

"Over-interruptive."

"Irrelevant. Algorithms of consumer behaviour are constantly changing and are hardly ever accurate. Of course, they are now helped with a fair dose of artificial intelligence."

A mention of AI should have drawn Qin's attention but he was instead turned by a gradual gradient running through the advertisements that he saw. Were they still brands? He tried to focus but the ads were changing too quickly. Suddenly amidst a flow of imagery, he noticed a disturbance that lasted less than a second. His eyes registered the information but his conscience failed to interpret. It was the outline of a big black fly.

Familiar words of an airline carrier appeared from within that passing outline. It bore the usual stereotype of "flying to over a hundred destinations." Immediately thereafter, walked another shadowy outline of an old man carrying a heavy brass vase more than half his height. Once again, the image passed quickly and was followed by a retail brand fashioning their in-house production of pocket trolleys over the message: "Are you waiting to get this old?"

He tried to focus but the images would not let him. They were replaced again by an undefined vehicle shown from the view of a passenger seated inside. Two other men looked rugged and in foul mood as they drove off the road, clueless as to their location, only to reach a dead end. The visuals had been designed impeccably with the perfect balance of ambiguity and focus upon their message which now promoted the use of Scinoi's advanced lenses in order to "not just see the world; talk to it."

It was all rather unclear at first but Qin felt a spark in his brain as if wheels were churning out unwelcomed memories of moments from his life that he did not wish to recall. There was something he could faintly connect with in that imagery of the turmoil that the old man had faced. There was a distinct shiver that ran through his spine at the sight of the driver, and there was surely a psychological mountain to climb each time the fly showed itself. *"The fly follows,"* he mumbled to the shock of his partner and in some way, his own.

Friuli let him observe. They continued to float as they came out the short pass to a wider corridor littered with brands unheard of, clearly audible as if reaching them through earphones over the violent cheering somewhere beyond the wall that lined the path. Yet, as more and more brands crossed them, Qin's excitement switched to visible stress firmly planted on his face and quietly making way for short stiff jerks of his head as if to ward off inconvenient thoughts. She knew she could not leave him to his clandestine chaos for long. Yet, in an absence of any protest, she was happy to see him fight those off.

"The one simple way for advertisements to be accurate," she addressed him, "was to know you and your fluctuating anomalies better. This was important for consumers as well, because advertisements were of true importance, provided they did not invade our privacy."

Qin found himself hit by that last word, for privacy itself seemed questionable in sight of the images he had seen.

Friuli continued, "They helped us learn of many different things and at the same time, contributed to the revenue of many services that we could then enjoy for free. In short, we could not escape them. So it was all about helping us embrace them. This was most crucial. It is why you see ads for available accommodations in areas that you have visited so far when you are logged in from my house as a fellow resident with no familiar connection to me. It's partly logical, computationally speaking, added on to by many other variables – like how I have mostly lived alone, the composition of my relationships registered online, the fact that it is a football game and not a romantic dinner, etcetera."

"Do these guys really know all that?" Qin was concerned.

"Apparently. It's tricky to avoid letting such information out. Once in the public domain, it is all about the analysis of data. The definitions of 'basic' and 'private' have changed."

"So basically," he summed up with the slightest sense of relief at the inference, "Ads have become more like personal conversations, which means you are not seeing the same ones as me?"

"No, I am not," Friuli confirmed as he breathed easier at having regained a sense of privacy, "That is the beauty of this virtual space. It isn't bound by the first three dimensions of space. Our individual projections can overlap if seen from a third eye. Only, there is no third eye, except for the organizers with monitory purposes. Remember, all you see is basically just a projection in the room in which you are seated, sourced from your own lens and combined with mine to give us a conjoined experience."

At the next right on a curving pass, they found an open gateway raised upon a few steps. The staircase was covered by huge walls that only revealed the northern sky to onlookers but as they drew closer, the huge stadium unravelled itself. Suddenly the cheer was no more a cheer but a giant pot of boiling roar that came from a slanting tapestry of people that appeared to stretch for miles. This was a larger stadium than any that could ever have been imagined. The path and the walls around them soon melted into two seats fixed amidst an ocean of that crowd, distributed along three tiers. The stadium looked painted largely in blue and red, thanks to the flags and the jerseys.

"Alpi?"

"Versus the Icisles," Friuli declared. "The former belong to-"

"The region around the Alps?"

"Yes."

"Just the Italian half or. . ."

"Pretty much the Swiss and the French too, which makes for some fierce domestic competitions. I suppose your questions will now waver to the political zone," she guessed; her smile remained intact.

Their conversation was suddenly dissolved in another loud roar as a player in white and green waved on.

"Those guys-" Qin pointed out.

"The Icisles. You may recall them by the lion holding a shamrock on their shirts."

Qin zoomed through his lens on to the crest and nodded. His lips were slightly parted and at a loss of reasons as to how things came to this. *How long could twenty three years have possibly been?*

"So who are you supporting?" Friuli asked, craning her neck as she tried to look at the players warming up on the ground.

"None in particular," Qin replied in kind but with a greater hint of a mumble. "What about you?"

"I am a fan of both actually. My parents belong to both regions. So let's say 'neutral'."

"So it's actually a draw you prefer?"

"Nope. A great game. Aah, here they come."

A huge applaud ran across as the home team came jogging around on their side of the pitch. Qin asked, "This crowd. It's almost unreal. Are they all-?"

"Yes. Virtual view robs the stadium of its conventional parameters. So you can fit in an infinite

[193]

number potentially. I mean, two viewers can easily be superimposed on the same seat if they are accessing the game through different channels. So the rush for tickets, if any, is really just based on the channels available in your region and of course, the carbons you can spare. Each channel keeps the number of heads fixed in order to properly accommodate the advertisements, the seating and the overall virtual experience to resemble a real one."

"That must be so effective."

"It was not always like that though. At first, the best experience was considered as one in which we were given complete privacy. Soon, they realized that the whole fun of watching a live match lay in experiencing the crowd. So they switched to this rather public mode, giving rise to a problem with expansion. Any game sold this way needed to ensure enough numbers to make the game worthwhile on each channel. A second division match in Vesuvia would probably not attract enough eyeballs to fill a virtual stadium in Icisles. This applied for other games as well. So the manner of ticket sales had to be revised, and the potential was found more limited than anticipated."

"So at other places smaller crowds watch it just like before."

"To an extent. All this fuss is only for those who wish to watch the game 'in a stadium'. The rest watch it in simple 3D visions at home."

"What's the difference then?"

"Apart from the obvious joy of a real stadium-like experience, and shelling out more carbons for that, we get to experience it in an environment where its ambience comes into play. Consider it like buying an advanced setup as compared to a normal one, like," she strained for an example, "LEDs invading a world of CRTs. The room you sit in has been designed by the company-"

"Scinoi."

"Bee. Yes, well, they made it to provide a real environment, complete with varying weather effects, like winds that can mimic the actual conditions that prevail – except rain and snow, which, unlike others, would only be experienced visually, and thankfully so; all that's old technology, to be honest. It is the degree and versatility of the connectivity that makes the difference."

"This could be very useful."

"Necessary too. Due to one specific change in the way we played sports, it became important to ensure all viewers had an online presence. So where the live audience would not go for individual 'box seats', they were instead redirected to a bar-like simulation where they would join in with other fans. This was quite pricey though. The other option was to actually go to the nearest bar, or other such licensed point to access the match. All this is irrelevant, Qin. Thousand minds, thousand ways," Friuli concluded with some impatience, "Now focus on the game."

"Wait, you just said there was one specific change in sports. What was it?"

She turned to him and reiterated, "Watch."

The players who had returned to the dressing rooms, walked out in their customary dual rows led by one referee. The latter floated along while the others walked. The incongruence gave much relieved amusement, given the exploits of Qin's day. The anthems followed and resonated fiercely across different channels around the world – mostly pre-recorded cheers with pre-recorded anthems tuned and managed by the broadcasters and made to appear as live sound. Flexibility was available in bagfuls. A coin toss, shake of hands, alignments on the field and a piercing whistle later, the game was on.

A massive roar sparked off the first kick on the ball. The game was fast, feet surging into one another as the little round world dribbled and bounced off those heads and legs across the length of the field. The players were unrecognizable, clearly the next generation that had risen to be the new age paparazzi magnets. Qin watched the ferocity at play and could not help but feel the level of the game to have grown a notch above. The players looked stronger, ran faster and had an army of tricks that could easily fetch them a performer's job at a circus. Yet, with all the smoothness with which they executed their tactics, he could also not entirely deny the slightest visual blur in their running every now and then. He passed it off as faults in the broadcast. There was not much to ponder anyway, given how he secretly revelled in the pinch of cold that mimicked the temperature on ground outside, helped further by the winds that blew in somewhere from the side. Suddenly it seemed as if a manual control to the ambience would have been more gratifying for the overall experience. It made sense and he became simultaneously sure that such a possibility was, in fact, on offer. He looked beside and noticed Friuli dressed in tight-fitting jeans that stretched to her well-defined calves, and a thin pullover that covered her strap-laden shoulders. She had clearly braced herself for the wind. Qin smiled and looked away, only to have his eyes now stuck on the crowd, starting with the ones immediately around him. They were all present only virtually but there was no distinction to be made. They looked opaque enough and screamed with a level of indifferent enthusiasm similar to the ones in the stadium as he remembered it. Nearly all of them wore jerseys in blue with stripes of red. Out of sheer curiosity, he extended his hand gradually towards another girl sitting beside him and watched as it penetrated through her sleeve and arm with ease. It was immediately followed by an incredulous "Hey!!" He looked up and saw the girl give him an ugly stare.

"Did you really think they would make it so easy for perverts in the crowd?" Friuli mocked.

Qin turned red and apologized to both of them but they didn't care, for the ground suddenly went out of view as everyone stood up at the seats. All he could see were erect backs under raised hands, jumping around in ecstasy. He looked up at the digital board towering over. *Alpi 1 – 0 Icisles. Alessi '15*. The game began once more and routine followed. Excitement had been over the top ever since the first goal and the fans were clearly anticipating another. Yet, Qin was once again lost in his preoccupations when another ear-deafening scream raced through the stadium many minutes later. He looked up but even the board was hardly visible now. Irritated, he tapped on his own projection and options appeared before him. He clicked on the last highlight – a clean volley from the edge of the box towards the near post, following which a towering figure led out his entourage towards the near corner flag in celebration. *Alpi 2 – 0 Icisles. Bueche '22*.

For that brief episode in the match, it was beginning to look all too easy. Complacency, though, can prove costly for the best of teams in even the best of situations. The next goal was not met with larger-than-life cheers as had been customary. It was instead marked by a complete drop of all excitement, replaced only by persistent groans and violent wave of hands that attempted to beat the air around. Icisles had taken the full length of those remaining twenty minutes to get on the score sheet and it came from an unlikely end of their defence. The score read *Alpi 2 – 1 Icisles*. The first forty five minutes had already seen three goals and yet, had managed to save drama for the last moments of its injury time.

A heavy collision occurred somewhere near the half-line and the game came to a halt. The Icislian striker, despite not having scored yet but buoyed by the possibility of a comeback before the break, dived rashly to steal possession from an Alpino defender. The challenge was visually brutal and invited an immediate red card. His send-off dashed the hopes of Icislians all over, for their striker was their lone front man. The coach was compelled to make a substitution to fill that role. The replacement was to be a teenager. So it was no less than a gift to him when, thankfully, the referee allowed breathing space as she blew the halftime whistle and led the players off the ground.

"The defender: he's all right," Qin pointed out.

"He is."

"That's lucky. He suffered a terrible challenge. Both feet planted, the guy could have had his leg broken!" Friuli shrugged to invite his speculation. Possibilities are what he was looking at – from inexplicable technologies to unexpected mentalities. He noticed the referee walk off the pitch with particular interest. She had held steadfast on her shoes elevated inches above the ground with immense effectiveness. With greater speed available at will, she could outpace the players and at times, the ball as well. Her tasks had been significantly cut down and that could explain the absence of her other two conventional compatriots. Both the offsides and the player conduct were monitored digitally and whistles indicated the stop of play. The 'Ref' received direct communication to her earpiece and she physically executed the rest. This implied all twenty-two men played under constant scanner for their behaviour and the referee was now more like an official representative. She still wore shorts though.

"Beer?" Friuli asked.

"Got it here, thanks. You?"

"The juice. Works well enough for me."

"Is it funny if I keep getting this craving for something sweet every once in a while?"

She produced a sly smile for no apparent reason. Many words intertwined themselves within her to create varying forms of an answer to the little rhetoric query, until the most important one showed itself. "No," she said and sipped on. "So are you enjoying it?" She asked, breaking the silence that followed.

"Yes, though I'd prefer a more even battle. I don't really know who to support. They are all new guys. What about you?"

"I like it."

"But Icisles are literally being rolled over. They are lucky to have scored."

"Instinct tells me they will pick up."

"Ooh, time is ripe to place bets," Qin mused. It was refreshing, for one half of his brain was well and truly preoccupied with images he had seen earlier: the old man, the driver, a crying child, a brown-and-cream coach and a fly. He kept them off effectively, and asked, "Do they still have that, by the way?"

"Sure."

"Really? What do they bet by? Carbons?"

"Yes, actually. That or several forms of online recognition and redeemable winner's coupons – all part of the marketing gimmick. There is no such need for them but bets still thrive. We like to risk things on varying levels for that excitement quotient."

The little trivia had not helped his grim spirit. He confessed, "I just cannot get it out of my head, Friuli. It is as if the erratic minds have been let loose with every measure of self-assurance arranged for. I keep thinking: This cannot possibly be the nitty-gritty of it. There must be more. There must be something distorted, something that ties it off; completes the circle; balances things out. Because if there isn't, then the fundamental concept of life as I knew it and experienced against all my wishes, would crumble." He paused.

She looked at him with the gentlest of smiles and turned to the projection with a most humbly pronounced remark of near-repulsive indifference, "Shall we entertain them first?"

The players were back on the field and the game began at its former pace right away. So did the voices

[199]

around them. They were all expecting more goals and had recharged themselves for the excessive cheering that lay in store. The screams went on and the flags waved like a curtain outstretched throughout the stands with blocks of bicoloured stripes. The enthusiasm was palpable and the home team came close to scoring on several occasions. Yet, it was around the sixtieth minute that the entire planet felt as if it had begun to rumble under the sound. Two goals came in quick succession, the louder of which had been the second, for it was scored by none other than a teenager now bearing the massive responsibility of keeping the spirits of his supporters alive. Qin tapped on his projection for his own personal highlight. *Alpi 3 – 2 Icisles. Best '60.*

It was turning out to be a violent play, with the referee having to reach out to her pockets several times in successive minutes. She was handling the game well, given the flaying tempers around, unperturbed by the jeering of home fans or the pressure for appeals. The steely resolve of the ref was something new to Qin but his thoughts scanned back to what Friuli had partially referred to in the park. An unsettling idea flashed before him. A very improbable manner of balance had risen to his attention and he shut his eyes as if to think over it in an attempt to not spare any more time on the irrelevant game. That was until a massive cheer swooped him away again as his eyes sprung back open. *Alpi 4 – 2 Icisles. Bueche '69.*

An immediate substitution was made on the other end. Formations changed and the attack began form the word go. Soon enough, the fluctuating wave of the noise around seemed to have nose-dived as rarely did so many thousands behave with such coordination. Everyone sat down and the score was clearly visible, unobstructed. The score read: *Alpi 4 – 3 Icisles. Best '75.*

The match was beginning to turn into a teeth-gritting affair and it was not hard to guess who the flood of blue was gritting them at. It took some time to get the spirits of the home fans up again. However, several missed chances converted them all to sheer yelling. The swear words had retained their flavour despite the years gone by. Men and women still enjoyed letting out the unnecessary build-up of frustration in chunks every once in a while. It was comical and proved as effective in diverting Qin's persistent preoccupation as the frenzy around had been. To swear was to be impolite. Yet, such rudeness was almost natural. To control one's emotions was professionally well reasoned. Yet, this was that un-detachable trait of our character. Swearing was one occasion of our distorted lingual behaviour when it was mutually understood and accepted to be potentially meaningless. The words used to swear varied across geographies and among people but Qin could not help but enjoy the natural rawness that the young and old expressed around him in moments when they genuinely did not care about anything but the one thing that they felt passionately about. That feeling in itself was otherwise impossibile in our everyday lives and, even if for a bleak moment, was a human proof of its attachment to life that did not dictate the words it could or could not allow. It neither cared and nor judged. Words were born, words died out.

Qin let out a grin despite himself and tried to stay in the match. It was a good time to turn his attention as another hefty blow was delivered soon after. Silence arrived again. It was brought about by a second yellow card that emptied the home team of one player and handed over a penalty to the other. The following seconds were simple and unexpected by any before the match. It read: *Alpi 4 – 4 Icisles. Best '88.*

Damien Best was the Icislian striker introduced just before halftime. Any of the thousands that watched could have gladly murdered him. He was just a kid and it seemed fascinating to watch him do all that he had in outpacing and outfighting the Alpini defenders. All his three goals had involved minimal assists as he had led the ball almost single-handedly past the centre-backs; once even having made the run from the middle of the pitch. Each time, the ball was struck with brutal force and Qin was amazed at his power and pace, wondering how he had come to achieve them at such a young age. It did not look natural but given all the restrictions and definite advances that physiology had made, it also looked unlikely that a player could get away with any unfair advantage. Best had managed to rescue his team and his teammates were only too glad to pass the ball over to him whenever they could.

The game was tense now with the ball staying mostly aerial in an end-to-end play. Qin looked at Friuli. She sat there with a misplaced sense of calm, detached from all that was happening. This was confounding, since she had been so excited about the match all day. He turned back. Everyone else was nervous. Ninety minutes had passed and the countdown began to the three minutes that remained in injury time. The fans around were glad enough to see the game through, even though a draw was a striking contradiction to what they had expected for most of the match. The ten men in blue were fighting hard against the ten in white, each of whose lions printed upon the shirt seemed to roar with added ferocity. The seconds slowed in anticipation and in the very last minute, the tragedy occurred.

The ball went out for a goal kick and the Icislian goalkeeper – a tall man with muscular build – kicked it far towards the opposite end. No one expected it to reach that depth as the players had hardly made their way back to the Alpian half. Pierre Bueche – the Alpino winger – had twisted his ankle in the preceding run and had fallen on the ground in his own half while his team had charged forward for that winning goal. Now with the ball coming back, he found himself in the unlikely position to save his team, with the two nearest defenders far wide. He made a strong run towards Damien Best who was a mile ahead of the pack and charging at extraordinary speed to reach the ball before the goalkeeper could, oblivious to the most unexpected Alpino running in from the sidelines. The three reached it with a second's difference. Best got the first touch as he managed to shove it away from a diving goalkeeper and shoot it in just before he suffered a heavy tackle from the last man that ran into the space between him and the goal. The ball hit the net and the world was overtaken by shock around Qin – one that could resonate for years to come.

Qin switched over to his personalized highlight to recapture the pristine moment. He could hear the commentator's excited voice as the ball neared its destined goal. The picture, however, stopped at the first touch that Best lay on the ball. It had hit his hand and was potentially subject to be disallowed. The player's intention was suspect but unproven and the commentators could only gawk at the way the play had concluded. It would cause uproar of epic proportions if Alpi were to get knocked out on foul play. As of now, it seemed like that was exactly what had happened. It all seemed quite heart-breaking but despite all our technologies and regulations at play, human behaviour continued to be a curious case of its own. The victorious hardly ever submitted to the other's plight. If he did, he would be termed foolish in every manner of judgement, which would come from critics and audience alike, more than they would have otherwise, unable to resist the opportunity to grab such a rare spice on offer.

So it was that normalcy resulted. Icisles had won the game. Everyone jumped around with no pair of feet able to hold itself to the ground. It was a huddle bouncing like a spring in white as players climbed over a fallen Best. One white shirt had not moved. Best lay static and flat on the ground.

It took the players some time to realize this as they began to leave the field and the other blues ran in first. The whites stopped their celebrations as reality dawned and one of them signalled for the paramedics. More feet came running in and inspections began. Something was wrong and the buzz around the stadium could testify to that. Stretchers were brought out while doctors pulled out the defibrillator. They treated him for a while but nothing changed. Anxious minutes passed before a doctor in that team signalled at the touchline. The entire team disappeared and was followed by each of the players thereafter.

"They were projections?" Qin asked, unsure as to what he was more startled by. The system was still running as the audience was subjected to what was a routine end-of-the-game protocol by the advertisers and organizers. Amidst it all, word spread around. Damien Best had been pronounced dead.

Qin was still struck speechless as the projections faded off in silence. The system waved a goodbye as the two were logged out of the stadium and off that jubilant world of tragedy. Blackness took over until lights and silence returned gradually around the room. Qin turned to Friuli with widened eyes. She was looking straight as if the visuals were still on. Shock took over as he saw her sit with lips fashioning the lightest version of a smile. It was as if she had found the events satisfying. It seemed heartless but Qin waited. At length, she stood up, still not looking at him, and declared, "The best game ever."

Chapter 15

What was wrong with people with reason? Within reason, what was so wrong with being wrong? Fridgeon's mind felt bound to the thought for much that followed her visit to the office. Her husband was back. Yet, she could just not feel the sense of relief and excitement a wife should have felt. She wanted to see him, to be with him and to get her old life back. The latest memory she had of him was devious but now she had a confirmation of all that she had doubted and knew that he was not to blame. All that had then remained were memories of the longer past that were sweeter and more homely. These were all ingredients of the perfect anticipation. Yet, she felt aloof and strangely sombre.

Home, she thought as she walked straight to a specific accommodation on the 5th floor. It did not feel like one by any means, not anymore, but that was the word that an entire vocabulary stacked in her mind churned out when summoned. It was inappropriate too, for home was supposed to be the one she had lived in for the past few years, one where her true family resided – not the one she had adopted for a few weeks. *What was this feeling then?* She felt clueless but walked along with a definite intention, towards the place that had little hope left to offer but still seemed to beckon her. Perhaps, the idea of going back to her house of old was discomforting, given how it would push her wait for Jelzan further, filling her mind with unpleasant memories of recent past. At least, on the fifth floor, she would have an objective to keep herself diverted.

So she walked on, arriving at Kanha's apartment, expecting a barren waste of urban commodities.

She entered as she had on the previous two days. The place looked cleaner but her mind was pulled towards the study. Without the customary inspection of the premises, she headed into the dingy room. Daylight had graced the space through the southern balcony and stalled her for a moment. Fridgeon stood transfixed upon the focussed rays of light that had slid across the room, illuminating the omnipresent dirt particles in air that floated in such abundance of space and in such dearth of direction that she felt submerged in an illusion of static water. She welcomed it, for she was tired; very tired, given the tides her senses had been subjected to in the recent past. All she would have preferred then was some solace. Sure enough, a beam of glee stabbed through her at the realization of how close she was to achieving exactly that. Solace and perpetual detachment from everything new or worthy lay at a horizon that her slow eyes could see and it spurred those few short steps she took towards his pile of sheets. The horizon, though, was merely a mirage.

The mess was in order as before but something was wrong. She scanned through the piles. Stacks 3 and 4 were visible. At some distance lay stack 2. Stack 1 was missing. Someone had already laid hands upon these things and she wondered if it was the work of Kanha or of Hope's men, stationed somewhere as her neighbour. She was supposed to call them upon the completion of her task and it made her feel secure, but the task itself required every detail to be present before her. If Kanha's laptop housed vital information upon which lay the prospective health of her husband and perhaps much more, then she would have needed every other stack to be available in order to figure out how to access those files. Stack 1 was missing and the two men were proven nut jobs if they had been behind this anomaly. If it were Kanha, the room should have been wiped out at the slightest intrusion. She crisscrossed her way to stack 2 and picked it up. The first page was blank, except for a two-inch vertical stretch at the bottom. Two stripes of light blue ran across the page here, coloured with crayon, with a small face of radiating sun crayoned in yellow in the centre. One line lay handwritten in the white space in between:

The one who loves you will make you weep.

She read it twice to gather the context and then thought it best to flip through the pages. There were poetries and short scripts randomly scribbled over. Nothing seemed to be of much importance, especially not enough to be labelled '2', given the hard-contexted '3' and '4' that had oscillated about the Hope and Bionic heavyweights. It was feeble and unjustified, unless one considered subtlety. Fridgeon stressed further. There was no name or headline that could hint towards a central topic. *Maybe the genre*, she thought. Each stack referred to one, after all. This one, with its emotional inclinations was bound to follow the same. At first, it had all seemed like the indulgences of a sentimentally preoccupied mind. The moods had differed through the write-ups, from longing to proximity to anger to reservation, but she noticed what she had initially taken for granted – the protagonist of those thoughts. None hinged upon their author. They spoke of someone else, possibly a woman. She read a few of them with greater care and in the seconds that followed, faced extended moments of vacuum in her lungs. Oblivious to how long each of her breaths and how rare her blinks had become, she read on, deeply driven by words that had been penned to pour out all elements of one's inner conscience. Few pages into the contents, she noticed another anomaly. The writings, dated in part but largely corresponding to serial events or moments of the long past, were unordered. For a man who would have taken care to preserve yellowed pages spanning decades, with numerals and categorization, this was a strangely undisciplined behaviour. *Unless*, she thought and raced towards the laptop.

It looked untouched since the previous day. Authentication was still required, and she was thinking hard into it. With lower lip bit under her front teeth, hands tucked to her sides and eyes tightly closed, she forced her mind through every instance that had passed her mind through the last fortnight. It was a vast pool of seemingly indefinite resources to scan through, unless a specific category could be found which perhaps, she had. Stack '2' had been helpful indeed but equally helpful had been, to her utter surprise, the absence of stack '1'. For, that had restricted her attention to apparently the second-most important stack which would not have otherwise been the case. She obeyed and began to search for peculiarities in the images that crossed her mind. There were tons but none of a personal nature. A password would be. Minutes passed but returned nothing of significance until she dropped her palms in frustration and a clink of metal against the table caught her attention. It was her engagement ring, thin as any could be. '*Jelzan,*' she muttered, reaching out for him in thoughts after what seemed to be ages. The shock of his behaviour in the latter days and the ones in pain thereafter had erased all memory pertaining to his ring that had accompanied her out of sheer coincidence. She fought her inclination to ponder over it, for it would have made her wait immeasurably difficult while he lay somewhere on an operation table. Suc*h a little thing with such universal value,* she thought. Rings had come to be a greater universally accepted expression of love than most other artefacts had. *Anywhere, everywhere.* It might have been exhaustion that had mellowed her thoughts to something so simple but simplicity was the precise ingredient missing from her data. *That's it!* Rings they were, belonging to two souls she had had the unlikely fortune of coming across in successive days. Love had brewed once, of this she was sure. Whether or not it had ever been expressed was an uncertainty thus far but not anymore, as the focus narrowed down to the two meaningless rings that Kanha and Hope had worn, both capacitated only with a ridiculously ambiguous explanation in return. She thought hard. Two capital letters and two unintelligible words didn't offer much separately, but if there were meant to express love, then they were meant to be together. *Could it be,* she wondered, *was Kanha really that nostalgic at the end of the day?* Why not? It would take one to observe both rings to devise his code and who ever got a chance to do that? A sly smile crept across as she eagerly typed in, with hope and a near-certain jubilation: Khaoriphea. *Invalid password.* The blood running through her vein stationed itself along with everything else. It must have been disappointment but she could almost sense being agonizingly close. She tried to remember again, carefully spanning through each letter now. If this weren't the password, there was none other she could possibly come across. It had to be, for her sake – a possibility that she both assumed and prayed for. "Two capital letters, so it may be two words," she said softly, "but then, a password doesn't accept spaces. Together then." She pondered more. It had been daytime. Every letter had been clearly visible and there was no mistaking what she had read. Two minutes went by challenging the apparent length of two weeks. Finally, that one-twentieth second struck with a sudden welcome. *No tittle.* "The 'I' had no tittle, Fridgeon, you fool," she remarked, slapping her forehead. She wrote the letters down and looked at them. Another couple of minutes pass by, revealing well a history she had only assumed thus far. The end this time saw a heavy exhalation and a short chuckle. She went back to the keyboard and typed in: KHaonphea.

It should have been a moment of relief, as the nagging dialog box disappeared and was replaced by icons. The background was plain black and she would have spared a moment to dwell on that, had a face not shown itself on the screen, complimented with a familiar voice: "Well done, Fridgeon."

She could not move as her hands fumbled with something. She then turned around in shock to face Kanha Evian standing by the door with crossed arms. He stood there like a teacher, judging her actions as if to prepare a final report. For a split second, her eyes drooped down. It was the second that had extracted her guilt out to the fore and despite all her reasons, she felt apologetic towards a trust that she had broken. Gradually, the second grew distant under the cover of several others that followed and her strength returned. It was he who had broken her trust first. The reasons began to take control once more and her guilt was replaced by defiance. Anger returned to her eyes but in every way, continued to battle an unspoken emotion that seated itself within her the moment her eyes met his. She stood up, shook the emotion off and faced him with a challenge. He smiled, moved in and pulled a little cord hanging from the ceiling that switched on the sole bulb in the room. There was no need for light in a mature Mediterranean afternoon, and Fridgeon sensed what he had just attempted. She raised her eyebrows faintly and looked at his laptop but turned again, alert and on-guard, as he moved about the room in slow steps, looking at his sheets and inspecting the space in general.

"I underestimated both of you," he said, every word dressed with calmness.

"You are not the only one who likes to play here," she said with words that stood firm but only partially decorated with that calm.

"Clearly."

"Disappointed?"

"Impressed."

"Did you think that badly of us? Or are you that proud of yourself?"

""Us?" I see that you have changed loyalties."

"So you did really bank upon musing me into your trap?"

"Was I that charming? I am flattered."

She smirked, rolled her eyes and exclaimed, "And I was too, very nearly, given how much you had trusted me with your little plan."

"I still do."

"With what? Your plan failed. You banked upon using my innocence with your act, and you failed."

Kanha did not say anything. Fridgeon continued, "Oh, wait. I get it. You believe you've managed to create a perfect gang of spies in me and those at Mongrando, and that you have ensured any link between Jelzan and you is taken care of, while ensuring his condition is blamed upon the heads at Scinoi. All tied off in your favour, right? Well, sorry to break it to you, but they have found him. In fact, we may also have the cure."

Kanha interrupted, "I am extremely happy for you then, Fridgeon. Is that what you were planning to get from my computer? The cure?"

"That, and anything that might help stop you if there's anything worth stopping you for."

"Oh, there certainly is but tell me, is that why you trashed my house two nights back - or was it just a routine search?"

"What? Two nights back I was working on your directions. Two nights back you had abandoned me."

"And conveniently left the access card to my house for you to find outside? Yes, that is exceptionally cruel on my part." The sarcasm pinched.

Fridgeon hesitated at the thought and asked, "How long have you been here?"

"Not long enough. It was difficult indeed to balance my work and the protection of my home, but I am glad I came back on time."

"What alerted you?"

[211]

"That," he said, pointing at his computer. "Someone fiddled with it. Would you know who?"

An answer wasn't really necessary but she replied with her defiance intact, "Me."

"Yet, you expect me to believe that you did not fiddle with other things too?"

"Yes, I do. Don't make me sick with how little faith you had in me when it's actually you who couldn't be trusted."

"Well, you were the little pawn of my play, as you just put it. Without you, what would I do? You were the god-sent key to a big problem I was trying to solve. I can't thank you enough."

Fridgeon felt like she could throw up. She was disgusted but every other feeling had been overridden by disbelief. How could he be so shamelessly forthcoming? Suddenly, she felt incredibly unsafe and scared. Images of his brutality and repercussions of confronting a satanic mind began to clog her. It was time to do what was needed.

"That friend of yours at Mongrando – he knew I was going to the factory that day. You alerted him, which was why he was there with his crew. Si?"

Fridgeon had spoken fast and her change of language seemed too misplaced to pass off. Kanha replied suspiciously, "I wouldn't know."

"Don't lie, Kanha! No such thing as a coincidence."

"Indeed. There may be none. I believe something does go on – an immense tapestry of events spread over the infinite space-time that we are ordinarily oblivious to, which leads to what appears to be sheer coincidence. But there must be-"

"Shut the bullshit. You told him. That's why he was present. The question is-"

"-Why I sent you there then."

"Yes."

"Well, you are doing quite well. By all means, go ahead."

"This is not a game, Kanha."

"I thought we mutually agreed to the opposite not many moments ago."

Fridgeon lowered her tone. "You think it's all just a joke? Even in defeat all you can think of is how to extract some fun!" Kanha looked at her without blinking, his smile remaining. Fridgeon continued, "You sent me because you wanted me to get a closer look at the factory, so that I could alert the police or testify to Scinoi's sins, if needed."

"Did you see anything in particular?"

Fridgeon's voice wavered at the memory of the decrepit half-woman. Her lips parted an inch, a thick chunk of saliva was forcibly gulped down the throat and the eyes blinked a bit too frequently for an instant. Kanha caught it and remarked, "What did you see, Fridgeon? I must know."

"Oh, do you? You know, in ordinary terms, they would call it nothing short of murder, except that that would imply death. So what can one say about something that falls in between? For, surely 'alive' does not fit the bill."

Kanha stared at her, unblinking, his smile vanished. All that changed in the seconds that followed was a prolonged dropping of his eyelids as he tried to drown a rising expression back within him. When his eyes opened, they no longer looked at Fridgeon. They were stationed far into the southern horizon, now glowing bright under the westward moving sun. Twice he shook his head. Fridgeon did not say anything, for she was unknowingly engrossed in his reaction. She had braced herself for something of a more violent nature. This was that of a highly troubled calm, as if he stood reserved to the repercussions of what her words had implied. It angered her further. For, deep within, she had hoped for an expression of cluelessness which might just have meant that he really, in a most unexpected way, did not know what she was talking about. She may have

[213]

believed him eventually, even if it had dragged on for the rest of the day, but the fact that Kanha had acknowledged what she was talking about even though she had only hinted at it, quite undeniably proved that Mongrando was his doing after all. It proved that he had had a hand to play in what she had seen. Suddenly it all fit – Kanha's reception on the first day amidst all strangers who had moved about in the subway, his quick focus on what might have gone wrong, his knowledge of Mongrando, the pictures in his study, his absence from the house while she went about his plan and the lack of panic he had shown on this day for most of their conversation. A feeling of disgust stabbed her heart at the memory of his hands crawling on her back and of those de-appetising breakfasts she'd come to cherish.

"Fridgeon," he said at length and was immediately interrupted.

"You can't hurt anyone else. You'll pay for this. Run wherever you can but you will. The tables have turned on you. I do not know if it will be prison or something much worse but I don't think it'll matter to me. Your files are in my command and being transferred as we speak. All your nuances and plots shall fall, along with any and every little secret of yours. You played with lives and as if that was not enough, with things that keep it sacred. This is how you pay for it." She ended her words with a final act of repulsion as her hand moved out of her pocket, holding a gun that now pointed directly at Kanha's eyes. Hope had armed her with a psitol in anticipation of an unwelcomed confrontation, and Fridgeon felt extremely thankful that she had been forced to keep it despite her attempts to deny the offer.

While the short barrel hid one of his eyes from view, the pain in the other was clearly visible. His eyebrows had sagged. Tranquility, instead of subliming, had exponentiated itself as if he had resorted to the prospect of losing out on everything, especially at the latest challenge from Fridgeon. He did not move to physically stop her but exclaimed, "So much hate, Fridgeon. I really did underestimate her. It took her two days to negate two weeks of an understanding we built."

"You dare speak of "we"," she stressed with virtually emboldened words, "There is no "we"."

"Why not?"

"Is that rhetorical?"

"Not at all. It's all very real. I want you to answer that, if not to me then to yourself at least. Why did 'we' die so suddenly?"

Fridgeon laughed at his audacity and said, "You really are presumptuous, aren't you?"

"I am rational."

"Then you should accept the outcome of cheating on the very essence of humanity. You ruined my life."

"I saved it."

"You had planned it."

"With that random driver you took a lift from?" Kanha exclaimed with strength in his voice for the first time that evening. "Which should then imply that I perfectly timed his arrival that night with your escape and therefore, by extension, with Jelzan's psychic outburst. That would then imply that Jelzan was in my team as well. How do you like that possibility?"

Fridgeon gaped at him for an instant. He continued, "Wait, since that vacation was your idea, I suppose you are in my team too. Did I operate you, erased all relevant memory and plugged in a chip in your head to make you act as I wished?"

Fridgeon was beginning to shiver. *Had he?* It was an unthinkable possibility but in the face of aspects of bionism that she had learnt of, it was no longer impossible. Suddenly, she couldn't feel the floor and the air thinned. The minutes that followed blurred out, then two heavy guys entered the house.

"Aah, so that's why you had switched languages," Kanha deducted from the trespassers, addressing her all the time.

She did not hear anything. Her mind was lost. Hope's men acknowledged her presence and moved quickly. One came to her while the other muscled Kanha out of the study. With a dropped jaw and widened eyes, she continued to stare blankly while the other took out the flash drive she had connected to Kanha's laptop before standing up to face him. The relevant files had been transferred into this little gadget of seemingly endless capacity. What was relatively unknown to her was that its wireless connectivity integrated to allow an immediate transfer of all files to the source computer. Hope had ensured that all means of risk were averted in this exchange of extremely rare information, for she had anticipated the sensitivity of any data from Kanha's files. She had looked forward to whatever she could use. The guys began to escort Fridgeon out of the apartment when she stopped one of them and turned to Kanha. He had been punched hard by the one who had held him and was now on his knees, holding his waist with one hand. He was in pain, given the couple of coughs and his audibly erratic breathing she observed. She freed herself from the guy escorting her, who in turn utilized the excess adrenaline to kick Kanha at the exact spot that he had cupped with his hands. His ribs rattled at the stroke of the heavy boot and Kanha fell to his side, crouched with his head dug towards his bent legs. Fridgeon did not move.

"Did you ever-" her words had risen out of an irritatingly unflinching emotion she could not explain but detested herself for.

Kanha punched the floor in pain and raised his head to look at her. A trembling smile spread across his lips and a solitary word came out with effort, "Etna." He then squeezed his eyes and dropped his head in pain.

Before she could think further, she was turned and led to safety by the men, as three pairs of feet walked out and shut the door to that fifth floor apartment.

Chapter 16

"Was that a joke?" Qin asked, as they sat in a restaurant Friuli had picked for them after the game. The question had graced his throat ever since but he had waited for her to explain on her own. She had not and he had left things for a more static moment to come by.

"What?"

"Your reaction at the end of the game. Is Damien really dead?"

"It appears so."

Qin said under a grave thought, "That guy, Damien, did not look normal, so to speak. He was clearly a notch above, physically."

"That he was."

"Bionism?"

"I wouldn't think so. That would have caused disqualification and any bionic change is easy to detect, though that does have a loophole."

"Such as?"

"Versatility. Consider a bionic eye. It sounds relatively harmless but if it were allowed unrestricted in play, a player could have the so-called supersight where he could track the trajectory or movement of the ball or of the players, as well as gather any physiological information on each competitor. He could also map the defensive movement of the opposition and understand both their original strategy as well as any changes to it in real time, giving his team a significant advantage by the end of the game."

"So obviously any on-field bionic involvement should be prohibited," Qin concluded.

"Should be, but it wasn't that easy to do away with, just the way phones or laptops could not be kept banned from classrooms after a period of time."

"Phones or laptops enjoyed a collective need."

"So did implants. Do you remember the part about Nature's nudge?"

"Yes," Qin replied, matter-of-factly.

"As a result of the series of cataclysmic events," Fridgeon deliberated, "there was virtually no inhabitation left unaffected on Earth. It didn't happen in one day, but in the pages of history, would largely been seen as a period of consistent and often fatal turmoil. The majority that came out of that phase were rendered paralytic on some level – subtle or pronounced. So bionic aid of some or other kind came to be quite common. Given the energy network, everyone could afford it too."

An idea arrived in Qin's mind, laden with dark humour. He cleared his throat and remarked, repulsed, "What limited its use then?"

"We did. You see, humans have evolved in different ways. A decade, for example, is nothing in terms of true human evolution but it still does occur, no matter how infinitesimal it is. Think carefully about the time before your accident. Did you notice a sense of greater understanding in people about human behaviour in general day-to-day conversation?" Friuli waited and rephrased in a more animated fashion when pursed lips were all that Qin returned, "terms like *'oh, that . . . yea, I know that feeling.'* Or something like *'relax, it's what people do.'*?"

"I guess," Qin concurred.

Friuli continued, "the point is that we get accustomed to anything that we observe regularly, even if it isn't pronounced or explained in so many words. The same was true for bionic implants but our history and successive decades of sudden rapid changes had left us very aware and conscious of certain fallouts. So the general public did not buy into the companies' marketing gimmicks as easily. Though what proved more helpful was the latter's own interests. The major stakeholder in this case was Scinoi. She had her hands full with many other prospects that needed far greater emphasis than bionism. She knew she could kill her competitors off, since all her core engagements were born out of niche concepts. Bionism, for a change, could wait because she held the patents as well as the expertise in the field by some distance, thanks to some careful planning. So she stopped wasting her time on this legal battle for the time being."

"So it's just a momentary pause."

"Evolution never stops, Qin."

He looked around the table. They were seated in the middle of a circular structure of stoned walls carrying holes in patches all over. The walls towered over them for over four storeys and were broken at places throughout the circumference. Stony steps stretched between the tallest point and the ground, diagonally covering nearly half its radius all along. The steps were broad and had allowed grasses to grow through the crevice between any two blocks of stones. The walls had accommodated bricks as well but the little blocks of red could barely match up to the enormous solidity of the greys. Yet, both held the grandiose in place in unison, with vast stretches of smooth bent stones and orderly sprinkles of rectangular bricks. This was an arena to behold and its story must have begun several millennia back.

The ground inside must have once stretched in plain to allow the human activities this arena had been built for. Violent gladiator games must have prospered for ages amidst the versatile and temporary onlookers and stories must have been written in praise of the grandeur of the impact they had had on men. That was the age of the structure's youth and it must have passed, as all ages do, to yield a phase of silent adolescence that would have eerily draped the hollow in the centuries that followed. Nothing would have survived then but those stories in soft whispers and amazed eyes that would have looked upon it from outside its perimeters.

Then, one day, Earth must have rattled on its own or in its superficiality to render the structure unstable. The ruthlessness of time must have imposed upon that unbreakable solidity of stones, a sense of humility. So must have fallen the very first brick and then perhaps, the very first stone, to remind its onlookers that even this majestic stadium of human effort was fragile in the pages of time. No matter how much we protect it, we could not outsurvive the threat of those undying seconds, which did not tire. This must have been the larger realization then, eclipsing all other thought over a span of mere decades that would have suddenly woken the inhabitants, returned to them their humility and dictated a nostalgic fear of preserving what had been an example of their own growth.

Thus, an age of adulthood must have finally arrived for the arena. The harmony between violent Gladiatorisms and the stories in praise of that violence must have come to fall, in order to give way to true harmony – true, as a human mind could define it. That time must have arrived to render this space that once stood as a beacon of unflinching prowess and unshakable mark upon Earth, as a fragile memory of what is precious and must be saved as long as is destined. Restoration must have taken place and stories, then returned to replace all else. Human activities would have risen again, this time of a different nature with women and men returning to watch others play, not to satisfy a brutal thirst but a pleasant one. For, these plays would correspond to the enactment of the former stories, theatrical in nature and emphasising heavily on the colours, the sounds and other peaceful senses of humanity. The resulting applause would then be without any trace of animalism in the eyes of their bearers, and before the nights ended, all would have walked out alive, in every sense of the word, for the first time in the history of that arena.

Qin looked at the imposing heights of the walls within which he now sat, sans the spectators or the actors. This was the final phase of its life. It was originally built to behold its superiority in terms of muscle and all else that we considered superior in that particular period of history. It had then been made to succumb to a visual fragility where it remained strong only through perceptions. Today it had arrived to a time when those very stones had transformed into a symbol of beauty and sensitivity. Qin sat watching it in its third phase – of retirement and of memories.

"Arena di Verona," he muttered to himself in awe.

"It is."

"Yet, not exactly," he said without looking at her. "This is just a projection, is it not?"

Surprise took over Friuli at Qin's quick analysis as he stationed his sight upon her once again. He had learnt well from his experience at the game earlier that evening. She looked away at a distance and ran her fingers through her hair in a most uncharacteristic fashion.

"I had told you about the need to incorporate the new amidst the old, had I not?" she said, "You can't keep making new cities every time a new idea hits you. To truly sustain any change, it has to be adopted by what already exists unless what exists breaks down entirely."

"This one suffered as well?" he asked, serious in demeanour and in continuum with an effort to scrutinize every word, object and event that came his way ever since his carelessness in the morning.

"Yes," Friuli clarified, "It suffered a blow in the last earthquake and since then, has been declared a heritage site. It is now preserved and kept secure from any intrusion and all activities inside have been stopped, but then, the Arena retains its brand power and the State uses it to good effect."

"Through sanctions on the usage of its virtual imagery?"

"Certainly. It is a good source of income each time any institution in the world uses this projection. Timelines and charges are fixed, and the brand image and quality is ensured in terms of the activities it is used for."

"That, I suppose, minimizes travel as well."

"Travel had already been minimized, especially to the endangered areas and under continuously tight schedules."

Qin pondered over the idea for a while. He then stated upon his own calculations, "I think this works more on account of the hedonic services it facilitates. Such spending is especially crucial in times of calamities to keep people calm and happy."

"Most definitely," Friuli said under an intangible hint of a smile. What she had not realized was a hidden rhetoric in his words. It was becoming increasingly difficult for her to contain his questions and the answers were becoming increasingly difficult to come by. It was a perfect moment then when the anomaly occurred.

"She lives in our memory as old age puts her to a feeble rest somewhere in her hometown," Qin exclaimed, lost in the realism of the imagery that lay around him. "It's a lovely end, coherent with our own conventionalism. This is how each great life must come to an end, and we have somehow-" His words suffered a hiccup as an unexpected blur ran through the walls. It was as if a scar had born and died in those walls in an instant, and it reminded him of the television signals of old. It was then that he remembered: he had seen it happen during the play as well. He finished without thought on the words, "-ensured it."

Qin was struck by the little disturbance when he turned towards a rumbling noise that had begun on the other end. There was a live kitchen area and a spot of intense movement in the restaurant. The moments that followed seemed to slow down to a buzz. It was a movement in the far corner that he noticed first. The waiter standing nearest stopped dead in his tracks, looking straight at nothing in particular with a tray still in his hands. Suddenly, all other waiters near him followed suit, joined further in complete and obedient silence by the chef, his team and the manager. It looked especially odd to Qin and he was sure that this was about to run down as 'bad service' to all who were seated inside. Expectant of some acknowledgement, he turned towards the other diners but it only increased his cluelessness. The shock had spread like a virus. For the briefest of moments, every individual in that arena was transfixed upon nothing in particular, looking straight but in random directions, without a word or movement. Qin could not decipher what had just happened until Friuli spoke. *Friuli*! He turned with a sudden burst of relief that she had been spared of whatever had taken over the rest.

"Oh my God," she spoke, almost pleading in tone, "Qin, they have you."

"Huh?" Qin begged for some sense to a suddenly distracted Friuli as she bent down, eyes shut and ears cupped with both hands. He was instead answered to by a different voice altogether.

"She's quick, isn't she?"

The voice was jovial and familiar but seemed to ring in his head. He shook and looked around for its source in panic. The voice continued, "Now that wouldn't help. What's the use of such fantastic technologies if people still seek boring conventional means with such fervour? I am in your head, Qin."

"Bree?" Qin remarked, having instantly recalled a name he had struggled to remember earlier in the day.

"Bree in your head and still wearing his tweed cap. How do you like that imagination?" Bree replied, partially chuckling.

Qin shut his eyes too and cupped his ears as if to prevent all sounds from entering. "How are you doing this?"

"Oh, you gave me permission to, although unknowingly so. Didn't I tell you about the brand of your inners? Honestly though, I could do without that bit." The voice teased, still as jolly.

"Is that what is happening to everyone else?" Qin asked, struggling against the echoes of that voice and looking at the mass transfixation on display.

"Yes, but not like it's happening to you. These people are just receiving an emergency news update from the State. That's something everyone is signed up for. You know, things like hurricane on its way, president died, 70% discount at Honeys & Stripes, et al. I thought your dear teacher had explained all this already. Not as quick then, is she?" He spoke again, before Qin could think of a makeshift reply, "Though, of course, in this case, it's nothing localized. It's the big national tragedy of a player's death. Damien Best, who died of cardiac arrest a few hours back, seems to have actually been murdered in a way similar as this."

"What?"

"Honestly, Qin, you need to do better than that at looking shocked. Or they won't believe you."

"They who?"

"The authorities, on their way to arrest you the moment one of these guys confirm your identification. As you can see, their news update is over and, well." Qin noticed, in utter fear, as a multitude of heads with straight, unblinking eyes, turned in unison towards him. Bree continued, under a tone of pity, "they have been told that it is you who did it. Their lenses are doing the rest as we speak."

[225]

"No," he protested and turned towards Friuli who looked back at him, without a word and without blinking, though with a look of sympathy.

"Yes. They seem to have identified you as the foreigner who met a highly dangerous, slightly fat suspect earlier today, laughed around, shook hands with him, and was later seen at the stadium. Normally, these are enough to go with, but wait," Bree reasoned, suddenly animated in voice, "looks like this guy had given an easy access to his data already. So sadly, a host of information linking the poor foreigner to that suspect was unearthed, including a barrage of conversations from the past."

"What did you," Qin stammered, "I didn't," before voicing a desperate, "How?"

"Of course you didn't. That's good. You know I did it. That's good indeed, although obvious. Frankly, Qin, we at Terrorist Inc. are quite disappointed and are planning to drop you from our next venture for such carelessness, that is, if you make it alive through this one." Bree was amused and very nearly excited.

Qin's mind was racing. By now, verifications must be complete and the authorities would be on their way. He argued, "That's it though. They will know, surely they will. A professional killer would never be as careless as to keep all information public."

"No, but those are true for terrorists of a different time, I understand. These are days of suicidal followers true to the new faith."

"The *new* faith?"

"Seriously? You really think you can afford to discuss this over coffee right now?!"

"No, but I do think they can distinguish someone with suicidal tendencies from ones without."

"Aah, but you forget. You *are* suicidal, Qin," Bree's words echoed in Qin's head, initiating hallucinations in a blurring memory. "Twice you attempted to kill yourself, did you not?" Bree paused as a faint overlap of images of fire and fall began to cross Qin's head. Images from his past came rushing back: There were strong, screeching winds and a woman screaming. A bottomless pit seemed to call him and he found himself stand in hopelessness and utter rejection of life. "And in the third, you managed to achieve it," Bree spoke again as the images evaporated to a whiff of moving metal. Then there was shock, a muscular effort, a short flight, a series of scratchy rollovers, and that determined fist. Qin could not speak but he no longer shook his head in panic. He accepted those thoughts with pain as Bree concluded, "Privacy laws keep changing. You should have known better than to have kept all this information accessible. Twenty three years are enough to bring all your data into the fray. Information is meant to last forever online. So it can always return even after decades or centuries to haunt and stab you or those who come after. That is the whole idea of storing all data permanently, isn't it?"

Qin dug his face in regret, not over the misuse of his memories but over the distinct recall of a past that he now wished, with all that he had, that he could mend – for others, if not for him alone. The hard fact was that the past was exactly that, and there was no going back in time.

Bree interrupted, impatient and crude in his voice now, "My apologies, but suicidal as you may feel yet again, I am afraid I can't let you die in their hands. So I invite you now to escape that arena and head straight to me. Make sure the authorities don't catch you and don't be foolish enough to head back to dear Friuli's already-captured home."

Qin nodded and queried, his eyebrows stiff and eyes poking through each other pair that looked at him, "What if they do?"

"Then I shall kill Friuli," Bree replied. Qin turned to face her with concern when the former added, "I suggest you bring her along anyway, because I really don't trust you to make it till here without help. She is being acquainted with your situation as we speak. So be quick."

"Wait," Qin prompted, gathered himself and then asked again in bitter sarcasm, "Where do you want me to come?"

There was silence and he thought Bree had hung up until the latter spoke and hung up nonetheless, "Where you woke to life."

Chapter 17

Three weeks had passed. Had the world changed again? She would not know. She could not know. Fridgeon had locked herself in her home – one that had always been so, save for the past few weeks and a darker few before that. She had hesitated at first. To come back was to live in an agonizing wait for Jelzan and to live in an equally agonizing fear for his recovery. Hope had assured her and she could trust the woman behind the desk who seemed to grace the Beehive with such dexterity as rarely encountered. Something seemed to drive that lady but Fridgeon could never surmise beyond this generic conclusion, not because of a lack of data but the lack of intent.

It was not so much the assurance as the shock that had brought her back. Even in those last moments of a helpless Kanha grieving on the floor in pain, the fifth floor apartment had not ceased to dispel its warmth on to her. What was it about that place? Or was it something else?

She had spent the first few days after the incident clouded mostly by anger and disbelief over the recent revelations but was thankful for those feelings because they had helped divert her from a larger, more pressing feeling of dismay at the lost memories of a settled married life, up to the moment of Jelzan's accident. It was with anger that she had paced towards her old home when she had left the fifth-floor with Hope's men. They had escorted her to safety and had dropped her to her rightful place – a bungalow nestled in a small alley of scenic value. Although all anger had vanished at the first sight of what would have pleased most onlookers, the beautiful house seemed to scream at her. That 'something' that had felt right on the fifth floor felt immensely repulsive in this bungalow. *Isn't this that same loving home?*

She had entered nonetheless, let some fresh air in, cleaned the place, bought in the groceries and spread out crisp bed sheets over the over-cushiony mattresses. By the end of it, the uneasiness had prevailed within those gleaming freshly-brushed surfaces but had been significantly replaced by the anger of Kanha's betrayal. She was thankful for it.

Twenty one days, though, are a long time to sustain a singular emotion that could battle through an idle mind. For, an idle mind seeks novelty and in that search, turns to the basic human craving for conflict. Denial within the brain can be parasitic but is often adjudged on more acceptable levels of humanity. The pain she carried these days was different from those that had preceded it. Those had been a concoction of physical scars and psychological stress. These, on the other hand, were more accommodating. Kanha, after all, was only a stranger she had met not long back. To think of it, he had never even proposed a sense of friendship in the times that they had spent together. All he had expressed was through all that he had done. She could not forget the run of his fingers on her back or the mess of a breakfast that would shout out the unwilling effort that he must have been expended while she had slept. Perhaps the very warmth in that apartment owed itself to the unspoken word and it was precisely this that had made this bungalow a case to the contrary. That was not all, and twenty-one days of an unfocussed routine are a long time to explore the rest.

Doubts had first crept into her mind at the remembrance of the last day once she had settled down. They could have come in earlier but she realized that she had not really allowed any analysis to incur over her heavily sentiment-led thought process. That was the problem with most people most of the time. To simply complain without analysing was often both satisfying and sufficient in terms of the energy one could spend in a finite period of time that defined each day. However, she had been forced to abandon such triviality. Twice she had believed in a truth and twice she had been convinced otherwise. What then could possibly guarantee its legitimacy this time around? Was there anything she had missed in the elaborately subtle play that had unfolded before her? The doubt, complimented with a good night's rest and an almost sinful breakfast, had finally managed to steal her attention and she had graced it with substantial respect once it began to show true cause. Her mind had wavered towards his finger, their nimbleness despite the strength that bionism must have blessed them with and then the trembling meekness with which they had gripped his waist as he lay beaten. It did not fit.

The centre clock had been running as usual and as it must have when left in the dark desolate state that the bungalow had recently endured. Yet, suddenly each tick seemed to echo like drum beats in her head. The permutations her mind had churned out were overwhelming and seemed to overlap with ease. Their edges blurred as one anomaly merged with a different possibility and vice versa. She cupped her ears with her hands as if to shut out all thought. She needed to get out and she did, to squeeze out a moment of respite to gear up for the next wave of similar thoughts.

It was a small courtyard that she had stepped out to, hidden from outside view by long walls on three sides, a metal gate on the fourth and a half-covering of the parapet above. While few taller buildings lay on either side, none lay in front. Open sky showed half of itself. Night had settled in and the moon was glowing diagonally above her. A car would often drive past beyond the opaque gate on the narrow street that stretched out as a mere offshoot from the main drive further outward. This was an ordinarily classy area, very close to the canals but secured from all commotion.

A long, flat building on the other side of the street housed offices and was separated by another deep body of water running along the road which was connected by two short, curving bridges made of stone. Stones draped the floor of the courtyard as well. Every step out here clicked off a sharp tap that would alert the cat that lived inside. Fridgeon had always liked her. Jelzan had always hated her.

The bungalow had three segments, excluding the little laundry room on the right. The entrance to the left stood two storeys above the ground, flowered with a spiralling metal-grilled staircase. On the north end lay the other two entrances, one on the left corner which led into the main section of the three-storey house and opened up to the long open-air balcony that the parapet bore its meaning for. Underneath this leisurely space lay the third quarter of the house – a loft that began two steps below the ground level from a small kitchen, the third of the house. It led to a living space perceived twice its size, thanks to the mirrors that had been planted along the entire length of one of its walls. It sat under a low roof to accommodate the open bedroom, visible from the ground floor, which one could climb up to using a thick wooden staircase on the other end. The entire loft was clothed in wood and mirrors, with mesh cabinets beneath the staircase and at every other idle wall. It was supposed to be earthy, relatively secluded and very cosy. Fridgeon, though, had needed an escape from all this.

The getaway though, could not be rendered complete, for outside lay arguably the most beautiful jewellery of the house – rows of slender climbing plants that adorned every wall and hung in disciplined rows from the parapet. Their leaves ruffled under the softest of winds and enjoyed the crown of tiny flowers for nearly two months every year, until everything would fall away, come the winter. Fridgeon stood out, holding a bunch of hanging stems and looking at the moonlight shine off a few of those leaves. She stood there embracing a break in her thoughts, gearing up for one that was soon to arrive to that beauty that stood on Via Argelati.

Mere minutes had passed before the fingers crossed her mind again. Much composed now, she thought about Kanha's compassion. For the briefest moment, it seemed a pleasant thought – to watch a man who had partially robotized himself still carry a touch of care. After all, every vision of the world had historically drawn a distinction between man and robot, save perhaps, for the Asimovians. "Isaac truly saw these machines as potentially us," she thought. Kanha stood somewhere on that thin line of division.

Curiously, it could have been that alleged superarm that had produced the silken touch and she was sure he would have strived to achieve that effect – fingers that had brushed through her hair and yet, got crushed so easily by two anonymous men. So *easily*, she thought, *how could it be*? It could not, unless the men had bionic arms just like he did. Yet, surely the initiator of such monstrosity would have ensured that he remains ahead of the pack over the years, in which case, he could have given them a match at the very least, unless he was compelled towards defeat. To a man of free will, that order could only have been self-committal. Wheels began to turn in her brain.

If the beating he took were really purposeful, then so was the surrender of his data. That would explain the absence of Stack '1' to ensure that she attended to the next-best Stack '2,' which in turn held key to his password. She asked herself in muffed voice, "Why would he do it?" Any incentive would imply that he was aiming to achieve something from Hope and since she had not crossed ways with him first, it could only mean that it was Kanha holding the stick that threatened to rattle the Beehive. Hope's concern looked legitimate then and Fridgeon found herself

[233]

back to square one. Kanha was guilty, and she was tired. There did not seem an alternative. *No, she pondered further, he had protected his data with their names.* That was a strong emotion unlikely in such circumstances. *They still wear their rings.* "Curious thing," she surmised. Rings held so much value in relationships, so much power. Her thoughts drifted to the one she had carried with her – another ring with a more personal connection.

An engagement ring came with a license to create intense emotional upheavals and it had been true so far for this one. Jelzan's lay somewhere in the house now but perhaps it was a good thing that it had followed her rather than bearing the brunt of its master's animosity towards everything around. She deliberated back to how it had come to be with her on both occasions when she had lost him. That little journey was filled with welcomed coincidences and cherished memories. Only one glitch sat crouched on the way, so far obscure and insofar trivial. It would have appeared coincidental, had it not followed the maze of Kanha's intentions. As her mind lay trapped amidst uncertainties and at a loss of logic, the faintest window in her story finally showed itself. Fridgeon would have jumped at it. Instead, she sat down on the wooden seat that stood behind her, facing the moon that intermittently shone through the curtain of leafy stems. To any other, the following hour would have been hardly more than a stationary picture. She sat still, flooded from within with racing blood and a blizzard of thoughts. It was only once the moon had risen considerably and had disappeared beyond the roof that she finally stood up, measurably solemn. The incongruity had verified itself. She would have to wait until Jelzan returned.

Suns set. Moons followed. The suns rose again. And both looked different each day, for it would bring in a new possibility until on one occasion, the sun brought with it a phone call. Everything that followed in the following lunar rise was inaudible in effect. Her senses went nearly numb in their solitary focus on the arrival of that long awaited resident who was to come bruised, battered and built back to an experimental perfection. She did not care how perfect he was, as long as he was alive, and well, and back home. Just as its predecessor had brought in the good news, the next sun rose with his footsteps. She was there to receive him in the silence of that early morning freshness when a car pulled over, and Jelzan stepped out.

Any among a hundred words could have served as the perfect greeting but none managed to intervene. They hugged, looked into each other's eyes for an age and slowly walked in with his accomplices who helped him settle down, delivered a piece of luggage and left the two alone. It was awkward at first. A couple, after any tragic separation, feels a sense of vacuum that needs to be filled upon its reunion. The tragedy in their case had been overly dramatic. It was a consequence, thus, when the very first time they set eyes on each other in solace, unspoken questions began to arise.

There was much that lay unexplained, much that deserved that explanation. Jelzan knew that it was he who held most of them and his eyes nearly spilled out a choking spirit of speechlessness as he sat there on a two-seater couch with one arm on its armrest and the other placed over one of his spread out legs. His exhausted head rested lifelessly against the velvety back but he continued to look straight at her equally expressionless face, waiting for a reaction. They spent several minutes battling their inner turmoil in silence, until Fridgeon finally broke it.

A faint shiver ran down Jelzan's spine when she stood up. He did not know what to expect, and for a man who had fallen victim to a series of unfortunate events, he bore a strange look in his eyes for a moment. All doubt faded when she walked straight up to him, bent over and planted a kiss on his lips. Without expression, she sat over

[235]

him with legs on either side, her skirt raised to her waist. With firm hands, she held his face in position and looked with eyes that would not blink. He stared back with slightest of smiles but she did not smile back. Without a word yet, they kissed – firmly, passionately and then violently, as if to churn out the urge that lay trapped inside this recently estranged couple.

Buttons broke, arms gripped, lips ran berserk and every trace of animalism poured out in the minutes that followed on that breezy night as they slid over each other under the unrelenting sweat as if no other space in the world existed beyond those sixteen square meters. Moans began to fill the air but they were mostly his. For, she was commanding that space as if with an uncontrolled urge for every inch of him, driving him to a pleasurably painful insanity and disallowing even a second's respite to his absolute fantasy. Yet, hardly a gasp of air ever came out of her lips, and even that was restricted to those culminating moments of finale when staying silent was beyond human capability. So they loved until night fell, and with it, so did they.

She woke up first the next morning. The wooden floor seemed colder than usual but she let Jelzan sleep as long as he wished to. Their clothes lay in partial tatters and spread all around. She picked them and repositioned the affected furniture nearby. On her way up the stairs though, she turned to look at him. He was lankier than average, height accentuating his thin frame. Short golden hair spiked out over his partly long face. Even the slightest of smiles was clearly pronounced on his face and the veins in the neck stood out when he did so. He lay on his back, fast asleep with an easy expression that revealed little about his state of mind. That was a problem as it had always been. Easily distinguished expressions on one's face often diverted others from the subtle ones that lay hidden underneath. It was tricky. For, contrary to the common perception, such

[236]

faces told far lesser about the person's feelings than the normal ones. While one could easily figure out those first couple of reactions that showed instantly in any of the hundred varieties of emotions, the ninety-eight odd ones were both absent and unrealized. These easy faces, then, were the most deceptive. Fridgeon looked at the bland peacefulness of Jelzan's sleeping face and realized – deception must have always been an oblivious part of their married life.

It could have been a sense of fear in both of them but no questions were asked initially. The speechlessness of their first night carried on for several days, except for smiles and customary discussions. Any doubt that had plagued their minds seemed to have begun to ease out as things slowly returned to normal. Yet, all instances of love, devotion or routine in that bungalow were preceded by a protocol of formal requests and permissions. It was welcomed by both, given the psychological exertion and a chain of bad memories that they had managed to survive. In fact, as a result of such conscious effort, they had turned softer in conduct. It could have been perceptual but Jelzan liked it that way. These were times of peace and he was glad to be closing in on that perfect home-office-home routine. Fridgeon, of course, would always be there to support him.

"Aren't you forgetting something?" She asked one morning as they sat at the breakfast table.

Jelzan was particularly buoyed, arguably under his returning energy levels. He asked, busy chewing on the cereals, "What?"

Fridgeon raised an arm from underneath the table and looked at him with his ring dancing between her fingers. Jelzan looked up when no response came and found himself caught off-guard. He smiled immediately and reached out for it but Fridgeon pulled it away, saying, "You don't have to wear it if you don't want it."

"Of course I want it, Fri. What kind of statement is that?"

"One that has waited days before revealing itself."

Jelzan held her arm and emphasized, "I'm sorry, sweetie. I forgot completely. I was just too happy to be with you again after all that had happened. I lost so many things on the way and assumed this was one of them. You understand, don't you?"

Fridgeon looked into his smiling eyes for a while and stated, "Of course I do." She handed it over to him but as she watched him slide it on to his ring finger, she jolted up. Still in that position, she mumbled, "Guys from your land always wear it on the right hand."

"Don't you know that already?"

"Huh? Yes," she confirmed and shifted topics, pointing at his right arm, "Does it hurt?"

"Sweetie, it's here, remember?" He replied, showing her his left. "It's in good shape, thankfully. I didn't expect such an excellent recovery."

Fridgeon gave a little smile under calmly drooping eyes. They continued to eat for a while, then she added:

"So did you really forget where the ring went?"

"I guess. I do remember you having kept it after the accident happened. It's been such a blur since. Sometimes I think I had partial memory loss. I mean, I distinctly remember wearing it for the year that followed but forgot entirely how I lost it again."

"You gave it to me that night in the woods."

Jelzan spent a while in thought and exclaimed, "Now that you mention, I do recall it. I told you I'd cook and had handed it over, right?"

She nodded but did not say much. Jelzan put his spoon down and turned to face her. He held her hand in his and said, "Those were hard times, weren't they? I'm really sorry for everything." He paused and then added, "What are you thinking, Fri?"

[238]

"Nothing," she replied, "Just that a night like that can't easily be forgotten. I thought about it every day. I still do. Given what you went through, it's amazing how you managed to keep it entirely off your radar."

Jelzan sighed and bent forth to deliver a peck on her cheek. She did not move. He went back to eating, with the words, "Difficult days those were." It was he, however, who broke the silence next with a more uplifting, "Oh, I never told you the good news."

"Which was?"

"I spoke to the office yesterday. We settled our joining date. Guess what?"

She contrasted his excitement with a hazy, "Tell me."

"I've been promoted," he exclaimed, ignoring her tone, "You are now speaking to the Head of Marketing at the Beehive."

The spoon slipped out of Fridgeon's fingers as she froze for a lengthy moment. Somehow she managed to etch out a smile plus a feeble, "congratulations." He smiled back and started chewing his cereal with excitement. She looked at him eat and inquired, "Beehive is all about that new IT venture, right? I hear it doesn't have any established market yet. Are you sure it's a promotion and not just a transfer?"

"Why would they do that?"

"Well, you may not be in a position to work as well as you did before. With your memory and physical issues, I suspect any company would have checked your performance first. To promote you straight away sounds quite unconventional then."

Jelzan looked at her with his broad smile and spoke empathetically, "It's an acquisition, Fri. I understand your concern, since you don't know much about these things. Put it this way, a niche market means greater scope for expansion and a lot of marketing to do with a lot of goals to reach. I, your husband, will be heading all of that. Isn't that great?"

"Yes," Fridgeon muttered, soft and polite as ever, "it is."

The excitement prevailed in Jelzan throughout that day, so much so that it conveniently eclipsed the soft sobs that Fridgeon dug herself in amidst a vague swish of the midnight wind on their deserted street.

Jelzan woke up the next morning to find the lady absent from the house. He expected a morning-walk delay to have accounted for this unusual absence and waited while he went on with his morning chores. When an hour had passed, he went out to the other, higher section of the house and called out to her but there was no response. He peeked inside the laundry room and then headed to their little loft. The kitchen had a low roof to accommodate a bathroom over it and he banged his head against the entrance at first. Fridgeon sat at the little round table in the kitchen, apparently lost in thought.

"Is everything okay?" he asked and semi-shouted, rubbing the little bump in his head, "I've been calling you!"

"Were you?" She feigned ignorance and added, "I didn't hear it."

"What are you doing here?"

"It's been so long since we ate together in here. This used to be our little vacation room, remember?"

"I do, but why were you sitting here like a ghost?" he asked, looking at her unconcealed red eyes.

"Oh, I was just lost. I did not want to disturb you sleeping, so I thought I'll cook breakfast. Look, we still have a little cylinder here."

"That? Gas cylinders have been phased out for years now. I can't believe we still have one."

"It's from our camping stock. Why don't you sit down while I cook us something?"

Jelzan seated himself on the left side of the table, closer to the stove. Everything here was quite conventional and stored more as emergency backup utilities. Light hardly entered the loft through the windows which remained shut to keep out the chill. She set the pan on the stove and took out a little cup of oil but in her haste, tripped on her next step, spilling a little along his left arm. Jelzan nearly barked at her morning clumsiness but quietened down when Fridgeon apologized. He had to respect the time that had elapsed since they had last had this breakfast. Nonetheless, he walked out to change his shirt, clueless to what was about to follow.

It was probably within the first couple of steps out of the house that he heard her scream. Quickly he rushed back, confident that the panic was petty. Instead, his body found itself cornered against the near wall, aghast and afraid as registered by what he saw. A flame rose from the top of the cylinder, slowly burning its way down through the leaking stopper. Fridgeon had stepped back and was screaming at him to do something. He did not know what. He shouted back at her to use the water but the taps were dry. The plug was gradually melting and the stopper itself could not shield out the fire for long from crawling inside the gas-laden cylinder. Merely a few seconds remained before everything would blow into oblivion. Desperate for the very life he had claimed to have so recently won back, he moved ahead, only to find Fridgeon grab his right arm as if trying to drag him outside. *How foolish! It had to be done!* He thought as he stretched out his left hand into the burning knob and turned it around. If he had to burn his way to safety, so be it. He clasped onto the melting rubber, bit his lips in agony that seemed to stretch each second for eternity. The wrist had turned as much as it could but the flame didn't subside. A last ditch effort went into it with force but the rubber broke off and half-fell on his hand. By this time though, the flame had caught on to his palm and had crawled up the wrist on the recently spilled oil, setting his sleeve alight. Amidst that panic and haste, he fell onto the entrance steps, twisting his ankle.

Under his agonizing screams, Jelzan hardly noticed when a blanket dropped over him and pressed against the burning flesh. It took a few additional seconds but once the fire on his arm had been extinguished, he looked up at the sky, wide-eyed and in disbelief. The steps felt like those to heaven with the view of clear blue sky above. The cylinder had surely burst by now and they were all dead. A trickle of relief ran through him at the thought of having died so easily but it persisted only till the white lights faded off to reveal the darker loft. He looked at his wife in shock and then at the cylinder. The flame had subsided.

Jelzan was glad, excessively relieved and sweating. He asked in significant pain, "What the hell just happened?" His eyes went back to her with the question but she stood still, suddenly without fear and looking straight at his charred arm.

"It was a miracle that you could be operated back to normal after that ghastly accident," she said like a zombie.

"Huh? Fridgeon, call the ambulance," he said, under constant groans.

"The left arm, you had said. A bionic arm, right?"

"Goddammit, Fri!" Jelzan screamed at the top of his lungs, "What the hell are you talking about?"

"The bionic arm. A super arm. Fire-resistant casing with many things unnatural. A curious thing. Funny," she said, "I can see your bone now."

His lips remained parted but the lines on his grieving face disappeared. All pain took backseat, excruciating as it was, as he looked at his arm and then at her, angry but also shivering at how she towered over him, seemingly without a trace of sympathy.

"Fridgeon-"

"I had removed your ring to keep it safe before they took you to the hospital after your accident. It was a torture. That little metal had your blood smeared all over it, if it was blood at all." Jelzan shook his head as if to outline the obviousness of that statement and her nearly hysterical doubt over it. She continued, "You always wore the ring on your right hand and it was that side that had drenched itself in red that day after the accident. How is it then that it was your left that ended up getting operated, Jelzan?"

Fridgeon was solemn and Jelzan, in his agony, could only follow suit. She spoke again, "They are right about our inclination to emotionalize things. It blinds us. An entire year you and I spent after that and it never crossed my mind." She then turned to him and reasoned, "How could it when there was actually never any operation at all." Jelzan's eyes widened again, partly in fear. He began to protest but stopped as she kneeled down and tilted her head to look carefully at his arm. She then grabbed it as he writhed in additional pain. Her touch was gentle but to a burnt arm, even feather felt sharp. Gradually, she dipped her thumb into his flesh and pulled it back. She then rubbed the blood on the tip of her fingers and stood up saying, "Nothing. Just blood, flesh and bone."

Jelzan knew his hope for any help was fading. He tried to get up but could not. The cold wind was beginning to burn itself through his charred skin. She asked, "There was never any operation, was there?" He did not reply, trying as before. She turned his face towards her, and ordered, expressionless as before, "Answer me."

More moments passed as the pain began to grow uncontrollable. She insisted a few more times in a flat tone until Jelzan finally shouted out, "No, there wasn't - none! Now please go and call for an ambulance."

"I will go," she said, "not to call anyone but to leave you here, exactly like this." She took a step forward but stopped when he pleaded. She then added, "Unless you tell me exactly what happened."

"Fridgeon, pl- please. It's unbearable."

"So were my scars."

"Please. I can't walk. I beg you."

"I shall heed. So tell me. The sooner you do it, the sooner you'll get help."

Jelzan was breathing heavily as he lay on the ground with his sweaty face raised to look at her tall stature. He gulped on a thick blob of saliva and brought himself to brave the inevitable moments of pain that he had no choice but to endure. He then revealed, "It was nothing against you. It was just office politics and you-"

"Were collateral damage."

"Yes. No. I mean, it was partly planned and it was necessary. Fri, it was nothing against you."

"That accident?"

"It was staged."

"Why?"

Another couple of seconds passed as Jelzan tried to gather his breath. He explained, "We had to create a genuine need for an operation that would look like a failed bionic experiment."

"So that you could get a valid reason to shut down the Mongrando facility?"

"Yes. It was necessary to make the case against its head."

"The one who was transferred to Dubai? Archer?" Jelzan nodded, to which Fridgeon questioned further, "Why? He was set to retire soon anyway. Why not just wait?"

"I don't know. You have to trust me, Fri."

"I don't, but go ahead."

"I swear," Jelzan reiterated, short of breath.

The objective was enough to help Fridgeon sum things up in her head. She queried, "How did you get involved?"

"It was a mess in Scinoi all these years. I had this one chance to make a big leap forward, Fridgeon. Within a year, I was to head the marketing of a new company."

"A flopped company. Why would you get excited about something like that?"

"Scinoi hasn't bought it randomly. They have plans that this project fits perfectly into. They don't intend to use it in its current form. It will be expanded and launched for a different purpose and gradually integrated as one of Scinoi's main ventures."

"With you as the spearhead," Fridgeon concluded. She had stood like a stone so far but her voice wavered as she asked, "Why me, Jelzan?"

"Because I was part of the plan," he tried to reason, "It had to be someone close to any one of the three plotters. Barring R&D and senior management, I was the only disposable one. I mean, one who could afford to be absent for long while the plan was being put to play inside the company. Bionism takes time to have its full impact and we could not make any sudden changes or we would run the risk of creating disbelief and doubt. Once the negative effects reached their pinnacle, they could justify any behaviour on my part."

"Like you waving your hand in mid-air, as if in illusion?"

"No, that was very much real," Jelzan said with a gasp of air as if in relief to substantiate that not all was fake. "A new type of lens – an improvisation of our wifi glasses with information that can still be operated with gestures. I was testing it and we assumed it would fit the plan well-"

"The plan to frighten me to desperation at the loss of someone close?"

Jelzan dropped his head again and murmured, "If you could not explain it, you would have no choice but to go to the police. One complaint and they would take care of the rest."

"Shutting down the plant, lodging a criminal case against its head, issuing a search warrant for you and finally bringing you to cure - all looking very natural."

"Yes," he said, looking at her with solemn apology, "I'm sorry, Fridgeon. I really am."

"No you're not," she said, firmly. "You're just in pain and desperate as you had rendered me to be."

"I am, I admit. Please, help me," Jelzan requested for the umpteenth time.

Fridgeon took a deep breath and walked back into the house. Minutes later, she came out with a duffle bag. She threw a cell phone at a corner and said, "There. Crawl over to it and call them yourself. I hope there's enough credit in it, by the way. You left me to rot. Consider us even. I am leaving, and everything has been taken care of. There won't be any trace of me, although I don't think there is any reason to find me anyway. There will be sufficient inconvenience in store back in the house though, but then someone had to teach you to deal with them, since dear mum probably did not. It's a pity since those at Scinoi will spit you out now that you have been chewed up. For the record, you were a fool to believe them, especially the one whose idea this was."

Jelzan looked at her startled, to which she added, "Yes, I know who it was now. Send her my regards."

Fridgeon spat the words and walked out with revulsion, without any inclination to turn back. She marched furiously on the pebble streets for many moments that followed, blinded to all else that passed her way. Gradually, a thought occurred: *What now?* There was just one person left in the dark, as a source of her hope in what she considered to be the most senseless thought. It was blind trust and she was angry, but this was a matter of instinct.

Chapter 18

Where you woke to life. The words had echoed once more. Before Qin could speak, Friuli had jumped off her chair and had rushed forth, dragging him by his arm. Two steps, an activated levitation and off they were now, at a breath-taking speed through alleyways, the likes of which she had termed dangerous for any high speed movement on their very first night out on the streets. She did not seem bothered about any sliding balconies. Such risks may have been required but would render all effort and purpose futile if an accident were to happen. Yet, she looked sure of where the balconies would spring out or not, as if each inhabitant was being conversed with in her head.

Quick and sharp they moved, stealthily making way to the house of bland, white walls where Qin had first opened his eyes. Every first glance at a new stranger irked him as an awareness positioned itself in his heart that every individual already knew all there was to know about him, including his greatest agonies and humiliating errors. He was the spicy gossip of the day. Yet, even in that rush, he observed for one last time, the structures and the communion of humans and nature that had been achieved as most could have only wished for. *It's a miracle for the world to have attained idealism*, he thought. After all, Qin had always believed in miracles. . . but Qin had never believed in idealism.

The thought struck his mind just as the little fact had. Idealism to him was about balance and it necessarily involved the positive and negatives to yield a sum zero. A marriage between Nature and people was positive. So there had to be fallout then. The marriage was the epitome of our imagination, a utopia in essence. So its negative must have been equally enormous, and any such thing could not as easily be hidden so as to escape his attention entirely, despite his complete focus on the new functioning order of the world. Yet, somehow it had. Traces or hints – Qin pondered over them all. *What didn't he know?*

His thoughts were interrupted by the screech of their destination as they slowed down at the door to face a familiar conventionally dressed man, waiting with his heavy, fleshy arms crossed upon each other.

"Come," requested Bree, as he kept Friuli close to him and led them inside the house and past the door after the relevant scan procedures. Qin entered into the corridor he had first made an attempt to float on like a baby taking his first steps. He was much more comfortable with it this time around. Bree asked him, "Do you know why you were removed from this house?" Qin shook his head, preferring to keep semi-accurate guess attempts to himself. Bree replied, "It should be obvious now. She knew we would come for you once it was confirmed that you were alive and well. As long as you were fast asleep, there was no point taking you away. She was your best bet to live and any effort from anyone else was fruitful only if you survived. Did it never seem curious to you as to how your own identification was concealed from you, even though a barrage of information was available on your lenses?"

The bulky intruder was at his undisciplined best and had every element of mischief wrapped around him but his logic was not as easily deniable as the validity of his grin. Qin considered his words and remembered the nervous blinks he had encountered after having woken up for the first time. He remembered that first look of his aged arms, the ensemble of stretched expressions and the goose-bumpy trauma of the unexpected. Only, he now remembered, there had been no goose bumps! He had felt the chill but hardly any assembly of spots suffering the miniscule pull of his skin. There had been none of those, not even at his first reflection as a middle-aged man on that all-knowing mirror on the wall that had identified him as "Unidentified".

The mirror, Qin thought and tried to move to his right before sense dawned upon him and he slowed his walk along that corridor they were now traversing. It was important to deter and to verify but more important was to do so as without raising suspicion. He gradually caught up to the two walking ahead. "Why did you want to take me, and," he asked after further deliberation, "who's 'we'?"

Bree was amused at how well his victim was playing along, too amused to notice when Qin, seemingly with an absent mind, turned right towards the corridor that led to his all-white room. He asked, "Did you ever hear of the age of calamities, Qin?" No time was allowed for any answer to come by. "Of course you did. It was a period of coordinated crises – an orchestra of natural disasters. If one could fast forward that time and sit down with a pair of earphones, one would hear such a marvellous rhythm of destruction and panic. It is just so beautiful, so pristine in its clarity and timing, so moving in its influence and so loud that it cut every other issue off our radar. Oh, you truly did miss it, although you are a lucky bastard, aren't you? Considering how you just slept and left it on others to save and carry you as they fled, indeed you are!"

"I didn't ask for it."

"Didn't you? Am I mistaken here or did you not throw yourself out of a moving train to your own doom? To say the least, you definitely did try your best, or as I just asked, did I get it all wrong?"

To impose upon someone a fact of brutal relevance was criminally defendable. To be the recipient of such ordeal, though, was infinitely more painful. Qin could not erase the specifics and his cluelessness of the world he had woken up to did not help things either. In a world that he had known, he had held power – one he never realized while he was in it. That was the power of information and like everyone else, Qin had gravely undervalued it. At that time, he had looked towards the more pronounced versions of authority and had allowed himself to be bogged down by their absence in him. He had not lived many years then, relative to how many he had now. Yet, out of his own drive to pace or perish, he had tried his hand at the former and then opted for the latter. What he had conveniently forgotten was that while pacing ahead was an effort with a finite boundary and controllable consequence, the fall was both limitless and uncontrollable beyond a point. So, 'perish' had abandoned him midway and had left him hanging.

Yet, something happened just then. The gravity of disappointment Qin carried at the remembrance of what he had sought and how lost he had felt before his accident should have left him crestfallen. Suddenly though, he remembered: He had begun to move out of that personal conundrum in the days that led up to his accident. The reasons had no longer met, even barely, the logic to give up on a life he was beginning to discover. *It was the fly that followed me*, he recalled. It had shown him that he would have grown, no matter how often he failed, if only he could remain loyal to time. For, that could never be meaningless even if it brought nothing of note. The understanding dawned upon him as he recited to himself, "Nothing is not insignificant."

He looked up at Bree, suddenly with a sense of power of an unexplained nature. He did not have enough knowledge of this new world but that was exactly what gave him a bigger incentive to learn and to grow. He had a lot to catch up on and to do so, he would need to survive the situation he found himself in at present. There were things unexplained, ones he could only guess at, but he was beginning to see light at the end of this short tunnel. The two individuals confronting him were both at ease in their space, aware at all times of the simple truth that in this world, they were older than him in knowledge and in power, regardless their age. To reach the light that now beckoned him, he needed to verify his assumptions. With that singular intent, he moved towards the mirror once they had reached his room. Bree would have noticed this but Qin diverted him with his question, "You know so much about me but you are still shy of telling me who you are. Isn't it unfair?"

Bree had been engaging in a play of virtual virtues. Challenged in his own play, he concurred, "It does. If you wish to know about me, you certainly shall." He tapped on his gloved screen while Qin did so on the mirror, feverishly reading through something over his reflection. The analysis was short-lived as the humble white walls dissolved themselves into a fuming mix of colours. Qin stepped back as the projections began to surround them. He was familiar to such change but still nested himself in a spot as the entire room widened its expanse to present a world that stretched farther than he could have imagined the new IT systems to ordain in their résumé.

Thunder sounded loudly. All of a sudden it felt too cold for comfort. Qin's amazement, Friuli's reservation & Bree's loquaciousness found their sources stand upon an apparent field of near-black gravel that seemed to slip beneath them. Its slope was gradual further downhill on one end but nearly exponential as it curved upwards on the other. Intermittent blocks of stone shining in absolute black over the ground which itself was draped in a gradient of black, brown and red, surrounded them. Somewhere far downhill, faint patches of green showed while the horizon was bordered with ripples of black. There lay the dark ocean, calm and hollow, but too far. Qin looked up, covering his chest against the biting chill so high up on the mountain. Much above, the peak stood, tall and commanding against the radiant night sky, gleaming on its edges in bright red. Every now and then its insides would

[252]

grumble and send an added shiver down his spine. It felt as if the earth would move or hiccup at any time beneath his feet and even the firm solidity of its surface could not be trusted. Wind was fierce and worsened both the cold and the wavering ground. Clouds were thick under the roof that had vanished well and truly over the dark humiliation of that covering of fumes and gases. The sounds were majestic and any intrusion was faint, as Qin realized when Bree spoke less than a foot from him, "You wanted to know about me? Here it is."

It had been a shout but was subdued by the thunder and roar in the sky. Qin looked at the tumultuous peak, flashing out warnings every second. He turned to Bree and asked, "A volcano?"

"Mungibeddu - my love, my tragedy, my home," Bree said, staring at the peak in awe. He turned to point at a distance, "Do you see that vast barren stretch along the coast? Cities of Catania and the ever-beautiful Siracusa lay nestled there once. On these deliciously fertile lands, we lived and prospered amidst olives and oranges lush and dripping with juices. Etna, however, likes to takes what it gives with equal ease. Her greatest ferocity spared none but came at a time when cure was at hand."

"Bionism, I know."

"Very good, Qin. That it was, but in a very nascent stage. So while few of us were certainly cured, many were resigned to the status of faulty experiments led by heartless professionals like your beloved nurse here. Isn't that true, Friuli?"

"Is that what drove the bunch of you to some arbitrary 'new faith', as you put it earlier?" Qin intervened.

"'Arbitrary'? The day these guys kept themselves excluded from risky implants, they forced us victims to stand together and ensure they do not remain unchallenged."

"Because that is always so very comforting," Qin remarked, shivering and sarcastic, "Anything is good as long as you have a lot of people join in, right?"

Bree normalized his tone, "You think you are detached from us, don't you?"

"If I am, I am gladly so. You haven't given me many reasons to feel otherwise."

Bree raised his chin to consider the statement. "You are right. I haven't. Well, how about I do so now?" He said, and took out a little tool from his pocket. It was shaped like a knife but was hardly an inch long. Qin gave him an uncertain look, to which he replied with an equally uncertain, "Aah," and pulled out a bag kept a few steps away. He then dropped the little knife in the sack and tapped on his gloved screen. The bag began to swirl from within and moments later, on the sound of a beep, he pulled out a much larger knife. He remarked when Qin could not understand what had just happened, "Robotic sands. They sculpt themselves into handy tools on-the-go, and when I say handy, I mean this will kill you not just through stab wounds but a host of physiological damage."

Qin stood alert with arms half-raised on both sides in defence. Instead, Bree pointed the knife towards Friuli and directed her, "Tell him, dear." Her silence seemed to make his smile echo around them above the overhead thunder. It was unsettling, to say the least. Its waning should have been welcoming. Instead, it gave way to a sudden shout in her ears, "TELL HIM!"

She shook from head to toe, her eyes wide in fear. Qin relieved her of the effort, looking still at Bree, "She does not need to. I know."

It was as if the words had suddenly encountered a big bang and reasons and assumptions had flown out of them in waves enveloping Friuli's thoughts. Her pursed lips intensified a sharp look that had overtaken her eyes but they moved for the slightest moment and seemed to resonate an

[254]

inaudible word in that chilly air – *"How."* Bree raised his eyebrows and repeated, "You do?"

"I suppose."

He nearly laughed out of doubt. Asking 'what' would have made it all too simple and he was in no mood to allow that. Instead, he asked, "How do you know, Qin? Did she tell you?"

Qin replied, expressionless as before, "In a way but it was you who confirmed it a while back."

"Is that so?"

"Yes. You said this visit has a purpose. There doesn't seem much that would move a psychopath other than something very simplistic, misdefined and social. I would say directionless but that would prove oxymoronic. As it turns out, I am not the one holding that knife. So what could it be then that I seem to be a naive part of and Friuli isn't? There are many differences between her and me at first, but one in particular seems of greater interest. In the name of introduction, your heart has poured itself out on bionism. It has all been about a divide between 'you' and 'us', not 'I'. So clearly, this is a social act where your bunch is allegedly the superior one, but that analysis is skewed towards a single parameter. Obviously, I smell bias. More importantly, though, you have kept an eye on me for some time and were particularly welcoming to me this morning. You needed me. I was a crucial pawn in this plan. Sure enough, now everyone would easily believe that I was a key conspirator in Damien's death not because of our meeting but a deeper connection that you have carefully avoided thus far. . . one that would prove that I am one of the treacherous lot. In conclusion, it all turns into a simple equation then, doesn't it?"

Silence prevailed amidst the continuing thunder and mountain roar but the intensity of their stare gave way to partial amusement. The eyes had constricted to the slightest and the edge of their lips had wavered equally slightly. At length, Bree spoke, "You have managed to startle me; I'll give you that. Quite a far cry from what I intended to do when I came to tell you-"

"That I am, in fact," Qin spared him the effort, "a bionic like you."

Bree endured several helpless moments of silence as they passed him untouched. Both he and his captive looked at Qin without any expression. Despite all his analysis, the latter could not decipher what it was that they were thinking. He looked back with the prior gaze, focussed solely on Bree but simultaneously very aware of Friuli.

"Well done," Bree gently applauded before a critical, "and now we can kill her."

"So that I can join your boy band?"

"Respect, Qin," Bree demanded but was obstructed by Qin's misplaced laugh that echoed through the wall-less room over and above the grumbling of the mountain. He laughed strong and hard, and closed in. "So I infer that you are not interested," Bree remarked, pointing the knife at him.

"I guess not."

"Well then," Bree sighed, shaking his head. In the next moment, he reproduced the gloved screen and tapped on it. The Earth shook once again, as the floor began to tilt on one end. As the gravelled surface began to shift and slip along the rough slope, the near portion of that floor cracked and spread into two, revealing flowing lava underneath.

"I thought this was virtual!" Qin screamed.

"Advanced systems. This was your room, wasn't it? Your access means my access, and this is what I have made for our tryst tonight. You see, Qin, you can either join us or die because naturally, I can't let you be taken in and be inspected. Such a two-edged knife called privacy!"

Qin stared at him wide-eyed, trying to muster a reply. Bree, standing on the safer end of that shaking ground, waited for an answer and said with another set of

[256]

taps, "Let us make your choice easier." In the very next instance, the ground shook again but restricted itself to Friuli's corner. The crack spread and reached her before Qin could react. He was pushed backwards but she fell and disappeared from sight. A loud yell was all that was heard.

"NO!" Qin shouted beside a grinning Bree and forced himself towards her. Suddenly the room felt far wider in its physical contours and while it was still nowhere close to the virtual spread, Qin noticed that the walls had actually shifted or perhaps dissolved to merge his room with others in the house. In every manner of thought now, he was faced with the crisis of a volcanic eruption. Of course, urban structures have their breaking point and thus, despite all attempts at reality, the lava was nearly not as hot as it should have been. All he noticed was fire. All he could think was Friuli's fall. All he wanted was to save her. The more he realized the fatality of the situation, the stronger his will grew and the greater his hopes of survival became. Qin let the feeling sink in, for he had arrived at his greatest triumph.

He reached the corner of that tilted land even as bursts of fire seemed to shoot out of that volcanic peak high above. The clouds of ash were flickering in red along their edges and growing denser by the minute, and the temperature had risen to abnormal levels near the Earth despite an extremely cold air surrounding them. He stretched his hand out to Friuli who was clinging on to a boulder sticking out of the grainy wall that the ground now was. Yet, for the space of one blink, Qin felt every inch of that surrounding change. The reds, the yellows, the oranges and the blacks merged to yield a humble off-white wall while the grainy ground switched to smooth tiles of a familiar kitchen. Friuli herself was replaced by a different lady, whose face was one of hope that had lain dormant for years. It was a face he had looked at after the longest of ages he could have ever imagined. The hallucination hardly lasted a second but delivered a finality of objective that closed a chapter that had stretched for years. The moment passed and Qin returned to the reality of that volcano.

"Reach out, Friuli," he ordered violently, stretching as far as he could.

"What are you doing?" she screamed back, "this is what he wants."

"This is what *I* want," he emphasised, "I want to save you, and I will."

She felt smitten but argued, slower and softer this time, "You may die."

"No, Friuli," he replied with absolute affirmation, "not here."

Qin had declared the closure of his turmoil and announced his steely resolve that was to stretch for the remainder of his life. Friuli watched the culmination of the longest adolescence a life could have suffered and she reached out, grabbing his hand with a wide swing of hers. He pulled her back, oblivious to his mellowing surroundings and a ground that had stopped shaking. Panting and charred in the intolerable heat, he tried to stand, hands supported on his knees. It took him a while to overcome his coughs and look around but when he did, he was startled. Friuli stood unusually at ease.

She turned to Bree and said, "He's ready."

Bree nodded, raised a gun out of nowhere and fired point blank at Qin's forehead. Two pairs of eyes looked at each other, unblinking in a silence that engulfed the warnings issued constantly by the volcano. Wind screeched itself around them, hitting at their bodies without any further impact. The sudden jerk had sent a shock through Qin's body. His head dropped backwards and his eyes closed with the last image of a faintly smiling Friuli, and of those darkened clouds glowing red across the violent peak of Etna.   Then,   all   went   black.

Chapter 19

Would he be waiting? Had he always known? Or was he one of the plotters?

Beliefs can be mere illusion at times. We all know a fact as the undeniable truth until we all come to know it as folly. We believe the words of those around us until we begin to believe that they were a lie. Days pass by in our oscillations between uncertainties and pseudo-truth but at no point can we rest without sticking our faith to any one fact in particular. That is our nature.

Despite being subconsciously aware of how fickle our knowledge is and how fast it may change, based on our own experience, we still make a choice to pick one of the available options and believe in it – wholeheartedly, until an alternative theory comes along. Be it our universe, our global businesses, our politics, our neighbours, our friends, family or at times, us – we believe what we believe.

It is a risk we take in such a beautifully convincing manner that our conscience refutes any contradictory theory at once or renders us aghast if the evidence is too strong. Where a contradiction does prove itself, there comes the flexibility in our nature, also tuned equally beautifully to gauge, absorb and balance the tragic shift in our allegiance to novel facts and allow the process of believing to re-initiate and to prosper. That is the world we live in – not the one we see but the one we perceive. It is a world that runs in parallel to the one we know and it runs in our minds. And in that mind, subject to our experiences, motivations and tragedies, reality is often merely an illusion we create en route to a convenient satisfaction.

Nearly five months back, Fridgeon knew Jelzan had been victimized. She also knew that no one was to blame. Two weeks later, she knew a stranger, by the name Kanha Evian, was a friend in need, uninvolved in every possible way to her turmoil. Three weeks later, she knew Hope was her friend but Kanha's intentions were suspect. Two weeks later, she knew Kanha was the culprit and Jelzan had been intentionally sacrificed. A month later, she knew she could not assume Jelzan's motives any longer but she could still rely on Hope. Now, she knew that the only one who had the remotest chance of coming out clean was Kanha once again.

"Three", Jelzan had mentioned as the number of conspirators. He was the one "barring R&D and senior management." Hope belonged to the latter while the third had remained a precautionary mystery. *It is precaution that often turns to paranoia.* Kanha could have made it all easy for her but clearly he had played a key role in adding to her confusion. His disappearance, the proofs in his study and the last conversation they had had – all adjudged him to be anything but ignorant. Why had he done this, if not to play a role in this entire setup? Yet, if he were truly involved, why had he not forced her to go to the police and had instead directed her to a facility where she could sniff the ugly possibility of what was going on behind closed doors? She was not the best judge of character but she trusted herself to judge a person's sentiments, and they had poured out of Hope's conduct at every mention of Kanha. That, she believed in. Then, there were also his fingers.

Oh, the touch was important. It was a simple act of contact, the pressure of which often determined the meaning delivered. The warmth of air that graced her lungs and the easiness with which it could escape out could both be potentially influenced by a touch and she despised her vulnerability towards it. Yet, hidden beneath that scorn was amazement and curiosity at how the tip of one's fingers could mean so much. Perhaps it was not the touch itself but something intangible that delivered itself simultaneously each time. It was important, for it was instinctive. Just like her beliefs, these instincts might have been perceptual but made all the difference to her judgements. Something so strong could not be all negative or ignored. To be decisive thus required one to trust these instincts. For, they would always prevail just as they had when a specific stranger had touched her back; just as they had when her own husband had done the same.

She felt powerful at the thought of the contrasting decisions she had managed to take. Now that she needed answers and was all on her own, that ability could be useful. She had timed her act in the morning. *Fire would be faintly visible and screams would be eclipsed by the noise around,* she had thought less than twelve hours back. As a wife, she must have hoped to be proven wrong but in truth, she felt glad to be rid of that maze of obscurity. Now she was out, with no choice but to find her own way. Her first destination was drenched with an objective to seek a vital clarification. If Kanha was one of them, she required a logical confirmation. So far, there wasn't one. With this final aim and with quick steps clicking on stony streets, the lady rushed towards the apartment on the fifth floor.

An unanswered welcome had become protocol. The card lay where it had been and the door still obeyed its authentication as easily. She stepped in to a clean but nearly emptied house. The study was open, was cleaner and was dark. She went in and pulled the cord to the lone old-fashioned bulb that hung from its ceiling. Immediately the laptop screen lit up and that was the first among the hints she had been waiting for. *Kanha used li-fi but why had he facilitated her theft of his files the last time they met in this room?* She tried tapping in but the password had been changed. *In fact, why would a man who continued to use outdated laptops leave one behind immediately after an*

[261]

attempted theft? She sat back hopelessly and almost angry at his aloofness. Was he still playing? Or did he just not care?

Nothing in his conduct justified how easy he had made her entry into his apartment. The first measure a plotter would take was to secure his backyard. Kanha had left it as if with an open invite. Thirst called and she dragged herself to the kitchen with a heavy head. The place seemed to have been left unused for several weeks now. She looked for a glass but there was none. She then tapped on one of the cabinets. On the slightest touch, its surface turned translucent and a message flashed on the screen. It read: *Welcome, Fridgeon Friuli.* Startled, she stepped back. She had used this space before but this had never happened till date. *It could not*, she reasoned, *unless it had been manually programmed to do so.* Only one could have done it and that would mean he was sure she would come back. *Why*? He was a curious man, delirious in conduct and much retired to his own world. Yet, he had welcomed her. A sudden thought crossed her mind and she rushed downstairs and out on the street. Midday had kicked in and the shops were hardly occupied. In the nearest bakery, the owner sat nearly bored while another served the only customer inside. She went up to the former, read his tag under a racing mind and requested, "Excuse me, Sir."

"Driss," he replied with a smile, "*dimmi signora.*"

Fridgeon turned her expression to one of disappointment and spoke in a meek tone, "Can you help me, please? I cannot open my door. It is jammed."

Driss had seen her a few times recently. He considered her statement and asked, "Are you sure the card is okay?"

"Yes, but it does not work. I know I am asking too much but can you please just come with me for a moment? Please!"

Pleading is an art and few excel at it. When the words mingle with suitable expressions and coherent body language, the rest hardly ever have a choice but to budge. It took him a moment of thought, some heavy exhaling and a final look at her face to concur. *"Va bene,"* he said, directed the other to stay in the shop and left with Fridgeon. Once at the apartment, he tried her card but the knob refused to turn.

He remarked, "It needs verified fingerprints and an ID, no?"

Fridgeon semi-nodded and slid the card with her right hand. The door did not open.

After several attempts, he gave up. She thanked him for his help, apologized for having taken his time and waved him an equally polite goodbye. Once he had left, she looked at the card tucked between her nimble fingers. A smile slowly creased across her face. With the head already half-shaking in disbelief, she took the card in her left hand and slid it in again. The knob turned with ease, the door fell ajar and she stepped inside.

"Kanha," she said, shaking her head under a broader smile and the thought of the only man in this city other than her husband who knew she was left-handed. Basking in the momentary realization, the next question was almost a prayer, "Where are you?"

Instinct told her he was where he had been when he had disappeared earlier but its services were not required this time. For, as she stood on the other side of that door, she could see his image – on the floor, in pain and with a single parting, unintelligible word on his lips: Etna. It was no longer meaningless although it could still be sufficiently misleading. Yet, that was the best shot she had and having scanned through the apartment in the thirty minutes that followed, she was sure that was the only word she could bank on. His study had been emptied and his last word, after all, had to bear some relevance. If it did, that alone might just vindicate him from her sentimental scepticism.

She rushed towards the airport – a restless sixty minute drive to the north-west outskirts of the city.

Malpensa looked calm as usual, pronounced in its desolation and bearing her faith in the frequency of its services. She addressed the lady at the counter, "Catania."

The smile was delightful; its response barely on the same platform, "Sorry, ma'am. The flights to Catania have been temporarily suspended."

"Since when?" Fridgeon shrieked.

"Since the eruption," the other replied in an apologetic tone. "But," she emphasized, "they have arranged for an aerodrome in Siracusa, as an alternative. Of course, we also have one to Palermo, though you'll have to."

"How long for the flight?" Fridgeon asked, visibly impatient.

"An hour."

"One ticket. Thank you."

Her feet tapped nervously as she stood at the counter and it was some three thousand feet above that Fridgeon began to wonder why she had been in such a rush. Excitement or nervousness – whatever it was – had drowned all other thoughts. It was perhaps more a lack of any restraining factor then than the abundance of a driving motive. Yet, as she walked out to one of the prettier Sicilian cities by the sea, her enthusiasm was shared by few. Etna had erupted a couple of years back and while the land had turned stable, the nearest habitation had suffered a mini-calamity. The threat still loomed and the authorities had been asked to brace for a quick clear-out under the slightest indication of a massive burst, which remained a theoretical possibility within the decade. With effort, a cab driver agreed, albeit at double the price.

The drive along the coast was welcoming and it alleviated her stress somewhat. The sun was about to set and had sprayed the sky with tinge of red, pink and yellow. As if with a purposeful run of brush strokes on a canvas, the clouds spread out in separate rows of coloured cotton, all sourced from one point in the horizon, directly above the sun. Underneath lay the ripples of blue water, flowing in a gradient of yellow. Short cream-walled houses lined the other side of the road. The edge of the sea was lined with black volcanic rocks that transformed the splash of tides to sprinkles of water that fell upon its onlookers who stood nearly fifteen feet above. Cars were plenty but parked on the sides; people liked to walk here. '*What's your rush?*' they seemed to ask. All Fridgeon had was a racing heart to answer with. That's all that she had had to answer herself as well, or so it had been until the car turned over on to the highway.

As the sea went out of view, Fridgeon found herself surprised by a sudden sense of longing for it. The sea had provided her with a desperately needed break – a deviation from the grind her brain had consistently endured. In those few minutes of its presence, it had finally established the answer that she had been seeking for so long. Kanha was her sea and she had never truly wanted to believe all that she had forced herself to.

It was going to be difficult, for she had had a vague destination in mind but she did not know how to find him once she arrived. Quietly, she continued to look out at the peak that had now come into view. It was silent but whitish smoke continually fumed out of it into the sky. As the road began to wave around, she caught the first glimpse of the city of Catania that lay in the distance, cradled within the stretch of the mountain and partly covered in black on its inner end.

As darkness began to spread over this part of the world, she noticed the scarcity of lights. Many homes had been abandoned. Those that still lived did so with hope. Was it some instinct that promised their safety, come what may? Would it help if tragedy was to befall in the future? Had it already done so in the past? She went around, partly concerned and partly appreciative of the courage and solidity of hope that the people prospered in. They worked towards a good life and towards growth, knowing how risky sustaining it was. Perhaps, then, it was not sustainability in the future that they sought. It was a productive life in the present. After all, who ever saw what the future held? Their houses were mostly ancestral and laden with aged wines – in effect, a mark of how they had braved the stabs of time, again, and again. Fridgeon prized their resistance until the realization dawned: It was not a hard-headed fight but a warm embrace with Nature that had allowed their survival. She did not know how exactly they had done that but under such a looming warning of that towering peak at every moment, she was sure that could have been the only way.

She was lost in her thoughts when the driver prompted her first. They carried on till as close as he would go to the mountain, now well and truly rising over them. Excitement had brought her so far although she had not planned her search out. She felt an inclination to walk back under the exhausting hopelessness, but as soon as she turned around, the option struck itself out definitively.

Two men stood at a distance, having stopped abruptly as if they had been following her. Their purpose felt alarmingly contrasting and Fridgeon could not risk trying to verify. Briskly, she began to walk towards the busier part of the city as they closed in on her, having watched their element of surprise fade and having sensed her urgency. With her sight clouded by her desperation, she tried to flee without a direction in mind. That, though, proved lethal. It was a bad mistake, for she took what she considered to be the worst turn of her life. Up ahead lay a dead end literally ringing a death knell on its dark brick wall. Somehow, within the past hour, a day of longing had comprehensively turned to one of fear, and possibly, the end. She turned to face her nemesis in that utterly abject moment, afraid to die under a finality of betrayal, had even one of them turned out to be Kanha. As they approached, she could see that he was not there. Nonetheless, a familiar face from the factory carried its own share of psychological blows.

"Az?"

"You remember me," he exclaimed, convinced on his planned attack. "I suppose you have met my colleague here already. He and his partner saved you the other day. They have been following you for a while now."

"Longer than I was told, I guess."

"Indeed, though you went a little out of reach once you were rescued at the subway – some luck you have. Anyhow, as you can see, luck runs out."

"As will yours," she said, imitating his defiance.

"I don't rely on luck, ma'am," Az declared under a false wear of consolation, "I don't claim to make or follow something I do not understand. I do, however, apply all that with other things, as I shall now, incidentally with you."

She shuddered at the thought, her voice trembling. "Wh-at do you mean?"

"I think someone who left a man burning shouldn't bother with that question. That was quite elaborate of you, by the way," he adjudged, amused.

She shook her head, as if to speak for the absentee, "I don't know how it came to me." The only response she received was a groan that marked the end of an unwelcomed conversation, and it was in that state of helplessness that a grave realization hit her:

She looked at the glaring reflection of disbelief in the face of her would-be tormenter and knew that nothing he chose to believe or do depended on what she actually said. His mind was made up, just like hers had been when she had confronted Hope, then Kanha, then Jelzan – each episode having followed a series of brainwashed brainstorming. Each time, she had confronted them with a pre-conceived notion of how right or wrong they were and every little thing they did or say thereafter was interpreted in

[267]

a way that only corroborated that idea. That in turn helped her to justify whatever it was that she had planned to do next. Such was the cycle of cause and effect that began with her inherent pessimism.

How then could anyone ever be genuine or fair in a world where the assumptions to the contrary ran so strong, and all our judgements at every step were so blinded by it? We continued to be unfair because we considered everyone else to be too – an assumption that left one with no choice but to follow suit. After all, to cheat or to lie was easy and when everyone began to do so, no one was left with an advantage. Could it be that an advantage had, somehow, now come to lie instead in *not* doing so? After all, why must anyone go through the effort of being genuine or fair if that option was neither easy nor gifted with a perceivable benefit? But if that were so, the real question would be why we created a world of morals in the first place!

It was to honour the answer to that question that there always stood a few in the crowd who chose to behave genuinely. They understood the profits well, and they were all who mattered, for they were the ones who decided to set an example and break that chain of pretence, thereby starting one to the contrary. Given how impossible it was to know who these souls were, we had no option but to set that example ourselves. It was a way that Kanha Evian had chosen to stick with despite being stabbed by the very stranger he had saved from the jaws of oblivion. *Why?*

There was an answer somewhere that Fridgeon could not decipher. She found the thought unsettling, for it breached the boundaries of practicality. How could she have ensured fairness with so much to lose, with so much at stake? How could she ever forgive one who chose fairness over the wellbeing of those who loved him? In the immediate absence of answers, she was compelled to accept the eventuality: She had chosen a path and this is where it had led.

With doubts over her recent past trivialized in the face of the broader view, her conscious mind was now squarely positioned in the present. The alley was dark and lonely and this was not how – or where – she had thought it would end. A tear drove clear out of her eyes and slid down as she raised her hand under a pointless attack, only to receive a strong blow from a palm larger than her face. The pain that followed enhanced itself further at the anticipation of more that was to follow. With hope strained out, she let her eyes close and her body fall under the impact. Fading voices of sudden panic was the last she heard. Then, all went black.

Chapter 20

A faint smell of charred wood was prevalent in the dark. While it may have been a minor indulgence at any other time, it alerted Qin's senses to reveal how futile his recent exploits had been. He did not agree. There was no way that he could have prized the smell of charred wood to this degree, had it not been for his prolonged inhabitation in a space nearly devoid of it. It did seem stupid but certainly not shambolic; and hopefully, not futile. In fact, he wished to return, for as soon as his senses opened up to that smell, so they did also to pain. Qin felt needles poke all over his body. His thighs felt locked while shoulders seemed a burden pinned to his arm. The back felt stuck to the bed, screaming at the slightest hint of movement. The eyes, though closed, issued warnings of severe inflammation if they were to open. His forehead was already engrossed in the same. The head was heavy and the elbows felt scarred. The skin forbade stretching at multiple places and even the generic air in that space felt chilly and very much a separate entity loaded over his body. His mouth, though, retained a sweet taste.

"I suppose you enjoyed that thoroughly," he inquired with eyes still closed, the voice notably weaker. It felt as if he had spoken after an age and his throat had lost all acquaintance with his vocal cords. He was clueless as to who he was talking to but was sure of someone's presence and his simultaneous involvement in his exploits.

"Actually, I enjoyed what led to it," came a nearly familiar voice, calm and in continuation with the smile Qin had last seen.

"So what happens now?"

"See for yourself." The reply carried a welcoming tone to it.

Whiteness had engulfed his eyes when he had opened them in that futuristic space with similar anticipation. A shade of yellow was all that breached the ensemble of black and brown this time around. Things had reflected back with pristine clarity and crisp edges back then. Here, things seemed settled conventionally in thick, unflinching timber glowing erratically under the light of flames somewhere to his side. A senseless feeling of floatation had threatened to betray Archimedes within the feathery ambience in those long gone moments. Archimedes had made way for an allegiance towards Newton as painful certainty of gravity bestowed itself upon him now. The former had been real as real could be perceived. This was real in absolute terms as he knew, but far less assuring than it had ever felt.

With effort, those eyes opened under shivering eye lids which slid back and forth as if in doubt over their capability to sustain stable vision after so long. At first view, Qin saw the three-dimensional edge in the top corner. It was dark and met by long slabs of semi-polished wood. Fire crackled somewhere to his right and cast a wavering light on the wall, on a worn-down sofa and on his own body. It was dim but yellow enough to emphasize that glowing stretch of bandage that Qin found himself wrapped in, covering a forearm, half-a-leg and possibly his waist under the loose cloth he was wearing. What was visible was scratched, partly streaked in red and partly covered in a new layer of pinkish skin. His body itched in several places and felt hot under the bandage even in the chill that had prevailed despite the fire.

There were no lights of electrical nature and little candles silently stood in the near corner of that wide old wooden room in which he now lay. Directly in front stood an open door, which housed hollow darkness, albeit with first couple of feet graced by the indirect light of the flames. On his left, the window was slammed shut by wooden pane and so was one of the two doors behind him. The other, although open, was equally dark. Only one window, on his right, allowed the outer view through frosty glass. It must have been cold outside and night had fallen heavily, judging by the mysterious curve of land he could see in the not-so-distant horizon. It did not give away much but the disappointment was limited in time, for diagonally behind him sat Fridgeon Friuli.

Qin noticed her crossed legs first and turned with excitement as his eyes ran up the warm cloak of rich wool that she had covered herself in. The restraint that followed was partly due to a sharp pain caused by his sudden movement and partly by what he saw in return for his effort. The face that blossomed over the wool collar was significantly different. The eyes still shone as they had but were surrounded by wrinkles. The hair had turned wavy and grey with sharp silver streaks in the front locks while the rest seemed to rest on her shoulders with the softest touch. Creases had developed in places and the lips looked sterner and less luscious than they had been till only sometime back. It felt as if decades had passed in the last few minutes. Friuli was old, still smart, and smiling, clearly well aware of what she saw in his eyes.

His calculating brain was led by inertia to unlock the secret behind what he saw and he narrowed his options significantly. He asked in jest, "Another twenty three years gone by?"

She let out a soft chuckle and shook her head, following it with the words, "Not exactly."

"I remember getting shot at," he continued, "but it seems that you ran havoc over me after I passed out. Care to explain these wounds on me now, and if I may add," he said

[272]

in a voice that broke as he shifted his weight on the bed, "a lot of pain."

"The truth is here, but first you have got to tell me how you figured it out," she said, eager as a child is for a bedtime story. She had bent forward with extreme interest, resting her chin on one hand which in turn rested on her crossed legs.

It took more effort to shift his weight again as Qin asked, "Did I do well?"

"Depends on what you tell me."

He let out a little smile and explained, "I had my doubts, although they were naturally quite out of place. After all, the change you showed me was quite improbable within two decades. Dirt-free surfaces and a scratchproof skin beg to question but as I learnt more of the world, I realized they weren't so unbelievable. If the skin was artificial and the surfaces were hydrophobic, oleophobic or microscopically ventilated, they were both very much a possibility."

Friuli raised her eyebrows with the words, "Go on."

"Still, I was never entirely satisfied. As I pointed out many times, there was too much perfection. Then again, it could just be a matter of partial knowledge. So I assumed I was yet to see the flip side of things and had no choice but to wait. Sure enough, bionism came along."

"That wasn't a negative thing."

"Not at all, but therein lay the catch. You wanted me to see it as something negative. You showed me the two big networks as on a field trip but left bionism to be explained by a mad man's antics. Speaking of which, where is Mr. Bree?"

"Around. Dramatising it was his idea. He remains in real life as you came to know him in the virtual one, I'm afraid," Friuli stated, half rolling her eyes.

"That was a nice touch and I wonder if he intended to let me figure it out or if it were just coincidence when he decided to call us to the old house."

"I'd say the latter but we were surely timing how long it takes you anyway."

"What if I had taken ages?"

"A question that had graced both our minds throughout this time, but someone seemed to trust you on this and was adamant. It was well worth it in the end. We must not forget that the only reason you could use that coincidence – if it was coincidence at all – was because you were already thinking in that direction. So my question to you is that if all that you doubted had an alternative explanation, what made you stick with those doubts? Surely you do not give scepticism such importance ordinarily."

"Actually, I do. However, in this particular case, I would say that it was partially you," Qin replied, ignored another rise of her eyebrows and clarified, "You were charged with a definitive objective, whatever it was. Many times you gulped words that nearly came out and many a times you reacted as if something was restraining you. Clearly, you held a personal stake in this matter. Twenty three years I had allegedly slept but you looked too young to have been with me throughout. So you could not possibly have had a historic connection with me. Yet, such a driving defiance could have only come from something as intense as that. Gradually then, I saw that you bore that connection not necessarily with me but with the new world. I was solemn due to the enormous unfamiliarity with the surroundings but you knew it all well. Yet, you resonated that feeling nearly every time I expressed it."

"Maybe I'm just a good actor."

"Perhaps you are but one with a sentimental purpose. New or old, it was a world of humans and the components of our everyday life, though transformed, were still the same in character and function. So why would I need a guide? Gradually, I came to learn of bionism and your objective became clearer. It was then that the frame on the old wall crossed my mind: One hand washes the other, both get clean. We were the two hands. So if you were trying to tidy me up, clearly I had been destined with a similar task. The questions began to grow a bit more specific. The frame had not been hung there out of coincidence. So someone was overlooking each of what I came across."

Qin waited for Friuli to ask, "Who?"

"It could be anyone but it had to be someone familiar. Whoever it was seemed to know awfully lot about me. He knew what would convince me convincingly."

"What do you mean?"

"That you had probably driven into my own sub-conscience. That, though, would also mean that it was a dream and everything would make sense. Sadly, it did not."

She gave a gentle nod, "Why?"

"You cannot dream about things that you have never had a clue about. That list includes you. I could not have summed up an entire character, nor could I have gone into technical details of all that filled the new world. That would require knowledge. Most importantly, though, if it was me, I could not see why I would render myself 'unidentified' by my own technology. Unless, you were driving that dream, in which case, my sub-conscience could not have driven it and the very first assumption would fail."

"So it was someone else then?"

"Or maybe my assumption was wrong. I was clearly missing out on something, and that little something was delivered to me by you, rightly and deservedly."

Qin smiled with the words, anticipating one in return. Friuli maintained her gesture and incited him to go ahead, having guessed at what he was about to refer to. He stated, "Your little quip after the game. I daresay that it did blow me away for a bit. That was truly a remarkable experience Friuli, thank you. Yet, to have such a brutal ending dignified as the best ever by a girl who was equally supportive of both the teams and was looking for a good match above all else - it wasn't right. I was perplexed and hopelessly lost for many moments. The answer lay in the hours that followed and only they would reveal it."

"How so?"

"Foremost, there was a behavioural issue. People had grown collectively fit, flashy and floatatious but they were still people – driven by their inherent need for spice. They still bet and they still went crazy in a football match. Now you had told me that we had reached an age of peak political instability at some point of time when Nature had intervened and had shut us up. In such a scenario, few things other than sports could have allowed a power play strong enough to satisfy our craving for a dose of adrenaline. Yet, back in the arena, there was no buzz, no expression of interest and no inclination towards what had just happened in the match of such extreme regional importance. Beyond the walls of the stadium, one was abject neither at Alpi's loss nor at the death of a player on field. Moreover, it was not just the crowd; it was you too: A girl so easily moved by so much every single day suddenly finds herself revelling in what she had seen, and if I can indulge further, is at peace with it. It could not be, unless you knew about it even before the match had begun. So the match, then, could not have been live but recorded, and recorded ages back so as to render every living memory adapted to its magnanimous controversial nature. That is when I remembered your mention of one specific change in the way we played sports."

Friuli shifted her weight in partial excitement and nudged him on with a smile finally. It declared to Qin the confidence she had held in him when she had chosen to not explain those last words of hers earlier.

He went on, "That change lay in the fact that we had begun to play all sports virtually. It occurred to me at the majestic, though unreal, arena when I noticed a blur just before Bree showed up. It was similar to the one I had seen in the players back at the stadium. I thought: if the viewers could move virtually and attend the game as live, why couldn't the players too? That would explain how they were able to defy physical limitations of their body and also escape challenges without a scar. Digitally connected, their virtual avatars could mimic them running around, diving, screaming, celebrating and playing in a secure infrastructure. Saved from injuries, infrastructural issues, weather issues or any physical obstruction, the game would go on – the surety of which would ensure sponsorships and imply larger revenues for all. It was magnificent and it would make sense, had it not been for the fact that Damien did actually die. Now how was that possible?"

Friuli wasn't willing to exchange words during his cacophony of rhythmic speculations. She just looked at him as he waited, streamlined his thoughts and entered the final chapter. "Bree probably just meant to emphasize how long your animosity with him had been but what he did not know was that you had dwelt over his picture earlier in the day with quite a bit of confusion. It could have been an act as well, which would mean that you two may well have known each other, in turn implying that both of you were acting in unison. With the kind of control over the projections that I saw, even the virtual information seemed unsecured. I was in a heavy doubt over all that my lenses were showing when he took us to the old house. Therein lies the coincidence – the verification. The place brought back memories of my first moments after having woken up. Cradled amidst those thoughts was the most disorienting memory of them all: that first projection of my lenses. I had used the password quite regularly but had forgotten the card I had seen it first on: QIn45. It was not a typing error, after all, was it?"

Friuli chuckled at the rhetoric remark, relaxed in her chair and confirmed, "No, it wasn't."

"I had had difficulty in remembering my name. I knew something felt wrong with Qin. As it stands, QIn stood for Quarto Internazionale. *Il Quarto Internazionale* – a tournament with a curious "international" name in a world where nations did not exist! And 45 was not my age as I had been made to guess. 4-5 was the final score line. You had gifted me that one big clue right at the beginning, knowing well that it's key lay in the end of your pre-planned journey."

"Did that explain why we chose that unfortunate match in particular?"

"Right in the end, once I had entered my room. I was looking for one particular headline in that old mirror when I came across it. The people might not have obeyed your plan but your IT systems surely did. Or you made them to. Right at the top lay the big breaking news of the day about how the most unfortunate event in sports had led to the most unprecedented result in history. The game had not ended at 4-5. It had ended at 4-4. Icisles, at the end of a humanly shocking conclusion, had equally shockingly decided to forfeit the goal that should have been disallowed in the first place. They did it as a gesture of goodwill, in respect for the player who had the misfortune of being at fault and paying for that attempt with his life. For starters, it sounded stupid. But that was the essence of the world that had come to be, was it not? A world extremely sensitized to matters of ethics and conduct, given how much it had supposedly suffered because of a lack in these two. Humans had evolved to consciousness towards the vitality of such aspects and while it would be bizarre in our world today, it was very much conventional wisdom in that future. It was a sign of our evolution and that match, I believe, was one of the first ones to exemplify this point. It had taken death for a team to publicly accept an error. Neutral as you were, it was this unimaginable expression of humanity that made this your best-game-ever."

Friuli's smile had turned retrospective. She looked calm and only gently nodded at Qin's words. He observed her for a moment in silence and brought his analysis to closure, "That was that. That news on the mirror reminded me of what I had read on the first day – about how Etna had recently woken up and had put everything to sleep. The very next minute, the mirror had dissolved to reveal her grand stature and Bree was explaining how her last eruption had been catastrophic, but had taken place years back. It added on to your statement about how Nature had nudged us all in the long-gone past. Either way, it could not have been a current affair. It was all cooked up. None of it was real. If players could play in a virtual setting, so could we. That's what we had done. I had been in a virtual world – a simulation – all along."

Friuli waited, and waited more with nothing but relief in her eyes, letting the old creases at their edge speak for her. Qin had not yet inquired her sudden jump in age, nor had he held grudges for the mask she had dawned ever since he had come to know her. He had not thrown himself into a shell as she had feared and while she knew he would have questions yearning to pour out of his throat, he had maintained his calm. She prized the moments of divine satisfaction that had overtaken her entirely. A heavy breath followed and the smile returned under drooped eyelids with an inaudible whisper, "Thank you," to no one in particular.

She looked up at him and, with smile persisting, pointed to the wall behind him. There hung a large mirror, slanting downwards to reveal the length of his bed. On the face of it lay his truth. Qin looked at his reflection wordlessly with unblinking eyes. It was not so much shock as it was catharsis. The face was scarred all over, few of which would never fade entirely. Colours of purple and black had patched up in corners, reminiscent of his deadly fall from the train. One end of his jaw was swollen and there was another bump on his forehead just under his bandaged head. He looked horrible, but he looked young. Amidst the ruins lay stretches of skin, unwrinkled and unfazed. His stubble had been neatly shaved, quite carefully and probably painstakingly so. He did not smile. How could he? A flurry of mixed emotions flashed around that riddled face in the mirror. There was relief, longing, memories and right at the top of the heap, reality - one in which Qin had not lost twenty three years of his life.

"Twenty three weeks to the day since your accident," Friuli revealed to ease his perplexity.

"Then why-" He could not complete his question.

"Precisely to make you feel *this*," she answered nonetheless, "and to save you from yourself."

He took his time, looked down at his body and noticed the reversal in age. It must have taken a large foot to put down and stop his inner assembly of sentimental inclinations but he fought them off to a disciplined order and culminated it with a long breath. He then asked her, "Why the future?"

"To prepare you."

"For what?"

"That which you were to face once you woke up. You had some confusion about that sweet taste, I believe."

"Yes."

"That has been your routine diet, mostly fluid but high in sugars. It's needed to keep your cells charged."

"The usual dose of energy?"

"Not exactly."

Caution returned as he asked, "Are you referring to-"

"Bionism, yes. Enough tissues in your body are now running on power generated by biofuel cells. These consist of electrodes – carbon nanotubes – that need sugars to produce an electric current – their main source of power."

He listened solemnly, not knowing whether to be glad or burdened by this information. "Those lenses-"

"-Are very much a part of you now. So are several other aspects of bionism. I hate to break this to you but..," Friuli paused and directed him to gently press on his elbow. He did as was told and immediately four flat rays of blue glowed underneath his bandage. They lit up and faded equally fast, leaving a resounding trace in his memory. He had felt them on his skin and was now silent. He was now a bionic in reality and he did not know what else lay in his body at that very moment. In those initial seconds, he felt repulsed and nearly depressed at the knowledge of having been deformed for life. He was a cripple in effect and had to depend on undetachable foreign entities planted inside him. Hopelessly, he lay back on his bed, facing the bland ceiling.

There were no lights or fans but the emptiness of that cold roof allowed facts to gradually dawn over: He had seen what he had always wished for - a future worth working towards. Was it all hypothetical? He did not know and even if he were to ask, he could not verify any response that would come his way. That was the nature of future in the present world – a space only time could breach, at its own preset pace. All he could vouch for was the basic truth – that he was alive. More importantly, he had been given back his twenty three years, each of which suddenly seemed more precious than it ever had. That, he agreed, was fortunate.

Amidst his thoughts, he mumbled, "I seem to remember things much more clearly now."

"That's because your memory is being aided by the smells in this place. This lodge has been attuned to house a specific set of smells for you."

Qin spared some time to grasp the distinction behind the overall smell that he could sense. He then asked, "How do these matter?"

[281]

"Oh, smells are important. They are the oldest senses us organisms have, and they have a rather privileged access to our brain. They can unlock memories and often help to do the job much quicker than we can surgically or experimentally hope to accomplish. I suppose you are wondering why it is required though."

"Because the accident damaged my cortex as well? Is that why I could not remember anything distinctly as long as I was in the simulation?"

"Actually, we had to marginally manipulate your hippocampus to ensure receptivity towards what we were to show you."

"Hippo-?"

"It is a convergence point for all information arriving from the rest of the cortex; like a hub-and-spoke model or a wheel. Smells help because the olfactory bulb lies right beside it and that is pretty much the reason why it is proving so effective now."

Friuli's deliverance was deeply unsettling Qin with every uttered word. His next words were filled with hiccups, "What else have you done to me?"

Friuli smiled and bent towards him empathetically. "We did nothing to your disadvantage, I can promise you that. I could prove it to you but my hands are tied for now. You dropped yourself into a mess and had conveniently chosen to sleep off the weeks of effort that we put into bringing you back. It has been a weird tapestry of events and has left us both with questions. The fact that we still feel we can trust each other with answers is in itself a miracle. I understand it but I am sure you don't, because there is no reason for you to. All I can say is that you will. You do have a number of corrections to make after the damage you had forced upon those near you. Does it help to know that you now have the opportunity to do that? If I guessed right, that had been your most pressing concern back in the virtual world. Was it not?"

Qin nodded within the pool of confusing anomalies. An analogous clock ticked under the cold, heavy air that had descended in that room. They were closer to dawn than to midnight now. Qin looked at it, hoping to get diverted from the oncoming thoughts in this uncomfortable silence.

"All I know," Qin said, almost inaudibly and without looking at her, "is that I had boarded that train with a singular objective."

"To come here, to say a goodbye to it all and to disappear for good."

"Yes," he confirmed almost immediately, but stopped as her words played once again in his mind. Startled but surprisingly hopeful, he asked, "What do you mean 'here'? Where are we?"

"Sandakphu."

Excitement and alarm rang in together. "How did you know?" he asked and realized the answer almost instantly but did not express it. He controlled a rising sense of urgency within and inquired, as humbly as he could but still with a hint of cautious emphasis, "Who are you, Friuli? I think I deserve to know that much."

"An unrelated accomplice who has been involved in this entire affair for a wish long held in her heart, and out of sheer concern."

"For whom?"

"You," Friuli spoke as instantly as she had been interrupted. "I suppose you will have enough trouble understanding this as long as we beat about the bush." Her words were calm and reflective. She looked at him and concluded, "I admit I have been reserved in what I could reveal but that time is now gone. My job with you is done and I shall take your leave soon enough. All that's left to be told is to be told by him and only he can do so fittingly."

"Who?"

"Kalki Evian. At the edge of this mountain, he waits for you."

[283]

Chapter 21

All stayed dark and silent for the hours that followed the fall. The silence was never breached and even though touch was the first sense that returned to her, she felt afraid of its implication. She could be dead already. If she wasn't, she was in the hands of those who would lure her towards it in the slowest possible manner. Hours had passed but her face still ached from the treatment it had received. The eyelids hesitated once the consciousness had returned but once they began to flicker in the brightness around, fear gripped her over hushed words that were being spoken in frenzy. One of the voices belonged to Kanha Evian but the other belonged to neither of the two tormentors she had met before. It was a sudden short-lived delight, attributed not so much to the return of her relief but to the uncanny fact that once again, her fears had been overcome by a stubborn instinctive faith that seemed to have no valid reason but refused to budge despite all that had happened.

The unknown voice spoke, "Is there nothing else we can do?"

No reply came at first. She hazily saw one shake his head as a familiar voice returned, "What good is light at the end of a tunnel if you never reach it?"

"That's hope, is it not? The light stays, regardless your reach. There must be some way."

"Just theories. We can pursue them, but to what end?" There was another silence, followed by that bleak voice filled with a familiar tone of love, "Go on dear Lana, the authorities need you more."

The other walked out without a word. Kanha turned to face Fridgeon's bed, unaware that she was now awake. His head dropped and hid between wide stretched out arms that were now resting on one end of the mattress. He seemed deep in thought and shook when her fingers moved to touch him. He gathered himself and said in a tone that had returned to normalcy, "You should choose your bodyguards more wisely."

"Where are they?" Fridgeon asked in breaking voice.

"At their rightful place - under custody. How's the cheek?"

"Aching like hell," she said, forcing herself to sit up partially. It took an extraordinary bit of effort under terrible weakness. She felt her swollen face and looked around. It was a white cottage – a temporary settlement, bright under the natural light of the day and with minimal amenities around. She looked at Kanha with a questioning glance, observing well the width of his strong forearm this time.

"It will subside. Here, drink this."

"What is it?" she asked, taking a short and thin glass from his hand.

"Almond wine. It's a dessert wine but you need something sweet and strong."

Fridgeon did not understand why but drank without question. Sweet it was, and chilly, yet smooth as it found its way down her throat, imparting a feeling of sipping on liquefied crystal. She then inquired, "What happened?"

"Nothing much. I settled scores, I suppose."

"So you decided to use your bionic arm finally?"

Kanha smiled to the slightest. "Did Hope tell you?"

"Yes, did you bank on me to find out on my own?"

"I banked on other things, to be honest," he said in rhythm as if their conversation had been rehearsed to shun both pretence and sentiment.

"Why couldn't you just tell me the truth?"

"It would have been risky, in case you spilled it to someone else. I did not know what you would choose to believe eventually."

"You could have helped me with that," Fridgeon asserted, though continuing the conversation under blank expressions.

"No, I couldn't. Logic fades where sentiment is involved. It was your husband we were talking about."

"Did you always know about him?"

Kanha sighed and dropped his head once more. "No Fridgeon," he said as if under pain, "I'm sorry. I had guessed initially – the day you told me your story, about how he had somehow managed to have blood on his right even though the drivers sit on the left side – but I chose to overlook all that. I wouldn't have let you go back otherwise. I shouldn't have."

"Why not?" She asked with a first touch of empathy.

Kanha looked at her for the first time. "Do you not wonder how the two men managed to track you down to Catania?"

"I haven't really had time to, frankly," she confessed, partly in jest and partly disturbed at the thought. The air felt heavy, both physically and in her head. That coupled to a stream of words being exchanged across blank faces precipitated the weight of the situation to an added effect.

"They had a chip planted inside you, inside one of your scars. I saw it soon after we met," he hesitated, "while bathing you."

"YOU NEVER TOLD ME! Why did you let it stay there?" Fridgeon screamed, but could hardly muster enough energy to see it through. Her eyebrows revealed her pain at the thought and she let it persist, challenging Kanha to match her gaze.

He continued, without much reaction to her words but lost in a consistent feeling of some pre-conceived

[286]

aggravation, "When you told me that Jelzan had given you those scars, it alarmed me at first. Something was fishy and for a moment, I suspected that you were part of the gang and that Scinoi had cleverly managed to sneak up on me."

Another sign entailed before her, now frozen and solemn as before. She spurred him on, "But?"

"I could not bring myself to believe that. It was instinctive, perhaps. I observed you and trusted myself on judging that well. Soon enough it became clear that it was you who had been victimized."

"Maybe I was a good actor."

"Perhaps you were, but the day I rescued you at the subway, I chose to take that risk; I had chosen to believe in the better nature of humanity and to trust. I had decided to cure you, even if it required me to safeguard myself."

"What if you failed?"

"Is life an exam that we must consistently pass at all costs? I chose to trust assuming that you may break it. I did my part."

Fridgeon dropped her stare and did not speak for a while. She then prompted, measurably sombre, "You could have let me go once I was healed and well."

"I could indeed have, but-"

"Hope stopped you. Isn't that why you wear that ring?" The words forced Kanha to turn away, half-nodding in return. She did not press upon his heart further but asked instead, "I can understand why you did not tell me about it but why didn't you remove the chip yourself?"

The reply was swift this time. "Because that would have alarmed them and made you consciously aware, and any chance of finding the truth would have been lost."

"The truth about Hope, about Mongrando?"

"Yes," he said with some analysis, "One can consider the beginning of the game you found yourself in to be the unlikely, intangible, unconvincing play of destiny which, to a calculative mind, should sound both bogus and

[287]

discouraging. Yet, it happened nonetheless – our chance meeting at the subway. So I played along but could not risk your safety."

"That's why you sent me to that horrible factory alone - to honour our chance meeting!" Fridgeon said sarcastically. Kanha simply looked back at her with the slightest hint of a forced smile. A lack of defence on his part, a lack of any clarification whatsoever, stabbed through her brain. The subsequent revelation showed prominently in her eyes. "You didn't. You followed me," she said, with unexpected joy.

He stressed further, "Fridgeon, it was important that you considered yourself alone to let them bring in the answers you sought, as one did."

"That old lady," Fridgeon remembered, "She was real, wasn't she?"

"I am afraid, yes."

Fridgeon stared at him in search for a longer explanation but it never came. The momentary joy had died out with as much affirmation as the very weight that she felt subjected to under latent despair. The only upside was to have a man finally clarifying every word he knew to her. Yet, layer after layer of hopelessness that had come to manufacture itself through every fold of pretentious human action began to dawn upon her.

"I sounded an alarm and those guys probably took care of the rest. I had to make my way out before they appeared though."

"You were the one who took the cab away?" Kanha nodded while Fridgeon continued her assessment without wait, "They dealt with her before I could wake up. They must have felt alarmed at what had possibly happened."

"So alarmed that the first thing Az did was inform Hope. It was she who asked him to direct you straight to her. She was playing this pretty close to her chest and had ensured it was all done in a way that you wouldn't suspect her to have known anything."

"She did it well," Fridgeon said, lost in thought. "Do you think she knew about your presence in Milano?"

"I doubt that," Kanha said but his eyes had wandered away at the words. It was not an expression of calm, nor was it one of disturbance. It neither was one of question nor did it carry an answer. He turned to her and answered, "She would not have planted her spies – your bodyguards – if she had known it was me you were staying with."

"You knew?"

"Yes. I tried to warn you, although in the weakest way. I had to be subtle to ensure you didn't think I was watching. That's why I messed my house up that night."

Fridgeon remembered her confusion, her concern and the cleaning she had had to do. Anger positioned itself in her eyes but who could she possibly direct it to? It felt inclined to pour out on her saviour and that seemed most unfair in a manner that she now found to be quite in sync with life itself. She nearly shouted again, "Why the hell were you absent in the first place?"

"To safeguard the plan, to guard against nature. If you would have met me, you would have inevitably discussed all that had happened and would have sought answers. If I had not answered you, you would have suspected me, and if I had, anything I said would have run the risk of being leaked out to Hope or to someone else. You have an example in Az already. More importantly, Hope had been hot on your heels from that very evening. I could not take chances. I did not doubt your sincerity, but I also could not doubt another's capability to play with your sentiments. I am sorry."

Fridgeon took some time to return her breathing to normalcy. It never did so entirely but she considered: If she had not managed to trust her own allegiance in the recent past, there was no reason to expect someone else to. Things quietened down until curiosity showed itself, "Az used to be your accomplice?"

"A friend. Frankly, there is no reason for you to believe it any more than you believed the previous version of the story."

"What happened?"

"His work happened. Obviously Hope has told you enough about bionism, given your little quip about my arm earlier." Fridgeon nodded and he continued, "Az wanted to take it further, beyond what had already been envisioned."

"Isn't that a good thing?"

"Expertise and freedom is of value only if you know how to control it. Az had vision but I daresay it was limited. He saw the very next step but could not see the repercussions in the longer term. Maybe he did not care. He's an intelligent guy and he wanted to utilize his expertise to its fullest. Such inclination to achieve often trumps the need to do it responsibly. That's why everything humans have done throughout history has gone in circles. By the time we reach the peak, we are so seduced by our rise that we don't stop looking up, even though any further step can only take us downhill. I tried to explain this, but Az was naturally blinded by his ability. All he needed was an investor."

"Enter Hope," Fridgeon concluded. Kanha nodded with some helplessness. She asked, "Why her? I mean, why not any other firm?"

"Az was already working at Scinoi. I hear he was one of the best but his ideas were uncontrolled. When Archer Piscoli refused to heed his plans, differences arose. Hope had been waiting for such a lead. So she enticed him with the prospect of fame and liberty in his intended research." Kanha was visibly disappointed now. "He's an intelligent guy but Hope's a better manager."

"So she basically wanted to climb the ladder. She waited until Scinoi had acquired the Bee to allow her to move out and distance herself from the affairs at Mongrando."

"Yes."

"I can't believe these were the people you risked letting me go to." A pause entailed. "Did you know I would need to come back? Is that why you told me about Etna?"

These were not the kind of questions that did not bear an answer, but ones that did not necessarily provide the right words to answer with. He replied, "Only because it was my business to save you in whichever way I could, within certain boundaries."

Fridgeon held firm with a steely resolve to not waver; perhaps even more so because she was so easily moved by such words at all times. Her straight expression continued, each word physically requiring more effort than the last, "You had your incentives too."

"Which you delivered well."

Her brows creased but it did not take her long. "Your laptop?"

Kanha nodded and explained, "The flash drive she had given you had an in-built connectivity to transfer information the moment files were added to it."

"So what did you do?"

"I switched on the light," Kanha said rather matter-of-factly. "The drive could not possibly outpace the connectivity delivered by the alternating current of those LEDs. I knew once she found out who you were staying with, she would be driven by greed towards this god-sent opportunity to hack me. So I let her do so, gaining access to her files in return. They are well protected, I daresay, and I could not extract much but I suspect that the feeling is mutual."

Seconds passed in reminiscence and were obstructed by clearly defined words, "You are lying." Kanha was taken aback but he did not protest. Fridgeon added, "Files, data, secrets – from what I have learnt, you have enough means to stay ahead of all that than having to steal them. You certainly wouldn't do that with someone like Hope, someone I know for certain is beyond petty gains and tiffs for you. You are lying, aren't you? It was something personal."

The conversation was unusual and Fridgeon sensed it. She had managed to quieten Kanha far too frequently and even through their brief history, she knew enough to find this behaviour rather unconvincing. He did not agree. He did not deny. She had to strain her nearly exploding head further until it churned out one word: "Password!"

Kanha's eyes spoke this time, without permission or delay. The involuntary expression was caught by their onlooker as the latter continued, "There was only one way any one could have figured out that password. My successful guess that day gave you perhaps the biggest answer that you had been looking for, isn't it? That she still wears the ring!"

Kanha softly blinked as his pupils shifted south. His lips pursed themselves with resilience. His gaze matched the depths of an ocean and it calmed Fridgeon down. It was brief, for soon enough, she jumped towards guilt. He had saved her life twice at least and she was only returning the favour with added sting. She tried to pacify the moment with a drift that was softer in voice, "the key to your apartment – it is a mini-bioimager, is it not? You had it registered to my fingerprints."

"I had its access allowed to them," Kanha corrected her with a disinterested tone. He had fought a mini-war in the span of seconds that had passed between her words. "It only allows access to registered fingerprints but it records all that fall upon it. The information is then sent immediately to me. That way, I know every time sometime tries to use it or to break in. Thanks to our social security systems, as long as the person carries a registered ID, his fingerprint comes along with it. Yellow pages, it used to be called. The world keeps changing-"

"I don't like the idea of it doing so. I certainly do not like being universally connected all the time. It makes me feel insecure."

"Maybe, but only time will tell how it turns out to be. As for now, it has helped me save you. Once my laptop logged into her server that day, your chip was as much a tracker for me as it was for them."

"If it were all that simple, Hope should have identified you much earlier."

"Well, I had taken measures to ensure anonymity-"

"-which you risked for me." They looked at each other squarely in the eyes. The smiles never came. She glanced away and exclaimed, "I hope you got all that you had wished for, although I can't say as much about Hope. That's why she sent those guys after me, I suppose."

"It has all worked out for her thus far but I don't think it worked out exactly as per her plan. She had banked upon some police action and an immediate removal of Dr. Piscoli, but unfortunately for her, you came home with me. The delay must have unsettled her and she could not make any sudden movements. It would have seemed unnatural, would have made you suspect an anomaly and would have ruined an entire year's effort that they had put into things. The little coincidence of our meeting forced her to approach another way and to adjust with a mere transfer rather than his resignation. Whatever he had that restricted her still exists in theory then."

Fridgeon rested her back against the wall and turned her stare to a blank one. The walls seemed to have turned whiter, accentuating the blankness of the room. Her eyelids ached and she spoke, under the air that forced itself out of her lungs, barely muttering to herself, "There was such a thing called life. I used to like it."

She allowed those eyelids to cut off the light with a muted hope to fly away to a never-land she had often sought before. The teleportation was automated, its destination was too, but Neverland never came into view. Instead, she found herself fixed towards a slideshow of the faces of statues, towering over her and staring with an inflicting layer of despondency. Each switched to the other before she could reason with one. All that was left in consistent proportions was that generic imposition of the feeling that there was a thing called life once, and that she used to like it. Quick and breathless, she opened her eyes again. Kanha stood calm, accepting and in a wait whose nature she neither knew nor had the inclination to analyze. Instead, she sighed and came at last to the point, "How long do I have?"

"Huh?"

"I have felt my lungs clog more and more by the second. I heard you speak earlier. Your gloom ever since is quite a give-away. I don't have long, do I?"

Kanha wanted to shout out to the skies. He wanted to question loud and clear the questions that graced his tongue so very often. It belonged to a simple category of arguments that began with a 'Why?' but never brought home an answer to. He had never sought them openly, for he had felt strangely at peace with those questions as if the answers lay just beyond the moment he was living in at all times. He had always been so utterly convinced of that fact that his inquisitiveness had never known a rush, never known the impatience that plagued every other soul with a lack of answers. To him, it had always felt as if he knew all there was to know but had just forgotten them somehow. He had seen desperate moments but had lived through them with a greater resilience to remember that which he was supposed to, leading inevitably to an even greater extent of patience. That, though, was not to be today.

He looked at Fridgeon. Her acceptance of a fact that had riddled, shook and disappointed him so far seemed strangely reflective of his own predicament. That was perhaps why he felt uneasy now. He felt out of place, out of patience and certainly out of answers. How long did she have? She had an eternity.

Fridgeon interrupted his thought, "That injection belonged to Az, did it not?"

Kanha turned with surprise to find the object lying on a nearby table. Her deductions had been at their best ever since shock and loss had robbed her of all other incentives of humility. They had added to her almost-blind belief in instincts and it proved to be an uncanny combination.

She continued, "What did he plan to do? Make me one of his experiments? I knew when I saw him and I guess he succeeded somehow. Am I right?"

Kanha looked out the window and said, "I don't know the cure, Fridgeon. If it were a virus or a transplant, the effects would have shown. It could be neither-"

"Or both," she said. She was calm even as he affirmed with his eyes. "Do me a favour, will you? Take me outside. I want to walk in Nature one last time and see with these eyes as I remember them."

He did as told and helped her out on the slope of that mountain. It was bright and daylight had thrown open two instant pleasures. First was the grainy push of Earth that had curved itself to rise with ambition from all sides to meet at the farthest that it could. That peak of Etna stood quiet and silently fuming in gentle white, every trickle of which rose up to meet with the clouds and become one. These clouds then flew in puffs of grey-bordered cottons, sparsely floating in the light blue sky. The blue and white were apt to soothe, moderate and support the majesty of colours that the soil beneath her feet had thrown around.

She looked at this second beckoning of amazement, as the land waved and overlapped for miles. It was all volcanic, all reminiscent of violent burning lava of the past that still flowed somewhere deep underneath them. On the surface, they had cooled in varying proportions on each set of slopes to render a brown soil that carried any one of the distinct hues of yellow, red, orange, purple and green. While green and yellow could be attributed to the resistance of vegetation, the others were just a play of frolic.

Decades ago, she remembered how she had felt strongly seduced to use all the colours in her crayon box in a little scenery that she had managed to draw as a little girl. However, she had been cautioned by the grown-ups and the impracticality of her idea had been explained to her rather convincingly. Here she stood now, observing the same art expressed unrestrained by the child in Nature in a world where everything was possible and every thought of every living organism was equally valuable. There were no rules if the heart was pure and genuine. It was upon Nature to accommodate such effort and on the plane of Etna, She seemed glad to have done so.

"Why here?" Fridgeon asked.

"Crateri Silvestri," Kanha said, pointing a few meters ahead, "a dead crater. It's to show you where I have been working for a while now. Remember PhU and PhD?"

A smile finally made its way to the surface. Fridgeon narrowed her eyes, partly due to the wind and partly in thought. The crater lay ahead, circumferenced like a saucer and covered with soil and stunted plants growing in patches, as if a couple of underground fingers pinched upon the centre had pulled the elastic land downwards. He led her up a shortish slope that bent towards the right along its edge, several steep feet away; the juncture marked by a single six foot boulder. It resembled a time-door, for the remaining twenty feet to the outer edge were rocked by incessant wind, so fierce that it could easily blow them off the cliff at the slightest wrong footing. They bent forward and forced themselves to the plateau-ish top as the outer edge on the other end of that bowl grew closer. The sea and inhabitation many miles away came into view. It was heartbreaking at first, for the inner quarter of the city wore a blanket of black soil that covered part of the buildings. The view was beautiful by all standard measures, were it not for the painful realization of some eruption not long back in the past.

"A narrow escape," she said, looking at how close the thick of inhabitation was to the earthy mess.

"Not exactly," came the reply. "The economy took a beating. Few left, others were ignored for long. At places, precautionary measures caused a collateral damage to their livelihood. The airport shut down indefinitely. So they ended up in a partial vacuum of socio-economic state as a fallout of the emergency agendas of larger governance." Fridgeon did not reply but continued to look ahead. Kanha pointed at the dark end of the city and then near the shores. "Look closely."

She did so with cluelessness at first. Gradually, like invisible cobwebs that show their distinct strands upon scrutiny, the anomaly showed itself.

There on the roofs as umbrellas, in the distant miniature balconies as hints, through pillars as barcodes and perhaps as much else in the internal veins of the structures lay thousands of sources trapping the energy gifted to the city in abundance. She did not realize what they did until she noticed the regularity of such tools on every building. PhU and PhD had arrived.

"Renewables?" she asked rhetorically.

"Prosperity," he replied, "or so it intends to be when all else has abandoned them. This is something that can't be taken away from them, from this place. They have the sun, the wind, and intense thermal activity beneath the ground. They have the sea, the tides and a fertile soil. Honestly, I can't think of a more perfect place."

"To generate energy and pass it on in return for the food they grow in abundance. You have turned this into an entirely self-sustaining city!"

[297]

"Just lent a hand, hoping that the experiment would work."

She tried to envelope it all with her eyes. Her pupils dilated in an excitement that she almost loathed herself for, for the very next thought was real and relevant to her own state. What she saw was precisely the kind of support that compelled men to drag through lives that did not appear to hold much meaning except in the continuity of that effort. The infrastructural boon seemed nothing short of a disguised bane and she argued, "I see only two eventualities to all this effort. Either some interested powerful party will come and take over or Etna will destroy it sooner or later. What good is it then?"

Kanha turned to face Fridgeon looking at him with tired eyes. He asked, "Do you like your school days? Your childhood?"

She shrugged, "Of course. They are the only trace of untarnished sweetness that lies in my memories."

"Yet you have hardly utilized the effort you put in at that age – at school, at home, at play; even the friends are long gone, are they not? So what was the point? What good did all those drawings do?" Fridgeon's eyebrows straightened to the slightest. She was without hope but hope did exist, despite all her efforts to the contrary. It was as if Kanha read that sentiment as he spoke, "Despair lies in your mind and you can control it based on how you reason yourself through. Hope, however, stays in some way or the other no matter how hard you try. Why do you think life designs itself as such? Your naivety, your ignorance and your appreciation for every moment that you live are the reasons that have left those days of quarrels, tears, laughs and a thousand other versatile emotions as the best – and ironically the most peaceful – memory you now have. In a way, none of them were productive but they are important all the same. So maybe life is not so much about what your actions lead to but those actions alone."

She blinked, at him with eyes that strained to see through a blanket of tears that appeared unrestrained as a mix of guilt, thankfulness, hope and everything unnamed that stood for something good, something more in this world. Fighting that little sparkle of spirit was the brutal reality of her future that stood dark, uncertain and possibly horrific. There in the depths of the psychological well she found herself grounded in, was the face of that mysterious deformed old lady but Fridgeon did not spare a moment to look at that face, for her eyes were fixed at the light that shone high above. It was then that the well felt like a blessing when for the first time ever, she saw: its bland walls acted more like a telescope, having shut out all distractions that Earth served up at all other times, thereby allowing her to focus on the infinity of a clear blue sky.

"There is something else I want you to know, something I wasn't supposed to tell you," he added as if in testament to what he had just explained to her, having arrived at a prolonged decision to spill the beans. "Kanha Evian," he said under sufficient hesitation, "has long been gone from all memory."

The brute forces, though, do not abandon one without a test and they certainly had no plans to abandon Fridgeon. Her brain felt itself stabbed with a sharp needle from within her head as she collapsed on the ground without further thought. Her accomplice jumped to cushion her fall midway and she looked at him with eyes that could not see much any longer. Light rays entered them only in name. Yet, the feelings were alive and all she wanted to ask was how many times he planned on saving her, unconcerned about whichever irrelevant truth it was that he had held on his lips. It was a thought that gifted her a final smile – one she was unable to translate on her lips. She squeezed those last drops of her life to utter words that were probably her last: "Save her. Save yourself. Kanha and Hope are meant to be together not just in passwords. She is driven by nothing

[299]

else than the pain of having lost love. Save your Hope or there would be no bounds to the number of Fridgeons she will sacrifice without thought."

Silence took over. Fridgeon had just told him exactly what he needed to know, and he cried; his tears strolling out in a defiance of their own as the words fizzed out in that wind. How could he save her? How could he ever bring her back? She had given in to the finality of a negative that threatens to eclipse this world every second of its existence even though in each of those seconds, the world fights back, unknown, unaware and uncontrolled. He did not believe in the pointlessness of hope. He would not. Yet, his tears had a mind of their own and rose out of his burning heart. Fridgeon Friuli lay still in his arms, having gifted something that did not lie in her words but in her, and only he sensed it in what was about to become his life's greatest incentive. Just like that, under that impulse, those tears began to subside. His heart began to wake up. His hands began to gather their strength.

"Kalki Evian, that's my name," he said as he picked her up in his arms and moved towards the crater to give Fridgeon Friuli a fitting farewell.

Chapter 22

The wind was cold. It revelled in the absence of the obstructions of an urban sprawl. The house, the hut, was made of wood, distinct in its snow-laden roof slanting down upon creaking doors. It stood singularly erect in a cluster of three huts further away. Qin stepped out in heavy boots; his limp exacerbated by thick uneven snow on ground and the darkness around. Three-quarters of his face was all that lay naked amidst the coat and wool, and even that was burdensome, for the face was scarred and the scars unhealed. His narrowed eyes found it quite unfamiliar to focus, given the weeks they had spent shut. Yet, he endeavoured to look at the smallest hut in the greater distance that flickered over a single candle flame somewhere inside. Qin smiled. A very old woman lived there once, several years back. He remembered her noodle soup – steaming, bland and life-saving. He remembered how it had proven nothing short of an elixir in the freeze that prevailed outside on his last exploratory visit. He hoped that she still served it. He wondered if she could. He wished now, above all else, to be able to tell her just how much her culinary effort in a lost world meant to each and every individual who had ever arrived at Sandakphu from the farthest corners of the world.

That faint flickering view at the back of his hut hid the path that brought trekkers up to this peak. His neck had turned that way by default until purpose knocked it back. Qin turned to face ahead. A stretch of land, some fifty meters in length and some fifteen degrees in incline, spread ahead. It sloped down from three sides, but nothing lay beyond its softly curving horizon in front, except the darkest a sky could be, adorned with the twinkle of brighter stars. The only sound was a howl – the hollow wave of the wind as on a desert. Its chill was delivered not by its flow but by a silhouette that interrupted the continuum of the horizon on that edge. The silhouette was that of Kalki Evian.

The darkness beyond felt defied by the borders of his silver hair neatly combed back and by the metallic cover on shoulders that stood still – broad and firm. The arms held each other behind him in a rigid, yet artistic curve. The feet – a foot apart – had not moved in the immediate past and yet, had managed to repel any apparent trace of snow. He stood facing the valley beyond – a valley so deep, its end could never been seen. Nor did he wish to see it, for his eyes were fixed upon the distant mountain range that stretched ahead – many, many miles away.

Slowly, Qin walked up to him, braving the pain in his joints and in each stretch of his bruised skin as he muscled his way over the snow around. It was a stiff climb of forty-seven meters when a voice – crystal, composed and heavy – came to him, "The sky's still as high. You can't go any higher, can you?"

Qin stopped in his tracks and replied in coherence, "Unless we begin to fly."

"That'll mark an evolution, but where is it that you would wish to reach?"

"The highest I can."

"So it's not a destination you seek, but the journey."

Qin was struck by the thought. He said, "Yes, a journey to a destination that is worthy enough . . ."

"Is that not?" Kalki asked, and raised half a hand to point forty-five degrees to the right.

"Mount Everest," Qin said and looked into the distance at the dark conical border on the other end of the ever-stretching valley. Solemnly, he answered, "it is."

"Then why is it that you decided to give up?" The voice carried no hint of curiosity. It was flat and factual.

"I didn't," Qin stammered, "In fact, it saved my life." It all came out as a justification. A justification it had been, the need to which was unknown even to Qin. Perhaps it was the discomforting chill, or may be the pain, or simply, a constant sense of guilt ever since he had woken up. Nonetheless, he added, "I was supposed to board a flight back home."

"The one that crashed, but you were not on it, as otherwise assumed by everyone else. You had decided to run away from it all, and took a train to come here." The questions of logic that should have breached Qin's guard from the very beginning finally arrived with a trace of an answer. Kalki added, "I do not mean to startle you as much as to comfort you with the knowledge that I know. There is not much use to this conversation if you carry so much guilt and scepticism with you."

"Still," Qin asked, "how did you find out?"

"Well, only one other knew about your plan but she would never speak of it to anyone. So how indeed, Qin?" Kalki left the question hanging as a mockery over Qin's head, for the answer should have been obvious to him now. He then added, "That's not really your name, is it?"

"No," Qin said with straighter brows.

"It is to me, Qin. I prefer it, and it's nice – short, simple and monotonous," Kalki mused.

It was as if the muse were to war with the gravity that prevailed upon its audience. Qin, serious and gradually finding his feet, asked, "Who are you?

Kalki did not answer, but he did turn, neither in haste nor in entirety. It did not matter, for his face now faced Qin's and even in that darkness, its shine was clear and unmistaken. An explosion in water reveals the exact ferocity of curls that the waves follow thereafter, and so did the ones inside Qin's brain; so did the blood within his veins. They were revealed by a flicker of his eyes. Only two

[303]

words escaped his lips, "Your eyes." They were interpreted well and accurately by the other. Kalki smiled with them.

"How old are you?" Qin asked rather naively and without thought, prey to the first question he could find to address his curiosities.

"Quite," came an amused reply.

"It can't be. It just can't. How is it possible?"

The question was expected, and planned was Kalki's reply. In one flash, as Qin's eyes stood watching evidently, Kalki's body flickered and stabilized. The eyes that watched it happen were contrastingly stagnant. There was no blink. There were no creases. There was a sufficient dose of amazement and it was next met by the magician's words, "What happened? In doubt once again?"

"Should I not be?" asked Qin.

"Well, there was that virtual world where everything was as real as reality could get. Here is reality marred by an illusion before your naked eyes. So yes, any person should find himself in a pool of doubts; any person, save you. After all, is this not what you had sought?"

"What do you mean?"

"A hint, an indication of possibilities, an excitement out of the ordinary, a purpose beyond what your contemporary world could give you. Are these not what lay at the very root of the crisis you found yourself in?"

Qin's stare dropped, his voice turned meek. "I did not come to know of the plane crash until much later that night. The flight had been significantly postponed due to bad weather, and my family wasn't expecting it to fly until next morning. Everything had been delayed. So I assumed they would be asleep. I decided to wait and figure out an explanation. I did try."

"But?"

"There was no easy way. I decided to call eventually, but the cellular network was nearly absent in those lands."

"Is that why you went out to the door in your coach?"

"Partially, and to get some fresh air."

"Because deep down, you were afraid that you'd have to cancel your plans if you called home."

Very softly, Qin confessed, "I can't explain how much I needed to come here. I do not know why. I only wanted to know that there was something I could look forward to. That the hopelessness of what I saw was not all that there was to see. I never meant to escape, although I know that's how it looks. It was best for everyone, especially for those around me. I know where I went wrong. I see it now, and I am sorry." Kalki's shoulders heaved as he turned to face the valley again. Qin gathered himself and asked simply this time, "You have travelled back in time."

"In a way; though I am standing very much in mine. I am just looking at yours."

"How?"

"Just the way you are doing it. Well, almost."

"What do you mean?"

Kalki looked up at the sky and asked, "You see those stars?"

Qin continued to look at Kalki and affirmed, "Yes."

"Light rays have taken hundreds and thousands of years to reach from most of those stars. What you see of them today was what existed those many years back. So aren't you looking at the past as well? We always have."

Qin's eyes travelled to the one that shone brightest, above the distant range of Himalayas. Kalki continued, "It's Beaming in effect, where unlike the virtual worlds of computer games, virtual avatars interact with real people in a real place. Our intelligence brought us to a little thing called television and within a century, we had learnt to transmit online data through light bulbs. How long do you think it could have then taken us to figure this out then?"

[305]

"You must have needed help in the present," Qin reasoned, "since you are just a projection."

"Indeed. A pair of knowing hands, to be precise; the others could be temporary labour. He's inside the house and I suppose we can let him have his sleep, wouldn't you agree?" Qin looked back at the hut and asked with a drifted mind, "Why save me?"

"I thought you said you understood your mistake."

"I did," he confirmed, "I do."

"Then you know what you must change."

"Yes."

"I doubt that," Kalki declared.

"I really do. I have risked their happiness, their safety, for the sake of my own uncertainties. They don't deserve it. My family is bound to me by fate, but Hope's not. She can go."

"What if I were to say that she is?"

Qin did not question what made Kalki so sure. In a way, he understood it already. However, he did ask why, through his eyes, for they seemed to converse well and effectively.

The other replied, "That fall was necessary for you to understand some things you otherwise wouldn't have. You conjoined your fate with her the moment you entered her life. She is naive, innocent yet hard-headed. You have seen this, haven't you?"

"Definitely."

"Then you have also seen how vulnerable she is to the flaws of human nature. She trusts too easily and believes in too much."

"That is not my problem," Qin argued, "I mean, it's not fair. Am I supposed to stay with her just for the sake of her happiness? What happens to my life, my decisions?"

"What about them? The only reason you wish to make alternative – even drastically destructive – decisions is because the one you prefer, and incidentally the one right

[306]

for you, is also the one that is being externally forced upon you. It's the same ego that any kid experiences against his parents."

"I think it's natural," Qin protested, though after an evident split-second gap. "So, say, that is true, but love doesn't follow such logic. It either happens or it doesn't. How can I love her this way?"

"Do you not already?"

Qin's words restrained themselves within him. He would have spoken for argument's sake but he wanted to consider. Kalki continued, "Love neither follows such logic nor common definitions. That which you speak of is fun and exciting. We read about it in fairy tales. Yet, that's not the only way it exists. Nor is that the most potent way in which it can survive and sustain itself. The love you have for her can. You are with her because you can't stand a hint of disappointment in her eyes, nor risk the loss of what she bears in her nature. In fact, her innocence is the only trickle of hope and faith you have in people. With that gone, there would be absolutely nothing that will hold you to any person in this world, the loner that you are. Most importantly, it must now be evident that the decision to leave her sent you rushing immediately to this uninhabited mountain peak. You did not come here out of disappointment. You came here out of hope to find a more purposeful life than the one that existed back there in the society. We both know it can't be found here. So perhaps it's not you who has been there to protect her; it is she who has been there for you, to keep you among people, ironically as it turns out, for everyone's sake. For, therein lies the anomaly, doesn't it? The most confusing bit of it all – your first love – your unquenchable drive to help the very people you can't live amidst."

A whiff of air left Qin's lungs as if he had been holding his breath thus far. With a slight shake of his head, he asserted, "it's not fair."

[307]

"It is profound," Kalki corrected him with a more compelling tone, "Your love for her is rooted in your passion for what you think is good and should be secured. Do not underestimate the potential of these two sentiments in unison, for I've never known anything stronger. This is what passionate love truly looks like - invisible, unflinching and never aspiring for ephemeral excitement of some preconceived story. It is also what had kept her from falling prey to the feeling that you know only too well; when you put everything at stake for something you want more than anything else and it abandons you – that free fall to a bottomless pit. You have felt it, haven't you?"

Qin did not answer, but it appeared as if something had driven him back to his senses. Kalki continued, "you came out of it nearly rejuvenated, having resolved to put things right. It was that determination that led you to so ardently try to protect and preserve the innocence you saw in her, as if she would lose them without you. You did not care about sense. You just did what you felt right. That is constructive determination, but it's not the only kind. Most of the times, the free fall instils a very different resolve in people - one to exact revenge, against their own fate or that of the world. Some are not capable of inflicting much damage; yet some are."

Those last words were unsettling. Qin asked quickly, "Is she?"

Kalki sighed and in a moment of vulnerability, suffered a petulant drift in his own thoughts. Qin was left to guess the rest. Yet, within that cloud of uncertainty, he found purpose and calm. He did not want any answer. He had only wanted to know that there was one that he could journey to.

Kalki spoke at length, "You only need to know and accept the truth about yourself."

"That I was naive?"

"That you *are* powerful. That everyone singularly is. You just don't see it. Most don't. But even the slightest of your actions lead to a chain of events snow-balled in a cause-and-effect of destiny that survives the length of time."

There was the confirmation of what Qin had only guessed at often and had, like everyone else, termed impractical each time. Yet, destiny, by definition, was pre-decided. *How then could any logic make a difference?* "What is destined to happen shall end up happening anyway," he argued.

"Though how and when it happens can very well make all the difference. An asteroid could have struck Earth in our time but it did not. It came when humans did not exist. Is that not fortunate?"

"Yes, but that wasn't my choice."

"That's where most err. We either believe in destiny or we don't. Not once do we realize that like everything in Nature, even this works in balance - through a combination of the two. Some supreme power does not have to exist either within us or outside. It is omnipresent and doesn't consider our skin to be some political power that it cannot trespass."

Qin chuckled despite himself, accepting the logic, and asked, "So how does my choice come into play?"

"Think about it this way: Every crossroad has four directions you can choose to go in."

"Is that our choice alone?"

"Well, if you turn left, the road ahead is laid out for you already and you must walk upon it, but whatever lay on the roads on your right, in front or at the back can no longer cross your path. Whatever comes your way then is because of a choice you made – the left."

"I could have been coerced into turning that way."

"Certainly, and that is where we would need to consider the forces external to you. You may have been persuaded by someone, a bad experience or an inexplicable

[309]

intuition. Maybe it was simpler. Maybe you just saw a pretty girl on the left. That would mean your choice was influenced by the choice of that girl who decided to stand there, which in turn may depend on the choice of one who dropped her there and of course, the timing of it all. These are not choices in your immediate control but also not your concern, because you will always have your own choices nonetheless."

"Ones that are inescapable," Qin concluded helplessly.

"For your own good. The roads are laid out so that you are not left directionless, as in a desert."

"Who decided that the roads should go in those directions?"

"Who decided that you should get heat and light every time you light a fire?"

Qin fell silent. He looked out towards Everest. The highest peak looked smaller in comparison to the others that stood nearer. Instead, he found his glance switch more yearningly to a set of triplets that stood far but stood challenging him tastefully. The Three Sisters glowed under the sky that had turned lighter to the faintest degree. Qin asked, looking ahead, "So we can save the world single-handedly?"

"He who plays the role of redeemer ends up getting crucified, Qin."

"Then what did Friuli mean when she said you wanted me to prepare for the future."

Kalki smiled, and said, "You have an entire life ahead to find out."

Even though Qin had wanted to come to Sandakphu, Kalki had brought him here for reasons much more rewarding. It was the perfect setup for revelations that would have otherwise burdened Qin and overwhelmed him, possibly to despair. Yet, he could not contain the feeling of having suffered en route this outcome. Kalki measured that thought well, for he clarified what rivalled the former as an undeniable truth, "We are all bionics on some level, Qin. The day we switched to artificial medicines and medical transplants, we changed our natural chemistry and biomechanics. We turned into something different than what Nature had made us to be. Changes have been too gradual but then, that doesn't mean they weren't destined."

Qin grasped the implied reality: Change was hardly an issue if it happened to all. Kalki elucidated, "Consider the lens on your eye, for example. It will become a common implant with time. To instantly know more than what you should or need, will deplete the very definitions of curiosity, incentives and above all, love. To realize then, the value of what is in true sense, real, normal, and beautifully ordinary over the glossy virtual world out there, you had to irrevocably miss out on the former first."

Qin did see, in the silent buzz of his mind as some fog cleared out, how he had fallen in love with what was conventionally real, what existed without human intervention, what seemed outdated and what even lay broken down around him. Through the initial moments of genuine effort, he could bring himself to differentiate those from what was novel, latest, upgraded and breakthrough. The world, however it looked, however it was or would be, even to the tiniest details of a little rusted piece of metal, covered with perfectly dispersed harmony of sand granules all over it, looked simply beautiful. It looked simply, perfect.

It was a rather poetic moment as the series of revelations had timed themselves with the pristine rays of a rising sun, fresh and ready for a new day. In all his exploits, he had nearly forgotten that his recent accomplices were neither an ordinary part of his days nor could remain so. It was pronounced quite strongly when Bree arrived, wordlessly but visibly nervous.

Kalki noticed him first and addressed Qin, "I am afraid it is time to conclude our tryst." Qin turned to find Bree look ahead without an acknowledgement of his presence, his focussed indifference contrasting the casual repertoire he had built with such deliberation in their recent past.

Kalki half-raised his face and affirmed to something with a nod. He gave one last look at the sunrise, breathed heavily and turned fully towards Qin, smiling visibly for the very first time. Without looking away, he raised his hands and adjusted a little piece of metal on one of his thumbs. As the ring rotated over his aged skin, engravings came to the fore and for the briefest of moments, seemed to reflect the sun's rays perfectly towards Qin. He looked at them in awe, having managed to catch just a hint - one that proved to be as comprehensive as any answer could be, one that spelt 'ɪphea.' Then, like the inevitably disciplined passing of a solar eclipse, the engravings disappeared once again as they moved back and away from light.

"The fireplace," Kalki said with love. Before Qin could respond, both men flickered in their stance and vanished.

Qin shook finally, his feet dragging themselves haphazardly and disturbing the perfect cover of dazzling white snow around. His thumb lay bare, his impatience at its absence suddenly pronounced. He rushed back to his hut in hope. Inside, natural light had illuminated every room but the central chair was now empty. Expectedly enough, Friuli was gone too. He pursed his lips at a lack of thought, or maybe at a convergence of too many. They weren't accorded time, for he was interrupted by another man, only a few years older to him, standing at the entrance of one of the rooms with a steaming cup of morning coffee. He bore an easy but reserved smile under rectangular, thin-rimmed glasses distinctly separated from his neatly-combed hair that

[312]

contrasted his morning drowsiness. He said, fairly doubtful, "They are gone."

Qin looked at the empty chair while the man looked at him, and concurred, "I suppose."

The other responded warmly, "It's good to see you walk, by the way. Quite an experience this has been."

Qin turned to him with interest, "Were you the one who helped them, and me with all of this?"

"With a few extra hands, yes. The Sherpa won't be back till lunch but he would be glad to see you awake. We couldn't have brought you up here without him."

"And you know about the time travel?"

"Theoretically," the man said and walked towards the fireplace as Qin's eyes followed him. "I don't know why they did it for you but they seemed abnormally familiar with all that had happened on the night of your accident." His brows creased under something he could not make sense of.

Curiosity gushed itself through Qin's heart but never showed itself on his face. He had learnt to control the drama and even though he did not have much to say, he had much to conceal. That was so, until his eyes fell upon the object the other had laid his hands on. There lay a book upon which lay a small ring.

"I believe this is yours," the man said, inspecting the little circle. "KHaor?"

Qin only meekly returned his smile but did not explain. His eyes were glued to what lay underneath it. Nostalgia overtook him and his stance remained stationary. In an absence of any acknowledgement in return, the other picked up the book. He looked at the cover with interest and smiled at the words written on them. "The fly that followed you?"

Qin was silent. He had no words, save for ones that were by now overdue. "Thank you," he said in return for days of unknown guardianship that the other had bestowed upon him.

The man chuckled, acknowledged Qin's need for some privacy and moved towards him, exclaiming, "Oh, don't worry. Like I said, I'm glad." He then extended his hands in their first formal introduction, "Dr. Archer Piscoli."

"Kanha Evian."

About The Author

Malay A. Upadhyay ordinarily works under a different pen name, reserved for pieces he has written in the future. Recently back in the present, he first dealt with the techno-economic genesis of Kalki's story at Bocconi University in Milano. It now stands ready to be winged with your imagination.

More importantly, he is your latest fan and probably smiling at having had your company for the length of this book. That elusively effervescent, ephemeral connection among people across space and time is after all, a belief that underlies every piece of literature ever written.

So, thank you.

www.kalkievian.com

Facebook: /kalkievian

www.ingramcontent.com/pod-product-compliance
Lightning Source LLC
Chambersburg PA
CBHW070222260626
47160CB00002B/644